ROOM MATES

with Benefits

new york times bestselling author

NICOLE WILLIAMS

Roommates with Benefits
Copyright © 2017
Nicole Williams

ISBN-13: 978-1-940448-17-6 | ISBN-10: 1-940448-17-4

ROOM MATES

with Benefits

CHAPTER One

I felt like all of my dreams had, or were about to, come true.

Waved farewell to Podunk hometown? Check.

Arrived in posh metropolis with luggage in tow? Check.

Signed to a top agency? Check.

About to roll up to my swanky new pad? Check.

The world wasn't just at my fingertips—I felt like it was clutched in the palm of my hand. All the obstacles—everything I'd had to overcome to get here—and I'd done it. I'd paid the price. Now I was ready to reap the darn reward.

"Oh, crap." My heart soared into my throat when I glanced at the taximeter for the first time since leaving the airport. I'd been totally preoccupied with staring at the bright lights and sights of New York City. "Is that how much it will cost for the entire ride? Hopefully?" My eyes widened when the meter tacked on another fifty cents.

The driver glanced at me through the rearview. He must have thought I was making a joke until he saw my face. "What? You serious, kid?" His meaty arm draped across the passenger seat. "That's how much it costs to get to right here." He speared his finger out the window, two bushy brows lifting. "There's still another mile before we hit the address you gave me."

"Pull over. Please. Pull over."

Digging inside my purse, I counted out what I owed the driver. Which left me with a whole two dollars and some cents to my name. Ever since I was a little girl declaring my plans to make it in the big city, everyone had been warning me that New York City was expensive. I guessed I hadn't realized that translated to public transportation as well.

Once the driver had pulled up to the curb, I handed him what I owed. He waited, blinking at me like I was missing something.

"Oh, yeah." I pulled out the last two dollars and handful of cents I had left for the tip. Even dropping the last penny to my name in his palm, it was a puny tip.

Heaving a sigh, he crawled out his door to pull my suitcase from the trunk. The dark streets looked different now that I'd be walking them alone.

"Do you have a map or anything I might be able to have?" I asked as he rolled my suitcase around to me.

The driver pointed his finger down the street we were on. "Keep going straight one mile. That will get you there."

I felt my palms clam up when I realized I was about to attempt to navigate on foot a city I'd never been to, with all of my personal belongings in tow, without a dollar to my name. The small-town girl I'd been wanted to cry and run to the first phone to call home. The big-city woman I was born to be had me clutching the handle of my luggage and lifting my chin. By the time, I took my first step toward my new life, the taxi was long gone.

Even though it was almost eight at night, the streets were still bustling. Unlike Hastings, Nebraska, where a person could hear the whir of their neighbor's washing machine by nine every night, New York looked like it was just getting warmed up. Cars whipping up and down the streets, horns blasting, people moving, bikes weaving in and out through it all; this was an entirely different life than the one I'd grown up knowing.

I loved it.

I felt like I passed more people on every block than had made up the whole population of Hastings, and the people here were dressed like they were off to a meeting with foreign dignitaries, instead of the 4-H meeting every Saturday morning at The Hastings Grange.

Fashion. God, I loved fashion. Designing it was my endgame, but first, I had to get my foot in the door however I could. Modeling would give me that opportunity.

By the time I'd rolled myself and my luggage down what felt like a million city blocks, I figured I had another three or four to go. My feet were killing me, since I'd worn heels instead of the comfy flats my mom had suggested when dropping me off at the airport earlier. I'd argued that I didn't want to arrive in NYC with faux leather loafers, but man, those discount store flats sounded pretty amazing right now.

Sheer willpower got me through the last few blocks, and I arrived at what I guessed was my destination, afraid to look at my feet for fear of finding them swimming in pools of blood or swollen beyond recognition. Or on fire, based on the feeling coming from them.

When I stopped in front of the address I'd written down, I had to triple-check that the numbers on my paper matched the ones on the outside of the building. They did, but this sure didn't look like *Big City Living at its Finest*, as the classified had listed. It more looked like *Big City Living at its Most Primitive*.

Then again, maybe it was one of those apartment buildings that looked like a dump on the outside but was a palace on the inside. You know, to keep the bourgeois away. That had to be it. There was probably a chandelier hanging in the elevator and the hallways were lined with gleaming white marble, but no one would guess that from the outside.

Doing one final check to make sure I was at the right address, I lugged my suitcase up the stairs. Someone was leaving as I made it to the front door, but either they didn't see me or didn't care to hold the door open for the woman in three-inch heels wrestling a monster-sized bag into submission. The door practically slammed in my face, heavy enough it almost sent me sprawling backward. I managed to snag the handle to keep it open long enough to shove inside.

Okay, so there were a lot of differences between Hastings and New York City.

I still loved it. A lot.

It would just take an adjustment period to get used to. Before I knew it, I'd be keeping up with the best of the city girls.

Once I'd made it past the front door, I paused to catch my breath and take in the interior of the apartment building. So the halls weren't exactly lined in marble. Or gleaming, whatever surface it was they were covered with. There was an elevator though, but as I took my first steps toward it, I noticed the sign taped to the doors. Out of Order.

Why not?

Shuffling toward the bottom of the staircase, I stared up them, thankful there were only six floors to the top. Kicking off my heels, I collected them in one hand and started heaving my suitcase up all six flights, one stair at a time.

The upside to arriving on the sixth floor in a panting, sweating mess? I'd just gotten my cardio in. For the whole week.

My chest felt like it was about to explode as I rolled down the hall, checking the number on each door as I passed. There wasn't any marble up here either. Or chandeliers. Or anything that held a semblance of shine, actually.

There was a smell though—a mix of mildew and garbage and . . . some other scent I didn't want to assign a name to. A couple of bulbs were burnt out on the ceiling, casting an eerie tone to the environment.

There were noises, too. Music, hammering, talking, screaming . . . other heavy breathing sounds. It was like the walls were made of plastic wrap and painted white'ish to give the illusion of privacy. I could hear every word of the heated conversation coming from the door behind me.

Number sixty-nine. That was a number nine, right? I checked the piece of paper in my hand just to be sure. Yep. My eyes weren't playing tricks on me. The door's paint was chipping, the numbers cockeyed, and from the damage done to it where the locks were, it looked like there'd been multiple attempts to break into it. There was nothing welcoming about this door.

This couldn't be the right place. No way. I had to have written something down wrong, or misread the address outside, or something—*anything*—that would assure me this wasn't the place where I was about to spend the next six months of my life.

As I debated knocking on the door or fleeing from it, a door screeched open down the hall.

"You finally made it." A young guy emerged through the door, his focus on me. "Have you been waiting there long? When you were late, I decided to swing by Mrs. Lopez's and give her a hand with a few things." He was still talking to me as he slid his feet into a worn pair of Converse. His fly was down too, but that didn't seem to be on his concern radar.

It looked like he'd decided to give Mrs. Lopez more than just a hand.

"Oh, god. You don't speak English, do you?" He exhaled, making his way down the hall. "You're one of those Eastern European chicks, right?"

I stepped back as he moved closer.

In another situation, I wouldn't have been trying to back away from the stranger approaching with a look that could make the most frigid of girls melt. He was easy to look at—a little too easy—walking that ever-so-fine line of cute meets hot. He was cute-hot. Hot-cute. Whatever. He was candy to the eyes, and had we run into each other at the Jolt Café back in Hastings, I wouldn't have been creeping away from him as I was now.

"Do I know you?" I asked.

He finally realized his proximity was making me uncomfortable, and he stopped right outside of Number Sixty-Nine. "You *do* speak English. Good. Because I'm not sure I have the brain space to figure out how to say 'The water bill's due yesterday' in Latvian."

I guessed the look on my face echoed my prior question.

"Soren Decker." He held out his hand then slid it into his jeans' pocket when it caught nothing but airtime. "And you are . . .?"

"Not at the right address. Clearly."

He leaned into the dilapidated door. "What address are you looking for?"

I had to lift the piece of paper in my hand to remember. Once I read it off, he shrugged.

"You have arrived at your destination."

That's what I was afraid of. "I must have the wrong apartment number then."

The way he was looking at me told me exactly what he was thinking—that I was mental. "What apartment are you looking for?"

Another review of the paper. Just to be sure. "Sixty-nine."

When his brows bounced, I felt my cheeks heat. I balanced my temporary embarrassment by narrowing my eyes.

"Sixty-nine." He rapped his knuckle below the crooked numbers on the door. "Home sweet home."

That was when the obvious started to settle in. "You're looking for a roommate? You posted the ad I responded to?" I swallowed. "*You*?"

He glanced down at himself like he was checking for a stain on his shirt. In the process, he noticed his fly was still open. "I really didn't think this would be so confusing," he said, pulling his zipper back into place. "Yes, this is the right address. Yes, this is lucky apartment number sixty-nine. And yes, I am the one looking for a roomie, who you replied to last week."

My heart had lodged into the back of my throat from the feel of it. *This* was the person I'd be living with? *This* was who I'd be sharing the same space with for the next half year?

He looked part California surfer, part vintage Hollywood film star. Pretty much the type of guy anyone attracted to males and in possession of a functioning set of eyes would drip some degree of drool over. Light hair, blue eyes that projected trouble, matching his smirky smile, good—*great*—body; he was pretty much the result of creation's best efforts.

Most girls probably would have been chanting *jackpot* in their heads, but I gaped at the perfection that was him, freaking out.

"You said you were looking for a girl," I said.

"I am." He motioned at me.

I motioned right back at him. "You're a guy."

"Wow. Okay. So much confusion." He shifted from one foot to the other, tipping back the red ball cap on his head.

"Why would you prefer a girl roommate when you're a guy?"

Again, the look that implied I wasn't the sharpest knife in the drawer. If he kept it up, I was going to start throwing daggers at him. Provided I had any. Or even one. Which I didn't, because airline regulations and all.

"For obvious reasons," he said.

"For obvious reasons like what? A built-in bedmate?"

His expression flattened as he realized what I was getting at. "You think I'm looking for some kind of 'roommates with benefits' type of thing?" He rubbed his chin like he was considering it right that moment. "I hadn't thought about that, but now that you mention it . . ." Whatever he saw when he glanced at me sparked an amused gleam in his eyes. "I'm not looking for that. I swear."

"Then why insist on a female roommate?"

"Because the female species tends to be neater than the male, ape variety. Plus, you smell better, too." His hand dropped to the doorknob. Before he opened the door, he tipped his chin at me. "And you're nicer to look at." When I didn't move after he motioned inside the apartment, he leaned into the hall and crossed his arms. "Come on, give it to me. I can tell you're dying to say whatever it is you've been biting your tongue over since I had the nerve to address you."

The way he said it, I realized I was maybe leaning toward the bitchy end of the spectrum. "It's just that I thought you were a girl. I didn't realize the person I'd agreed to room with was a guy."

"That's not my fault." As soon as my mouth opened to argue, he added, "You could have asked. But you didn't. You assumed."

My teeth chewed on the inside of my cheek, hating that he was right.

"If you're uncomfortable moving in because I'm a guy, okay, no problem. I'm not going to force you to move in. Even though I took down the 'roommate wanted' ad when you placed dibs. Losing out on a whole week of finding someone."

My fingers pinched the bridge of my nose as I struggled to form one rational thought. If this guy would shut it for one minute, I could think.

"You know, and what's this whole thing about gender equality and erasing those lines that used to separate the sexes? You're pretty much saying you're okay with moving in with a total stranger, sight unseen, just so long as that stranger doesn't come equipped with a scrotum."

"What?" My hand dropped back at my side. "Gross.

Just stop talking. Please. Give me a second to try to figure out what is happening right now . . ."

Squeezing his lips together, he tipped his head back against the wall, making a "carry on" motion in my direction.

Okay. Think.

Swanky new pad was more a nasty, biohazardous dump.

Hip New York roommate was more a crass, vile entity of dubious intentions. Who came equipped with a scrotum, as he'd so articulately put it.

I had an appointment in the morning with the agency, potential go-sees right after, and a whole zero dollars and zero cents to my name. A hotel was out. A really shady motel was out. I supposed I could sleep on a park bench, but instead of just one man, I'd have to be worried about the rest of the city sneaking up on me as I slept.

I didn't have many options.

Actually, I wasn't sure I had any at all.

Taking another good look at him, he didn't seem so bad. He wasn't tattooed from head to toe, didn't have that predatory look parents taught their daughters to identify from twenty paces back, and he didn't reek of alcohol or other substances of questionable repute.

He was no Boy Scout, that was for darn sure, but he didn't have the look of an axe murderer either. Besides, I was a tough chick. If he tried anything, he wouldn't walk away with that cute-hot face unscathed.

"I'm Hayden." I rolled my shoulders back and crossed the distance. "Hayden Hayes."

"Soren Decker. In case you missed it the first time."
He held out his hand as I approached. "By the way, I'm a
dude. You know, to clear up any confusion you might
have on the subject."

"One of those creatures that comes with a scrotum?"
My eyebrows lifted as I shook his hand.

He cracked a smile as he shoved off of the wall. He
didn't have a terrible smile. Not even a little bit.

"Wow. Dang." He twisted his cap around so it was
backward as he stood as tall as he could. "You are tall.
Like, please don't wear heels around me tall."

I held up the pair of heels I was still clutching. "Just
missed them."

"Good. I can't have a girl roommate who's taller than
me. It might emasculate me."

"More than you already are?"

"A fellow smartass." He made a face of approval as I
moved inside the apartment. "We're going to get along
just fine."

"So long as I don't wear heels when you're nearby?"

"See? You get me. Two and a half minutes into our
relationship and you understand me. Why can't the rest of
the girls on the planet seem to get it?" He didn't give me a
chance to fire back my idea on that topic. "Seriously,
though, how tall are you?"

"Five ten." Once I rolled my suitcase inside, he
closed the door behind us.

"Liar, liar. Designer jeans on fire." He waved his finger at me as he moved into the apartment.

These were designer jeans. The one pair I owned and

12

would be living in until I could afford a second pair. It had taken me three months of mucking out stalls to make enough to afford them.

"Fine. Five eleven." When his brows disappeared into his ball cap, I sighed. "And a half."

"My six one is suddenly not feeling so big and bad."

The inside of the apartment was an improvement on the outside. Somewhat. Paint wasn't chipping off the walls, and the funky odor wasn't quite as strong in here. Although there was a different one—that sweat-and-dirty laundry man smell with the faintest hint of aftershave or cologne mixed in.

"So. Here it us. My humble abode."

Emphasis on humble.

There wasn't much to see. A shoe-box-sized kitchen was right inside the door—at least there was a stove and a fridge—with a same sized bathroom across from it, and what must have been the main living space, which we were standing in now, was made up of a line of windows, a couch I would not sit on unless a sheet of plastic separated me from it, a couple of room dividers, and a rectangular metal table with four mismatched chairs.

It was semi-clean and super small.

"Where's the rest?" I asked when he stopped beside me, nodding at the space like it was the definition of opulent.

"What do you mean? This is it." He indicated the room.

My gaze circled the space again. A secret hallway. There had to be one of those hiding in here somewhere.

"Where are the bedrooms?"

He made a clucking sound with his tongue, leading me to one corner tucked behind a sad divider. "Here's mine," he said, letting me peek behind the divider.

My heart did that hiccupping thing again when I noticed a twin mattress lying on the floor, a whirl of blankets and pillows scattered on it. There was a big plastic bin too, which looked like it served as a dresser.

"And yours is over here." Guiding me to the corner across from this one, he proudly waved at the empty space behind the second divider.

There was nothing there. Unless you counted the dust bunnies.

"You're kidding, right?" I blinked, frowning when I found the exact same scene in front of me.

"About what?" he asked, straight-faced.

"This being a bedroom." My arms flew toward the empty space. "This is a stall. Actually, I've mucked out stalls twice as big back home."

His brows pinched together. "Like a bathroom stall?"

"No, like a stall inside a barn. A horse stall. A cow stall. Shoot, even the pigs get a better deal than this." My voice was rising, as I realized he wasn't messing with me. This was supposed to serve as my bedroom, and there were a few big things missing to make it my definition of a bedroom—for starters, a door.

"Wait. So you're one of those small-town girls?" He appraised me with new eyes, like everything was finally making sense.

"Yes, I'm one of those small-town girls, but not small

town enough to realize I'm getting the big city runaround."

"The runaround?" His arms crossed. "What do you mean the runaround? I didn't say anything about there being a private bedroom straight out of the Four Seasons, girlie."

I tried to remember the "roommate wanted" ad I'd seen online last week. Specifically, the wording. "Yeah? And what about the penthouse views?" I crossed my arms just like he was. "This is the opposite of a penthouse, and the view sucks." I glanced out the row of windows, where there was a view of the building across the street.

Soren's eyes lifted before he moved toward the windows. He waited for me before pointing his finger up. Way up. "Penthouses." His finger was aimed at the tippy top of the buildings around us. "We have a view of penthouses."

My mouth opened. "That's not how you meant it to be taken, nice try."

"How do you know how I meant for it to be taken? Penthouse views. That's the truth." He was still pointing out the window. "You make a lot of assumptions. Might want to work on that if you plan on surviving in the city."

Turning away from the window, I scanned the apartment. Had it shrunken in size when I'd turned my back? "You said it was a generous living space."

He indicated the same apartment I was looking at. "Are you kidding me? This *is* a generous living space."

"Compared to what? A cardboard box?"

His mouth snapped open, but he closed it before whatever was about to come out, did. He rolled his head a few times, his neck cracking in a way that made me cringe.

"Listen. You are obviously from a different world than I am. I grew up in Brooklyn. My definition of generous is clearly different than yours."

"I grew up in Hastings, Nebraska, raised by a single mom with a high school education after dear old dad bailed on her and his three daughters." I paused, staring at him. "I was not raised in the lap of luxury, nor am I a spoiled brat, but this . . .." My hand waved between his and my "bedrooms," my stomach churning when I counted off maybe ten feet of separation between them. "This is not generous living space."

"Then fine. Don't move in. It's not like you've unpacked your things. You're the one looking for an apartment, not me. Go find some other place to live in the heart of the city for less than eight hundred dollars a month. Good luck with that."

When he started toward my suitcase, I intercepted him. I didn't have anywhere else to go. No friends. No family. No money. My first rent check here wasn't due for a couple of weeks. Accepting that should have made this place seem much more appealing, but instead I felt more like an inmate resigned to their cell.

"It's been a long day. There have been lots of surprises. I'm feeling overwhelmed." I rolled my suitcase toward my barracks so he didn't roll it out the front door.

"You're not in Nebraska anymore. You're in New York City." He indicated out the windows before storming toward the kitchen. "Buck up, buttercup."

I bit my tongue when I wanted to fire something right back. My life had not been easy, and I hated that he assumed it had been because I was shocked I'd be sharing a room with a strange boy. This wasn't normal. This was five thousand percent *not* normal.

"You want a sandwich?" he called from the kitchen as he started tossing things onto the counter.

"A sandwich?" I repeated. Hadn't we just been in a moderately heated conversation? And now he'd moved on to sandwich-making twelve seconds later?

"You know, meat, cheese, condiments? Two slices of bread holding it all together?" He shot me a smirk as he twirled open the bag of bread.

My stomach answered for me. "Actually, yeah. Thanks." Leaving my suitcase behind the divider, I moved toward the kitchen.

"What brought you to the biggest city in the country from Nebraska?" he asked, glancing at me.

I stopped behind one of the plastic chairs around the table. It didn't feel right to just make myself at home . . . even though this was my new home. "Modeling."

He made a sound like everything made sense now, then stalled with the knife in the mayo jar. "So when you say you want a sandwich, you mean two pieces of celery smashed together?"

My eyes lifted. I'd been called a stick, a twig, a pole, a *bean*pole, accused of being anorexic, bulimic, a drug addict, you name it, because I was genetically predisposed to having a thin frame. Now that I was officially a model, it was only going to get worse, I guessed. "I hate celery."

Soren spread a thick layer of mustard on one piece of bread. "Too many carbs?"

"You're annoying."

"So I've been told."

Of course my roommate would be one of the few people on the planet who was capable of getting under my skin. Who better to share a six-hundred-square-foot space with than someone who couldn't look at me without triggering mild irritation? The more he talked, the less cute-hot he became. Silver linings. I didn't need to harbor some minor attraction to the guy I was sharing an apartment with.

"Don't you have any questions for me?" I asked after a minute.

One shoulder rose as he layered on what looked like pastrami. "You don't smoke?"

"Nope."

"You don't stay out late partying, getting your drink on, and come home smelling like the city barfed on you?"

"Definitely not." I wasn't straitlaced, but I wasn't a hot mess either.

He pulled a couple of plates from a cupboard, tossed the sandwiches onto them, and moved toward the table. "You aren't prone to stealing other people's property? Namely my Nutter Butters?"

It didn't seem like a serious question. The look on his face told otherwise. "No," I answered.

He held one plate toward me. "Then we're good."

When I took the plate, my stomach growled. The last thing I'd eaten was the pretzels on the plane.

"Thanks," I said, feeling a stab of guilt for the way I'd acted since meeting him. He was the only person in

New York who'd offered me a place to live, and he was giving me a free meal.

"You don't look like you could afford to miss one more meal," he said. I didn't miss the way he inspected my arms as I took a seat. "So now that you've had the grand tour, do you have any questions for me? And by that, I mean actual questions, not accusations."

When I shot him a look, he gave me a big smile right before stuffing his sandwich in his mouth. Let's see. I knew his name, his gender, where he'd grown up, that he was a smartass, and that he was cute-hot when he wasn't talking.

"What do you do?"

He lowered his sandwich. "I model," he said, his expression flat. "Men's underwear mainly. Sometimes women's. If they pay me enough."

I smiled at my sandwich as I lifted it. "I thought you looked familiar. I just didn't recognize you without those big wings and the million-dollar diamond bra."

He chuckled, tearing off another bite of his sandwich. "I play ball," he said, still chewing.

"Like dodgeball?" I took a small bite of the sandwich he'd made me so it wouldn't seem like I was starving.

He shot me a tight smile. "Like baseball." He waved his sandwich toward his "bedroom," where a big red duffel was, a mitt and bat hanging out of it. "I play at one of the junior colleges close by since none of the D1 schools wanted to take a risk with me."

"A risk?" I took another bite, this one bigger. I wasn't usually a fan of pastrami or mustard, but dang, this was the best sandwich I'd ever had.

"Let's just say I was a bit of a hothead in high school, and D1 schools would rather have the golden boy with some talent than the wild card with mad talent."

"Hothead . . .?"

"I got into a few fights at some games."

I circled my sandwich in the air. "Like pushing, name calling type fights?"

"Try fists flying, dust spinning type of fights." He must have guessed where my mind was taking me. "Don't worry. I never have or never would put my hands on a woman like that, and I've calmed my shit down a lot since then. Nothing like being forced to eat a slice of humble pie at junior college to get a player in line."

Nibbling off a corner, I curled my legs up onto the chair. I'd been too busy freaking out over my new living arrangements to notice how chilly it was in here. I couldn't see my breath or anything, but it felt only a few degrees away from that.

"What are you studying?" I asked.

He dropped the last piece of sandwich into his mouth before wiping his hands on his jeans. "I'm just banging general requirements out of the way right now. I don't care about becoming an accountant or a project manager or whatever the hell else other guys go to college for. I want to play ball. I go to school because it's a package deal."

"So your plan is to transfer to a D1 school to play ball after you're finished?" I asked, like I knew what I was talking about. Which I didn't. Sports weren't my thing. Watching or partaking in them.

"I want to get drafted by the best professional baseball team in the whole wide world. *That's* my plan." He shoved out of his chair, carrying his plate into the kitchen.

"You want to play professional baseball?"

"No. I'm *going* to play professional baseball. And the one good thing about playing at a junior college is that I can be drafted any time they want me. I don't have to wait until I graduate like I would have if one of those D1 schools had recruited me." He rinsed his plate in the sink before setting it on a drying rack. He hadn't used soap, but I supposed it was better than licking it clean and sticking it back in the cupboard. "Want anything to drink? Another sandwich?"

I lifted what was left of my first sandwich. It was only halfway gone and I was already feeling full. It wasn't because I was a small eater either—he made his sandwiches like he was entertaining a team of linebackers. "I'm good, thanks."

He lifted a package of Nutter Butters, one hanging from his mouth, a half dozen clutched in his other hand.

"I just promised I wouldn't steal your Nutter Butters."

"But I'm offering you one. There's a difference."

"Thanks, but no thanks. Looks like you need them." I eyed the stack in his hand as he stuffed the package back on the top shelf.

"I play ball two to four hours a day. I go to school four to six hours. Homework on top of that, *and* a part-time job in between. I have to take advantage when I have a minute to stuff my face." He padded back to the table and set one cookie from the pile in his hand on my plate.

"For dessert."

I thanked him, even though I wasn't a fan of Nutter Butters. I was more a chocolate person than a peanut butter one.

"You want a hand bringing up the rest of your stuff? I've got some time before I should hit the books. I have a biology test tomorrow morning." His nose crinkled as he stuffed another cookie in his mouth.

For his apparent love affair with cookies, he sure didn't have the body of a cookie enthusiast. Thanks to his light-colored tee, which hugged particularly nice parts of the male anatomy, he looked like the type who ate egg whites and kale in his sleep.

"Oh, I don't have anything else. Just my big suitcase and me." I set my sandwich down after taking one more bite.

"So you don't have any more stuff to move in?" When I shrugged, he frowned. "No more stuff as in a futon or mattress or . . .?"

My head shook as I moved toward my suitcase. I needed to throw on a sweatshirt before I gave myself frostbite. "They don't let you check mattresses or futons on the airplane. But I brought a pillow and a sleeping bag." Setting down the suitcase, I unzipped it and pulled out those very items.

"Hardwood floors." His foot tapped the floor.

"I've slept in barns, train depots, and the backseat of a '77 Malibu." Shaking the sleeping bag open, I shot him a smile. Whatever had happened or was about to, I was chasing my dreams. Life was pretty damn good. "Buck up, buttercup."

CHAPTER Two

Today would be a great day. The best.

That was what I thought as I stirred awake . . . right before my heart stopped mid-beat. My alarm wasn't going off. And I was awake. That was my first warning sign.

I did mornings if I had to, but I didn't have fond feelings for them. Especially when I hadn't slept well and I'd set my alarm for six New York time, which was five Nebraska time.

Lurching awake, I grabbed the tiny alarm clock I'd set beside my pillow last night. Blinking to clear my eyes, a shriek squeaked from me when I saw the time. Just after seven. "Crap!"

Throwing the sleeping bag off of me, I dove into my suitcase and tore out a fresh pair of underwear and a clean camisole. I'd be wearing the same pair of jeans I'd worn yesterday because, yeah, one designer pair of jeans.

"What's the matter?"

The voice surprised me, making me jolt. I'd momentarily forgotten about my new roommate.

"My alarm. It didn't go off. I'm going to be late."

When Soren stuck his head out of the bathroom, I ducked behind the divider so he couldn't see me changing. "Yeah. I turned it off. It kept blasting and you weren't waking up, so I figured you needed a little more rest."

I froze in the middle of yanking my jeans up over my hips. "You turned it off?"

From the sounds of it, he'd moved on to brushing his teeth. "Yeah. It was seriously going off for ten whole minutes, twelve inches from your face, so I did you a favor. Feel better?"

I stuck my head outside of the divider, my eyes already narrowed. "No, I do not feel better. At all. I've got to be at Park Avenue on the twenty-second floor in under an hour. For my very first meeting with my new agency. It's one of those times I planned on making a good impression instead of, oh, I don't know, showing up late with my hair a mess and morning breath."

Soren was gargling in the bathroom. "You'll make it, no problem. The subway station's just down the block, and it's a five-minute ride from there. That gives you time to brush your teeth and hair."

My jaw ground as I wrestled into my cami then grabbed my jacket from where it was hanging over the divider. "You had no right to turn off my alarm like that."

"You had no right to wake me up an hour early because you wouldn't turn off your alarm." His voice wasn't really argumentative, just matter-of-fact.

"I promised I wouldn't touch your Nutter Butters. You don't touch my alarm." Freeing my brush from my toiletry bag, I ripped it through my long dark hair before throwing my hair into a ponytail.

"Okay, so you wake up cranky. Noted. I'll keep my distance from here on out." As he emerged from the bathroom, he was wearing nothing more than a towel around his waist. A small, thin white towel. He was still wet from the shower.

I froze in the middle of searching for my toothbrush and toothpaste. I had been born and raised in the heartland of America, where corn-fed, All-American boys ran rampant, but dang . . . Nutter Butters did a body good.

When he caught me looking—*gawking*—at him, I got back to wrangling my toothbrush free. "I'm only cranky in the morning when someone turns off my alarm on one of the biggest days of my life."

As soon as I had my toothpaste, I went charging into the bathroom. The mirror was still fogged up from his shower, the scent of whatever soap and shampoo he used lingering in the air.

"The biggest day of your life? I think that should be reserved for your wedding day or the birth of your firstborn or something other than posing and walking for a bunch of shallow people who think the label on your shirt is synonymous with a person's worth in life."

After wiping off the steam with my forearm, I squeezed a blob of toothpaste onto my brush, glaring at my reflection in the mirror. The one positive to getting into an argument with him was that it warmed me up. "Oh, yeah?

Because being drafted by some baseball team to swing a bat and catch a few balls for millions of dollars is so much more enlightened?"

He was quiet. For all of two seconds. "Listen, I'm sorry I turned off your alarm. I really thought I was doing you a favor by letting you rest. It won't happen again."

When I popped my head out of the bathroom, brushing my teeth, I saw that flimsy white towel drape across the top of his divider. My toothbrush stopped moving. Giving my head a shake, I finished brushing, took a minute to do what I could to my hair and face, and rushed back to my suitcase. The alarm showed seven fifteen, which gave me forty-five minutes to figure out where I was going, get there, and compose myself before shaking hands with one of New York's biggest modeling agents.

"I'm never going to make it," I whined, shoving my feet into the same heels from last night. My feet felt swollen and the blisters on the back of my heels had popped, but beauty was pain. At least some of the time.

"Stop freaking out. Of course you're going to make it. You've got plenty of time." Soren reemerged from behind his divider, wearing a similar outfit to last night's: dark jeans, light shirt that hugged his body, low-top Converse, and a backward red baseball cap. He was sliding on a backpack, strapping it around his chest and waist. "If you're ready to go, I can walk you to the subway and tell you which stop to get off at. The stop for my school's a few after the Park Avenue one you'll want."

As I threw on my jacket, I grabbed my purse and started for the door. "I can't take the subway."

"Everyone in New York takes the subway. I know it can seem intimidating to out-of-towners, but I was riding the subway, by myself, from the time I was ten." Soren caught up to me and made a stop in the kitchen to pull a box from one of the cupboards. It was a pack of Pop-Tarts. Strawberry with sprinkles.

"I'm sure it is easy to figure out, especially if the ten-year-old version of you could do it."

He shot me a wounded look after pulling open the door.

"But really, I can't take the subway," I said.

"Really, you can." He paused at the door to lock it, pulling an extra key from his pocket and holding it out for me.

"Soren . . ." I grumbled as we started down the stairs. He was able to move down them quicker since he wasn't balancing on quarter-foot high heels, but he waited at the bottom of each flight. "Any idea when the elevator will be fixed?"

"Yeah." He motioned at it when we made it to the first floor. "Never."

"Never?"

"It's been busted since I moved in last year. It will probably still be busted when the apocalypse moves in."

I made a mental note to pack a pair of flats for traversing the stairs every day. Heels were one thing on sidewalks, a totally different thing on a steep pair of questionable-looking stairs. When we shoved through the door, the cold New York air blasted over us.

"Holy cold." My teeth were already chattering as I

went to zip up my jacket. It was one of those coats created with fashion in mind, instead of function, so it didn't provide much warmth.

"Insulation helps." Soren walked down the stairs with me before pacing down the sidewalk toward the subway tunnel.

"This is the only coat I brought."

"I was talking about the insulation that goes under the skin."

I aimed a fake smile at him. "Another model joke. Any chance you're getting close to running out of them?"

He grinned at the sidewalk, but I didn't miss the way he angled himself enough he was blocking some of the wind cutting down the street at us. "Just getting warmed up."

It was only a couple of minutes before the subway entrance came into view.

"See? How handy is that? Public transportation practically right outside your front door." He indicated back at our apartment building, which was still in sight.

"Okay, good to know where it is. Have a nice day."

When I kept moving down the sidewalk, he gave me another one of those looks. "If you actually want to be late to your appointment, walking's the way to do it. Park Avenue is not just a hop, skip, and a jump down the block. Especially in those shoes." He grabbed my wrist and started guiding me down into the subway.

"Soren, I can't," I protested, though my feet kept following behind him.

He didn't say anything as he kept guiding me through the maze of people, before stopping at a ticket counter. Even though he was holding a monthly pass in his hand, he purchased one ticket from the agent. When he held the ticket out for me and I noticed it was a round-trip, another knife of guilt stabbed right into my stomach.

Whether he was right or not in turning off my alarm, I believed he'd done it because he thought it was what was best for me. Now he'd bought me a subway ticket without me even needing to embarrass myself by admitting I was totally broke. I'd been nothing but a crabby pain in the butt since arriving.

"Soren . . ."

He winked at me as the subway pulled up to the station. "I know."

"Did you just pull a Han Solo on me?"

He lifted his arm in front of me when I moved toward to the car. "You better believe it, girlie."

As I nudged him, I saw why he'd stopped me from going any farther; the moment those doors opened, a wave of people surged out. Getting stampeded wasn't the way I wanted to start my career.

Once the last people were trickling off, he wove his arm through mine and moved us on board. There weren't any seats available, so he grabbed one of the vertical poles, indicating I should do the same. Even when I did, he kept his arm twisted through mine.

Being so close and still, he let out a groan when he examined how I wasn't at eye level with him. "The heels. I thought I told you they were a no-fly zone when I was around." The toe of his Con tapped my heel. "I'm feeling less like a man every second you hover above me."

I made it a point to stand as tall as I could. "I'm on my way to work. Models work in heels. The agencies would probably nail them to the soles of our feet if there weren't humanitarian laws against it. I can't slide on a pair of flip-flops because my roommate's got masculinity issues." I took a moment to scan the subway car. "I'm hovering over just about every guy in here. Do they look like their egos are taking a hit?"

Soren didn't look. He was busy wrestling the box of Pop-Tarts open. "I can't help it if I'm more macho than most guys. It runs in the Decker blood." He ripped open one of the foil packets, pulled one Pop-Tart out, and offered the other to me. "My mom, god bless her, gave birth to four boys. My grandma gave birth to five. Macho is tantamount to the Decker name."

"You talk a lot in the morning," I said, taking the Pop-Tart. A person didn't turn away free food when they were flat broke.

"That's not just a morning problem." He bit off a quarter of his "breakfast."

I set my breakfast into my purse, saving it for lunch. I'd just brushed my teeth and didn't want to chance showing up to meetings with pink-stained teeth and sprinkles in them.

"What's your schedule like today?" I asked, my heart hammering from experiencing my first subway ride. It was everything they made it seem like in the movies, but grittier. Plus, there were the smells a screen could never recreate. It felt like every part of the planet was somehow represented in odor inside of this small subway car.

The familiar ones, to the not-so-familiar.

"I have class, baseball, work, homework, sleep." Soren moved more behind me when the next load of passengers crawled off and on at the next stop. "That's my schedule most every day except for the weekend. Then it's all baseball, homework, and sleep."

"When do you have fun?"

Soren chuckled like that was a cute question. "Sometimes I have a few hours on Thursday to go home. Makes my mom happy, and I chow down like I'm not going to see a meal for a month. Dad and my brothers bond by shouting and gesturing at whatever game's on television. That's about all the time I have for fun in my life these days."

The car was getting more packed the closer we got to the heart of the city. A guy who'd climbed on at the last stop was standing uncomfortably close to me. I knew I'd grown up in a small town with probably five acres to every occupant, but this dude felt like he was trying to drape himself around my back.

Soren must have noticed the dude was pushing his boundaries too, because Soren slid around me and into my spot so the guy was sandwiched up against him instead. Weird how the perv melted back into the rest of the crowd.

"That sounds nice, and I bet it makes your mom happy."

Soren checked over his shoulder to make sure the guy had backed off. "It's more an exercise in survival of the fittest, but yeah, it makes Mom happy. The burden of being the favorite." He stuffed the last of his Pop-Tart into his mouth, pointing at the door. "The next stop's yours. Are you comfortable getting off on your own? Won't get lost in the great city of Oz?" He checked the time on his phone, the skin between his brows creasing. "If we hustle, I can get off and take you there myself, just to make sure you know where you're going. My professor's pretty cool about students being late to class."

My head shook as I felt the subway slow. "You've already saved my butt a half dozen times this morning. I can navigate a few blocks on my own."

He glanced at me, giving me a second to change my mind. I still hadn't when the doors started to open.

"Just head up the stairs. That'll put you on Park Avenue. Depending on your address, head up or down a few blocks." He lifted his chin at the doors. "Those doors don't pause for anyone, not even a supermodel in the making." His hand moved to my back, gently guiding me toward the doors as people started to shove on.

"Thanks for everything," I shouted back at him, shouldering through the wave of people. "Have a great day."

"Make today great!" he shouted before the doors closed.

When I waved over my shoulder at him, I barely caught him winking at me before the subway moved down the rail.

The clock on the subway wall read 7:40, which gave me plenty of time to make it three blocks. Provided I didn't get turned around. Which I wouldn't. Soren had saved me this morning. Now the rest was up to me.

Following the herd of people up the stairs, I emerged onto the sidewalk as the winter air blasted over me. This city was so dang cold. With all these tall buildings and people, how could it possibly feel like the cold was knifing through me straight to the bone?

Taking a moment to get my bearings, I checked the address for the agency. It was on the 1480 block, and I was currently on the 1450 block. So I was close, but I didn't have a clue if I should head straight or turn around.

Everyone back home had told me how people in big cities weren't like people in small towns, especially when it came to helping one another out. Whether they were right or not, I was going to ask for help until someone marching down this sidewalk gave me some.

It only took a few *excuse me*s before one lady paused.

"Can you tell me if 1480 is up or down?"

She kept moving, pointing over her shoulder. "It's back that way. Few streets down."

"Thank you," I called after her as I started moving down the sidewalk.

I felt like I was going against traffic as I shoved through the crowds headed in the opposite direction, but I finally made it to the building I needed. It was one of those massive structures that seemed to go up so high, it broke through the atmosphere. The windows were gleaming so much, they seemed to ripple, and the people whisking in and out of the doors looked like they'd just stepped out of one of the fashion magazines I was hoping to one day have photos of me in.

Covering my stomach with my hand to try to massage the butterflies away, I took a deep breath and moved through the doors. It was gleaming inside too. This was how I'd pictured my new living space, but at least I was getting it in some capacity.

After checking the building directory, I moved to the wall of elevators and waited. With everyone else. Move. Wait. Move. Wait. I felt like a farm animal. As soon as one set of doors opened, people would spill out, shove in, and I'd be left lingering in the hall. This repeated at least six times until I realized I was never going to make it up to the twenty-fourth floor if I didn't take the New Yorker approach and shove, shoulder, and slide myself where I needed to go.

The ride up was even more smashed with bodies than the ride on the subway had been. Some lady was pressed into my back; I was pressed into some guy's back. I'd never been so aware of body odor—others and my own.

"Excuse me," I announced when the doors pinged open on the twenty-fourth floor. "Coming through," I added when no one was willingly "excusing me." The shoulder-slide-shoulder got me out of the elevator before the doors closed on me.

I hadn't expected the elevator to open right up into the agency. Buildings back home—you know, the five- and six-story ones—had elevators that opened into halls that led you to office doors. Not this building. Not this elevator.

To my left was a sprawling reception desk, modern,

fashionable-looking—if furniture could be described as such. A couple of women who I assumed were receptionists were behind the desk, but from the look of them, they could have been models had they been born half a foot taller. Behind all of that stood an opaque glass wall where K&M Models had been etched onto the glass with matte black lettering.

Standing there in my one pair of designer jeans, my faux leather jacket, and my heels bought on the clearance rack at the mall back home, I'd never felt so small town as I did right then. What on Earth did a place like this see in some Nebraska girl like me? Some some-town tall girl who'd known her share of hardship?

It made my stomach drop, wondering if this was all some trick. Or they'd see me here under the scope of New York City and not see the same thing they'd seen in Omaha that day I'd been wandering the mall.

I couldn't go back home. That wasn't the life for me. I couldn't spend the next sixty years going from part-time job to part-time job, struggling the way my mom had to support her family. I wasn't content to settle down with my high school boyfriend and start popping babies out the way a lot of girls in my graduating class already were. My goal was to work the job I loved, in the city I was hoping to fall in love with, and make enough money to support myself with extra to send home to ease some of the financial stress on the family I already had. My mom was getting by just fine on her own, but I wanted more for them all. More than just getting by. I wanted more than that for myself as well.

That was what had me lifting my shoulders and putting on an air of confidence I was not at all feeling as I approached the front desk. When the girl greeted me with a smile, I said, "I'm Hayden Hayes. I have an eight o'clock appointment to see Mr. Lawson."

She pulled up something on her computer and gave a brief nod. "I'll let him know you're here. You can take a seat over there if you like."

She indicated a line of see-through plastic chairs lined against a silver wall. A few dozen magazine covers had been framed and hung, presumably featuring models represented by the agency. After thanking her, I moved toward the wall to inspect the pictures. Some big magazines were represented up there, featuring some just-as-notorious models. It was impossible to wrap my mind around the fact that the same agency representing some of the biggest names in the modeling world was the same one representing me. Hayden Agatha Hayes from Hastings, Nebraska. The gangly, awkward girl who'd been teased and dubbed a freak by the intellectually-stunted turds in middle school. I couldn't wait until I made it. Until it was my face on that magazine cover. Until I made my first million. I'd make sure to have them make that check out to Miss Freak.

After staring at the covers for a while, I took a seat and flipped through magazines. I was done going through those and still hadn't been called in for my meeting, which was now running a half hour late.

The girl at the counter set the phone back on the hook and swallowed. "Miss Hayes? Mr. Lawson has been held up in another meeting and asked if I'd get you everything you needed." Coming around the desk, she was holding a portfolio. "Here's the go-see schedule for the day. Make sure to arrive a few minutes early, but no more than five." She held out a sheet of paper with a list of times, companies, and addresses.

"This is all today?" As I scanned the sheet, I counted seven different meetings. Scattered throughout the area.

She smiled at me like I was teasing her, then she held out the black folder. "This is the portfolio we put together after your photo shoot last month. There aren't a lot of shots, but we'll schedule another one soon to build up your portfolio."

Taking the folder, I flipped through a couple of pages. When I'd signed with K&M last month, their scout had a photographer do a simple shoot back in Omaha. A couple beauty shots, one profile, and a few full-body ones. Jeans, T-shirt, heels, hardly any makeup or posing. I didn't look like a model in my portfolio, or at least not how I pictured one, but I knew that was the point. The clients wanted to see a blank canvas, not one already drawn and marked all over.

"I just need to double-check your measurements to make sure there are no surprises there." The girl whipped a fabric tape measure out of her pocket and cinched it around my waist first. When I lifted my arms, she moved to my bust, then finished with my hips. After checking the measurements included inside my portfolio, she nodded. "You're all set."

When she started back toward her desk, I clutched my

schedule and portfolio close to my chest. "So that's it? Off I go?"

She rolled the tape measure back up, appraising me like I was every bit as naïve as I felt at the moment. "That's it. If any of the clients you meet with today decide to book you, they'll contact us, then we'll contact you. I'll have a fresh list of go-sees for you tomorrow as well. I can email them to you, or you can pick up the schedule here again in the morning."

"I'll pick them up," I said, because I might have had an email address, but I didn't have a way to access that email at the moment. "Thank you for everything."

Her face softened a little, giving me the impression gratitude wasn't a regular sort of thing around here. That soft look faded as soon as the phone rang. Talk about wearing multiple hats—that poor girl looked done and it wasn't even nine yet.

After climbing onto the elevator, I checked the address of my first meeting. It wasn't until ten, which gave me time to slow down and put together a plan. I would be on foot all day. I'd already accepted that. My goal was to plan my trips as efficiently as possible, but as I read the seven different addresses, I didn't have any idea if any of the streets were close together or on opposite ends of the city.

Crossing my fingers, I approached the desk at the first-floor entrance. "Excuse me, sir?" As soon as the man at the desk glanced up, I continued. "You wouldn't happen to have a street map of the city, would you? One of those touristy ones that make it simple enough to understand that a small child could navigate the streets successfully?"

The elderly man gave me an amused look, then something dawned on his face when he noticed the black portfolio clutched in my hands. Reaching inside one of the desk drawers, he pulled out something. "Must be your lucky day."

He winked as he set a brochure in front of me. Sure enough, it was one of those maps made for the navigation-impaired tourists swarming the city. Or in this case, the small-town rookie model who was attempting to traverse her new home.

"Thank you." It came out sounding like he'd just saved my life instead of handing me some free paper map, but I felt like he kind of had saved my life.

Taking a seat on one of the benches beside the doors, I scanned the map for a few minutes, familiarizing myself with the streets. Then I pulled a pen out of my purse and circled the general areas I had appointments at, along with numbering them based on time. None of the appointments were way on the outskirts of the city, thank goodness. There must have been a centralized fashion part of the city.

The trek to my first appointment looked like it would take the longest, so I started moving that direction, pausing every few blocks to check the map to make sure I hadn't gotten turned around. The sidewalks weren't quite as busy as earlier, but there were still swarms of people moving along them.

This was all so different from where I'd come from. The noises, the sights, the people, the smells—I wasn't sure two places could be as opposite as New York City and Hastings. Even though I'd spent my whole life in one town, this place had an odd sense of home. An air of belonging. Everything was new, but it had a familiarity—like I'd experienced it in another life.

New York City. The place that was home to millions, yet it felt like it was all my own at the same time.

By the time I made it to the address for my first go-see, my feet were numb. I couldn't tell if that was from the cold or the walking. Tomorrow, I was definitely bringing sneakers to change into for my biped commuting.

Zelda Zhou was the name of the client. From what I recalled from scouring endless magazines, she was an up-and-coming designer known for courageous use of color and unapologetic attitude toward mixing patterns. At least that was how I recalled the writer describing her designs in last month's *Mode*.

As soon as I stepped inside her shop, I felt like I'd been transported into some psychedelic hippie rebirth. Coming from the monochromatic streets outside, it took me a moment to adjust to all of the color inside the studio.

Similar to K&M's, there was a reception desk and a young lady working it, but she was dressed like she was auditioning for the circus. When she noticed me, she adjusted the feather boa on her neck. "Her Highness will here shortly. Please take a seat." The girl pointed her long, neon green fingernail at a few beanbags shoved against a wall. Two of them were already taken.

The fashion world—designers especially—were a unique bunch. A breed that embraced the freak-flag-flying motto. As "vanilla" as I considered myself when it came to my own inner freak, I loved the whole creed. Be yourself. Whoever that is. To whatever extent that was. Individuality was frowned upon in Hastings, at least in its extreme cases. But here, it seemed to be celebrated.

The two girls sitting on beanbags were talking, clearly about me. When I dropped onto the beanbag beside one of them, she twisted toward me.

"We were just taking guesses," she explained, glancing at the way I was clutching my portfolio to my chest. "On what number go-see this is for you."

The girl beside her leaned forward and waved at me. "She thinks it's your third. I say it's your first."

Okay, first model-y-model run-in. I'd read the horror stories, of course, but I was determined to approach this new life with a give-the-benefit-of-the-doubt philosophy. Neither of them were giving me serious side-eye, and they'd been upfront about what they'd been whispering over.

"It's my first."

The girl two beanbags down thrust her arms up in victory.

"What number go-see is this for you guys?" I asked.

The girl beside me lifted a dark eyebrow. "The number So-Many-I've-Lost -Count."

"That's because she's ancient." The other girl pointed at the corner of the girl's eye, but I didn't see a single wrinkle.

She shoved her "friend's" finger away. "Twenty-two is not ancient."

"It is if you're Her Highness Zhou. If you don't look

fourteen, she'll toss you out the back door like last season's designer handbag."

It felt like these two were just getting started, so I cleared my throat. "I'm Hayden. I just moved here a whole . . ." Checking my watch, I did some quick mental math. "Fifteen hours ago."

"Hey, I'm Ariel, and this is Jane," the girl next to me said. "She's a plus-size model."

"You hear that note of bitterness?" Jane leaned farther forward so she could look at me. "It's because having no fat on one's body turns a person into a miserable bitch."

Ariel's eyebrows lifted. "And who's had more boyfriends in the past two years?"

"You." Jane motioned at her like she was accusing her of something. "Because I'm not looking for a boyfriend. Why would I want one of those when I can have a new boy-toy in my bed every night of the week?"

"You sure they're not just hanging around one night because in the morning when they sober up, the beer goggles from the night before fall off?"

Jane didn't look the least bit insulted, leading me to the impression these two had plenty of experience giving each other a hard time. "You know what's another side effect of no body fat? Diminished sex drive. Might be why Jon's right hand's been looking extra soft and supple lately."

Ariel elbowed Jane as she crossed her arms. I stayed quiet, because that seemed like the safest option.

"She's my best friend," Jane explained, tipping her head at Ariel. "We give each other a lot of shit, but it's all in love. Plus, it makes anything nasty these designers or photographers say about us seem like positive affirmations in comparison."

"Is that why you came home and bawled after your last photo shoot and the photographer said you looked like you'd been stuffed with cottage cheese the day you were created?"

"Oh, please. Kind of like the day you came home ugly-crying because a designer said you walked the runway like a methed-out drag queen?"

Again, I stayed quiet. It seemed like the safest option.

"Clearly we're in need of extensive psychological help," Jane said when she noticed me kind of gaping at them. "But this industry is all rejection for the most part. You have to grow a thick skin and make some good friends to kick you in the ass every now and again when you need it. I'd have given up years ago if it wasn't for Ariel reminding me why I got into modeling, and that a rejection from a designer didn't mean I needed to reject myself." Jane motioned at her own frame. "Because I'm a glorious beast, darling." She instantly lifted her pointer finger at Ariel. "And don't you go adding nothing about having the beast part right at least."

Ariel shifted on her puce beanbag, checking the trippy clock on the wall. "What agency are you with?"

"K&M," I answered.

They both gave an impressed look.

"I used to be with K&M until I started photographing too 'old.'" Ariel stuck out her tongue. "Now I'm with a different agency."

"One that specializes in the special needs of our senior citizens." Jane dodged Ariel's elbow just in time.

"Who's your agent?" Ariel asked.

"Mr. Lawson," I said, not knowing his first name. I had yet to meet him, since I'd signed on with the scout who'd discovered me.

Ariel's and Jane's heads twisted my way, their eyes scanning me in a new light.

"Ellis Lawson is *your* agent?" Jane said.

"Yeah?"

"Holy shit." Jane reached across Ariel to grab my arm. "Ellis Lawson is a god. The Modeling God."

My nose wrinkled. I knew he was one of the partners of the agency, but I'd only recently found out he'd be my agent. "He is?"

"You want to know how a model becomes a supermodel?" When my shoulder lifted, Jane added, "Ellis Lawson. That's how. Dude, he's responsible for churning out more supermodels than any other agent out there."

"He's also known for *doing* more supermodels than any other man alive."

Jane rolled her eyes at Ariel before giving me a serious look. "That's his other reputation. He's a bit of a ladies' man."

"And by 'a bit,' she means the toilet seats inside the public restrooms at Grand Central don't get as much ass as Ellis Lawson."

My face drew up. "Wow. Could have done without that vivid mental gem."

"If he decided to be your agent, you're going to be big. Huge." Jane shifted her beanbag so we were in more of a circle than a line. "Hey, we should swap phone numbers. You're new in town, probably looking to make some new friends." She pulled her phone out of her clutch. "We're the best type of friends you can find in this city."

"And she doesn't only say that because we have connections to get into the hippest clubs in the city," Ariel added.

"I mean because we keep it real." Jane punched a few things into her phone. "In an industry full of phonies and fakes, you need friends who tell it like it is. We're really good at telling it like it is."

I returned Jane's smile. "I noticed that."

"So? What are your digits?"

"Actually, I don't have a phone yet. I plan on getting one, but I am currently digit-less."

Jane and Ariel gaped at me.

"No phone?" Ariel sounded as though I'd just told her I had a month to live.

When I shrugged, Jane pulled an old gum wrapper from her purse, along with a pen, and wrote down some numbers. "Well, here's my number. Once you get one of those phone things, you know how to reach me." She winked as she dropped the wrapper into my palm. "Us small-town girls need to stick together."

"How do you know—"

"It's that wholesome thing you have going on." Jane's finger circled my face.

Ariel huffed. "If wholesome's the definition of 'small town,' you sure as hell weren't born and raised in one."

Jane's hand dropped to her curvy hip. "Just because I like entertaining gentlemen in my bed on a regular basis doesn't mean I'm not wholesome."

"My bad. I thought it meant you were a promiscuous lush."

Jane was ready to fire something back when the studio door burst open and a blinding mass of color and movement whisked toward us.

"Your Highness." The girl behind the desk came rushing out, automatically holding her arms out to take the woman's coat and purse.

Zelda Zhou, aka *Her Highness*, screamed to a stop in front of the three of us situated on the beanbags. She was barely pushing five foot, but I felt like she was towering above me. She was dressed to blind. And shock. And wow. She looked like she'd just come from Mardi Gras and was on her way to Carnival.

Her finger lifted. "Too top-heavy," she said of Jane, moving on to Ariel. "Too old." When her finger landed on me, she paused. I resisted the instinct to cower and expose my throat. "How old are you?"

Instead of flinching from her terse voice, I sat up straighter. "Nineteen."

Jane and Ariel were already moving toward the door, but they waved bye before leaving.

"How tall?"

"Five eleven and a half," I answered, standing when she motioned me up with a flick of her wrist.

She scanned me up and down. "Measurements?"

"Thirty-four twenty-five thirty-four."

The corners of her mouth sank even lower as her appraisal paused at my midsection. I'd never been as self-conscious about that part of my body as I became right then.

"Your waist is too big for the dress I have in mind for you." Her eyes lifted to meet mine. "Can you lose two inches off your waist by next week?"

"Maybe if I don't eat," I answered with a smile, joking.

She nodded, like she assumed I was being serious about starving myself for a week to lose two inches off an already small waist.

"Probably not," I added, holding out my portfolio for her.

She didn't take it. She just turned and marched away, her clothes causing a racket as she moved. "Okay, come back and see me when you have an actual model's waist that will fit into an actual sample-size couture gown."

I stood where I was for a good minute after she'd disappeared, blinking at the spot she'd last stood in. This was my very first go-see and I'd bombed it because what? I was too big? My waist was too fat? Good grief, how could it get any smaller without removing some non-essential organs?

Part of me wanted to cry. The other part reminded me that rejection was part of the business and to log this first one in the books and keep going. Checking my next appointment's address—it was at eleven—I consulted the map for a moment to make sure I knew where I was going, then I left Zelda Zhou's studio with a flourish.

Someone really needed to tell her that it didn't matter how "bold" the industry had deemed you, it should still be considered high treason in the fashion world to mix a chevron skirt with a paisley blouse.

The rest of the day continued in a similar fashion—at least in the sense of it being unusual and surprising. I thought I'd known all about how eccentric the fashion world was—I'd been reading about it since the first time I opened a fashion magazine at the age of seven—but reading about it was entirely different from being thrown into the three-ring circus with them.

Some clients treated me like I was the sibling they had been separated from at birth, and some behaved like I was no more human than the cell phone glued to their hand. Some wanted me to walk, some asked me to pose, only a couple actually glanced through my portfolio, but all of them were what I'd classify as supremely unique. I didn't know if I'd booked any jobs, but I definitely knew I hadn't booked a couple.

By the time I left the studio of my last go-see a little after seven, I was so tired I was half tempted to curl up in one of the lounge chairs inside the women's restroom waiting area and fall asleep. The bathroom was warm, and the thought of taking to the streets in my heels again, finding a subway station, and praying I made it back to the apartment felt like being tasked with solving the equation for nuclear fusion.

With the help of a few strangers, and a whole lot of help from luck, I somehow managed to make it back to my new apartment building. Before I climbed the stairs to the sixth floor, I took off my heels. When I glanced down to see the damage, I winced. I'd rubbed a few blisters raw, and my feet looked like I was nine months pregnant in the dead of summer. Swollen, blistered, and red. Hopefully no one wanted to book me for a barefoot photo shoot.

After I walked up six flights of stairs, I pulled out the key Soren had given me earlier, unlocked the door, and walked (hobbled) inside.

"Hello?" None of the lights were on inside, but it didn't feel right to just come in without announcing myself first. This might have been my apartment now too, but I still felt like the stranger. "Soren, are you here?"

When there was no answer, I flipped on some lights. I should have just left them off. The apartment looked like someone had held a party and invited the whole city. Clothes were strewn around, dirty dishes were scattered everywhere but inside the sink, and junk was littered between the rest of it. I'd only been gone a day, right? This morning, the place had been mostly tidy. How had it gone from that to this in ten hours?

Wandering into the bathroom to throw some cold water on my face, I found the sink coated in shaving cream and scraps of facial hair. Wet towels clumped on the floor. Dirty clothes in another pile. Toothpaste spots dotting the mirror above the sink. The toilet seat lid up, the toilet paper roll empty to boot.

Deciding I'd had a long enough day without trying to process just what degree of a slob I'd moved in with, I clomped to my "bedroom." After shimmying out of my jeans, I slid into my sleeping bag, closed my eyes, and imagined I was going to wake up and everything would be better.

CHAPTER Three

Everything was worse.

That was what I woke up to the next morning. Soren was one of those heavy-breather types when he slept, which I probably wouldn't have even noticed if we had actual walls instead of flimsy, bamboo dividers.

I woke up when my alarm first went off, wondering why I still felt tired after getting ten full hours of sleep. My feet looked worse than they had last night, but I was hoping a warm shower and some movement would help with that.

Sliding out of my sleeping bag, I gathered my outfit for the day before moving toward the bathroom. Soren must have been working last night, because I hadn't heard him get back. It was kind of creepy to realize I hadn't stirred when some guy I barely knew crawled into a bed no farther than fifteen feet away from my own.

The apartment was dark, but a hint of morning light cast through the windows, revealing an apartment that had gone from messy to warzone. What in the hell? My feet rolled to a stop when I saw the table covered in books, to-go boxes, soda cans, and an assortment of baseball paraphernalia. Something hanging from the blades of the ceiling fan caught my eye.

My face pinched up at the same time I covered my eyes. Jockstraps. He was hang-drying his jockstraps from our ceiling fan. Trying to erase the image of Soren's unmentionables dangling from a ceiling fan from my mind, I darted for the bathroom before I could take in anything else that would cause permanent mental scarring.

I'd barely made it three steps before I tripped over something right in the middle of the hall. My hand managed to brace against the wall to keep me from falling, but the incident had my blood pumping and my anger stirring. What was his giant duffel bag of baseball crap doing in the middle of the hallway? Probably the same spot he'd let it fall off his shoulder, then decided that was as good a spot as any to store one's personal objects.

As I took my shower, I reminded myself what he'd done for me so far. He might have taken messy to a new level, but he was a decent human being. That didn't do much to make me feel better. I was living with this messy, decent person. In a confined space. For at least the next six months.

Given I trended toward the neat-freak end of the spectrum, I found myself entertaining the knowledge I'd rather be sharing an apartment with a tidy, not-so-decent individual.

My shower went extra long, thanks to yesterday's lack of one and today's necessity of working out some irritation by loofahing the heck out of my skin. I came out looking pink from all the scrubbing.

Once I'd dressed and gone through my standard morning ritual, I left the bathroom. Soren was still asleep, which was probably for the best since I likely would have greeted him in an unpleasant way to start a new day. Especially when I noticed the carton of milk left out on the counter. From back here, it looked like it was already growing mold.

As I packed up what I needed for the day, I made as little noise as possible, then I tiptoed toward the door. From a few steps back, I noticed something taped to the door. It was a twenty-dollar bill. A yellow sticky note was attached to it. *Just in case. You can pay me back by introducing me to your future supermodel friends.* That was followed by a smiley face with its tongue sticking out.

I didn't want to take the money. I hated owing a person something, and I felt guilty taking it after all the things I'd grumbled about him in the shower. I didn't want to take it—*borrow* it—but I needed it. If having to accept some favors from my roommate was what it took to get me on the right track, that was worth swallowing my pride.

I took the twenty down, grabbed the pen from my purse, and scratched my own note onto the yellow sticky. *Now I owe you twenty dollars and a subway ticket.* After adding my own smiley face with its tongue hanging out, I slipped out of the apartment.

Today was the same as yesterday. Subway. Agency. Go-sees. A pattern seemed to be emerging, and with each client I met, I became more comfortable with the process. I got a better overall response from today's meetings than from yesterday's, so by the end of the day, I was feeling pretty amazing when I returned to the apartment building. Having sneakers for my commute made a big difference too, not to mention having a couple dollars in my wallet when my stomach staged a protest and would not let me pass the next food cart without getting a soft pretzel with cheese sauce.

My stomach started its protest again when I reached the fifth floor and the smell of something fantastic became present. It got stronger the closer I got to the apartment. The sound of pans clamoring was echoing in the hall as I unlocked the door.

"Hayden?" Soren's voice chimed from the kitchen.

"What are you making? It smells amazing." I paused beside the entrance of the kitchen, checking him out as much as I did what was on the stove. He was in a pair of light grey sweats that barely clung to his hips. The shirt and shoes were missing, but the ball cap was in place, backward and resting low.

"Chicken marsala. It's my mom's recipe. You like Italian?"

"I like Italian," I said, having to force my eyes to look away from him. *And I liked whatever nationality the person cooking Italian tonight was.*

When I realized I was having marginally dirty thoughts about my roommate, I gave myself a mental thrashing. Crushes, fantasies, and dirty thoughts would not be entertained where my roommate was concerned.

"Do you usually cook like that?" I asked after dropping my bag off at my bed space.

He glanced down at himself. "How do you cook?"

"Usually it involves more clothing."

"This way, I don't have to worry about staining my shirt." Right then, a bubble of sauce popped in the pan, sending a splatter onto his abs, causing him to flinch. I was so not staring at their muscle definition or the web of veins trailing into the waistband of his sweats. After running his fingers across his stomach, he licked off the sauce. "Easy cleanup."

I'd been so distracted by him licking sauce off his abs, it took me a minute to realize the state of the apartment. Nothing had been cleaned up from earlier. But more mess had been added to the mix.

"We need to talk." I slid into the kitchen doorway, figuring it would be better to address some apartment rules sooner rather than later.

"Don't mention it. Really."

"Don't mention what?"

His shoulder lifted as he reached for the last two clean plates in the cabinet. "The twenty I spotted you."

"Thankful as I am for that, it's actually something else I want to talk about."

He started plating the chicken. "Shoot."

"The apartment . . ."

"What about it?" He licked more sauce off his thumb as he moved on to scooping mashed potatoes onto the plates.

"It's a disaster." So much for trying to be delicate about it.

He kept working. "If you think this is a disaster, you should have seen the place when it was me and my old roommate."

That thought made me shudder. "The apartment was clean when I moved in."

"Yeah?"

"Why was it so clean then and not even close two days later?"

"Because I was trying to make a good impression." Grabbing the two plates, he moved past me toward the table.

"So you were trying to trick me into moving in with you? Making me think you cleaned up after yourself instead of . . .?" I kicked at his duffel, which was right back to blocking the center of the hallway.

"Instead of what?" He looked up as he set down the plates.

Half of my face pulled up as I debated how to word it without causing offense. "Instead of you *not* cleaning up after yourself."

"Are you calling me a slob?" He flattened his hands on the table and stared across the room at me.

This was blowing up in my face, and now I was questioning myself for bringing it up. I'd never had a roommate before—that I wasn't related to, anyway—and wasn't sure how to make it a successful partnership. Was it better to be a laid-back type or was it better to bring stuff up before it drove me insane and I exploded on him? "No. I'm not calling you anything. I'm just saying you seem to have a tough time cleaning up after yourself."

"Translation—I'm a slob." He settled into his chair and motioned at the one he'd set the other plate in front of.

"You've got your jockstraps hanging from the ceiling fan. That's above the dining room table." I pointed at the fan as I moved closer.

"I hang them there to dry." He motioned at the fan too. "If I'm such a slob, you should be grateful I'm at least cleaning them."

"I'm not calling you a slob. I'm trying to address this in a mature, respectful way."

He was cutting into his chicken like he had some sort of vendetta against it. "I go to school, play ball, and work. I even try to do my homework on occasion." He circled his fork at where his backpack looked like it had vomited its contents on the couch. "I'm busy. I don't have a lot of free time, and what I do have I'm not inclined to spend it cleaning." He stuffed a bite into his mouth, continuing on as he chewed. "If you had some sort of expectation that your roommate be a neat-freak, you should have mentioned that before you decided to move in."

"I didn't have neat-freak expectations, but you did make sure the apartment was clean and organized when I first saw the place." As I sat down in front of the second plate, my stomach growled. I was hungry, but something felt wrong about eating a meal he'd prepared for me while we were arguing.

"What? Are you accusing me of tricking you now? Taking advantage of you because I wanted the place to look nice when you arrived?" He snorted as he cut off another bite. "It's called wanting to make a good first impression. That's what I was trying to do, but next time the inclination to do that hits me, I'll make sure to save myself the time and energy. Since you're probably going to find some way to turn it around on me."

Rolling my neck, I inhaled to give myself a moment to think before I snapped back. "Okay, I'm sorry I accused you of trying to trick me." Another pause to give myself a chance to word it right. "But do you think you could at least try to clean up some of your stuff? Some of the time?"

He stopped chewing mid-bite, giving me a look. "Sure. I'll go ahead and hire a housekeeper to come in every day to make my roommate happy since she's one of those people who have a fetish for everything being clean."

My eyes narrowed. "I don't have a fetish for cleanliness."

"You obviously do because this"—he circled his arm around the room—"is not that bad."

My gaze circled the same room. "This"—my nose wrinkled when I noticed the same milk jug on the counter—"is a few spores of mold and grime away from becoming condemned."

Soren's silverware clattered onto his plate. Then he shoved back from the table and stood. "I lost my appetite," he announced before stepping onto the chair to pull his undergarments from the fan blades.

A sigh rose from inside me. So much for trying to have an adult discussion about this. "Soren . . ."

He didn't answer. He just kept moving around the apartment, picking up one item of his at a time.

"Soren, come on, stop."

His neck was rigid, his jaw set, and he only seemed to get more upset with each thing he picked up. Once he had a heap in his arms, he stormed over to his bed area and dropped it all in there. Then he came back for more.

"Soren, I mean it, stop."

"Sorry, can't stop. Need to get my stuff cleaned up. My roommate is throwing a fit."

"I'm not throwing a fit. You're the one acting like a child right now."

He yanked the duffel off the floor. "Oh, nice. Now you're accusing me of being a slob *and* a child?"

"I'm not accusing you of being anything. All I did was address the state of the apartment and request you make a bit of an effort to clean up after yourself." I twisted in my seat as he moved around the room.

He was acting so immature. How could he go from cooking chicken marsala one minute to behaving like a five-year-old the next? God, and that line of hair he kept tucked out around the sides of his head so it curled beneath the brim of his cap. Couldn't he tuck those chunks in with the rest of his hair? It looked ridiculous.

And could he pull up those sweats already? Any lower, and I was going to get to know him on a whole new level.

And why was I nit-picking the way the end of his hair curled under his hat? Or his low-hanging sweats? Crap. Maybe I was being petty. Or maybe it was something else —something I didn't want to assign a name to.

"And look at me now? Making an effort to clean up my shit." He showed me the contents in his arms this round before making another dump behind his room partition. "Happy now?"

"Please just come and finish eating." I stared at his half-eaten meal.

"I don't think so. You'd probably criticize me for the way I eat or something stupid like that."

A long groan rolled out of me. This had gone so entirely wrong. "I'm not going to criticize the way you eat."

"Maybe. But for your information, having manners around a table growing up with three older brothers made you a target." He marched back out, scanning the apartment for anything else of his. "By the time my mom got around to me, she was so worn out, the only manner she was still preaching was respecting women."

My head was starting to pound and my stomach was still growling. I wasn't sure if I was wrong for bringing this up the way I had, or if he was just taking it wrong, or if it was some mixture of both. I just knew having a roommate was hard. Especially when Soren and I had been mere strangers a few days ago.

"Please come eat. I'm sorry."

"No, no. I'm going to finish cleaning up after myself so I can sit down and eat a meal in peace without being nagged at." He moved into the bathroom next. "We're not even married and I already feel like I can't do anything right."

"Okay, now you are being immature." I cut into my chicken and took a bite. If this was how he was going to deal with every issue we needed to resolve, I wasn't going to waste too much time feeling guilty.

"Excuse me for thinking that someone like you wouldn't have all of these crazy expectations when it comes to a roommate."

I froze in the middle of cutting my next bite. "Someone like me?" Then I twisted in my chair, my eyes narrowing in the direction of the bathroom. "Someone like me? A girl who grew up poor in a poor town? That automatically means I have low-to-no expectations in life? That I don't have any standards?"

His head appeared in the doorway. "Putting words into my mouth now too?" His eyebrows carved into his forehead. "Someone like you as in someone who gets it. Someone who's down to earth and knows what's important in life. *That* someone like you." He held my stare a moment longer before disappearing in the bathroom again.

I turned back around in my seat and rubbed my temples. What was wrong with me? Assuming the worst? Jumping to conclusions?

Since he was still making a racket in the bathroom, I worked on my dinner to give myself a chance for some self-reflection. Dinner was good. Really good. He knew what he was doing, and the longer I sat there eating, the worse I felt for bringing up the whole messy state of the apartment in the first place.

"The bathroom's cleaned. My junk is picked up." He emerged out of the bathroom smelling like Windex. He wouldn't look at me as he took his seat behind his dinner again. "The kitchen's all yours."

My fork froze midair. "The kitchen's all mine?" I repeated, just to make sure I'd heard him right.

"Shared space. I tackled the bathroom. It's only fair you get the kitchen."

I blinked at him. He was serious. "I haven't stepped foot in the kitchen since I moved in."

One of his shoulders lifted like that was beside the point.

"I haven't used one dish."

"You're using dishes right now." He motioned at the plate and fork in front of me.

Wherever the boil button was installed inside me, he'd just hit it. "I'm not cleaning up after you. Nice try." I glanced toward the kitchen, cringing when I thought of how much time and sweat it would take to get all of those crusty plates and pans cleaned.

"I just cleaned up after you." His arm thrust toward the bathroom. "You had a bunch of long hairs stuck on the shower walls, already clogging up the drain." Before I could say anything, he kept going. "And come on, I cooked dinner for you and gave you carte blanche to raid my snack stores."

My fork dropped to my plate. "So what? I'm indebted to you now? I owe you?"

"Most people don't expect everything and give nothing in return. Most people would realize if I cook, you clean." Soren was talking and chewing at the same time. He really did have the manners of a caveman. "It's called a partnership. Not a dictatorship."

Every word that came from him made me madder and madder until I couldn't stay in my seat another moment. Bursting out of my seat, my fists curled at my sides. "No, this is a misogynist regime. I know why you really wanted a woman as a roommate. So you could have her clean up after you. So she'd be happy to scrub your crusty dishes and nasty pans because you threw a meal together and shared some of the extras with her." I found myself glaring at what was left on my plate, wishing I hadn't taken a single bite. "You're two centuries behind. Time to catch up and clean up your own damn mess."

For as upset as I was getting, Soren stayed totally chill. Eating his dinner, his expression indicated he was having a normal conversation. "If I was two centuries behind, I'd expect you to do the cooking and the cleaning. Instead, I'm asking if you'd consider doing the cleaning since I did the cooking." His eyes moved from his dinner to mine. "Any questions?"

One by one, my arms folded over my stomach. "I'm not cleaning the kitchen."

He made a face that indicated he didn't care. "Fine. Then I guess that's the way it's going to remain until somebody does because after I finish demoing my dinner, I have to finish a lab and study for a test."

My shoulders lifted. "Fine by me."

Soren's head tipped. "Then why did you bring up the messy state of the apartment in the first place if it's 'fine by you' that the kitchen stays looking like a crime scene?"

When he smiled in gloaty victory, I let out a frustrated groan I hadn't wanted him to hear. I didn't want him to know he was getting to me or irritating me or making me want to create my own crime scene.

"I take it back. You *are* a child."

As I marched toward my partition, he chuckled. "And who's the one marching away after throwing a tantrum?"

My teeth ground together to keep the next scream of frustration to myself. The moment I got behind my partition, I adjusted it so it concealed more of my area than before. It wasn't even eight yet, but I didn't know what else to do besides go to bed. I didn't want to hang around where I could see him or he could see me. I sure as hell didn't want to clean the kitchen. What I wanted was a real door I could slam and lock, a room of my own I could escape to when I needed to cry it all out. What I wanted was a different apartment and a different roommate. One that didn't make me jealous of a splatter of sauce that had touched his abs one minute, and emotionally unstable the next. I was used to being the low-key, even-tempered one, but Soren had a way of bringing out emotions I hadn't known I was capable of expressing.

I had to make it big. I had to make it happen soon. The sooner I could get away from Soren Decker, the better off I'd be.

CHAPTER Four

My head was still throbbing the next morning. I'd fallen asleep to a headache and waken up to one. I beat my alarm this morning, so after turning it off so it didn't disturb my "roommate," I grabbed my outfit for the day and moved toward the shower. It was dark outside, but there was still one light on in the apartment—the torchiere beside the dining table. Soren was in the same chair he'd been in last night, books and notebooks scattered around. He'd fallen asleep studying.

His head was on an open book, a pencil still clutched in his hand. He was doing his typical heavy mouth breathing. Every time he exhaled, he made the sheet of paper he'd been working on rattle. Still shirtless, his cap was sitting backward on his head, that light fringe of hair still curling beneath the brim.

Seeing him like this, I almost had the urge to drape a blanket around him or something. He was cute when he was sleeping, sweet when his mouth was shut. Too bad he couldn't stay like that for the next six months, I thought as I noticed the kitchen. It was in the same condition it had been in last night. The milk that had been left in the gallon had now turned from white to some shade of greenish-gray.

Gross. It was a miracle the place wasn't crawling in rats yet.

Moving extra fast today so I could escape before he woke up, I was out the front door a little before seven. I had another meeting this morning with Mr. Lawson to go over how my go-sees had gone, and hopefully he'd actually be there for this one.

By day three, I felt like I'd already mastered the art of the subway and felt like I almost blended in with the rest of the hardy New Yorkers ready to tackle another day. The wide-eyed Nebraska girl was becoming a city girl. I still had twelve dollars left over from the twenty Soren had left me yesterday, and when I took it out to pay for my subway ticket, another one of those guilty pangs hit me hard in the gut.

He might have been a barbarian, but he was a decent enough one where it counted. So he left the toilet seat up and dried his jocks from the ceiling fan—he also cooked me dinner (when I couldn't have afforded a package of ramen on my own) and left me a twenty-dollar bill taped to the front door. And helped me navigate the subway. And . . .

I didn't want to think about it. I needed to focus on getting through the day, doing my best, and booking some jobs. I could work out all things Soren later.

The K&M Models office was buzzing at seven thirty in the morning. A cluster of models was lining the chairs in the waiting area, and the same young woman who'd helped me a few days ago was there to greet me when I strolled up to the front desk.

"Hello again," I greeted. "I'm—"

"Right this way, Miss Hayes." The girl slid out of her chair and came around the side of her desk. "Mr. Lawson is ready for you."

She knew my name. No one had referred to me by name yet in this business. It was more of a "you" or a pointed finger. "My appointment isn't until eight."

"It's okay. Mr. Lawson asked that I bring you back whenever you arrived."

The girl moved down the long hallway like she was working an actual catwalk, with four-inch heels and everything. Five more inches, and she would have been one of those models on the covers. Genetics had so much to do with the people we became, the positions we were put—or forced—into.

We didn't stop until we'd reached the end of the hall. The smoked glass door was closed, E Lawson etched in large, bold lettering. For some reason, I suddenly felt more nervous to meet my agent than I had at any go-see I'd been to.

"Mr. Lawson?" The woman rapped on the door a few times. "Miss Hayes is here to see you."

"Send her in." The voice on the other side of that door had an air of authority, the kind I wasn't sure I'd ever heard rivaled.

The woman opened the door halfway, stepping aside to let me pass.

"Thank you," I said. I wanted to say, "Aren't you coming in with me?"

She gave a little curtsy then closed the door the moment I'd cleared the threshold. I felt like I was being trapped. Or herded.

The first thing my eyes were drawn to was the man looming behind the desk. Like his voice, everything about him exuded the kind of confidence that demanded to be acknowledged. He hadn't said a word since I'd stepped in —he hadn't even looked my way yet—but I already knew this was a person who didn't often hear the word "no."

Ellis Lawson must have been in his forties, but he didn't look it. He'd clearly been a model before starting the agency. He had the chiseled sort of face that screamed couture, and he filled out a suit the way designers envisioned when creating their designs.

All this, and he had yet to lift his gaze from his sleek gunmetal laptop.

"Miss Hayes." Finally, he rose from his chair and moved toward me. "Nice to finally meet you. I apologize for my absence early in the week."

"It happens. Nice to meet you too."

I held out my hand as he approached and was totally taken by surprise when he leaned in for the hug. My arm kind of got lodged in between us, my other one hesitantly moving around him to pat his back.

Awkward.

It was one of those longer hugs too, tight squeeze and all.

Super awkward.

Rubbing my back one last time, he finally stepped back. I'd been so distracted by the hug, I hadn't noticed how tall he was. Like, the kind of tall that almost had me feeling short. In my heels and all.

"How has the city been treating you so far?" he asked, his eyes roving up and down me.

"It's been good. I like it." I took a few steps back because again, he didn't seem to get the personal space concept. Being as big as he was, with as much confidence as poured off of him, he really should have been respectful of people's bubbles.

"Homesick?" He backed up to his desk and leaned into the edge of it.

"I miss my family. I don't miss Nebraska."

His smile suggested he knew how I felt. He had a nice smile, one that had probably cost tens of thousands to perfect. He even had nice lips, which was just strange to think about a guy. But Ellis Lawson did. He had nice everything. Even the silver that was starting to streak through his dark hair was nice.

"That's good to hear, because your family you can move. A Midwest state, not so easily transported." Mr. Lawson rolled his fingers along the edge of his desk, fighting a smile, though I wasn't sure why. It was like he was in on a secret. "I've heard back from almost all of the clients you had go-sees with the past couple of days."

My stomach hiccupped. I wasn't sure if I'd booked a single client; that was how much any of them had indicated their like or dislike of me. Fashion designers could have been the world's best poker players, I swear.

"Would you like to know who you booked?" Mr. Lawson prompted as my silence continued.

"I booked someone?!" My voice went higher.

He gave me an amused look, still rolling his fingers along the lip of his desk. "You booked them all," he said, a dark eyebrow lifting. "Well, all except for Zelda Zhou, but I don't think 'Her Highness' has ever once booked a model who didn't look like an emaciated little boy."

My mind was struggling to catch up to what he'd just said. "I booked them all?" I echoed, my feet starting to bounce. "Except for Zelda Zhou, I booked them all?"

When I looked at him, needing the confirmation, he pointed at me. "You did."

"Holy crap," I whispered, feeling light-headed and heavy-headed at the same time.

"I hope you're a hard worker, because I'm going to be asking a lot of you over the next few months. I've seen a dozen supermodel's careers go from nothing to every-thing, and this, right here, is how it starts." His finger moved to point at the floor between us. "If you already have this many designers seeing something in you when you're a nobody, every major designer in the world will want you for their campaign next year. You're going to be an icon. The kind of model the whole nation knows by name."

My head was definitely moving more into the light-headed territory, so I slid to the side to fall into the chair in front of the desk.

"I'll have Jennifer print out your schedule for the next couple of weeks so you know where you need to be when, and I'm going to give you my private number so you can get a hold of me whenever you need to, day or night." Grabbing a business card on his desk, he flipped it over and scribbled down a number. "Text me later so I have your number on my personal phone as well."

Taking the card, I shifted in the chair. "Actually, I don't have a cell phone. Yet," I added when he gave me a look that suggested I'd just confessed to not being able to read.

"Why not?" he asked, not waiting for an answer. "You're a professional model now. You need a cell phone. You need a way for people to get a hold of you."

"I promise, it will be the first thing I purchase once I cash my first check." After paying this upcoming month's rent, utilities, and stocking up on ramen. And a winter coat.

"Your first check will take weeks before it's issued."

Heart-stopping moment number two of the meeting. Though this one wasn't brought on by the warm happies.

"Weeks? But I thought you just said I booked all of those clients. They're going to pay me, right?" I didn't mean to sound so stressed, but I couldn't hide it. Rent was due in ten days, and there was no way I could ask Soren for another favor, especially not one as big as covering my rent next month. Provided he even could, which was assuming a lot of a college kid working a part-time job.

"Yes, they'll pay you, but first, you have to do the job. Then they have to write the check. To us. Then we take our cut, draw up a new check, and that's when you get paid. These things take time. It's not like you're working at Burger King and getting regular checks every two weeks."

Thankfully, I was sitting down. I'd just gone from feeling like my dreams were falling out of the sky into my lap, to having them stolen away a moment later.

It was quiet in the office for a minute. I felt Mr. Lawson watching me, trying to figure out if I was in as tight of a spot as I was making it seem.

"Tell you what? I'll pay an advance on your first check." He pulled a money clip from inside his jacket. I didn't realize people carried that much cash on them at one time. I'd felt like a baller the one time I had fifty-three dollars in my wallet after I'd worked all day in a cornfield last summer. "Would a thousand be enough to get you by for a while?"

When he held out ten hundred-dollar bills, all I could do was gape at it. I'd never seen that much money in one person's hand at one time. Not once. Here he was, holding it out for me to take.

"Of course not, this is an expensive city." He pulled some more bills from his clip to add to the pile. "Here. A two thousand-dollar advance on your first check. If you need more, you know my number." When I didn't move to take the money, he reached for my hand and placed it on my palm.

"Mr. Lawson—"

"It's Ellis, and yes, you can take it." He put his money clip away again—it still looked just as thick. "Might I suggest you make a stop by a cell phone store as soon as you leave here? Text me your number right after."

My eyesight was going blurry, which meant I was getting close to crying, but I wasn't going to cry. Not in front of my agent. "Mr. Lawson—" I tried again. "Ellis, I think I'll be giving you my next ten paychecks to pay this back to you."

He was grinning at me, almost smirking. "Believe me, your first one will more than cover this little cash advance."

It was impossible to conceive of that kind of money —the kind that could change the course of my family's lives and my own.

"You're going to be big. I've never been wrong before, and I won't be wrong with you. Just do what I tell you, and this city will be chanting your name by this time next year."

CHAPTER

Five

Wandering the streets of New York with two grand in my purse made me feel like I was trying to make it through Sherwood Forest without running into the Merry Men. I swore everyone who passed me could read on my face how much money I had on me. On the subway, I clung to my purse like the mothers clinging to their toddler's hands.

After stopping at a cell phone store, I made a quick stop at a pizza take-out place. Exchanging money for something felt so good. It was the first thing I'd been able to pay for with my own money as an official resident of the city.

By the time I reached the fourth floor of our building, I could smell the scent of cleaners. It became stronger with every stair I took, until I realized where it was coming from. Juggling the giant pizza box in one hand, I unlocked the door and stepped inside.

The smell inside was intense. A combo of fake lemon, Windex, and vinegar. Still, it was better than eau de dirty underwear.

"Soren?"

I heard him talking, but I didn't realize he was actually singing until I moved a few steps far enough inside to peek into the kitchen. With a pair of headphones covering his ears, he was humming along to some song and moving his body in ways that had me close to blushing. In one hand he held a bottle of cleaner. In the other was what looked like an old shirt he'd turned into a rag.

The sink was spilling over with suds and dishes soaking, and the old food and boxes had been tossed into the garbage. He was scrubbing the stove right now as he started to belt out some lyrics. At the same time, he moved against the stove like it was a dance partner who liked to get freaky.

So my roommate knew how to move his body. So he knew how to dance. Why was I feeling that fluttery stomach sensation from watching him grinding against an outdated appliance? I didn't really want to answer that question, so I dropped the pizza on the table and stepped into the kitchen to help. He was singing again, twirling his shirt-rag in the air.

When he finally noticed me, he didn't jolt or seem surprised to see me.

"Nice dancing," I said, loud enough I thought I was speaking over his headphones. "And singing."

Soren slid his headphones behind his neck, continuing to dance. "I'm a double threat."

"Not a triple?" I asked doubtfully.

His head shook once. "I can't act for shit."

"Really?"

"Do I seem like the type of guy who's good at pretending?"

Moving toward the sink, I pushed up my sleeves. "Double threat it is."

He chuckled and got back to scrubbing a crusty spot in one of the burners. When he saw me dip my hands into the sink to start washing, he moved up beside me and tried to hip-check me out of the way.

"I got this," he said, bumping his hip against mine again when I refused to budge. "You were right last night. This mess is all on me. Pretty sure this is the first time you've stepped foot in the kitchen."

"No, you were right actually. You cooked your food for me. The least I could do in return is clean the kitchen after." I started scrubbing the first dish my fingers touched.

When he accepted I wasn't going anywhere, he stationed himself as the rinse-and-dry guy. "I'm not going to tell my mom you just said that."

"Why not?"

"Because I just spent two hours this afternoon being lectured by her on things a guy can and can't say to a girl, and according to her, I committed one of the great offenses of all time last night when I suggested it was your responsibility to clean the kitchen." He winced like he was remembering the conversation. "Apparently it's very not okay for a guy to suggest it's a woman's job to clean a kitchen. Even if he didn't mean it in any antiquated, gender-profiling way."

I smiled into the sink as I handed him a clean dish. "But you didn't say it was my job to clean it. You merely suggested I might be willing to do it since you'd cooked the meal. There's nothing wrong with that."

"According to my mom, there's everything wrong with that." He dried the dish and tucked it away in the cabinet. "And I'm also supposed to tell you that it won't happen again. She said that was important. Oh, and to apologize. Which I think I already did, right?" He paused, his forehead creasing. "Just in case, I'm sorry for being a prehistoric asshole last night, Hayden. It won't happen again." His head shook as he rinsed the next dish. "Actually, I can't guarantee that one hundred percent because I'm not the actor type. I say what I think. I express how I feel. I'm not good at playing a role or pretending. So if I fall into that asshole mode again, just throw one of those heels of yours at my face or something."

When he nudged me, his arm running down mine, my hands stopped scrubbing the pan I was working at. I'd brushed up or passed thousands of people in my life, but this was the one instance where I felt an odd, buzzing warmth exchanging between us. I slid just enough aside so our arms weren't touching.

"You weren't the only asshole last night. I was too. Let's just file it away as roommate growing pains and move on." I finally managed to get the last of the crust off the pan, then I handed it to him. "Tonight, *I* made dinner and guess what? No dishes to fight over who should do them." When I glanced at the dining table, Soren noticed the pizza box.

"How did you know I was craving pizza?"

"I didn't. I just knew I was and figured you wouldn't argue if I shared."

As he dried the pan, his brows came together. "How did you manage to pay for the pizza?"

"By the exchange of money for goods," I answered, giving him a funny look.

His eyebrows lifted. "Where did you get the money? You couldn't have enough left over from the twenty I left you to have paid for an extra-large from Fultano's."

"I paid with my own money."

Soren glanced at me. I could still hear whatever music he'd been rocking out to buzzing in the headphones draped around his neck. "Your own money ran out before you made it to the front door of my apartment. Nice try."

My scrubbing became more vigorous thanks to him calling me out and also being right. "How do you know that?"

"Why are you trying to hide it?"

There were only a few more dishes in the sink, so I took my time washing them. "Because it's humiliating."

"Why's it humiliating? We all know what it's like to have empty pockets. Well, most of us do. Those silver-spooners who've never had to worry about money a day in their lives don't come out nearly as well-adjusted as the rest of us. It's the hard times that make us who we are. The rough stuff that shapes us." He nudged me and took the cup that had been clean twenty swipes ago.

"I got an advance on my first paycheck from the modeling agency. So now I'll be able to afford food, subway tickets, and rent."

"That's a sweet deal. I wish I could get the restaurant to pay me an advance on my checks."

"I don't think they normally do it, but my agent must have made a special exception when he realized I was so broke I didn't have a cell phone. I don't know what he would have said if I'd told him I didn't even have a few dollars to pay for a subway ticket."

Soren stopped drying the last glass. "He? Your agent's a dude?"

Pulling the drain, I glanced at him. "I mean, I didn't do any anatomy checks to confirm it, but yeah, pretty sure he's a he."

"And this 'he' gave you an advance on your paycheck?"

"Yeah," I said, drawing it out a few moments longer than necessary.

"Was this a cash type of advance?" He tucked the glass away then turned toward me, crossing his arms.

"Considering I don't have a bank account here to cash a check at yet, yeah, it was cash." Why did I sound so defensive?

Soren's brow cocked. "Did this cash advance come directly out of his wallet?"

"No," I answered immediately. When his brow only went higher, I groaned. "It came out of his money clip. *Not* his wallet."

He made a noise. One of those that didn't suggest much, but made me feel like he was suggesting everything. He continued to stand there, leaning into the counter like he was waiting for an explanation or something.

He was my roommate. He wasn't my dad, my brother, my boyfriend, or my spiritual leader. I didn't have anything to explain to him. There was nothing to explain anyway. I needed money. I was going to be making money soon. My agent stepped in to help.

"I don't like what you're suggesting," I stated, crossing my arms the way he was.

"I'm not suggesting anything."

My finger tapped his elevated brow. "This is."

"What do you think I'm suggesting then?"

"That he gave me money in exchange for sex."

My bluntness seemed to take him by surprise. For all of one and a half seconds.

"That's the way the modeling industry is, right?" I continued. "No one made it to the top without putting in the time on their back first?"

I'd taken him by surprise again. This time for two and a half seconds.

"Why would some guy you just met give a woman a couple hundred dollars, Hayden?" Soren followed me out of the kitchen. "You might be innocent, but you're not naive."

"Who said I was innocent?"

"That stamp you have stuck to your forehead." When Soren's finger came around to tap my temple, I pushed it away.

"It wasn't a couple hundred dollars, by the way. It was a couple thousand."

Then only my footsteps continued toward the table.

"Two grand? That guy fronted you two grand out of his own bankroll?" He let out a low whistle. "Please don't tell me you took it."

When I motioned at the pizza, I guess that answered his question.

"You really are that naïve."

"It's fine, Soren. Let's eat." I pried open the pizza box.

"Not fine. He wants something from you."

"Yeah, he's my agent. He wants me to book jobs."

"Something else."

"Please."

"No, you'll thank me later when the creep proves me right."

"So any guy who offers a girl he just met money has some expectation for sex in return?" I paused just long enough, giving him an accusatory look. "It's not like I'm standing five feet away from someone like that."

Soren shifted, jabbing his thumb into his chest. "I'm your roommate."

My arms flew out at my sides. I was not eager to get into an argument over dinner again tonight. "And he's my agent."

His mouth opened to say something else, but he managed to catch himself before it came out. Swallowing, he cleared his throat and moved closer. "So what does it mean if some girl I just met brings me home free pizza?"

I fought a smile as I pulled him out a slice. "That she's so expecting sex in exchange for all of this cheesy goodness."

He took it and tore off a healthy-sized bite. "You get two grand, I get a few slices of pizza. Damn, I'm one cheap lay."

We were both laughing, but the topic we were circling made me uncomfortable. Not sex by itself, but sex as it related to Soren. Because now I was thinking about it. Picturing him moving under a sheet, imagining the sounds he made, visualizing myself as the one he was with.

"You're blushing." Soren pointed his half-eaten pizza slice at my face.

"I'm hot."

"It's an icebox in here."

Yeah, it was. Instead of confirming or denying that, I grabbed a piece of pizza to distract me.

"So, honey, how was your day?" Soren nudged me as he came around the table to sit in what must have been his favorite chair. It was the same one he always sat in, the one he'd been sleeping in this morning.

"Great, actually. I booked every single one of the clients I met with except for one." I scooted into the chair across from him, the one that I guessed was becoming my favorite. "And I got my very own phone."

"And two thousand dollars from some dude you just met," he muttered between bites.

"A two thousand dollar *advance* on future earnings."

Soren gave me that same look that suggested the money was given in exchange for something else. I ignored it.

"How was your day?" When he circled his hand, waiting, I tacked on, "Honey?"

He grinned when I said it—even though I'd paired it with an eye roll. "Fantastic, thank you for asking." He dug another slice from the box. "I killed it at practice today. I'm surprised the pros aren't already knocking on my door."

"I'm sure they're on their way." When I tore off a chunk of crust, I knew New York style pizza and I were going to be good friends. That processed five-dollar junk back home was an offense to actual pizza.

Soren checked his wrist as if he were wearing a watch. "Any minute now."

When I laughed, he beamed his massive grin at me before sawing off another bite of pizza. My stomach did the flutter thing again. Why was it doing that so much lately? Why was it only happening around Soren? If I could just focus on his personality instead of his physical features, that would help. His personality that was . . . generous, fun, considerate, the kind that apologized, and still talked to his mom. Damn, he was as attractive in the personality department as he was on the outside.

Pizza, I thought. Focus on the redefining pizza. Not on what's sitting across the table from you, grinning like he was game for anything and everything.

"Look at us." Soren waved his finger between us. "Just a couple of big dreamers in the big city."

"Just like everyone else our age."

"Yeah, but unlike everyone else our age, we're going to do it."

"Do what?" I asked.

He leaned back in his chair, his eyes sparkling. "Dominate the shit out of our dreams."

I lifted my half-eaten slice of pizza. "To dominating the shit out of our dreams."

He lifted his. "I'll eat to that."

Then we both took a ceremonious bite, which made me laugh again.

"Okay, so I'm going to work on the clean thing. I promise. It's not going to be easy, but I'll make an effort. I've got twenty years of slobbery I'm fighting to over-come." He rested his forearms on the table and leaned into it. "Fair enough?"

"More than fair. And I promise to work on being more chill about that kind of stuff and not trying to control everything. I've got years of controlling and supervising to overcome."

Soren slid his headphones off his neck and punched the music off on his phone. "Oldest child?"

I nodded, kicking my sneakers off to get comfortable. "Yeah, and Mom had to work multiple jobs to support us, so that left me in charge of my younger sisters."

He was quiet a minute, his face serious for one short-lived moment. "So I'm like the annoying little brother you never had?"

"Pretty much."

My response was met with a feigned wounded expression. "My mom always used to say she pitied the women her sons would one day marry. She said they'd all have their work cut out for them, training us to clean up after ourselves and adopting some manner of decorum."

I fought my smile—he'd been chewing with his mouth open and his elbows on the table ever since sitting down. "Your poor mother."

Soren nodded. "She's a saint. And she said you'll earn your saint status by the time you and I are done."

"Logic behind that?"

"Because you're like that future wife she's been pitying all this time." Soren moved in for his next slice. "Except now she pities you too."

I shifted in my chair. "How am I anything like that future wife?"

He was looking at me like he was wondering why he had to answer that. Finally, he pointed his fresh slice of pizza at me. "You're going to be the one who whips me into shape."

"Soren. I yelled at you *once* about cleaning up."

"Yeah. And look around." I felt him smirking as I glanced around the mostly tidy apartment. "I cleaned up."

CHAPTER

Six

For going eighteen years without a cell phone no problem, I already felt dependent on it after one week of ownership. Like, the thought of losing it brought on a mini panic attack kind of dependent.

That might have had a lot to do with how many calls I took every day from the agency or clients. I wasn't sure how girls had modeled before cell phones. How did they find out that an appointment had been moved up an hour? Or that a client wanted to snap a few final pictures? Or that your agent needed to meet you for a power lunch between meetings?

I'd known no one in the city ten days ago, and now it felt like everyone had my number. Whether my new cell phone was a lifesaver or a beast of burden, there was one number I was always eager to answer whenever it came in. My mom and sisters were so excited for me and made me list every last detail of my day, but those calls were easy. I could just be myself. I didn't have a part to play.

ROOMMATES WITH BENEFITS

They were all doing well, and I promised to send a chunk of my first check so Mom would have some breathing room in her tight budget, and the girls could take a few bucks to the mall to shop with their friends. It took a few rounds of convincing to get mom to accept it, but when I told her I wasn't backing down on this for the sixth time, she gave in with a sigh and a heartfelt thanks. Having expendable income would be a new concept for us all, but it was a welcome one that had me working harder and longer than the next model.

It had been a long day of photo shoots and fittings, and it would be another early one in the morning. Soren was working tonight, and he'd been trying to get me to stop by the restaurant all week to see where he worked. His bribe of free unlimited fries had finally worn me down.

Sullivan's Pub was about a little over a mile from our apartment, so I took a different subway stop, which put me right there. The streets were buzzing in this little hub of the city, lots of people off work and grabbing a bite or a drink with friends. The pub looked busy, which was never my scene, especially after a long day, but before I could change my mind, Soren walked by one of the big windows and saw me. He waved me inside with his free arm. The other one was loaded down with a tray full of food.

It had been a crazy cold day for February, so the pub felt extra inviting when I stepped inside. I'd never been in an Irish pub before—not a lot of foreign culture in Hastings—but Soren had said this was your everyday classic-style pub except this one's food was good. It seemed strange a restaurant could survive if the food sucked, but Soren had assured me people went to Irish pubs to drink beer and have a laugh. The food was an afterthought.

"I knew the lure of the fried potato would get you eventually." Soren paused by me just inside the door before moving to a full table close by. "Any seat in the house. Just not in the bar." He eyed the No Minors sign hanging inside the bar area nearby.

My eyes lifted. "Like you're old enough to sit in the bar."

"Yeah, but I have a fake ID. And facial hair." He kept talking even as he dropped the food off at the table.

"Not sure facial hair's a good look for me." I tapped the back of his heel with my toe as I moved by him toward a free two-seater in the back.

"What do you want to drink?"

I glanced back at him, but he was right behind me. He'd already dropped off a half dozen dinners and caught up to me. "My usual poison."

"You models and your water. I don't know how you drink all of that every day without drowning yourself." His nose curled as he turned toward the back station. He tapped my back with his tray first, then he hustled away before I could smack him.

Soren and I had managed to settle into a kind of friendship that had sibling-like characteristics . . . and something else. We still got into it—over the stupidest things usually—but once we got it out, we moved on until the next thing came up. I'd grown up with two sisters, so I was no stranger to constant bickering. He'd grown up with three brothers—he was just as familiar with it.

The silver lining to all of our heated debate was that we'd pretty much already called each other out on our annoying idiosyncrasies and said exactly what we thought about them. He'd cleaned up his crap more and didn't randomly belt out some chorus that jumped into his head in the middle of the night while he was studying, jolting me awake in the process. And I'd gotten faster at taking showers to save him some of the hot water the building had in short supply every morning and didn't run my blow-dryer with the bathroom door wide open if he was still asleep.

Common courtesies we were working out for each other. Or, as Soren called it, getting each other into shape for that amazing future spouse.

I was still in my heels from earlier, so I slid out of those once I sat at the table in the back. My feet had quickly formed callouses from the amount of heel wear, so I navigated the streets in stilettos as often as I did sneakers now. Plus, I had a subway pass, which made all the difference in the world when it came to bolting between ten different addresses in a day.

"The hemlock you ordered." Soren slid a glass of water in front of me, then he dropped a full pitcher behind it.

"Busy place. I like it." I scanned the restaurant, understanding why Soren liked working here. It was loud and busy and friendly, just like him. Plus, there were plenty of college-aged girls who, gauging by the appraisals they were giving him, seemed to be under the impression that Soren was an itch that had to be scratched.

"I knew you would. Just wait until you try the fries. You're never going to leave." He disappeared again, seeming to fade in and out of the tables like he was made of air.

While I waited for the fried, starchy dinner I knew Ellis would frown upon if he was sitting across from me right now, I found myself watching the cluster of girls. I noticed petty, stupid things, like how one had on jeans with frayed hems, or how the other had a wild chunk of hair out of place, or how one laughed like she was part hyena.

Stupid, catty girl stuff, which I liked to consider myself well above. Apparently not in this situation though. When I realized why I'd transformed into a mean girl nightmare, I squirmed in my chair. Soren might have been an annoying, loud, brother type, but he was also insanely nice to look at and had boyfriend potential slapped all over him; loyal, generous, fun, attentive, killer smile. He was pretty much everything a girl looked for in a guy, save for perhaps a few annoying flaws, but I was trying to convince myself I saw nothing appealing when I looked at him.

I really needed to hone my ability to lie to myself.

A few minutes later, Soren appeared at my table and slid a plate of food in front of me.

"I didn't think the French fries would be enough, so I had them fry up some fish for you too. See if we can put a little meat on those arms of yours." Soren's fingers wrapped around my bicep. "I asked Tommy to fry up whatever else he can back there for you too, so if a plate of fruit salad with an oily, golden crust arrives next, you'll know why."

"You know, body-shaming applies to all types of bodies." I put on a straight face as I glanced at him, determined to maintain it. "Do you think I felt any better about myself because kids were snickering and calling me different names than the other girls? Do you think my self-esteem took less of a hit because a person called me concave?"

The easy smile Soren lived with dwindled. "Shit. I'm a prick."

I nodded solemnly.

"For the record, I don't think you're too skinny or that your arms are scrawny or anything like that." As he said scrawny, his face drew up. "I mean, you've got a great body. A really great body." He winced again, his processing a moment behind his words. "And I'm going to do what we men should do more of and just shut up and walk away." He flashed a wave at me, backing away from the table while shaking his head.

"You're kinda cute when you're self-deprecating." I grabbed a fry and twirled in the direction of the group of girls. "Might want to play to your strong points."

Soren glanced over where I'd indicated at the front of the restaurant. "Oh, them. The Thursday night fan club." His brows bounced.

"You have a fan club for certain nights?"

He dusted off his arms theatrically. "I have a fan club for every hour of the day."

My face went flat. "You're not so cute when you're full of yourself."

"I'm cute because my boyish charm still radiates through my rugged manliness." He circled his face as he backed into the kitchen. "Irresistible."

When I got back to my meal, I realized I was being stared at. By the Thursday night fan club. They didn't seem to be fans of me. More whatever the opposite was. When I waved, all of their heads turned. Look who was playing the catty card now?

I'd barely finished my second fry before Soren appeared at my table again. "Pick a condiment." He was holding a tray with an assortment of different sauces. When I moved to reach for one, he pulled the tray back. "But pick carefully."

"I'm not picking what I want to put on my tombstone. I'm picking the kind of sauce I want to dip my fries in."

"What kind of condiment a girl likes says a lot about the kind of guy she's into."

"What? Where did you read that? *Moron's Illustrated*?"

He slid the tray in front of me again. "Oh, just the small print on The Holy Grail."

Suddenly, I wasn't so sure I wanted to reach for the same condiment. What did it say about my taste in men? What would I be giving away about myself if I choose it?

Why was I actually sweating what kind of condiment to pick? Nothing like a reality check to clear the crazy.

"Hmm." Soren nodded. "Interesting choice."

"How is hot sauce an interesting choice?" I did my best to ignore him as I shook the bottle of hot sauce over my fries.

"Because now I know."

"Now you know what? I like spicy French fries?" I kept shaking the bottle as a distraction.

"That you're looking for a good guy, but one who isn't so good he's boring. You want a little danger. You crave some crazy in your life." When I groaned, it only seemed to encourage him. "You want someone who will stay hopelessly devoted to you, the kind of guy you can imagine sharing a glass of Metamucil with in the mornings when you're old, but the type who lives in the moment. You want someone who isn't perfect and doesn't pretend to be, a guy who might have some irritating quirks but has enough redeeming qualities to make them easy to over-look." He shifted like he was trying to get comfortable. Once he got going, it could be a while before he finished. "You're looking for a guy who's close to your age, some-one who's six one'ish, one-ninety, blond hair, blue eyes—" When I realized what he was doing, I looked at him. He was grinning. "Nice face, smokin' bod"—he gave a body-builder pose—"he loves baseball, pizza, and his family. The All-American boy."

I continued to stare at him, blinking as I finished a few more fries. "You just summed up exactly what I'm *not* looking for in a guy. I think you got your hot sauce mixed up with your mayonnaise."

When he made a face, I cleared my throat to keep the laugh down. Soren hated mayonnaise. So did I. To us, mayonnaise was root evil in gelatinous form.

Swiping the bottle of hot sauce, he carried it toward the kitchen with the rest. "Side of mayo coming right up."

The next couple of hours passed in pretty much the same fashion. Soren buzzed by regularly to tease, talk, or mention something, and even though I'd finished the fish and chips a while ago, I lingered because . . .

I wasn't sure. It wasn't like I was sitting with anyone else like everyone in the bar was. It wasn't like I wasn't tired and should probably get some rest for another harrowing day tomorrow. Sullivan's was the first place I'd been to in New York where it felt like I was surrounded by friends—or the illusion of them. I felt like I fit in with this rowdy bunch because everyone seemed to be accepted. I knew that feeling was because of him. Soren was fast becoming what home felt like here in New York.

The last few guys were sitting at the bar, finishing their dark beers, when Soren slid into the chair across from me with a tray of salt and pepper shakers. He started unscrewing the lids, topping them off as he went. "You've been busy lately. Booked the cover of *Maxim* yet?"

I made a face. "My goal isn't to book the cover of *Maxim*. At all."

His forehead creased.

"Try *Vogue*. When I book the cover for them, that's when I will freak the heck out."

"*Vogue. Maxim*. What's the difference?" One of his shoulders lifted.

I tried not to look too insulted. "Only that one's a fashion magazine for women, and the other's a spank bank for guys."

Soren paused in the middle of marrying two pepper shakers. "Fair assessment." He got back to working on the peppers, so I decided to help with the salts. He slid the pitcher of salt toward me. "Okay, so this is probably one of those times I should keep this thought to myself—"

"Uh-oh," I interjected.

"But modeling? You?" He was searching for words, at least trying to say whatever it was with some degree of sensitivity. Last week, he'd been about as sensitive as a rhino's hide. He was making progress in the Neanderthal department. "I don't know. Isn't it maybe just a little . . . shallow?"

When he chanced a glance across the table at me, I was already looking at him. He exhaled when he realized I wasn't about to throw a shaker of pepper in his face.

"More or less shallow than a bunch of guys playing with bats and balls into their adulthood?"

His mouth fought a smile. "Point taken."

"I get it. I understand what you're saying. It's not curing cancer or building houses in Third World countries. The clothes, pictures, poses. It's what I love. That fire inside, you know?" I didn't need a confirmation from him because I knew he felt the same thing about baseball. "If more people listened to that, the world would be a better place."

Soren lifted a full pepper shaker. He waited for me to lift one of my salt ones. "From one person chasing their dream to another, cheers." He clinked the shakers together.

"Cheers." I checked the time on my phone, my eyes going round when I saw it was almost midnight. "I better get going. I've got to be up in six hours." When I got up to pull on my coat, I felt Soren giving me a look. I zipped my jacket all the way up. It would only be colder out there than it had been a few hours ago. "What?"

"Where do you think you're going?"

"Home."

He shook his head like I hadn't understood his question. "Where do you think you're going *alone*?"

"Home," I repeated.

Another head shake. "The answer would be 'nowhere.'"

"What do you mean nowhere? I have to get back so I can get some sleep."

He finished screwing on the rest of the shaker lids. "And you will get back once I finish up here and can go with you."

"Soren, please. I'm a big girl perfectly capable of making it home by myself."

His eyes lifted. "At midnight in one of the biggest cities in the country?"

"In one of the *safest* big cities in the country."

He started moving around to the empty tables, sliding the full shakers into place. "Doesn't change that you're a pretty young woman walking by herself in the kind of shoes that were not designed for running in the event she needs to." His gaze dropped to where I'd kicked off my heels under the table.

"You're being crazy," I said, sliding back into my heels.

"No, *you're* being crazy. This isn't small town Nebraska where everybody looks after everybody." The more he talked, the more upset he seemed to get. "I mean, come on. Did they teach you anything about safety and common sense back there?"

Grabbing some of the salts, I followed behind him to help. "Let's see. I was taught not to run with scissors, not to talk to strangers, not to put my drink down at a party."

Soren sighed. "Child's play. That might have gotten you through adolescence back there, but it's not enough for you to safely navigate your twenties in New York."

"So I need a reeducation on safety?"

"A total rehaul from the sounds of it."

I followed him to a back station, where he grabbed a towel and some cleaner. "And who do you have in mind to be my teacher?"

Sticking his thumb in his chest, he winked. "This hunk of hardened, big-city meat."

Grabbing another towel and bottle of cleaner, I moved to the table beside the one he was cleaning. "What's your first lesson then, Professor Decker?"

He grinned when I called him that. "First lesson is— you don't walk anywhere alone at night."

"Define night?"

"If the sidewalks are mostly empty, that's night." His arm motioned out the windows at the quiet streets. "Otherwise it's just dark, and then it's okay for you to be out walking by yourself."

"You've actually put some thought into this, haven't you?" I said as we moved to the next couple of tables.

"And while I'm on the topic of important life lessons, here's another one." He turned to face me, pointing the spray bottle of cleaner at my chest. "If some guy you don't know comes up and offers to buy you a drink, what he's really saying is, 'I don't have enough money for a hooker, so I'm hoping this twelve-dollar cosmo will serve the same purpose.'"

My hand moved to my hip. "Oh, well we had guys like that where I'm from. Except we didn't have drinks that expensive. They were like five dollars, or half price on Ladies' Night. Or so I heard from older friends because, yeah, I never would have snuck into a bar." When I bit my lip, that's what gave me away.

Soren grinned. "Wait. You, Naïve in Nebraska, used to sneak into bars?"

"If that's some epic surprise, I think it's you, Naïve in New York, who has a few things to learn."

Soren moved beside me, cleaning off the chairs as I wiped the tables. "You really used to sneak into bars?"

"It was either that or go cow-tipping. Both involved figuring out how to handle large masses of meat, but usually the guys in the bars smelled better than the cows in the pastures."

Soren was looking at me with a new set of lenses. "Maybe you're the one who needs to teach me a few lessons."

CHAPTER Seven

"**M**y home opener is tomorrow night. You're going to be there, right?" Soren hollered from the bathroom after turning off the shower.

Finally. He'd been in there forever and I needed to pee. Sharing a bathroom with a member of the opposite sex provided its challenges. If I had a girl for a roommate, I would have just walked in and peed, but that wasn't exactly appropriate with a male roommate.

Especially the one who'd been in my deliciously filthy dream that might have involved the bathroom counter last night.

"For the thousandth time, yes, I'm going to be there." I turned off the kitchen sink once it was full. The dishes would need to soak for a while before I could even attempt scrubbing them. Someone had been slacking on cleaning up after themselves lately, but I tried to be more chill about it. With the season getting underway, Soren had been crazy busy. I saw him in ten- and twenty-minutes chunks most days.

"Good, because I got you front-row seats."

"I didn't know I needed to have tickets for the game."

"You don't. But I taped a big sheet of paper that says reserved on the front row bench."

"And you 'reserved' enough space for me and a couple of friends?" I added another squirt of dish soap to the sink.

"I reserved one spot."

"Soren, I told you I was bringing Ariel and Jane."

His head peaked out from behind the door. "You told me you were bringing a couple of model friends, so between the three of you, one spot should be plenty of space."

"The model jokes were old two weeks ago. Time to move on to something else." Pulling the fridge open, I looked for my Bing cherry yogurt. I was craving something sweet before bed and I'd finished the last of my dark chocolate squares last night. There wasn't a lot in the fridge, but I scooted stuff around to make sure my yogurt wasn't hiding behind the tub of margarine or the bottle of lemon juice. No luck. "Did you eat my last cherry yogurt?"

He was quiet just long enough for me to have my answer.

"Did I?" His tone gave it away too.

"Soren, come on. I don't want to have to label every little thing I bring into this kitchen." My stomach growled, making me crankier than I normally would have been over a missing yogurt. I had some money coming in now, so I could afford to feed myself, but time was my problem. I didn't have much extra to swing by a grocery store every few days.

"I was planning on making it to the store tonight to replace it for you, but life didn't go as planned." He walked out of the bathroom wearing nothing but that same small, white towel cinched around his waist. It was practically a singlet for all the coverage it provided.

I looked away from his wet, nearly naked body, focusing on the empty fridge again. "Well, because your life didn't go as planned, now I have to decide between chemically engineered butter or fake lemon juice to satisfy my sweet craving."

"You can have some of my Nutter Butters," he suggested, pausing in the doorway of the kitchen. "Actually, no, you can't. I ate the last of those earlier too. Dipped in the cherry yogurt."

When I groaned and shut the fridge, I waited for him to move out of the way. I didn't want to have to rub against him to pass. My feelings circling Soren were complicated enough without adding the knowledge of what his wet skin felt like against mine.

"But I did do the laundry."

"How does you doing your laundry help me feel better about stolen cherry yogurt?" Since he wasn't stepping aside to let me move by, I slid past him as quickly as I could, smashing myself into the doorframe so my skin came in as little contact with his skin as possible.

"Because I did yours at the same time. Your laundry basket was overflowing worse than mine, so I just did them both." He sounded proud of himself, but I froze.

"You did my laundry?" My stomach swirled as I tried to recall what had been in that basket. "You went through my dirty clothes?"

"Well, yeah, I had to sort the lights from the darks from the delicates. I might be a caveman, but I don't want my loincloth dyed pink on accident." He motioned at his white towel which was slipping lower down his hips. Low enough I could just make out . . .

Giving my head a shake, I looked away. "I can't believe you did that."

"I know, right? Who would have thought I'd willingly do laundry that wasn't my own?" Soren's footsteps padded behind me. He clearly wasn't getting the clue that I was pissed at him for going through my laundry. "By the way, in case you want a dude's opinion on the matter, your underwear is smokin' hot. Like seriously, the things wet dreams are made of."

"Soren!" I didn't realize I was pitching my jacket that was draped over the sofa at him until it hit his face.

"I didn't know they allowed that kind of underwear to be bought, sold, or worn in the Bible Belt. How are the guys going to spend all day working those fields when all that's on their mind is plowing something else?"

"You are . . ." I grumbled, so flustered I couldn't think of the right word to sum up exactly what he was.

"Cool down, Hayden. I'm paying you a compliment. You have nice underwear. It wasn't like I was trying them on or sniffing them or anything creeper'ish like that."

My face was red, I could feel it, so I kept my back to him. "You just used my underwear in reference to wet dreams. That's full-on creeper."

"Full-on creeper would have been jacking myself off with them and then putting them back in your panty drawer. The only full-on I can be accused of is being a splendid roommate for going out of my way to do your laundry."

"You're disgusting." I marched for my "room," another flush of heat shooting through me when I noticed the folded piles of clean clothes sitting on the plastic rolling drawers I used as a dresser. A stack of folded panties was sitting on top. Crap. That assortment made me look like I was a call girl.

"I probably shouldn't ask this, but my curiosity will not be silenced"—I was already bracing myself for his question—"but isn't that uncomfortable? Wearing underwear that rides up your butt crack like that?"

Shoot me. Just shoot me. "What? Like it's comfortable having your junk stuffed in a plastic triangle?"

Silence. For a second. "So is that your way of saying thongs are or aren't comfortable?"

"That's my way of saying I'm not talking about my underwear with you."

When I started putting my clean clothes away, I realized I was shaking. I wasn't sure why. Soren was like my brother in a way—what did it matter that he'd seen my underwear and was asking a few dumb questions about them? Soren was not like my brother in one rather large way though—the thoughts and feelings I had for him at times. No sister should be wondering what the rest of her brother looked like beneath that towel. No sister would be feeling tingles, in more than one place, when her brother grazed by her.

Soren may have looked after me like a brother, but the ways I wanted to look after him were not sisterly in the slightest.

I needed space. To clear my head. With a shortage of doors that actually closed in this apartment, the bathroom was my only option since it was "night" according to Soren's rules. Too late to be out walking the streets by myself.

"I'm taking a shower," I announced, already heading that direction.

"You might want to wait on that for a while. Unless you feel the need for a cold shower."

"Why would I feel the need for a cold shower?"

Soren gave me a funny look. Probably because I sounded defensive after he'd mentioned a cold shower. "I'm not saying you need a cold shower. I'm saying if you want a hot one, you're going to have to wait."

"Why?" I asked, right before it clicked. "Because you took a thirty-minute shower and used all of the hot water that struggles to make it up to the sixth floor."

He stepped behind his partition, and the towel flew over the top a moment later. "Sorry. If I'd known you wanted to shower tonight, I could have quickened things up."

The way he said it, like he had some checklist to go through, made me pause. "Quickened things up?" I waited, but he was quiet. "Why do you take such long showers anyway?"

"I have to shampoo my hair."

My forehead creased as I stuffed my clean underwear into the back of a drawer. "You have, like, a tenth of the hair I do. You don't have to shave your legs or armpits or anything else. What could you be doing in there that takes so long . . . oh." My eyes widened as another thought cross my mind. "*OH.*"

"Not a lot of privacy out here. The bathroom door is the only one that closes and locks."

My head dropped against the plastic storage bin as I squeezed my eyes closed. "Great. Now I'm going to have to bleach the thing before I step foot in it each time. And wear flip-flops." The harder I tried to erase the mental images from my head, the more vivid they became.

"Stop acting so appalled." Soren's footsteps moved out from behind his divider. "Where do you do your business?"

"What business?"

"Your self-love business?" he said, padding into the kitchen.

"I don't masturbate." My hand moved toward my nose. I was half surprised it wasn't growing.

"Why not?" The sound of the fridge door whined open. "Yourself doesn't like yourself enough to let her get close?"

"Or maybe you spend so much time with yourself because you're the only one who can stand being close to yourself." I was banging my head against the storage bin now. What kind of conversation was I having?

"Positive endorphins. Just sayin'. Would do you some good."

Sticking my head out from behind the divider, I aimed a glare in his direction. "Excuse me? Is that your way of saying I'm a bitch?"

"What? Jesus, no." He was rummaging through the same scant fridge I'd just been searching for something appetizing in. "Get those panties untwisted before you open your mouth to bite my head off next time." The fridge door slammed shut. "Oh yeah, you can't untwist them, they're already riding up your butt."

CHAPTER

Eight

"I never knew how much I loved sports until today." Jane was staring at the diamond with a grin.

Ariel rolled her eyes. "You hate sports."

"Yeah, but that was before I'd been to this kind of sport, where the guys are hot and wear tight white pants. What's not to like about that?" Her hand circled the air in the direction of one of the back-up pitchers warming up in front of us. Then she made a squeezing motion.

"I do like to watch them wrap their hands around their big, hard sticks," Ariel added with a shrug.

Jane nudged her. "And the way they play with their balls."

The two shared a giggle while I focused on keeping my attention on the game as a whole, instead of the one component I'd been focused on since the three of us arrived at the start of the game. I was in the same boat as Jane—I'd never realized I liked sports until today. It had little to do with the actual game and everything to do with a certain someone with the number twenty-three stamped on the back of his jersey. Watching Soren play baseball . . . did things to my mind and my body I wasn't eager to acknowledge.

Things were complicated enough between us without adding physical exertion and tight white pants to the mix. He was good. Stand-out good. I didn't need to know the ins and outs of the sport to recognize that. When he was up at bat, he hit the ball. Far. When he was crouched behind the plate, playing catcher, he caught the ball, tagged incoming runners, and threw the darn thing so hard I could hear the smack it made when it landed in his fellow players' mitts.

Every time he jogged off the field, before dropping into the dugout, he aimed a smile at me. Every time he emerged from the dugout, same story. I wasn't sure how many more times I could shift in my seat without looking like I had an acute case of hemorrhoids.

And what was I doing thinking about hemorrhoids? I'd clearly been spending too much time around Soren Decker, the one person on the planet who had no boundaries—when it came to anything really. From confessing to his female roommate that he jerked off in the shower, to fanning the air in my direction after he farted, he had no boundaries. I felt like I knew everything there was to like and not like about him.

So why did I find myself still warring with feelings for him? The sensation of being drawn to him, inexplicable as it was?

"Your roommate is off-the-charts hot, Hayden." Jane grinned at home plate, where Soren was squatting, holding his mitt at the ready. "Please tell me you've hit that already."

"It's what puts the spring in her cat walk," Ariel sang as I groaned.

"Come on though. Be real with us." Jane's head turned my way. "You're getting a piece of that action, right?"

My eyes moved to the diamond. "No. He's my roommate."

"Is he gay?"

"Yeah, right. Have you seen the way he dresses? The state he keeps the apartment in? No. He's not gay." That would make things easier though.

"Are you?" Ariel's gaze roamed me, her forehead creasing.

"No." That would also make things easier.

"Does he have a girlfriend?"

"No."

My instant response had them glancing at each other with raised eyebrows.

"And you don't have a boyfriend . . ." Jane continued.

Soren was shifting around behind the plate, distracting me and making me do some shifting on my own. "What? So because we're both straight, single, and sharing a space, we should be getting it on?"

Jane blinked at me a couple of times, her hand turning over. "Exactly. It's not like you have to make it anything official or hold hands down the sidewalk. You two are young and in your sexual prime. You need to exercise more than just your heart to stay healthy and happy."

Ariel leaned in like she was going to whisper something. It didn't come out a whisper though. "That's her way of saying you need to exercise your vagina more."

"Yeah, got it."

I glanced over my shoulder to make sure no small children were close by. Just a couple of older guys with small smiles, pretending to focus on the game.

"No need to start dropping an anatomy lesson on the entire stadium," I hissed.

"There's only one possible reason you two aren't boning then," Jane said.

"The fact that we're roommates and that's complicated enough?"

Her finger waved between Soren on the field and me in the seat beside her. "That you have feelings for each other that go beyond routine boning."

The guys behind us were smiling wider when I checked this time.

"Yeah, I have feelings for him," I said under my breath. "Ones that stem from annoyance and disgust."

Ariel and Jane stared at me, their expressions needing no explanation.

"We're here to watch a game. Let's watch the game." My arms flailed out at the field before I dug into the bag of kettle corn Jane had stuffed between her legs.

"I'm here to admire fine asses. But you feel free to watch the 'game.'" Jane cleared her throat dramatically.

"Or Soren Decker's package bulging through those teeny-weeny white pants."

Ariel leaned into Jane, jabbing her finger Soren's way. "Except that bulge is not teeny-weeny."

"Not the slightest bit teeny-weeny." Jane's eyebrows bounced as she popped a piece of popcorn in her mouth. "That weeny's a hugey-hugey."

"That's it. I refuse to sit beside you two until you tone your hormones down to a public-setting level of appropriate."

The moment I burst to my feet, Jane grabbed my arm and yanked me back down. "They're leaving the field. You wouldn't want Soren the Huge to start asking questions as to why you're so flushed." Jane patted my cheek I could feel heating.

"He's wearing a cup, you know? That's not his actual"—I leaned in so I didn't have to say it out loud—"*package.*"

"Yeah, and the only reason a guy wears a giant cup is because he's packing a giant cock." Jane covered her mouth before I had the chance to do it for her. "I mean penis. Sorry. That was too far for a public setting." She shot an apologetic look at the grinning guys behind us. They didn't seem to mind.

"Hey, Jumbo!" Ariel hollered as Soren jogged closer.

He turned toward the fence, sliding off his catcher's mask. "Did you just call me Dumbo?"

Ariel's head shook. "Jumbo."

When Soren's brows came together, I reached behind Jane to smack Ariel. "Don't ask," I yelled at him, pointing at the dugout where the rest of his team was heading.

He moved a few steps toward the fence instead. "A few of the guys on the team are having a party tonight at their place. Want to come?"

Soren's face was streaked with sweat and dust, and his uneven smile was making my throat go dry. I shouldn't have feelings for my roommate. I couldn't. But the thing about feelings was that they couldn't be controlled—nothing that came from the heart could be controlled. The head was a different matter.

"She'd love to come. And so would her friends," Jane answered for me.

"Are you going?" I asked, finding my voice.

Soren tucked his mitt under his arm. "It depends."

"Depends on what?"

"Your answer." He moved closer until he stopped against the fence.

I could smell the sweat clinging to him. It felt like it was drawing me nearer instead of repulsing me as it should.

"Yes," Jane filled in for me again. "Her answer is yes."

Soren winked as he shoved away from the fence. "Same here."

The three of us watched him turn and jog away. It was one of the rare moments there was actual silence when we were all together.

"Since you don't seem to be in a hurry to stake your claim, I'm staking mine." Ariel raised her hand like she was bidding at some auction.

"That choice specimen can claim me with his stake whenever he wants," Jane said.

I settled back onto the bench and tried to chase away the strange new feeling I was experiencing while watching them gawk at Soren. "You two need to get your libidos under control."

"And you need to let your libido get out of control," Jane fired back, aiming a piece of kettle corn at my head.

"So partying with a bunch of ball players tonight." Ariel shimmied as she took her seat again. "I'm not used to athletes. I spend more time around male models and photographers. Got any advice for us?"

Soren reemerged from the dugout, sliding on a batting helmet before taking a few warm-up swings. Another odd feeling rolled over me. Possession.

"Yeah," I said. "Stay away from my roommate."

CHAPTER

Nine

reat. Missed called number twelve was coming in. My texts must not have been enough for him—he wanted to talk. I would have answered this one except I was almost to the address he'd texted me after the game. If he wanted to talk, I was fifty feet away from being face to face.

Also, great—judging from how quiet the sidewalks were in this part of Brooklyn, it was more night than it was dark. He was going to go all overprotective, big brother on me, and my patience was running on fumes.

Ellis had called me sometime in the sixth inning, informing me I needed to come in for a "quick" photo shoot. He'd caught word that one of the big Italian designers was shopping for a new face for their black label line. Ellis seemed to think my face was exactly what they were looking for, and he wanted to add a few more simple, European-type shots to my portfolio. I wasn't sure why that couldn't wait until Monday morning, but Ellis made it seem like it was make or break.

Like most things in this industry, it took longer than I'd expected and it was now pushing eleven. I'd wanted to go back to the apartment and crash, but I'd promised Soren I'd come tonight and that seemed important to him for some reason. Plus, Jane and Ariel were here and I had to make sure they didn't get into too much trouble because, yeah. If trouble was lurking in the bottom of some puddle five blocks over, they'd find it.

This was an older part of the city from the looks of it, and all I had to do was follow the echo of music and laughter to find the right place. It was a chilly, early spring night, so everyone was stuffed inside the small house, but I noticed a shadow move beneath the porch when I passed through the opening in the fence.

"Please don't tell me you walked all the way here from the subway station. Please tell me you took a cab." Soren moved down the walkway to meet me, his face drawn up.

"Okay. I took a cab." I stopped when we were a few steps from each other.

"Really?"

"No, I walked from the subway."

"Hayden," he sighed, thrusting his arms toward the street behind me. "I told you to call me when you were done at work so I could come meet you. Do you remember anything I told you about walking alone at night?"

"I do, but here's the thing—what makes you think I'm safer if I'm surrounded by people versus nobody? Isn't that counterintuitive?" I crossed my arms, staring at him. "If there's no one around to do whatever harm you think I'm in danger of, doesn't that make me safer than being caught in a swarm of bodies marching down the side-walks?"

His jaw moved, probably from holding himself back. Soren and I were naturals when it came to bickering and pushing each other's buttons. We weren't afraid to chal-lenge each other or call the other out, but he'd been learn-ing impulse control where I seemed to be loosening mine.

"The people who hurt others don't march down side-walks. They hide in the shadows. You don't see them until they're on you, so next time, save me the heart attack and call me so I can come meet you. Got it?"

The warming in my veins started again. It was a fa-miliar sensation when Soren was around. Brought on by usually anger or annoyance, it was also spurred by emo-tions I was less eager to admit to. This latest episode was probably a combination of a lot of things.

He was wearing a clean jersey hanging untucked over a dark pair of jeans. He had on his standard Converse and backward red ball cap. Even outside and a body length apart, I could smell the hint of his favorite soap on him. I could make out the light splash of cologne he must have put on for tonight. It was tempting me closer, but I needed to keep as much distance from Soren as possible.

"This is a party, right?"

His hands slid into his pockets as he shrugged. "So I've heard. I've been a little busy trying to look after my roommate."

"It's not your job to look after me. I'm a big girl." Moving around him, I started for the house.

His footsteps followed after me. "Then stop acting like a child and prove it."

"You first," I snapped, pulling the door open and stepping inside before we could go any deeper into this heated topic.

Compared to outside, the packed house was sweltering. Bodies were everywhere—pressed into furniture, walls, each other. The space had easily exceeded its fire code maximum by a hundred bodies. I noticed Jane and Ariel toward the back of the living room, which was serving as a dance floor tonight. They were in the middle of a handful of guys wearing the same kind of jersey Soren wore, so they looked happy. Jane had said she wasn't going home tonight until she'd cured her curiosity regarding baseball players' supposed reputation of being good in bed. She claimed they knew they had to hit every base before thrusting for home plate, and that was where I'd tuned out.

Sweat was already starting to bead to the surface of my skin, so I untied my trench-style jacket and unzipped it. When I slid it off, I didn't miss the way Soren's head whipped toward me.

"What in the hell are you wearing?" He blinked, swallowing when his eyes reached where the hem of my dress fell.

"I didn't want to take the extra time to change after the shoot, and Ellis said I could have the dress." I smoothed my hands down the sides, not about to let my confidence waver from the way Soren was staring at me. And some others were staring now that I was moving through the room.

"That's not a dress. That's a tank top." Soren fell in behind me instantly, shoving aside some guy who made an interesting noise when I passed.

"Oh, yeah, because the guy who lives in Levi's jeans and Hanes T-shirts knows all about couture fashion." I smirked back at him, biting the inside of my cheek to keep from smiling when he got in another guy's face for checking out my backside as I passed.

"I might not know a damn thing about couture, but I know if you lean forward two inches, you're going to be flashing the whole room your underwear." Soren's face went blank as he realized something. "Tell me you're not wearing—"

"Do you see any lines?"

When his gaze lowered to confirm or deny it, his face drew into lines like he was being tortured. "Do me a favor and don't lean forward two inches."

I turned my head back around so he didn't see the smile I'd lost the battle to. "So I shouldn't do this?" I barely leaned forward.

The hem didn't have a chance to ride up before his arm swung around me, pressing me against him to straighten me out. "Hayden, for the love of god. I don't want to have to beat every ass in here for checking out yours."

Soren's head was beside mine, his breath warming my cheek as he spoke. With his chest firm against my back, I could feel it moving, hard and hurried. Or was that my chest moving quickly?

His arm didn't untie from around me. His head didn't pull away when he was done talking. I didn't want him to pull back either. I wanted him to come closer. I wanted his other arm around me, his mouth warming my skin with more than just his breath. Inside, I felt a match being lit, a flicker of light as it struck. I knew I'd explode in a ball of fire when that match dropped—from weeks of fuel being spread inside me, waiting to be ignited.

Behind me, his body moved. Even, methodical waves rolled against me.

"What are you doing?" My voice wasn't my own.

"It's a party. I'm dancing." His other hand slid into the bend of my hip, no hesitation in his touch.

"Where did you take your dance lessons?" I tipped my head back at him, trying to look unimpressed when I was feeling very much the opposite. The man could move. His body. His hips. He could *really* move his hips. "The School of Bump and Grind?"

He huffed, moving against me in true bump-and-grind fashion. Having his body moving against mine the way it was, feeling the way it seemed to fit into the bends and dips of mine had my mind drifting to other ways our bodies might fit together.

Roommate.

Obnoxious.

Short Fuse.

I listed off as many discredits as I could. Then I repeated the list. But it wasn't working. Thinking about

Soren's shortcomings while his body was moving against me so closely I could feel his heartbeat thumping against my back, was about as effective as throwing a thimble of water at a forest fire.

Useless.

That's what my attempts to confine my feelings for him felt like right then.

"You giving me the brush-off, girlie?"

Soren turned me around so I was facing him. At this proximity, I could smell the minty sweetness on his breath. I could see the silver shards in his light eyes. I could see the three light freckles scattered at the bridge of his nose, probably from playing baseball every summer since he was five.

"I thought you loved to dance?"

"I used to," I said, avoiding eye contact.

Up until this moment, when I felt like every feeling I shouldn't have was about to detonate through the room for everyone to see.

"You used to?" He spun his ball cap around like he usually wore it.

"Now I hate it."

"You hate dancing now?"

"Things change."

"How can you hate dancing with me as a dance partner? I mean, I paid attention during *Magic Mike*. I might have even taken a few notes."

I had to bite my lip to keep from smiling. "You watched *Magic Mike*?"

"I went with my mom. I was the only male Decker secure enough in his manhood to go with her." His hip movements became a little more "obvious" as his back arched back a bit. "There's this one move I've been working on—it takes about a half hour of stretching first, but it makes the ladies go crazy." His brows bounced, something flashing in his eyes.

"What move is that? Putting the toilet seat down when you're done using it?" My arms folded in front of my body, having nowhere else to go. "Because, yeah, I do go crazy when you, on occasion, remember to do that back at the apartment."

"Hey, Ball Buster, time to give them a break for one night—before they fall off. What fun would you have if that happened? Got to remember to take care of my proverbial balls you like to crush in the palm of your hand."

"Your balls, proverbial ones included, will never get anywhere close to the palm of my hand."

"You're saying that to convince yourself, right? Because you sure as hell didn't convince me."

Even though I wasn't looking directly at him, I could see his grin from the corner of my eye.

"Because my balls are fantastic. A masterpiece. A real testament to manhood. Symmetrical, grandiose, soft yet firm. They're a damn sight to behold, my balls."

My teeth were still working at my lip to keep me from snorting at his confidence or laughing at his antics. "How do you think they'd like the caress of my knee joisting into them?"

"Your proverbial knee?"

Lifting my leg, I skimmed my knee up his thigh. The steady movement of his dance hiccupped then stalled. A moment later, he'd recovered, but now I was wondering if he felt the same kind of "something" I did when our bodies were this close.

"This knee. My literal one."

"Well, I was referring to my proverbial balls. So if you want to caress them with your knee or the palm of your hand"—his grin stretched wider—"you're going to have to do so with your proverbial ones."

My teeth released my lip, and I let myself smile. I was tired of holding back my feelings for him. A smile wasn't going to set off some avalanche that led to the two of us becoming more than just roommates.

"Why are you scared?" Soren asked, his hands slipping down my back until they fell onto the shelf of my backside. The pads of his fingers were just barely touching what was roughly butt territory, the rest of his hands resting securely in lower back land.

"I'm not scared," I answered, glancing around the room. The scariest thing around was that ratty, old sofa that had clearly seen its share of action. All kinds.

"You're scared of me."

My forehead creased as my eyes met his. "If I was scared of you, I sure wouldn't be sharing a closet with you."

His head shook. "You're scared of something about me."

"Well, if you want to break it down to micro, yeah, there's a lot about you that scares me. I can put together a list if you want. I can section it off by category and subcategory if it would be helpful."

Instead of smiling from me teasing him, his face got all serious. That was never good. "You're scared to touch me." His eyes dropped to where my arms were still crossed. "Why?"

"I touch you all of the time," I argued, my voice a few notes too high.

"Yeah, when I'm at arm's length, but not when I'm close." He moved closer, his chest pressing against mine causing a chain reaction of sensations spiraling through my body. His expression was still frozen in seriousness. "Why?"

We were connected at the chest, hips, and thighs. I could feel his energy breaking over me, siphoning into my depths. I could feel my own dispersing into him, burrowing deep. I'd been close to other guys before, at least in physical proximity, but I'd never felt this.

Sure, the aching pulse of desire was making me shift, that desire for more was arousing what a person typically associated with feelings of lust . . . but this went beyond that. I didn't feel my want for him only at the apex of my legs; I felt my desire in every part of my body. From my small toe, to the underside of my forearm, to the column of my neck. My need or want or whatever this was for the man holding me was so all-consuming, it felt as though it could devour me whole.

Unwinding my arms, I wound them loosely behind his neck. I had to. If I didn't, he'd keep harassing me about why I was so scared to touch him, and if I didn't say anything, he was bound to jump to some of his own conclusions. I didn't want him even inching toward those types of conclusions.

"Was that so bad?" he asked.

One side of my face drew up. "Worse."

He just grumbled and pressed me closer, his body moving against mine in ways that were testing the integrity of my knee strength.

As we danced, I did my best to imagine I was somewhere else, some place serene. Anywhere but here with him, our bodies tangled together, because I couldn't let him see what having him close did to me. I couldn't let him know the feelings I'd been wrestling with for weeks now. I couldn't cross that line, because once it was stepped over, there was no going back. Sure, we could break up, but we were roommates. We'd still have to see each other every morning and every night for the next four months until the lease was up. No, thank you. Breakups were hard enough without the added component of sharing the same roof.

And then there was the fact that I didn't believe in relationships. Sure, I'd seen a few people have seemingly good ones, but I knew firsthand how badly a heart could be broken. I always swore I wouldn't be like my mom, crying for months after my dad left. I wasn't looking to open myself up to that kind of pain.

When I caught Soren staring at my mouth, the skin between his brows drawn into a deep line, I panicked. "It's hot. I need some fresh air."

My arms were untying from him at the same time I broke out of his hold, cutting through bodies toward the back door. I heard him shoving through the party after me, snapping something at the guy who'd just whistled at me when I moved by.

I didn't stop to wait for him. I couldn't. I felt like I was suffocating, and even though I knew it wasn't from lack of oxygen, fresh air seemed like a good place to start. Besides, what antidote was there for someone suffocating from their closeted feelings for someone?

Once I shoved through the door, I rushed to the back of the yard, leaned into the rusted cyclone fence, and focused on breathing. So much had happened in the past couple of months. Getting signed. Moving to New York. Booking jobs. *Good* jobs. Being on my own. Sharing an apartment. Realizing I had feelings for my roommate. Trying to kill those feelings. Only to have them grow with each new day, instead of withering away like I'd hoped.

Now this—feeling all of my control over my mind and body become lost when he drew me close. This was perhaps the scariest realization of all. At a distance, I could keep my guard up with Soren, but up close, I lost total and utter control. Walls crumbled. Barriers fell. Resolve evaporated.

I had only one solution to keep Soren from realizing my feelings—keeping him at a careful distance. At least as much as our living situation allowed. An actual arm's length should work, especially with as long as my arms were. I couldn't let him close again. I couldn't let him get his arms around me or put mine around him.

Soren had to be avoided. As much as possible without making it obvious.

"Nice emergency exit back there."

The sound of the door closing behind him made me flinch. How was I supposed to avoid him if he made it his mission to find me every time I escaped?

"You okay?" His feet crunched over the dead grass dotting the yard, pausing when he was a few steps behind me.

"Yeah, I'm good. There are just a lot of bodies in there. Generating a lot of heat." *Or, truthfully, one body generating way too much damn heat for me to handle.*

"Yeah, it's way better out here than in there." Soren shouldered up beside me, leaning into the fence. "It's quiet out here. We can just be alone."

My breath hitched. "I feel better now. So much better. We should probably get back to the party."

"I only came to this party because you said you'd come. The way I see it, the party's right here." He bumped his elbow against mine, inching closer.

Shifting, I leaned away from him. Not too obvious, but just enough so our elbows weren't touching anymore. "Don't you want to introduce me to your friends?" He'd mentioned me meeting his teammates a couple of weeks ago but had yet to do so. I figured tonight would be the perfect opportunity.

"No." His head shook firmly. "Especially not with what you're wearing." When his gaze wandered in the direction of my dress again, he frowned.

"What am I wearing?" Straightening, I glanced down at what I had on again. Short, yeah, but it wasn't skintight. Cut low in the back, but not in the front. It fell into the stylish category, not the sexy one.

Angling toward me, he gestured at the dress I was still inspecting. "Man-Nip. That's what you're wearing."

"Man-Nip?" I pinched the material, my eyebrows coming together.

"You know like catnip, except for bros? It'll drive them wild." Reaching for his shirt, he started to pull it over his head. "Just put on my jersey or something. This one's clean." Once he'd peeled it over his head, he pulled his undershirt back down over his stomach and held out his jersey for me.

"I'm not putting on your jersey."

"Please."

"No, thank you."

"Pretty please?"

"No, pretty thank you," I replied with a fake smile.

"Well, I'm not introducing you to my friends dressed in that. That's a way to lose friends, and I'd rather keep the ones I have since we play on the same ball team and the season's just getting started."

"Just because you're having a tough time with my dress doesn't mean your friends will. They can't all be like you."

Soren chuckled. "I'm the upstanding, good guy of the bunch. You know, if that gives you an idea of the type of animals I call friends."

"Wow. You really know how to pick them." I sighed, snatching the jersey from his hand. I really did want to meet his friends, and if I had to slide into Soren's jersey to achieve said goal, there were worse things in life.

"They make me look good. It's essential to hang with people who make you look good." The fence whined when he shoved away from it.

"Yeah. I follow that same policy," I said, keeping a straight face as I shoved my head and arms through the big jersey.

"You're referring to me, aren't you?"

"So quick," I joked then glanced down at my new Soren-approved, friend-introduction outfit.

When Soren's eyes followed mine, a sound vibrated in his throat. "I'm not sure that's any better actually." He stepped back, rubbing his chin as his inspection continued. He was almost smirking, definitely smiling as he took in the sight of me sporting his jersey.

When he lifted his finger and twirled it in the air, my arms crossed. "You can twirl yourself around me if you want to see the back view."

The smile turned more into a smirk as he started to wind around me. Another throaty sound came from him when he paused behind me. When he stayed back there, I twisted my head to see what he was doing. He was staring at my back, the top of it, his hands behind his head.

"I know I'm going to sound like one of those animals I just warned you about, but damn, my name on a beautiful woman's back is doing things to me I'm not sure are twenty-first-century approved."

I spun around so fast, I teetered thanks to the high heels and soft ground. "Should I call the Feminist Police? Because I know the chief."

"Yeah? Who's that?"

My eyebrow lifted. "Me."

Soren fought a smile, still staring at his jersey wrapped around my body. "Then I'm definitely not going to tell you what I'm thinking about now."

"Dear god, please don't."

Soren stepped toward me, something in his eyes inviting me closer. So I took a step away.

"Seeing my name on your back, the way it's making that damn beast inside all of us dudes throw its head back and roar, makes me want to ask the woman I marry one day to tattoo it on her back. In big, bold letters. We're talking so giant, a satellite could pick that shit up in outer space."

My mouth had fallen open from the start and kept dropping with every word.

He moved around behind me again. "'Decker.' Seriously, I'm going to start looking into tattoo artists now. Feel my arm. I've got goose bumps." His arm appeared beside me, but I didn't touch to confirm that yes, goose bumps galore. "I mean, I'm fucking hard—"

He abruptly cleared his throat and went in a different direction with his body's "approval rating," but I didn't hear it. At least not at first.

Had he actually said that?

I mean, was he really?

He was still standing behind me, still drooling over his name, so I couldn't confirm it. Not that I should be confirming if he was hard anyway, but curious minds . . .

Peeking over my shoulder, my gaze dropped to his zipper. *Damn, damn, double damn.*

So he really was. Hard.

Hard to hide something like that. Hard.

Stop thinking the word hard, Hayden.

My cheeks were already flushed enough without getting redder from singing a soliloquy of "hards" in my head.

He really was Jumbo.

Jumbo.

Stop thinking the word jumbo. So much worse than hard.

And there it was again. Since I clearly was incapable of not saying it to myself . . .

Fine. Soren Decker had a hard, jumbo-sized dick.

Like I cared.

That part of his anatomy had no relevance where I was concerned. It was more our poor shower's concern than mine.

"See something you like?" Soren stuffed his hands in his pockets and rocked his hips forward.

My head whipped back around, my face feeling hot. "See something I'd like to forget."

A sharp exhale came from him. "Please. Like that part, *any* part, of me is forgettable."

"And now I'm going to move on to trying to forget you just said that." My arms crossed again, as was my typical reaction most of the time when Soren was around. Why did I like this guy? Why did I feel some pull toward him when I should have been backing away in revulsion? Okay, so maybe revulsion was a strong word, but exasperation wasn't.

"Damn. I keep thinking I'm going to eventually reach some limit to staring at my name on your back, but it's not happening."

Groaning, I swept my braid over my shoulder. There. At least now half a letter would be blocked. "What is it with you men getting all hot and bothered when you see your name on a woman's back? I mean, this isn't lingerie with strategically cut holes or anything. It's a baggy, frumpy jersey."

"I guarantee it dates back to caveman times." He cleared his throat like he was getting all factual on me. "Has seen a resurgence in current times." When I sighed, he laughed. "I don't know, Hayden. It's just, like, marking a guy's territory or something. I'm probably going to hell or about to get stoned by a mob of women, but there's just something that gets to a guy when he sees his name on his woman."

My heartbeat was so strong, I could feel it in my palms. "But I'm not your woman." My head tipped back just enough I could make out his figure.

"You're the closest thing to it."

I am? How? Like in the romantic way or the non-romantic way?

"What makes me the closest thing to it?" I asked, confirming yet again why curiosity was going to be the death of me. If, at least, in my love life.

"You know, how we look after each other. The way we spend our free time together. We live together. Eat together. Get into arguments. Know all about our families, our pasts, our goals . . . you know, all of that stuff."

Replaying in my mind what he'd just said, I realized how Soren and I were more than roommates. We were more than casual friends too. Good friends? I wasn't sure that was right. Best friends? A person shouldn't dream about sliding into bed naked with their best friend, right? Lovers? Definitely not.

I didn't know what we were anymore. Didn't have the faintest clue.

"Marking your territory, eh?" I slowly turned around, arms still crossed. "I didn't peg you as the chauvinistic type. Caveman kind, sure, but—"

His head shook. "My name on a woman's back isn't just about her belonging to me." His eyes found mine before I could look away. Now I was stuck. "It's about me belonging to her too."

Everything started to soften. My expression, my heart, my posture. How could he say all the wrong things, yet have it all exactly right when it counted? The name on my back wasn't just about staking his claim; it was about taking himself out of the game.

"Say something. Say something dumb. Hurry." My hand rolled, encouraging him. "Say something that will stop making me wonder if you really are this sweet, thoughtful person you're coming across as right now."

He gave me a funny look, giving me a chance to take it back. When I didn't, he shrugged, a crooked smile working onto his mouth. "And maybe I might be thinking about how insanely hot the view of my name on my girl's back would be while I'm fucking her from behind."

My eyes widened as I felt my knees slacken. Hearing him say that should have earned him an eye roll and a groan like I'd hoped whatever "dumb" thing he said next would do. Instead, I was picturing the very act he'd described. I saw Soren naked, moving inside a woman from behind. One hand cradled around her waist, the other pulling her hair, a smirk on his face as he stared at his name on her back.

It wasn't picturing Soren having sex that was screwing with my head though. It was who he was having sex with. Me. I was the women he was driving inside of, spread out on all fours, panting his name like pleasure was a cute little notion compared to whatever it was I was experiencing.

"What's the matter? Your face. You're red. Like, *red, red.*" Soren's expression took on a serious tone as he hurried toward me.

"I'm fine. Just stay there." I whipped my arm out in front of me, hand raised.

He stopped, but my unusual reaction had caught his attention. "Are you blushing? Is that the blush to end all blushes?" He squinted as he moved his head, inspecting my face. "I think it is. Here I was worried you were having an allergic reaction or something, and it's just you blushing because I brought up doggy-style fucking." His brows bounced as his chest pressed into my hand. I was keeping him at a literal arm's length right now. "Turned on?"

"More like repulsed. But thanks for playing the Name That Emotion game." I took a deep breath and moved back a few steps, trying to drain the color from my face. "Might want to work on that before you find that lucky lady you want to have your name tattooed on. You just mistook arousal for revulsion. Going to want to get that figured out."

That damn grin. I hated it. I was obsessed with it too.

"And if I were to ask you to hand over your panties right now, they would confirm your claim?" He held out his hand, like I was just going to whip out of my panties and hand them over for inspection.

My hand settled on my hip. "Like the Sahara."

His hand stayed in the air. "Prove it."

"I don't need to prove the truth. I'm not the one who cares anyways." Turning to escape from this whole nightmare of an exchange, I opened the back door. "I'm going to go introduce myself to your friends now. I'm sure they're far less animal than you."

"Sahara," he scoffed, following me through the door. "Try the Amazon instead."

"God, Soren, will you stop? I'm not giving you my panties." I hadn't meant to shout that as loudly as I had, but the crowd in the kitchen didn't seem to mind.

"I wouldn't give them to him either. Not when I'm here," one of the guys jeered as I shoved by.

"Where do I throw my name into that hat?" another hollered, making a lewd motion with his tongue at me.

"Keep it in your mouth, asshole." Soren shoved up beside me, pushing the guy into a wall so I could pass. "Before I pull it over your nose and staple it to your head."

No one mentioned anything else about my underwear after that.

"Staple it to his head?" I nudged Soren when he showed up beside me again. "Props for creativity."

"That was nothing, believe me. That wasn't even digging deep into my threat arsenal."

I didn't miss the way he seemed to be corralling me into the side of the room, the way his arm floated behind my back like he was shielding me from your everyday to your record-setting douchebags. Soren waved at a cluster of guys toward the front of the room. They were all wearing jerseys like him, beers in hand and shoving one another with their free ones.

"Friends are over there. Sure you're still up for the intro?"

"Hey, I'm a fan of the team." I drew my finger across the Devils cursive lettering going across the front of the jersey.

"Yeah, and they're going to be big fans of you once they meet you."

I was starting to figure out why he'd been hesitant about making the introduction tonight. Especially with the way his arm went around me as we approached. He didn't like the idea of any of them flirting with me or making some play for me. Like they even would—there were plenty of aesthetically pleasing girls here tonight—but I could tell by the way Soren was acting, he felt differently.

Big brother warning his friends they better not even think about little sister?

Or was it something else? The same something else I felt when Jane and Ariel talked about Soren like he was something they couldn't wait to test drive?

His friends noticed us coming, a couple of them stabbing their elbows into the next guy's stomach. By the time we stopped in front of them, all of the guys were staring at us. Like they were trying to figure something out.

"Now I see why you've been so close-lipped about your roommate," one of the guys up front announced, giving Soren a look like his secret was out. He pointed his beer at me, a goofy grin moving into place. "You've been trying to keep her all to yourself."

Nothing was subtle about the way Soren angled in front of me. "You know shit, Derrick."

"Come on. Cut the defensive thing." Derrick moved so he was able to see me again. His beer pointed at the tops of our heads next. "She's too tall for you anyway," he said, before pointing his beer at his chest and stretching a little taller. Derrick was tall—a couple inches taller than Soren. He was trying to make those two inches seem like two feet.

"Yeah. Well, she's too smart for you." Soren slapped the bill of Derrick's hat down so it covered his eyes, then he stepped in front of him. "Okay, listen up and listen good. I'm only introducing you bunch of thugs to my roommate because she asked, not because I think you have any merits or admirable qualities that deserve an introduction to her."

"I'll show you my merit, Decker," one of them popped off, working at his fly.

"Merit, Callahan. *Merit.* Not miniature." Soren patted Callahan's face a few times. "Keep your bean in your pants. Last time you went searching for it, five reruns of MASH were over by the time you found it."

A chorus of jeers followed, the herd of guys shoving at "Callahan" like he'd just been schooled. He didn't even look fazed; he was heckling right back at them.

"What's your roommate's first name, Decker? I already know her last."

"How do you know my last name?" I asked, trying again to step out from behind the wall Soren seemed to have put up in front of me, compliments of his body.

"I might not know what your last name is right now. But I definitely know what it's going to be," the guy replied, lifting his chin at me. "The same one as mine, *mamacita.*"

"I'm going to *cita* your mama, Mateo, if you keep hitting on my roommate." Soren didn't budge when I shoved him. I didn't think he'd even felt it.

"Soren, dude, are you going to introduce us or are you going to continue the act of making yourself look like an idiot?"

When Soren didn't answer, I ducked out from behind him so quickly he didn't notice. "So, hey, I'm Hayden. Soren's roommate."

I waved at the newly quiet crowd of guys, starting to understand why Soren had been so hesitant to introduce me with the way I'd been dressed before. Even with his ginormous jersey hanging off of me, most of them were staring at my legs like they were contemplating how far they could wrap around their back. Long legs had their advantages on the runway—not so much when being introduced to a half-drunk team of college baseball players.

"And when you say Soren's roommate, how would you define that?" Mateo asked, earning a death threat issued in the form of a glare from Soren.

"As in we share an apartment?" I answered.

"Do you, on occasion, share anything else?" Mateo continued, handing his beer off to the guy next to him before moving closer. As soon as he did, Soren's hand planted in Mateo's chest, shoving him back. "Say, perhaps, a bed?"

"Mateo, for real, man. Do I treat your sisters like this when you bring them around?" Soren asked.

"No. Because you know I'd whup your ass if you did."

"And I'm about to whup yours if you don't adjust your line of questioning. Or the alignment of your eyes." Soren stepped back in front of me.

"She's not your sister though, man."

"Where all of you tools are concerned, she is. Got that? Hayden is my sister, and if you fail to show her the sister-code we uphold on this team, I will destroy you." Soren jabbed his finger in the direction of each of his teammates. "Slowly."

A unified lifting of hands followed as they took a collective step back. "Little Sis Decker. You got it, Captain."

Soren waited a minute before introducing me to his teammates. I didn't hear any of it though. Sister. Little sister. That was all I heard as he listed off names. That was what I was to him. A responsibility. Someone to look out for.

How many more reality checks did I need before I accepted that Soren didn't have the same kind of feelings for me? I saw someone I wanted to take into my bed, and he saw someone he could tuck into bed.

Great. My life was festering in a steaming pile of win tonight.

It was too loud to hear my phone ring, but I felt it vibrating inside the small purse on my shoulder. I'd take any distraction I could find. Even if it was my agent calling me late on a Saturday night, I thought with a frown.

Tapping Soren's arm, I pointed at my phone before I moved toward the front door. When I waved at his teammates, they waved back. Their eyes were on mine for the first time since our meeting, giving me the little sister code of conduct treatment.

"Hello?" I answered. When Jane and Ariel saw me and flagged me over to where they were dancing with an even larger group of guys, I pointed at my phone.

"Hayden? Is that you? I can barely hear you." Ellis replied just as I moved outside.

"It's me. Sorry. I'm at a party, but I'm outside now. Better?"

He was quiet for a moment. "You're at a party?"

"Yeah, but I'm leaving now," I replied, glancing through the window. I could see Soren's teammates still clustered around one another. Sister Code. I was *not* Soren's sister. We'd shared an apartment for barely eight weeks—that made us acquaintances, not blood relatives.

"Did you go with friends or with a boy?"

"Both," I said.

"And are you and this boy serious . . .?"

"No, definitely not. He's my roommate."

"Oh, yes. That boy."

My eyes lifted. By now, I was used to Ellis drilling me about both my professional and personal life. He said he'd seen models ruin their careers more often by making bad decisions in their personal lives than the poor ones they made on the job. So he asked how much sleep we were getting, how "hard" we'd partied the night before, what our workout routine looked like, what our boyfriends were like. There wasn't much sacred where Ellis was concerned, but he'd kicked my career off faster than I could have hoped, so I tolerated his intrusiveness.

"The reason for my call is that I wanted to invite you to my own party I'm hosting at my place tomorrow night," Ellis continued as I walked circles around the front yard. I wanted to leave, but I couldn't before checking in with Jane and Ariel. "Top industry professionals will be here, a Michelin-star rated chef will be preparing the food, and I've had enough cases of champagne flown in from France to fill the swimming pool out back."

I could hear his smile; I could see it. Measured, compulsory. It was an attractive smile. I just wasn't sure it would win any genuine awards.

"That is, if you're not too partied out from tonight's jubilee," he added.

My finger tapped the outside of my phone as I thought. Ellis gave the kind of parties all of New York talked about. Rumor was that he'd turned down certain A-list celebrities who'd vied for an invite. Going would be a smart career move if some of the top designers, editors, and photographers would be there, so I couldn't understand where my vein of hesitation was coming from.

"Don't think, just come. I promise, you'll have fun. I can also promise you won't have to worry about intoxicated frat boys groping you and trying to drain cheap beer down your throat." Ellis paused. "No offense to your current company, of course, but I think we both know you're on a different level than they are."

My feet stopped moving. "I consider myself to be on the same level as every other human being on the planet, actually." Okay, so I'd kind of just talked back to my agent in a not-so-pleasant tone. Maybe not the most superlative call in the world, especially since said agent held my future in the palm of his hands.

"Just because you believe that, doesn't make it true." His voice was calm, even. "We might all be created equal, but it's what we do with our lives that sets us apart from the rest."

I wasn't sure I agreed. I wasn't sure I disagreed. But I knew better than to dig any deeper into the topic with him. "What time's the party tomorrow?"

"It starts at eight o'clock. It ends when it ends."

The thought of rubbing elbows with possibly hundreds of strangers made my stomach turn. I was nineteen. Most girls were my age were working part-time jobs at the mall and hanging out with their boyfriends, not partying with fashion icons and expected to carry on intelligent conversations with them.

"Can I bring a friend?" I asked.

After a momentary pause, Ellis asked, "What kind of a friend?"

"My roommate." My forehead lined when I heard what I'd just said. *Soren?* Of all the people in the world I could have come to some fancy party, Soren was the one I picked? But it wasn't really a conscious decision; my subconscious had been responsible for that pick.

"Your *boy* roommate?"

It made me smile that Ellis made *boy* sound like some unsavory disease. "That's the one."

What followed was a minute of silence where I felt like he was waiting for me to retract my request or change it, but I stayed quiet too.

"Yes, of course it's fine if you want to bring a guest," he said at last. "Perhaps request he leave the beer bong and keg at home." He followed it with a chuckle, but Ellis wasn't joking. Not that Soren had a beer bong or keg lying around anyway.

"We'll see you tomorrow night then. Thanks for the invite." I could see Soren watching me from the window— he hadn't taken his eyes off of me since I'd moved outside. You know, had to make sure little sis didn't get kidnapped out of the yard.

"You have my address, correct?"

"I do," I said.

He'd texted it to me a few weeks ago, basically giving me a free pass to come use his home gym or indoor pool whenever I wanted. I knew what a nice offer that was, but at the same time, it made me wonder how many of his clients got a golden ticket to his legendary estate just outside of the city. He took a helicopter to and from work every day, though he'd offered me a ride as well if I ever wanted to take him up on his offer to utilize his hotel/home facilities. I'd never brought up what I was supposed to do when it was time for me to leave and the helicopter only flew back to Manhattan in the morning.

"Oh, and Hayden, this is a black-tie affair. You're welcome to borrow any of the samples lying around the office, but please let your roommate know sneakers and a ball cap won't cut it tomorrow night."

The line was dead before I had a chance to say anything. Sneakers and a ball cap? Ellis and Soren had never met, but he had him pegged in the fashion department. Looking through that same window again, I realized most college guys could be put into that fashion category.

Black tie? How was I going to convince Soren to put on a tux? The fanciest thing I'd seen him in was a polo shirt that he'd worn untucked over his dark 501's, sneakers and ball cap included. There was no way he had a tux lying around in his rotting pile of laundry. Heck, there was probably no way I could to convince him to put one on in the first place.

Provided I could convince him to attend the party with me anyway.

Soren. *Soren?*

Of all the names I could have said, his had been the first? The only one on the tip of my tongue? I hadn't made a load of friends yet, but I still had a decent handful I could call on in the event a wingman or wingwoman was needed. It wouldn't take much convincing to get any of them to an Ellis Lawson party.

When I stepped back inside, I noticed Soren trying to get my attention. I pretended like I didn't though. I needed to get out of here. I needed some space to reflect and realign my brain so it accepted Soren as my roommate and friend and that was all. I needed to pull the drain on wherever that pool of desire I had for him was buried inside.

"Jane!" I hollered, tapping her shoulder and squeezing in between the legion of frat boys piled around her and Ariel. "I'm out. Are you guys ready to leave or are you staying?"

Jane waved her finger at the man circle around her. "I'm not leaving until I've had a bite of every last one of them."

"You staying too, Ariel?" I asked, interrupting the modern recreation of a scene from *Dirty Dancing*.

She didn't look away from the guy she was moving against. "I'm definitely staying."

My head shook. For a couple of girls who thought college boys were in the "to be avoided at all costs" pile, they both were getting awfully friendly. "Okay, well, text me when you make it back to your place later."

"Wait. You're not leaving by yourself, are you?" Jane stepped away from the football-player-looking type grinding up against her, coming toward me.

"I'm fine. I came here alone. I'm good leaving alone too."

"Yeah, but it's late."

When I started for the door, Jane's hand wound around my wrist, earning her a sigh. "It was late when I got here too."

"Hayden, you're not leaving this party by yourself."

Someone came up behind me then, replacing Jane's hand around my wrist with his. "No. She's not."

Soren's fingers were warm and solid. Five fingers, that was all he had on me, but I felt him everywhere.

That was maybe what had me shaking my wrist free.

"Would you stop with the overbearing protector thing already?" I snapped, moving toward the door. "I can take care of myself."

"Soren?" Jane called from behind me.

"Yeah, I got her."

Hearing his answer, like I was a duty or something, had my pace picking up. If I hadn't had heels on, I could have tried to outrun him, but how foolish would that be? Running away down some dark sidewalk from my roommate who wanted to make sure I got home safely?

My life made negative one sense.

"Hayden!" Soren hollered when I made it out of the cyclone fence. "Stop."

"*Stop* telling me what to do," I fired back, super mature-like.

His footsteps pounded down the walkway, only making mine move faster. "God damn it, Hayden. What is your deal?" Soren's footsteps slowed once he was a few steps behind me. "One minute you're laughing and letting me close, and the next I'm afraid you're going to go praying mantis on my ass. What am I not understanding here? Please. Enlighten me so I can fix it."

The words *little sister* were rising from within me when I clamped my mouth together so hard, my molars felt about to creak. "I don't need a personal security guard. You can go back to the party and enjoy yourself. The subway station isn't far."

"I'm not trying to be your personal security guard."

"Then what it is? You're trying to be something. What?" The sound of my heels clacking against the sidewalk echoed into the quiet night.

His sneakers hardly made any noise behind me. "I'm trying to be someone who cares. That's all. But you're making that damn near impossible."

My eyes were starting to sting. Must have had to do with the windspeed from the pace I was pounding out. It definitely wasn't because he was saying the right thing.

"You can't protect me from everything." My arms drew around my body. To keep myself warm and to keep myself together.

Moving up beside me, he sighed. "You make it a habit of underestimating me way too much." Nudging me, he slipped something over my shoulders.

"What?" I glanced at the jacket he'd covered me with.

"It's Derrick's. I didn't bring mine and figured you'd get cold since you know, it's early spring in New York, which is pretty much nothing more than winter going into overtime."

My fingers went around the collar of the jacket, pulling it closer. "Thanks."

"See? There it is again. That tone of surprise. Underestimating me." His hands went into his pockets as he matched his pace to mine. Now that I wasn't trying to run away on four-inch heels from a college athlete, I'd slowed down.

"I don't underestimate you," I replied.

"Then what is it you do? Because you definitely don't overestimate me."

I'm trying to note every flaw you have so I don't fall for you any more than I already have. I'm trying to inflate every flaw you have. I'm trying . . . but I'm not sure I'm succeeding.

I went ahead and kept that explanation to myself.

"Who were you talking to back there?"

"My agent, Ellis," I said.

"Didn't you just see him a few hours ago? And what's he doing calling you after midnight?" Soren's attention focused ahead of us, where a couple of guys had just stumbled out of a bar.

"He wanted to invite me to a party tomorrow night." Perfect segue.

"And he thought the middle of the night was the ideal time to extend that invitation?"

"This profession, it doesn't keep regular business hours. It's an any day, any time type of gig. I knew that getting into it."

When the guys crossed the road to the other side, Soren's eyes came back to me. "Yeah, but that wasn't a business call. That was a social call."

"You make that sound so scandalous."

"He's a single dude in his forties calling a nineteen-year-old in the middle of the night to invite her to a party. That's the definition of scandalous."

"He's my agent."

"He's a man first and foremost."

Exasperated, I indicated at him. "If I followed that string of logic, then what in the world am I doing living alone with you?"

"Ah, but I'm a man with a moral code. There's a difference."

"How do you know Ellis doesn't have a moral code?"

Soren blinked at me. "Do I need to restate for a third time the call he just made?"

"So how do you tell the guys with moral codes from the ones without? Am I looking for some halo, badge, or insignia?"

As we approached the bar, Soren draped his arm around me and drew me close. It was one of those biker bar looking places that had just as many people outside smoking as they did inside drinking.

"You *feel* it, that's how," he answered.

"You feel it," I echoed, blinking at him.

"Yeah, you know, in your gut. You can look at a person and feel what they're really about."

"In my gut," I said, not masking my sarcasm.

"Come on. You felt it when you met me that day you moved in. You might have been surprised and apprehensive, but you could feel—in your gut—that I was one of the good guys."

"You read the sports section of Mr. Matthews' newspaper every morning and put it back before he gets his paper."

Soren glanced at the sky like he was looking for divine intervention or something. "Yeah, but you knew I wasn't the type of guy you had to worry about waking up to find him towering over you, touching himself, while he watched you sleep, right?"

My nose curled for him. My toes curled for me. "I guess?"

"No, you know. And I know you know, so let's move on to your agent."

As we walked by the bar, a few whistles sounded and a couple of motorcycle engines revved.

Soren's response was waving his middle finger and tucking me closer. "So what's your gut tell you about him?"

My brain wasn't ready to acknowledge what my gut told me about Ellis Lawson. My shoulder lifted. "I don't know. He's my agent. It's not like I'm moving in with him or anticipating a marriage proposal."

Soren huffed. "Come on. You know."

"Will you stop telling me what I know and don't know already? You might want to add Know-It-All in that character column of yours."

Soren didn't drop his arm once we'd passed the bar. I didn't slide away from it either. "Your resistance to giving an answer *is* an answer. I don't need you to say it out loud."

I looked at him, my eyes drawn to his jawline. He'd nicked himself shaving in a few places, probably because he'd been trying to get in and out of the bathroom quickly so I could use it too. "Don't need me to say what out loud?"

Soren cleared his throat as we approached the subway entrance. "That the guy's a creep."

"Ellis is not a creep."

"Want to try that one more time? Sprinkle a little conviction into that tone of yours?" When I elbowed him in the ribs, he laughed. "Okay, okay. Enough about your creeper agent. You know it, and I know it. Let's move on to another topic, like what fast food joint we're going to hit up on the way back to the apartment."

Soren came around me so I could use the handrail to climb down the subway stairs. "Actually, I have something to ask you. Kind of a favor." My teeth worked at my lip.

"Name it." Soren hung beside me, matching every step I took.

"The party tomorrow night, at Ellis's—"

"Aka, Super Creeper," he mumbled.

I kept going. "I asked if I could bring someone with me, and he said that would be okay."

"Yeah?" His voice gave away a hint of surprise.

Ask him. Just ask him. You're not asking for him to be your baby daddy or anything. You're asking him to be your wingman at a party. "Would you go with me?"

Soren leaned in. "Sorry. I didn't hear that."

Yeah, I couldn't even hear that.

My back straightened as I took a breath. "Would you go with me? To the party tomorrow night?"

Soren paused on the step he was on. When I turned to see what was the matter, I found an odd look on his face.

"Me?" He pointed at his chest. "You want me to go with you to this fancy party? Not one of your model friends?"

I could have invited Jane or Ariel. I could have invited a few of the other friends I'd made from seeing the same faces at go-sees and waiting in the same waiting rooms over the past couple of months. I wasn't sure how to explain that he was the only person I'd thought of when I asked if I could bring someone.

"If you don't want to come, or can't, that's okay. I can ask someone else—"

"No. I can come. I want to come." He moved down the last few stairs to stop beside me. "I'm just surprised is all."

"Surprised why?"

"That you voluntarily invited me to spend a night with you." When my eyes widened, he lifted his hand. "To spend an evening with you. *Evening.*"

"Why is that a surprise?" We were roommates; we were together a lot.

153

"Because usually I'm the one forcing myself on you"
—his eyes squeezed shut, the other hand lifting in the air
—"*imposing* myself on you."

"I came to your game tonight. Willingly. And to the
party after. Also willingly."

"Yeah, but this is different." When I glanced at him
as he moved toward the subway platform, he elaborated.
"Because this time you're inviting me to something."

"I invite you to things."

He turned to face me. "Like what?"

My mouth opened before my mind had generated a
response. I couldn't think of an instance. There wasn't a
time I'd invited him to go do something with me—it had
always been the other way around. Of course I'd done that
in my quest to keep some distance between us, but I was
surprised he'd noticed.

"I'm sorry," I said.

"No apology needed. It's just nice to know you might
actually kinda like me." He winked as the subway
screeched to a stop. He took my hand to pull me away
from the doors so people could climb off. "I was starting
to think you hated my guts and were just too nice to say
so."

"Okay, that's the second time you've talked about
guts tonight. And zombies haven't once come into the
conversation. I'm calling a gut armistice, at least for tonight."

Soren smiled at the ground, waiting until the last person had climbed off before leading me in the subway car.
The subway pulled away from the platform, and I found

my head lolling into Soren as sleep deprivation caught up to me, now that I wasn't moving. His arm tucked around me so I could rest my head on his shoulder. I felt his head turn toward me, his breath warming the top of my head.

"Yes."

My eyelids fluttered but couldn't open. "Yes what?" I said with a yawn. "Yes to the party?"

His head bobbed beside mine as his hand curled around my arm. "Yes to that, and yes to anything else you ever need from me."

CHAPTER
Ten

"You know what a tux is, right? Suit, jacket, bow tie?" I rambled from behind my partition as I shimmied and stretched into the gown I'd borrowed from the sample collection at the agency.

"What? The dude at the tux rental shop told me it was a speedo, top hat, and bow tie. Damn." Soren grunted from behind his own partition. "Think anyone will notice?"

My eyes closed. With Soren, I wasn't sure if he was joking or serious about something like that.

"Before you go searching for the sharpest heel you have in your arsenal to lob my way, let me throw out a quick 'just messing with ya.'"

The sound of a zipper came from his side of the room. Which had a direct effect on the rate of my heartbeat. Which sucked for me, since my secret crush was under the impression I was the kid sister he never had.

"You got a black one, right?" I asked after I'd finished wrestling the long gown into place.

"Oops. Thought you said blush."

"Soren," I groaned, reaching for my bottle of ibuprofen. I was already stressed about tonight without his relentless quest to annoy me.

"Of course I got black. I reined my mom into tux-shopping duty with me. She's got great taste and wouldn't steer me wrong."

"You took your mom with you?" I reached for the earrings I'd picked out to match the champagne-colored gown.

"There was no way I was taking lead on tux selection. She had the day free, so she offered to come into the city to help me pick something out."

"That was nice of her."

"Please. Any of her sons calls up and mentions tux and girl in the same sentence, and Mom would rip the cape off Superman's back to get here lightning quick."

"Someone excited to get four sons married off?" I asked, slipping into the T-strap heels I'd picked for tonight.

"Someone's excited to have grandchildren. And another woman around to help even the balance."

From the sounds of it, he was pulling on his dress shirt. Soren made a lot of noise dressing. In fact, I never knew dressing or undressing could create so much noise until I'd moved in with him.

And no, the logic that perhaps the noise level might have been attributed to how keyed in I was to his every movement was not lost on me.

"Did she know you were going out with me tonight?"

I asked, hoping my voice sounded more innocent than my face looked.

"Yeah, I told her."

"And was she still just as eager to help you pick out that tux?" My eyes clamped shut when I replayed my question to myself. Hello, Fishing For Information. Now scoot along before he figures it out.

"Well, I didn't tell her until she'd already met me at the tux shop, so I'm not sure how to answer that." From his voice, I could tell his face was pulled up with mild confusion. "She did say to tell you hello though, and extend an invite to their place next weekend for my brother Ben's birthday. She makes a huge meal. We do demonstrations trying to prove who's manlier, which usually results in some kind of verbal or physical brawl, after which Mom bribes us with more food for good behavior. That type of thing."

I chuckled as I finished strapping on my shoes. "Sounds like a lot of testosterone."

"That's why Mom could really use a little extra estrogen on her side. Take your time. Think about it. I can come up with some good excuse if you don't want to come." The sound of his arms sliding into a jacket followed. He was almost ready. Good timing, since so was I.

"Sure. I've got the weekend off as of right now, though that could change in five seconds. I'd love to come meet the saint who put up with you for eighteen years."

"Please. I'm the angel of the bunch."

"And those two horns sprouting out of your head are there because . . .?"

158

"To hold up my halo. Obviously."

Another laugh as I took a moment to check my reflection in the stand-up mirror. I had it balanced against the partition, so the image was a little distorted, but for doing my own hair and makeup, along with picking out the outfit all by myself, I'd done a pretty damn fine job.

Except for . . .

Reaching behind me, I tugged at the corseting crossing down the back. I needed it tighter or I was going to flash someone at the party tonight, guaranteed. Downside to not having much real estate in the chest department to keep a dress in place.

"Can you give me a hand with my dress?" I asked, giving up. There was no way I was going to be able to contort my arms enough to get the corseting tight enough. Moving out from behind the partition, I pulled the dress up a little higher in the front. "I can get your bow tie for you in exchange for your assistance."

"I can give you two hands"—Soren emerged from his partition, buttoning his arm sleeves—"but I got the bow tie whipped into submission already. I think." He glanced down at it, double-checking, before realizing I was in front of him. He stopped moving mid-step. "Jesus Christ." He blinked a couple of times, staring at me. His hand was still frozen where it had been buttoning his sleeve.

My head tipped. "Jesus Christ . . .?"

Soren gave one more dramatic blink before blowing out an uneven breath. "Jesus Christ, I'm glad the rumor on the street is that he went and died for humanity's sins because I just committed about fifty-four in my head right now."

My lips pressed together to keep the illusion of a stern face. "Fifty-four?"

Soren's gaze swept down and around me. "Fifty-five."

"What sin is fifty-five?"

Soren gave a crooked smile. "That's for the priest's ears, not an innocent lamb's like yours."

Innocent. Was that what he thought I was? Was that how he viewed me? He wasn't looking at me like he was thinking innocent thoughts, that was for sure. I sure as heck wasn't thinking innocent thoughts about him either.

"You look insanely pretty, Hayden. Like, so insane, I'm an idiot for even trying to tell you how pretty you look." Soren rubbed his face with one hand, the other indicating at me. "And that dress . . ."

"Jesus Christ?" I suggested.

His eyes flickered to mine. "Jesus Christ exactly."

I'd been so focused on the look on his face as he stared at me, I hadn't even noticed he was in a tux. A nice-fitting one that made me think of James Bond and Italian runways. "Your mom picked that out?"

"Well, I picked it out. She just gave it the female stamp of approval." Soren glanced down at himself like he was expecting to find some garish stain or tear. "Am I way off the mark?"

"No." My hands folded together in front of me because they wanted to reach out and touch him. "You look . . ." *Like sin in flesh form? Like sex wrapped in a suit?*

160

Lickable? "Nice. You look nice."

"Nice?" He held out his arms and took himself in. A hint of dejection settled into his expression.

"I take it back," I said, giving him another once-over. Nice was the last word I'd use to describe the way he looked. "You look . . ." My eyes met his and I tried to mirror the same crooked smile he'd mastered. "Jesus Christ."

Soren tipped his chin. "I knew it."

"Well. you've never been one to lack in self-confidence."

"No, siree." He moved toward me, his shiny dress shoes drumming across the floor. "So what help did you need with with the dress?" He paused in front of me, appraising the dress like it was a sophisticated equation.

"Oh. Actually." I took a breath and turned around. "I need help with the back."

A rush of air hissed from his mouth. "Fuck me with a crowbar and call me Daddy."

"What?" My head twisted toward him.

"Exactly." He shook his head, eyeing the corseting trailing down my spine. Then he held out his hands and popped his knuckles. "Okay, okay. So you're working the whole temptress in the front, seductress in the back thing. Good look for you," he said, his eyes narrowing as he reached for the corseting. "But would you mind wearing a jacket tonight and just keeping it on all night?"

"Why?" I tried not to grin at the way he was clearly stumped by what to do next. His hands were frozen in the middle of my back, unmoving.

"I don't really want to spend the first night of ten life sentences in prison tonight."

"What does that have to do with the back of my dress?"

"It has to do with me gouging out the eyes of every creeper who runs them over you with a certain look in his eyes."

"Just start at the top, pulling each place the ribbon crosses tighter. Work your way down until it ties at the bottom," I instructed when he started tugging at one of the end pieces of the ribbon. "What certain look in their eyes?"

"You know what certain look. The one that says he's picturing doing the nasty with you right then and there." Soren's fingers tugged at the top of the corseting, just hard enough to force a gasp from me. "You know, the way I just looked at—" His throat abruptly cleared, his fingers tugging on the next section of ribbon. "Yeah, so, don't forget a jacket, okay?"

Don't smile. Do not smile.

I was totally smiling. Thankfully, he couldn't see it. "I'll bring a jacket."

"*Wear* it. Don't just bring it. Wear it." He'd almost made it to the bottom of the corseting, and for a guy who'd been a corset virgin before this, he'd picked it right up. "This corset thing is kinda kinky, girlie. Like, it's got me wondering if you keep chains and whips in one of those bags of yours. The type who will keep a guy chained in her basement when she's older."

162

My head turned over my shoulder. "I thought I was an innocent lamb?"

"So did I. But now I'm not so sure."

"The dress changed your mind on that? One small component of a dress?"

"The dress, and maybe other stuff."

My heart stalled. What other stuff? Could he read minds? Had he been listening in on me late at night when I thought he was asleep and maybe giving that self-love thing a try? Crap. Had he seen the underwear I'd bought that still had the tags on them? The ones I might have been saving in case anything ever came of us?

"What other stuff?" My voice squeaked as I said it.

Soren tied the ribbons into a bow at the bottom. "The chains and whips you keep stuffed in your bag."

I sighed. He was messing with me. He wasn't serious. I needed to get a grip.

"Anything else?" he asked, lingering behind me for a moment before coming around in front.

"I'm all set."

His face pulled up at the same time he stepped closer. "The heels. You're killing me with those things." Soren waved his hand above our heads. With my heels, I was taller than him. "My ego is relying on you putting on something that doesn't look like it was meant to hunt wild boar with or, better yet, flats. Aren't those in fashion right now?"

"Sure, they're in fashion. If you're wearing jeans and visiting the park for the day." I made it a point to stand up even taller.

His frown deepened. "Fine. But I'm sending my therapy bills to you."

"Fair enough." The mermaid skirt swished around me as I hustled to grab a jacket and clutch from my room. "All set? Because we're already going to be late even if the cab goes twenty over."

"Fashionably late? You fashion people invented the term, for crying out loud." Soren helped me into my jacket, making sure to tuck the back down so it covered the corseting.

"Fashionably late is fifteen minutes. Not an hour," I replied, wincing when I saw the time on my phone.

He waved it off like it was no big deal after locking the door behind us. "Ah, shit. I forgot to stop by Mrs. Lopez's apartment." He paused at the top of the stairway, glancing down the hall.

That familiar stab of jealousy cut me. "What was it today?"

"Drippy kitchen faucet." Soren sighed before turning his head and following me down the stairs.

"The apartment manager's supposed to take care of that kind of stuff. Why does she call you every other day when she needs something?" I hadn't known jealousy had a sound until I heard it echoing in my voice. Mrs. Lopez. Soren was down there "fixing" something every few days, it seemed. I'd never seen her, but in my head, she was an exotic beauty with voluptuous curves that reduced the male species into a drooling, fawning mob.

"The apartment manager fixing stuff. That's a good one." Soren snorted, coming up beside me to help hold up the hem of my dress as I moved down the stairs.

"I just don't know why you're the only one who can *fix* whatever it is she needs fixed."

Soren's head turned toward me. "She doesn't have anyone else."

"But she has you?"

"Ye-ah." The corners of his eyes were creased in confusion.

He had a right to be confused. I'd done my best to keep my Mrs. Lopez jealousy to myself. I had no idea what went on behind that closed door when Soren visited. I might have paused in front of it a few times to listen in, and I'd certainly never heard any sounds that would lead me to the conclusion he was engaged in manual labor. Physical exertion . . . that was trickier to pin down.

"Why the Mrs. Lopez interrogation all of a sudden?" Soren helped me down the last few stairs before shoving open the building door.

"No reason. It just seems weird that for someone who's so strapped for time would choose to spend so much of it tending to a woman's plumbing."

Soren rubbed his mouth, his eyes smiling. "What warm-blooded guy wouldn't want to spend his free time tending to a woman's plumbing?"

My cheeks flamed when I realized how I'd worded it; they heated even more when I replayed his response in my head. What did he mean by that? Was he getting it on with Mrs. Lopez? Was he really just doing home improvement when he visited her . . . or was he *doing* her?

I had no reason to believe he was. But I didn't have any reason to believe he wasn't.

Soren stepped off the curb to hail the first cab that came speeding down the road. As it pulled over, I scrolled through my phone to find Ellis's address to give to the driver. Soren helped me inside, making sure not to step on my dress, before sliding in beside me and slamming the door.

When I listed off the address, Soren let out a low whistle. "Never thought I'd make it to that part of town in my lifetime."

"No? Even with your dreams of playing professional ball?"

"I have dreams of playing pro ball, not dreams of living in the biggest house money can buy." Soren shifted closer to me, the length of his body running down the span of mine. He'd put on cologne. I could smell it in the confines of the taxi and damn if it didn't feel like it was luring me in.

"You don't want a big house?"

"What do I need a big house for?"

I thought about that for a minute. I supposed a person really only needed a big house if they were planning on having a big family. Even then, I'd seen a dozen people share a one-thousand-square-foot space harmoniously.

"Okay, so maybe not a big house, but one of those expensive, flashy cars, right? The kind footballs players roll up to clubs in, shiny wheels, Italian makes, zero-to-sixty in two seconds or something?"

Soren gave me a funny look. "I've never even gotten my license. I'm a big city, public transportation kind of guy."

"What if you get drafted to some team in a place that doesn't have the same kind of public transportation? Like, I don't know, Texas? What are you going to do then? Hire a full-time cab driver to haul your butt around?" I twisted in my seat so I was facing him, which wasn't the best idea.

In the darkness of the cab, fractals of light cutting across him as we drove, he looked so good, smelled so good . . . to take a term from his book, he was the epitome of Hayden-Nip. Driving me totally out-of-my-mind wild.

I scooted toward the door and cranked the window down an inch.

"If that happens, then I'll get my license, buy a car, and haul my own butt around. Thanks for checking."

"Yeah, but it'll be one of those flashy, expensive foreign ones right?"

His face drew up like he was considering it for the first time ever. "Nah. I'll probably just get one of those hybrids. The ones that get crazy good gas mileage."

"A hybrid?" The image of him squeezing into one of those little cars drew a smile.

"They're good for the environment, too."

"Now you're an environmentalist?"

"'Saving the ozone, one hybrid at a time.' That'll be my bumper sticker. Well, that, and another that says 'My Carbon Footprint is Bigger Than Yours.' You know, just to keep them guessing."

I elbowed him. "You're such a child."

"Thank you."

The rest of the drive passed in the same way—the two of us bantering, teasing, or laughing about something. I'd never known another person like Soren. I'd never experienced a relationship like the one we'd formed. We had an intimacy that came naturally, a simpleness that took me back to childhood. I felt good when I was with him. I felt a hundred other things too, but at the core of it all, I felt good. Happy. Content.

That was perhaps what scared me more than my physical attraction to him. The emotional attraction was dangerous. It couldn't be so easily severed or excused away. Soren Decker was one fine-looking man, but my soul craved him more than my body did.

"Holy snikkies." Soren stretched over me to look through my window as we pulled up to Ellis's home. Which was more estate than home. "Think this guy's compensating for something?"

"I'd rather not think about my agent's gender-identifying body part, thank you very much."

Soren huffed, still gaping out the window. "Yeah, can't blame you. Especially since it must be the size of a mustard seed judging the size of his manor."

When the driver stopped, Soren came around to open my door. I was suddenly nervous. I hadn't been expecting that. Why? Nervous because of spending the evening with Soren? On the closest thing to a date we'd been on? Nervous because I was at Ellis's place and expected to mingle with the social elite of the city?

Nervous because of something else? Because of something I wanted to get off my chest, even though it felt like it might rip me open in the process?

When I opened my clutch to pay the driver, Soren beat me to it. "Thanks for the lift." Then he held his elbow out for me, waiting.

"I was planning on paying for the cab," I said, lacing my arm through his.

He tucked my arm close to his side, which pulled me close against him. "So was I."

"But I'm the one who invited you. You did me the favor."

"Exactly. You invited me." His shoulder rose as we moved toward the front doors. "You did me the favor."

"By inviting you to some black-tie party with a bunch of people you don't know?"

His head stayed forward, but he looked at me from the corners of his eyes. "By inviting me to spend it with you."

"The dress. You're saying that because of the dress, right?"

"You. I'm saying it because of you." The corner of his mouth twitched. "And maybe because of the dress too."

My free arm lifted. "I knew it."

"It's a damn fine dress." He leaned in like he was about to tell me a secret. "But only because of the woman wearing it."

My heart stalled, but before I could figure out what he meant by that, or ask him, a man was there at the front door to greet us with a tray of champagne and instructions to where the party was being held.

"Ballroom?" Soren whispered to me. "This boss of yours has a ballroom?"

"Not your style?"

"Oh, no. Every room in my house one day will be a ball room. Baseballs, footballs, basketballs, the male anatomy type of balls."

My head shook. Whispering romantic things in my ear one minute to referencing his testicles the next. I had no idea where I stood with Soren.

"They didn't card us." Soren lifted his glass of champagne, clinking it against mine.

"We're not in a bar."

That was when we rounded the corner into the ballroom. We both came to a halt. I'd never seen anything so lavish, not even on television. There was an actual symphony playing music at the other end, people *waltzing* from the looks of it, and waiters dressed in tuxes holding silver trays with an array of finger foods I couldn't name.

Everyone looked expensive. The air even smelled expensive, whatever that scent was. There were dozens of other tall, young women milling around, models no doubt, but I didn't miss how the arms they were hanging off of belonged to men two, if not three, times older than they were. Soren was by far the youngest guy in attendance. Other than the servers.

"Yeah, about the bar." Soren took in the scene with me. "Can we go to one? Now?"

"You'd get carded there, you know."

"Don't care. I'd rather get kicked out of some dive than spend a night in this place. With these people," he added under his breath when a guy wearing a floor-length fur coat passed in front of us.

Truth be told, I wanted to leave too. Yes, I loved the fashion industry, but I couldn't say I loved the parties if my first two minutes at this one gave an indication to how they went.

"Just mingle with me for a little while, and then maybe we can sneak out," I whispered, my hand covering my stomach as we moved into the room.

People were starting to notice us, though they made an effort to make it seem they weren't. Thank god I'd brought Soren. I couldn't imagine walking into this viper's den alone. I had yet to see a familiar face, though I recognized a few from magazine covers. None of those faces seemed particularly welcoming either.

Soren leaned in. "Take a drink. It will help." When I took a sip of my champagne, Soren took a drink of his too. "You're going to leave your jacket on, right?" He shot a thumbs-up at a couple of guys looking at me and whispering to each other. I thought they were a couple of photographers.

"Soren," I sighed.

"Just . . . I can take a few guys at a time. A dozen of these kind, no problem." Soren's eyes landed on a group of guys wearing matching polka-dot bow ties with their tuxes. "But I don't really feel like being held down and glittered to death."

He held his champagne glass in the direction of a guy whose tux looked like it had been hand-done in gold glitter. We're talking the kind of stuff kids love to get their hands on and make a mess with. That kind of glitter. This was my first industry party, but I supposed I should have known formalwear had a generous definition in this group.

"So, yeah. Guess I could have gone with that powder blue tux I was really itching for, right?"

"But at least you look like James Bond instead of Peter Pan," I whispered.

He choked on a laugh. "This whole night, totally worth it now."

"What's so funny?" My face went blank as Ellis appeared from behind me. He was dressed in a tux similar to Soren's, though his was clearly custom tailored and had probably cost as much as the hybrid Soren was planning on one day cruising in. Ellis waited, a measured smile on his face, his eyes aimed on me.

"Me. I'm so funny," Soren answered.

Ellis's attention drifted to Soren, appraising him like he was an inconvenience. "What's so funny about you?"

Soren circled his face with his champagne glass. "The way I look."

A laugh choked out of me, making an unattractive sound.

Soren nudged me. "Nice of you to agree. *Friend.*"

Ellis didn't seem to find anything amusing about our interaction. "Ellis Lawson." He held out his left hand for Soren, which meant Soren had to unwind his right arm from me.

"Soren Decker."

"The roommate."

"The agent."

The way their hands seemed locked in some kind of death grip had me shifting. Testosterone was literally seeping from their pores from the tension I could feel building in the air.

What was going on?

"What is it you do for a living?" Ellis slid his hand into his pocket, making a point to stretch every inch of his six-foot-four frame. "Hayden never talks about you much."

Soren gave me a good-natured raised-brow look. "I go to school. Work part-time at a pub."

Ellis's head tipped. "NYU?"

Soren huffed. "Just one of those regular ol' community colleges."

"Soren plays baseball," I interjected. "He's really good." When I glanced at him, I found him staring at me, a hint of a smile in place.

"I'm sure he is." Ellis took a sip from his drink, eyeing the arm Soren was linking through mine again. "Hayden, I'd like to introduce you to some friends. Believe me, you're going to want to meet them." When we started to follow him, he paused. "Soren, would you mind if I stole your roommate away for a while?"

Soren wound my arm from his, giving me the go-ahead when I was about to object. "As long as you bring her back."

"I'll bring her back." Ellis was already guiding me away, his hand on the small of my back. "Eventually," he added, smiling at me.

Glancing over my shoulder, I found Soren in the same place we'd left him, watching. In a roomful of people, he stood out. In this city, he stood out. As different as we might have been and as much as we got on each other's nerves, I was drawn to him. From the look on his face as I walked away, I was starting to wonder if maybe, just maybe, it wasn't just me who felt that way.

Ellis introduced me to so many people, my head was spinning with names and titles. Everyone seemed eager enough to meet me, a few of them referring to me as Ellis Lawson's latest "it" girl. A few of them said that like it hinted at more than our professional arrangement, which made me all too eager to make my way back to Soren.

I felt like a jerk for inviting him to a party and ditching him. He didn't know anyone here, and the only thing he had in common with them was the state they resided in. He seemed to be mixing it up okay though. Every time I managed to catch of glimpse of him, he was chatting with someone or charming the sequins off some girl.

When I noticed another woman casually make her way up to him, I felt my hands curl into fists. He was like a model magnet, and please, her? He could do so much better than that.

And cue the jealousy theme song.

I hated this trivial, bitchy side of me that had emerged out of nowhere. I'd made it through high school without being reduced to this kind of behavior—so why was it cropping up now?

Of course I knew the answer to that—Soren. Specifically, my feelings for him.

"Hayden?" Ellis's voice cut through the haze. "Hayden?"

"Yeah? Sorry," I added, when I realized he'd introduced me to a new group of people I didn't remember stopping in front of.

Ellis didn't miss the reason for my distraction.

"I hear you're walking in Fashion Week in Paris. How exciting," one of the women said, giving the once-over I'd quickly gotten used to in the industry. Similar to the same way a butcher looks at a cut of meat to grade it accordingly.

"Yes. I can't wait." I mustered up the level of excitement I gauged was fitting.

I was excited, but Ellis had been booking me for a lot lately. Half of the bookings were in places I'd need to travel to. As a model, I'd scored the jackpot, but I was still that Nebraska girl who'd never flown on a plane up until two months ago when I boarded one to fly here.

Paris. Milan. Buenos Aires. I didn't even know how to pronounce half the places I was going.

"And would you look at that dress," the woman continued, waving at me. "You were made to wear that dress."

"It would be even more impactful if she'd lose the jacket," Ellis added under his breath.

My tight smile was my answer to that. He'd been suggesting I ditch the jacket all night, but I'd held my ground. It wasn't like the jacket was a bulky, frumpy thing that didn't match. I'd made sure to pick the right one to complement the gown.

"Why not?" he whispered to me while the woman turned to her friends and started speculating on who the designer was.

"Because I promised someone I'd leave it on to-night."

A deep-throated chuckle came from him. "College boy? *Community* college boy? That's who you promised?"

My eyebrows came together. He was getting more brazen with his insults aimed at Soren, and I wasn't sure why he felt the need to go so out of the way to degrade him.

"*Soren*," I said slowly, my expression serious. "I promised him I'd leave it on."

"Why?"

"Because the dress is a little revealing." The corner of my mouth lifted when I remembered the way Soren had staggered back a few steps when he saw the back of my dress.

"You're a model. You should be used to revealing. A little, a lot, all if need be." Ellis turned to face me, one dark brow carved into his forehead.

Warmth drained into my veins. He might have been Ellis Lawson, the man who'd given the world more su-permodels than anyone else, but he was still *my* agent. I had to remind myself of that when I felt him trying to hold his position over me.

"I'm not a model right now. I'm me. Hayden." I blinked at him, my hand going to my chest. "My life as a model is different from my real life."

He chuckled, clinking his glass against mine. "Forgive me. I forget you're still in the idealistic phase of the business." Before I could say anything, he lifted his glass in Soren's direction. "I'm only saying this because I'm your agent and have your best interest at heart, but it concerns me when I see this kind of controlling behavior. Even if it's only in the form of a jacket staying in place throughout the night. That's how it starts." Ellis scanned the jacket wrapped around me like it was a pair of shackles. "Tonight, he's telling you to keep your coat on so no one can see your body. Next month, he's ordering you to stay home so no one can see you at all. It's not healthy, and I've seen too many models fall into controlling relationships."

I'd only finished one glass of champagne, so it couldn't be the alcohol messing with my head. But surely I hadn't heard him right. Only one way to find out.

"Controlling relationship?" I repeated the term I thought I'd heard. "He's my roommate. We're not *in* a relationship."

Ellis steered me away from the women still going on about my dress and leaned in closer than seemed necessary. "You might look at him and see a roommate." His hot breath coated the side of my cheek, his hand adhering to my back again. "But when he looks at you, it isn't a roommate he sees."

As if Soren knew we were talking about him, he glanced over. He seemed to know exactly where I was in the room full of people. He didn't wave or wink, tip his head or smile, but something in his eyes acknowledged me; something in them that had my lungs petrifying for half a breath.

He looked away a moment later, but it took me a while longer to recover.

"How does he look at me?" I whispered, but Ellis was meandering away. "How does he look at me?" I repeated, louder this time.

Ellis glanced over his shoulder, a gleam in his eye. A gleam. What was I supposed to do with that?

CHAPTER

Eleven

"Think I'm okay to impose my existence on you now?" Soren shouldered up beside me, holding out a fresh glass of champagne and taking my empty one.

I shot him an apologetic smile. "I'm sorry. For dragging you here and then ditching you."

"It's all good. I'm an expert at mingling."

Something on his cheek caught my attention. Lipstick.

"Yeah, *mingling*." My eyes narrowed as I scanned the room, searching for the lips that matched the shade on his cheek.

"You okay?"

Why was I so upset? Why was my blood boiling? Why was I still staring at the mark on his cheek?

"I want to leave," I announced before chugging the fresh glass of champagne as I whisked out of the room.

"I'm on board with that decision. This bow tie feels like a noose." Soren pulled at his collar and bow tie, falling into step beside me.

We were almost out of the ballroom when someone stepped in our path. Well, she stepped into *his* path.

Matching lip girl.

Jealousy felt like a living thing inside me right then. A putrid, crippling stew of tar-like substance. She was obviously a model, but not one I recognized. I found myself targeting in on her every flaw as she rested her hand on his chest, laughing about something he'd just said.

I was bigger than this. Better than reducing myself into a spiteful, bitter person who pinpointed the flaws in others.

"I'll meet you outside." I shoved by them, dropping my empty glass on one of the serving trays at the doorway. "Take your time."

I was still wincing as I whisked down the hall toward the doorway. It was one thing to think the thoughts of a raging bitch and another to vocalize them. By the time I'd made it through the front door, I heard his steps jogging behind me. He even called my name a few times, but I kept moving. I couldn't let him see the emotion on my face, the hurt in my eyes. I had to recompose myself before I let him see me.

"Hayden!" His footsteps pounded across the concrete walkway, catching up to me.

I focused on hailing one of the cabs waiting in a line in the driveway.

He paused beside me, his breath coming quickly from his chase. "What was that about?"

Sniffing, I crossed my arms, still gazing down the driveway. "What was what about?"

"Back there? That crazy shrew moment?"

Shrugging, I played it off. "What? I wanted to let you know I'd be waiting out here." When I glanced over, I noticed a folded napkin in his hands, and I could just make out some numbers on it. I swore I felt like there was a volcano about to blow inside me. "Since your new friend clearly couldn't let you go so soon."

"My new friend?" He pulled the cab door open when it stopped in front of us. "Are you talking about Penelope?"

Penelope. Who named their kid Penelope? Who lived their life being called that every day instead of getting a name change?

Oh, god. My inner bitch was really having a field day.

If you don't have anything nice to say, just don't say anything at all. I could hear my mom's words echo in my mind. She'd raised me up better than this. Better than some insecure-acting girl who thought mean things about total strangers.

"Do you know her or something?" he asked.

I slid across the backseat of the cab, burrowing against the far door. "No. But it looked like you were getting pretty comfortable with her."

As Soren entered the cab, he appraised me with a look that suggested I was an injured wild animal. "Oh-kay. There's something I'm missing here. And I'm a guy, so

I'm going to need you to spell it out for me. Slowly. In small words."

I knew better than to open my mouth without counting to ten first. At least I was learning how to tame my inner "shrew."

"You're not missing anything," I said slowly. "I was just making an observation. Looked like you two were good friends."

The skin between Soren's eyes creased as he finished giving the address to the driver. "Let's see. I know her name, that she loves using the word *like* every other breath, that she's a born-again vegan—whatever that is—and thinks people who wear fur should be burned at the stake. Oh, and she once dated some guy whose name I can't remember anymore, but she said it like it was one of those names I should know."

I made a sound with my mouth. One of those really mature ones a teenager gave their parents when they were being lectured. "You know something else about her too." My eyes dropped to the napkin still clutched in his hand.

"Oh, yeah. Her number." He unfolded it and held it out for me.

My arms stayed folded around myself. She'd planted her lips on the napkin too.

"She said we should get together some time and 'hang out.'" He did the air quote thing, his brows moving in time with his fingers.

She'd just met the guy and was already throwing around her number and suggestions for "hanging out." What kind of guy did she think Soren was? He wasn't that type . . . was he? My stomach churned, the champagne bubbling inside not helping the situation. I could feel the two glasses I'd had on an empty stomach bleeding into my system, fogging my head and relaxing my body. "You know what that means, right? Hanging out?"

"She wants to use my body for vulgar purposes?" When my mouth dropped open, he chuckled. "Hayden, relax. I'm a big boy. I know the game. It wasn't like I was born in Hastings, Nebraska, or anything."

"You don't have to make fun of me. I'm just trying to look after you. That kind of girl is only looking for one thing from a guy like you."

"Gee, okay, Dad. Thanks for the words of wisdom." Soren lifted his voice an octave, batting his eyes at me. "Why don't you just have a chastity belt welded to my special lady parts so no person of ill repute can deflower me?"

I couldn't believe he was behaving so childishly. He looked after me—why couldn't I do the same without being treated like I was way off base?

"Can we just not speak to each other for the rest of the ride? I'm getting a headache." My fingers rubbed my temples, the mix of alcohol, jealousy, and tight corseting making me feel like my head was being attacked by a herd of elephants.

"Wait. What is this?" Soren's voice changed, growing serious. He leaned closer, studying my face. "Why do you care who I make 'friends' with or who wants to stuff their phone numbers into my hands?" He paused, still studying me.

I sealed my eyes closed and angled myself toward the door. I didn't like where he was going with this line of questioning. "Silence, please. Migraine en route."

"You have my word that I will seal my lips for the rest of the night as soon as you answer my question."

I heard him shift closer. His cologne hit me again, this time combined with the light hint of champagne on his breath and the faint scent of sweat clinging to him. I found myself experiencing that magnetic pull feeling again.

He wasn't going to let this go. Soren was as obstinate as I was.

"I don't care who you make friends with or who passes you their phone number with their lips stamped all over it."

He leaned forward. I twisted farther toward the door. "You're acting like you care."

"You're *pretending* that I care. But I don't."

I heard him shift back into his side of the cab. "Wow. Ouch. Okay, good to know. Thanks for clearing that up." He sniffed, scooting a little farther away. "I'll keep my mouth shut now."

An amoeba? Was there anything lower on the life scale than that? If there was, that's what I was. That's what I felt like.

My whole life, I'd been the mature, responsible one, and now that I was on my own in the big city and falling for some great guy, I'd morphed into a child. Great timing.

He kept his word the rest of the ride back to the apartment. Not a word. The tension became so thick inside the cab, the driver actually rolled down his window a crack.

When the driver pulled up in front of the apartment, Soren already had the money ready before I'd checked the fare. After crawling out, he waited beside the door. He didn't give me his hand to take as he had on the ride to the party, but he waited for me to climb out, and he closed the door behind me once he'd pulled out the hem of my dress.

He followed me as I unlocked the front door. After we made it through the door, he stayed one step behind me on our climb to the sixth floor. The silence stretched on— nothing but the sound of his shoes echoing on each step, the sound of my own barely making a noise.

"Would you hold onto the handrail? Please? That's what it's there for."

I looked back and saw his jaw move as he eyed the handrail beside me, still lingering a step behind. His arms were kind of open, like he was ready to . . . catch me if I fell.

Even when I'd pissed him off, he couldn't lay off the big brother routine. Paying for the cab, opening doors, making sure I didn't fall down the stairs.

I didn't take the handrail. Instead, I moved up the stairs faster, taking a couple of them at a time. It wasn't him I was upset with—it was me. Having my roommate show such concern for me should have made me grateful. Instead, I felt let down. Because I didn't want my roommate treating me like a family member—I wanted him to be like some hero in one of those classic stories I'd read in high school. I wanted him to pursue me. To crave me. To

185

lose sleep over me. To be mad with sickness if he couldn't be near me.

I wanted Soren to *want* me. The way every woman in the world desired to be wanted.

"Hayden, be careful." His footsteps hurried behind me. "Slow down. I don't need you tripping on that dress and spilling down the stairs."

"I'm fine." My feet moved faster, my heel strikes filling the stairwell.

"No, you're pissed. And pissed people trip and fall down stairs." He caught up to me, his hand circling around my arm in an attempt to slow me.

I shook off his hand. "Don't touch me."

"Why are you acting like such a child?" He kept moving up the stairs with me, one arm braced behind me just in case.

"A child," I stated, twisting around to face him once I'd reached the top of the stairs. I held my arms out at my sides to show him I'd made it up six flights in four-inch heels and a floor-length gown all on my own. "Because that's what I am to you, right? A helpless kid who needs someone to look after her?"

Soren clearly hadn't been expecting me to stop. He bumped into me when he reached the top. "A child? What? No."

He steadied me with his hands after knocking into me, but again, I shrugged them away. Having him touch me now was painful since I'd accepted what I'd been trying to deny for weeks. I liked Soren. I really liked him.

"Where is all of this coming from? My head feels like it's about to break off from all of the whiplash I've sustained tonight."

"Whatever, Soren." I moved toward our apartment, searching for the key buried in my clutch. "You're not the only person with whiplash." I thought of all the looks, the comments, the moments where I'd thought, when I'd hoped . . .

My gaze dropped to something resting on the floor outside of our door. A plate of cookies. Homemade peanut butter ones. His favorite. Stuck to the plastic wrap was a yellow sticky, signed Mrs. Lopez. There was even an XOXO.

At least this note didn't have a desperate lipstick kiss on it.

Why did all of the women of New York have to want the first man I'd ever wanted? The same one I was forced to share a small, confined space with?

The stars were screwing with me. Big time. Although with the way I was acting lately, I totally deserved it.

Soren crouched to snag the plate of cookies, already peeling back the plastic wrap and going in for one.

"Mrs. Lopez left some of her goodies for you," I said, stating the obvious. "And why does she go by Mrs.? Is she married?"

Soren held the plate up toward me, one cookie already shoved in his mouth. "Not anymore. And what do you have against Mrs. Lopez?"

"Nothing. It's you who's had something against Mrs. Lopez." As soon as I had the door open, I powered inside.

"Your body," I added under my breath, the very essence of mature.

"Great, and now Mrs. Lopez?" The door slammed shut behind him, his footsteps rumbling after me. "First the chick back at the party, and now her? You're acting kind of—" His footsteps came to a halt at the same time his voice did.

I ducked behind my partition and yanked off my jacket before he could get in my face to make me confirm or deny what he'd just silently accused me of. "No, I'm not."

"Whoa. Yes. You are." Two footsteps rang toward me. "You're jealous."

There it was. He'd said it. It was a nasty word. A highly flammable one.

A true one.

"I am very unjealous," I announced, capping my response with an insulted huff.

He was quiet after that. Quiet was bad. Especially where Soren was concerned. It meant he was thinking. Contemplating.

After tossing my jacket onto my new mattress, I yanked the bow free behind my back and started working to loosen the corseting. Even with all of my nervous energy, I made barely any progress. Looked like I was going to be sleeping in the gown tonight.

"Why are you jealous?"

His words made me freeze. Not because of the question, but because of the way he'd asked it. I didn't know a person could sound that vulnerable. When I leaned my head around the partition just enough to see him, I found his whole exterior matching. Vulnerable. Exposed. Bared.

I didn't understand why he looked the same way I felt. How he looked even more so.

"Why, Hayden?" His forehead lined as his throat moved. "Why are you jealous?"

I had to slide behind the partition again. It was hard to hear his voice—it was hell to see him at the same time.

"I can't answer that, because I'm not. Jealous," I added, just to make it clear. Clear to him I was telling the truth, clear to me I was lying.

Getting back to yanking on the ribbons of the dress, I let out a frustrated yelp when I wound up tightening a link instead of loosening it.

"Need some help?"

No.

"Yes."

My answer surprised me. For once, I felt like my words matched how I really felt where Soren was concerned.

The sound of his heel strikes moving toward me gave me goose bumps. When he came around the partition, I felt my throat dry to cotton. He'd yanked his bow tie loose and popped the top couple of buttons of his dress shirt undone. I so rarely saw him without his ball cap, I found myself staring at his hair, mussed from the way he'd styled it earlier. Probably from running his fingers through it in frustration from dealing with me the last hour.

I wanted to run my fingers through it. To feel it slide across my skin, curl over my knuckles—I wanted to hear the sound that would spill from his lips if I gave it a solid pull.

My heart was beating so fast, I felt like it was about to split out of my chest.

"Turn around." His voice was distant, tired.

Turning in place, I felt his hands drop into place before I finished moving. They went straight to work, moving deftly, precisely. More raised skin. More prickles spilling down the column of my spine.

He didn't say anything. Neither did I. The only sound was that of the ribbons being manipulated by his hands. Each loosening should have made it easier to breathe, but instead, it made it harder. The more freedom my lungs had, the more strained they felt.

I guessed I knew why. Before, Soren had been helping me get dressed.

Now, Soren Decker was helping me undress.

That realization drew an uneven exhale from with the next loosening tug of his hands.

"Almost done."

I nodded, concentrating on my breath.

He'd just made it to the last few crosses at the top when I lowered my hands from where they'd been tucked across my chest, holding up the front of the gown. They trembled as I dropped them to my sides. A test. It sounded like a good idea.

If he let the dress fall to the floor, I'd know.

If he caught it before it did, I'd know.

Either way, I'd have my answer.

A guy who was into a girl would definitely let the dress fall, right?

A guy who viewed the girl as a sister would definitely *not* let the dress fall. Right?

I didn't know. My reasoning had been misfiring for weeks now.

When I felt Soren give the top of the corseting a hard pull, I sucked in a breath and held it. Here came the answer to my harebrained experiment.

The dress started to slide down and, no lie, his hands cinched around the sides of it so quickly, he had to have broken the sound barrier.

The breath drained from my lungs all at once.

"I've got you," he said, slipping the dress back into place, waiting for me to take it so he could give me some privacy.

"Yeah. You do."

My hands lifted to hold the dress, then he stepped out of my room. Area. Space. Whatever this was now.

Letting the dress fall to the floor, I grabbed the first article of clothing that was pajama-like. An oversized shirt of some '70s' band I'd picked up at a yard sale back in Nebraska. After tugging it on, I pulled the bobby pins out of my hair and let it all fall into a messy heap down my back. I didn't comb my fingers through it to try to tame it or lay it down. Then I kicked off my heels as fast as I could before marching toward the kitchen. Food sounded like a good idea. The sugary, fatty, salty variety.

The lights were still off, and I didn't bother to turn any on. There was enough city light streaming through the windows on any given night to light up the whole apartment enough to move around without running into a wall.

"Want a cookie?" Soren appeared in the doorway as I was rifling through the fridge. Yogurt, berries, and almond milk. Yeah, that wasn't going to cut it.

"No. Thanks," I added, shoving my inner bitch into a cage. Hopefully she'd stay there for a while.

"They're good." He waved the plate in front of me.

"No, thank you." I scooted the almond milk aside, just in case a jug of chocolate milk had decided to magically appear in the back of the fridge.

"Come on. Have a cookie. It will make you feel better." He pulled one out and held it in front of my face.

The volcano inside that had stayed dormant for nineteen years of my life started to erupt. Slamming the fridge closed, I spun on him. Whatever he saw on my face had him backing up a couple of steps.

"I don't want a cookie from you, Soren."

"Okay. Noted." He stuffed the cookie in his mouth and set the plate on the counter. "Forget I mentioned anything about cookies."

"How can I? You asked me half a million times!"

He shifted, blinking at me. "Okay. I give up." He freed the buttons on his sleeves then slid his hands in his pockets. "What did I do?"

What had he done? Just made me fall for him. That was all.

That was enough.

"Nothing," I answered.

"What did I do?" As I headed back for my room, he followed me, right on my heels. "And if you give me one more 'nothing,' I'm going to lose it."

When I kept moving, his hands caught my shoulders, stilling me at the same time he twisted me around. His eyes aligned on mine, his face moving closer. I'd never seen his eyes like this before. Inches away from mine, emotions played in them that made me dizzy.

"What? Did? I? Do?"

My mind lost its foothold. "I don't want cookies from you."

Imaginary head smack. Commence now.

Soren looked as confused as he was amused. "Okay, okay. You don't want cookies from me." He moved closer; I moved away. He stalked closer still. I slammed into the wall behind me. One side of his mouth twitched when he appraised my current situation. One arm braced beside my head. The other fixing to the wall on my other side. "Then what do you want?"

My lungs faltered.

My heart followed.

My mind last.

"You." The word fell from my mouth. "I want you."

And cue the fuckity-fuck-fuck chorus.

All signs of amusement blanched from his face. A deep crease carved between his eyes as his throat moved. "You want *what*?"

Don't you dare say it again, Hayden. Dignity. Hold onto whatever you have left.

"Forget it." When I tried ducking beneath his arm, he slid it down to keep me detained. "It's late. I'm tired. I'm two glasses of champagne into the night." When I ducked lower, he did the same thing.

"Forget it?" His head shook once. "No way."

"Soren," I exhaled when I tried to escape beneath his other arm, only to find him caging me in on that side as well.

"Stop." One of his hands formed around my shoulder, positioning me so I was facing him straight on again. His head moved closer, aligning with mine. "Explain."

His mouth. I was staring at it. Wondering what it would feel like moving with mine, how his lips would feel, how his tongue would explore. My face rushed with heat, a crimson sign giving away my thoughts. I moved to duck beneath his arm again. "I don't know what I meant by that. I meant *nothing* by that."

Soren's hand caught my shoulder again. "Turn," he instructed, waiting. "Look me in the eye." He waited again. The instant my eyes met his, he continued, "Explain."

Tired of fighting it.

Tired of hiding it.

Tired of pretending it would go away.

"I want . . ." My stomach was in knots. "You."

He didn't say anything. He stood there, bolstered in front of me, studying my eyes. "You want me? In the way I'm thinking you mean?"

My fingers worked at the hem of my sleep shirt, nervous energy pouring out of me. "Probably, yeah."

"For how long now?" he asked, his expression giving nothing away. He could have been disgusted. Embarrassed. He could have felt the same way about me. His face was that veiled.

"Too long," I answered. A month? A day?

"Why didn't you say anything before?" His light eyes glowed with curiosity.

My arms lifted before falling at my sides. "Because it's embarrassing. I didn't want to tell you tonight. I didn't want to tell you ever. I didn't want you to know because . . ."

Soren leaned closer. "Because why?"

I'd already confessed the worst. The rest was nothing. "Because of the way you treat me."

His forehead creased. "What way do I treat you?"

My finger motioned between us, expecting him to realize it. It was obvious to me. "Like I'm your little sister or something."

"My little sister?" The look on my face managed to wipe whatever amusement had been about to surface. He took a breath. "What's wrong with a guy treating a girl like a sister?" His shoulders moved beneath the tux jacket. "Respect comes with that, protection, taking care of her. Having her back, chasing off the cheese-dicks of the world. What's wrong with that?"

After I got past the cheese-dick reference, I took a minute to consider that. Respect. Concern. Loyalty. My mind felt muddy from all of the conflict raging inside of me. One moment believing one thing—the next invalidating that belief.

"Nothing's wrong with that," I answered quietly.

"You just don't want me looking at you and *only* thinking little sister—is that what you're saying?" My eyes answered him. "How do you want me to look at you then?"

My mind stalled. The answer to that should have been easy to give since I'd been consumed by the topic for weeks. "Like I'm . . ."

Soren's body drifted closer. "Like you're someone I have feelings for?"

My head bobbed. "But I know you probably don't, and I know I'm an idiot for telling you all of this because we live together and now it's going to be all awkward, and . . ." I was sweating, that was how nervous I was. "What am I even saying right now? God. Just shut up already, Hayden." When I realized Soren was still standing there, arms braced around me, eyes unyielding, I slouched into the wall. "What?"

"Just waiting to see if you're serious."

"Serious about what?"

His mouth twitched. "Shutting up."

"Soren!" I slugged his arm. I'd just bared my soul—this wasn't the time for his wit to run free.

"I just want to know."

"Why?"

"So I can finally reply to everything you just said."

Sealing my lips, I shrugged.

He had to fight another grin, but as he did, his feet slid closer, one settling between mine, the other outside my foot. His arms bent as his body pressed into mine. His chest rose and fell against mine with each breath, sending a cataclysm of sensations loose inside my body.

"What are you doing?" My voice quaked as his hands moved from the wall to the sides of my neck.

Soren's eyes dropped to my mouth. "Answering your question," he breathed as his index fingers skimmed my neck, causing a tangle of goose bumps to charge down my spine.

"Soren—"

"Still answering your question," he whispered right before his mouth touched mine.

Every nerve in my body fired at once. A moment after, I lost control of them all.

My hands found themselves on his chest, sweeping beneath the lapels of his jacket. My lips found themselves parting as he kissed me, taking the lead, guiding me as our mouths came together and fell away like waves breaking on the beach.

I'd kissed a few boys back home. I'd made out with a couple of them too, but that had felt different than this did. Maybe it was because my feelings for Soren were stronger, or maybe it was because Soren didn't kiss like a boy— sloppy and unsure, hands a groping, untamed mess.

No, Soren definitely didn't kiss like a boy. My god, I wasn't sure what to compare his knowledge of kissing to.

Soren kissed like a . . .

Deity. The damn deity of lust.

His hands stayed framed around my neck. His thumbs swept along my pulse points when he kissed me harder, and fell away when his intensity waned, allowing us each a moment to recover.

Five minutes went by. Maybe more. His mouth never once left mine, his hands staying secured to my neck. This was the best kiss of my life. I knew that. No kiss in the future would ever compare to the one happening right now in this small apartment in this giant city.

This was more than what I'd ever hoped to get in return from Soren—but still, I wanted more.

So much more.

My hands circled behind his neck as I leapt just enough to encircle his waist with my legs. The surprise of it drew a sound from deep in his chest, his mouth working against mine at the new pace I'd set.

Combustion. I was on my way, in the process of, or experiencing it. I'd never felt this way before to know for sure.

My tongue collided with his as his hands loosened from my neck to loop behind my backside. He pushed me harder into the wall, this time more with his hips than his chest. I could feel him straining through his slacks, fitting his warmth against mine.

Something uneven and low vibrated in my throat when I pitched my hips against him. The same type of sound, a few octaves lower, emanated from him.

He pressed me harder into the wall, pinning my hips to it, making it impossible for me to move. His tongue untangled from mine, his mouth slowed, and he pulled back just far enough, a ribbon of rational thought could form again.

"What?" I panted against his lips.

He was breathing hard, like he'd just finished sprinting the bases. His eyes were feral, the pupils almost swallowing his irises. "Did I answer your question?"

My breaths were just as fragmented, so I nodded my answer.

One side of his mouth pulled. "Good."

His mouth. It wasn't just nice to look at; it was capable of performing nice—really nice—things. Which made me want to get back to doing those nice things.

Soren pulled back when I moved back in.

"What's the matter?" I asked. For one insecure moment, I wondered if I was a total letdown in the kissing department. Was I a bad kisser? The slobbering, messy kind?

"I just think that we should maybe slow down." Soren's eyes dropped to where my hands were still draped on his chest. I'd managed to get three of his shirt buttons undone, my fingers frozen on the fourth. I didn't even remember reaching for the first.

"Slow down?" I repeated. That didn't mean I was a bad kisser.

"Slow down." His eyes moved lower, to where our hips were joined. My shirt had ridden up, my white underwear was showing, and something of his showed behind his zipper.

This didn't seem like the time to slow down. My body was racing. I was ready; he was *clearly* ready.

"Why?" I asked, letting go of his shirt, which my fingers looked about to rip off.

His face pulled up like he was trying to answer that question himself. "I just think that we might be moving a little fast. Maybe," he added, looking as unsure as he did sure. "Like you said, you've had champagne. You could totally be turned on by the sight of me in a tux because, well, no explanation needed right?" He leaned away so he could motion down at his tux.

Damn. He'd looked good all polished and pristine. But now, bow tie undone, shirt halfway open, hair mussed, his erection pushing against his zipper . . . this was what a girl's dreams were made of.

"I only had two glasses of champagne."

"You never drink."

"Over the course of four hours."

"You weigh nothing."

I exhaled, accepting he'd have a rebuttal to every point I tried to make. "I felt something for you before I saw you in your tux."

His brow carved into his forehead. "Yeah, but the tux didn't hurt the feelings, right?"

He took my lack of answer as one.

"Plus, the whole jealousy thing could be swaying your . . ."

"Feelings?" I suggested.

His eyes dropped to my sleep shirt, where my nipples were popping through the thin material. His eyes swept lower, where my hips were still fighting to form against his. Letting go of his hold around my backside, he set me back down on the floor.

"Libido," he stated, taking a few steps back, his hand lifting when I moved to close that distance.

"You think because some other chick was hitting on you, that's the reason I want to . . ."

"Have sex with me?"

My arms crossed, my legs trembling with what felt like withdrawal-like symptoms. "That isn't the reason."

"Good. I will be happy to let you prove that to me at a later time. When alcohol, a tux, and another 'chick' aren't part of the same evening." When Soren's eyes ran down me again, he rolled his neck and took a few more large steps back.

At least I wasn't the only one fighting temptation.

"Did you seriously just suggest slowing down?" More of my mind was coming back with the farther away he got.

He looked like he was replaying it in his head. "Yeah, I think I really did."

"Why?"

"Because I'm a moron hell-bent on making sure I suffer and strangle any measure of happiness out of my life."

Leaning into the wall, I tried to catch my breath. "That sounds about right."

His face creased. "Then why does it feel so wrong?"

"Doing the right thing's hard?" I guessed.

Soren's eyes dropped to his belt region. "It's hard, all right. So damn hard, I'm going to have to take a cold shower if I want to get any sleep tonight."

My eyes roamed the same region, but I forced myself to stay where I was. "We both know what you do in the shower."

Soren fought a smile as he kicked out of his shoes. "Tonight, in the shower. Tomorrow night"—his eyes met mine—"we'll revisit this . . . topic." His hand motioned between us.

"You're not saying that because you're not that into me and don't want to hurt my feelings?" I worked at my lip as he slid out of the tux jacket and settled it over the back of a chair. Nice of him to do the Soren Strip Show ten feet in front of me.

"No," he snorted, making a face like I was insane. "I'm into you. So way into you, I'm still kind of in shock you just admitted you were into me. So way into you, I'm fighting every instinct and muscle fiber begging me to push you back up against that wall and finish what we started."

My knees quivered. More from the way he was appraising me, his jaw working, than the words he was speaking.

"I'm into you, Hayden. I'm not saying slow down for my benefit; I'm saying it for yours."

"For mine?"

"If I was only looking out for mine, I'd have you in my bed and screaming my name right now." He pulled the bow tie from his collar, giving me a look that dared me to challenge him.

"Screaming your name, huh? Confident in your abilities."

"I could try to convince you with my words. Or I could just actually convince you tomorrow night." He smirked as he unbuttoned what was left of his shirt. "You got a preview of what my tongue can do, right? Believe me, screaming my name's just the start of what I have planned."

That man. Good god. I swear, if I barely touched myself through my underwear right now, I'd come from the way he was appraising me like he wanted to possess me. "Tomorrow night?"

"Sleep on it, think about it. You still feel the same way tomorrow night—minus the alcohol, tux, and other chicks—yeah." He nodded, slipping out of his shirt one arm at a time. "Tomorrow night."

"Twenty-four hours? That's the difference between taking it slow and rushing into things?"

"Eighty-six thousand, four hundred seconds. Each of those feeling like a damn lifetime to a man waiting to be with the girl he's into." Soren worked at his belt as he started for the bathroom, winking at me when he caught me staring at his bare upper half. "I'd wait tens of thousands of lifetimes for you. *That's* the difference right there."

I turned to watch him, my heart trilling. "It's still only twenty-four hours. One day."

"I'm trying to be romantic."

"I'm trying to get laid."

"I'm trying to be a gentleman. A good guy here."

"I'm trying to be a bad girl. A very bad one."

His hands gripped the frame of the doorway before he banged his head against it. "I'm going to take that cold shower now."

"Have fun with your 'self-love.' I prefer to do mine in my bed." Shoving off the wall, I wandered toward my room. "Come to think of it . . ." When I glanced over my shoulder, I found him watching me, mouth hanging open, his body angling like he wanted to follow. "Good night, Soren."

A few more thumps sounded. "Sweet dreams, Hayden."

CHAPTER Twelve

My dreams had not been sweet. Not even close.

The next morning, I woke in a panicked frenzy, my sheets twisted around my legs, sweat clinging to my skin. All night, I'd dreamed about Soren and me, but it hadn't been the kind of dream I'd been hoping to have. Us fighting and yelling, being petty and childish. Then when it seemed we'd never be free of this endless loop of arguing, we were torn apart. He went one direction; I went the other.

He left me.

That was when I jolted awake.

I gave myself a few minutes to let the clutches of the nightmare drift away, but this one didn't retreat the way most did. Instead, it clung to me, refusing to let me shuffle it into the back of my mind.

Soren had early morning practice and was already gone by the time I forced myself out of bed. The pieces of his tux he'd scattered like damn bread crumbs last night had been picked up and were gone. He probably had to return it today.

However, the wall we'd gotten all hot and heavy against was still there. Not going anywhere. Glancing at it, I swore I could see my impression carved into the drywall.

I'd kissed Soren. I'd *made out* with Soren.

I'd been ready and practically begging to do more with him.

My stomach contracted, a wave of nausea rolling through me.

I'd told him I liked him and wanted him and . . . shit, I'd gone and ruined everything.

Soren and I were roommates. We had to live together. How was confessing feelings for one another and letting those feelings physically manifest going to make this arrangement any easier? Being in a relationship was hard enough at our age. Sharing an apartment was just as hard. But combining those two challenges and expecting everything to come out okay? Yeah, right. World peace had a better chance of making it.

As I rushed through showering and getting ready, I couldn't stop thinking about my dad. I hardly ever thought of him anymore, but there he was now, ready to take up as much of my head-space as he had when he'd first left us.

Soren wasn't my dad. The rational part of my brain knew that. The irrational part linked the two, comparing and contrasting until I felt half-mad. Soren was a man, just like my dad. He wore jeans, just like my dad. He had blue eyes like my dad.

It was endless. Ridiculous, but endless.

I had the day off, but I needed to leave the apartment. I had to avoid him for as long as possible because while he was expecting one thing from tonight, I had to give him the total opposite.

I cared for Soren. Now I knew he cared for me. But this, us . . . we wouldn't survive if we let our friendship take a back seat to our other feelings. I'd rather have him in my life in some capacity forever than in no capacity one day soon.

Besides, what did I know about relationships? Other than what I'd watched my parents go through and the superficial ones I'd seen back in high school? I'd come to New York to model, to work hard, and to go far in this business. To make a name for myself in the fashion industry and turn that into a long-term career. What was I doing getting tangled up with a boy with just as lofty of a dream?

He was right. Last night, the champagne, or the tux, or the jealousy, or something had clouded my judgment. I might have harbored feelings for him, but confessing them and wanting to act on them . . . that was something I should have kept to myself.

There was a note taped to the door, my name penned on the outside in Soren's handwriting. I didn't take it down, unfold it, and read whatever he'd written. I left it where it was, needing to clear my head and figure out some way to explain away everything I'd confessed last night.

Even though I'd showered, I could still feel where his hands had touched me. The taste of his lips seemed to cling to mine no matter how much lip balm I applied.

Today was warmer than it had been, which meant the park was busier than usual. All of the noise and action made for a welcome distraction though, so I spent a few hours meandering around. I took a break to relax on a bench so I could call home and catch up with everyone, and just as I was about to hang up with them, another call came in.

After saying bye to my mom, who had not stopped reminding me to send less money back home, I answered the call. I'd been avoiding Soren's, but this one I couldn't ignore.

"Hi, Ellis," I said.

He gave one of his typical greetings. "Where are you?"

"At Central Park. Why?"

"I just caught wind that one of the giants is looking for a fresh, new face for their line."

"What company?"

"The giant of the giants."

The skin on my arms raised. I'd been landing good gigs for weeks, but this—something like this was big. Booking a campaign like this took a model from the masses and set her on a platform. I needed a platform. I needed people to not just recognize my face but to know my name. Fashion was a business of names, and that was my long game. Model, gain experience, get recognized, make connections, then launch my own fashion line one day.

"Can you meet me at the agency in thirty minutes?"

The time on my phone showed two. On a Sunday. "Yeah, I guess. What are we meeting for?"

The sound of movement in the background came through the phone. "I want to add a few new shots to your portfolio. Ones that will appeal to this client."

That made sense, and it wasn't like I had a whole lot else planned for the day. Other than having to eventually confront my roommate and deliver an, "oops, I lied" speech and make it convincing.

Impromptu photo shoot sounded like a much better option.

"I'll see you there in thirty."

The line was already dead by the time I rose from the bench.

A moment later, a text from Soren came in. "I got Trish to close for me tonight, so I'll be home by nine. Can't wait to see you."

My throat burned from reading his words. I couldn't wait to see him either, and that was the problem. We couldn't both feel the same way about each other.

I'd mess things up. Or he would. Or we both would.

We'd totally ruin everything because we'd been foolish to think that of all the doomed relationships out there, ours would be the one to make it.

Right after that text, he sent another one that read, "You left your phone at the apartment again, didn't you?"

He was going to go through the whole day looking forward to tonight, thinking we'd . . . pick up where we'd left off. He was probably going to stop and get flowers or bring me home one of my favorite truffles from the chocolate store down the road or something sweet like only Soren was capable of.

The thought of having to look him in the face and tell him I didn't have feelings for him made me physically ill. I couldn't go home tonight. I couldn't lie to him about not having feelings for him, probably crushing him, when he'd been expecting the night to go totally differently.

I couldn't go back.

A hotel or a friend's or something. I felt like I'd sleep on a park bench before going back to our apartment tonight.

Once I made it to the agency, I turned off my phone. I felt like such a coward doing it, but there was no way I'd be able to focus on the photo shoot if the sound of Soren's texts coming in kept breaking me in half.

Ellis had beaten me there, and he already had the lights on. It was quiet throughout the office as he led me to one of the big rooms used for shoots. "Thanks for coming in on a Sunday. Especially after a late night at my place."

He wasn't wearing his standard suit and tie today, instead in a pair of dark slacks and a light, button-up shirt rolled up to his elbows. The sinews of his forearms were hard to miss, as was the rest of his body. Ellis played to his every advantage, from the way he did business to the way he dressed.

It was what had made him so successful. It was also what had earned him such a womanizer reputation.

"What photographer did you manage to bribe to come in today?" I slid my purse over my head and dropped it on one of the chairs stationed around the room before I moved toward the dressing area.

Ellis moved around the lighting equipment, turning things on and adjusting them. "Me."

I paused outside of the curtains. "You?"

"It's what I did between modeling and this. Taking photographs of beautiful women. Exotic locations." He fired a smile at me as he pulled a camera from a bag. "It wasn't a bad gig."

I smiled back before sliding into the dressing area, but I felt uneasy. Ellis was my agent. I was used to seeing him in that light, not the photographer one. I was worried it might affect my performance—that having him behind the flashing camera might make my poses stiff and unnatural.

Just a photo shoot. Just Ellis, I reminded myself, taking a deep breath. No big deal. None whatsoever. We were so used to working together, this would probably be a snap. Quickest photo shoot in the history of ever.

That was what I was convincing myself of as I scanned the dressing area for what I was supposed to wear.

There was nothing.

"Ellis?" I called from behind the curtains. "There's nothing back here for me to change into. Did you just want me to go with the simple jeans, tank thing?" I started peeling out of my sweater, guessing so. "I'll need to borrow a pair of heels from wardrobe though. Don't think my sneakers are what you have in mind."

I heard a few test shots fire. "It's okay. You won't need shoes for this shoot."

That was a first. I'd take it though. I was used to shoving my feet into uncomfortable shoes that were usually two sizes too small. Barefoot for a photo shoot was like being told I'd be given a massage at the same time.

"So jeans and tank then? Hair in a ponytail?" I was already gathering my hair up, a twisty tie between my teeth, when Ellis cleared his throat.

"This is a nude photo shoot, Hayden. I'm keeping it simple for you. You can decide if you want your hair up or down."

The twisty tie fell out of my mouth. "A . . ."

"Nude. You heard me right the first time. This company's headquarters are in Paris. They view nudity differently than us Americans." Ellis paused. "Trust me. I know what I'm doing."

"Okey-dokey," I replied, feeling the opposite of confident as I reached for the hem of my camisole.

Some models had staunch views on nudity, but I floated somewhere in the middle. I wasn't so in love with the idea of it that I traipsed around my apartment in my birthday suit, but I wasn't so against it I'd signed some moral code in my own blood, swearing I'd never get naked in front of a camera. This wasn't *Playboy*. This was fashion. Tasteful nudity.

If that made any sense.

As I worked my jeans down my legs, I realized it wasn't the fact I was doing a nude shoot that had me panicked—it was that I was doing the shoot with Ellis. Alone.

He was Ellis Lawson though. He'd probably seen thousands of naked women—in photos, in front of his camera, and beneath him in bed. He was probably so used to naked women, they were no different to him than the clothed ones.

That was what I told myself as I finished sliding out of my underwear and bra. I left the twisty tie on the floor. At least having my hair down provided some coverage.

"Are you ready?" My voice was high. Because I was nervous. Because I was about to emerge naked from a dressing room in front of my agent and his camera. They didn't prepare Nebraska girls for this kind of a situation.

"I've been ready," he replied, sounding like he was fighting off a yawn.

If nothing else, the fact that he was on the verge of a yawn when a woman was about to pose naked in front of him gave me the courage I needed to emerge from the dressing room.

He didn't even glance my way as I shuffled across the room, fighting the instinct to cover my chest or my something else with my hands. "Where do you want me?"

He was messing with the dials of his camera, totally focused on that. "Up front. Start posing however you want —I'll guide you from there if we're not getting the right shot."

My eyes flickered to my purse, where my phone was. Soren. Why was I thinking about him right now? Why did I want to call him and talk to him or have him come here to be with me right now? I was working. I was naked. This was exactly not the time to call him.

"What did you do last night after the party? You must have left early." Ellis was still making some adjustments on his camera; he hadn't once looked up.

"We just went back to the apartment. Sorry I left without saying good-bye. It was a good party." I moved in front of all of the lights, feeling the heat of them breaking down on my skin. Talk about feeling exposed. Every light in the room was aimed my way.

"That boy. Your roommate?" Ellis finally looked up. His eyes strayed nowhere but mine. "He likes you."

My throat moved as I swallowed. "Soren? No. He's just protective. He looks after me."

"He's protective because he likes you. He looks after you for the same reason."

Being naked, I wasn't feeling at the height of my de-bating best. I elected to keep my mouth shut and hoped he'd get the shoot started.

"Have you slept with him?" Ellis's gaze found me again, but this one strayed slightly.

"No." I made a face to sell my disgust. "Definitely not."

Ellis lifted the camera, so I could no longer see his eyes. He still could have been looking at my eyes. He could have just as easily as been zeroed in on my chest.

"He wants you. If you don't feel the same, you might consider moving out. I'd hate to see him take advantage of the situation. If he ever tried forcing himself on you . . ."

"Soren would never do that." My tone had a defen-sive edge. Why?

Ellis chuckled, the camera flash firing. I hadn't been ready. "You might find men will do just about anything when it comes to serving the interests of their cocks, Hay-den."

Ellis's blunt words lingered in my mind when the next flash fired. Crap. We weren't going to get one good shot if I didn't get my head right. "Can we please not talk about Soren anymore?"

"What would you like to talk about?" Ellis lowered the camera to inspect the images and made a few dial adjustments.

"Nothing," I said, sitting on the floor and angling my body so my chest and nether region weren't showing. "I just want to focus on the shoot."

Ellis lifted the camera, firing another shot after crouching in front of me. "Works for me."

He checked this image too, then scooted forward a few feet before taking another shot. He kept shooting as I made small adjustments to my face and neck.

"Why don't you lie back?" he suggested a few shots later. "So it's like you're lying down in bed?"

Except I wasn't in pajamas and I didn't have blankets to cover me.

Rolling back, I stretched my spine across the floor, letting my legs swing to the side, bent and zippered shut. I hung my arms above my head, looking at the camera dead-on as Ellis appeared above me. There. European.

"Yes. Perfect." He leaned over me, his camera firing as I held each pose for a few shots before making a small change to my face or hands. "They're going to book you the minute they see these shots. You're exactly what they're looking for."

Ellis floated around my side, lifting his leg over me so he was directly above me. My neck suddenly felt stiff, the rest of my body following. Nowhere was Ellis's body touching mine. Nowhere. But the stance, the way I was stretching out between his legs as he towered above me, his camera aimed at my exposed body . . . the instincts Soren had been suggesting I hone started to fire.

"Are we almost done?" I blinked, the heat coming from the lights stifling.

"A few more shots, just to make sure we've got it." Ellis crouched over me, the camera still snapping, but in his new position, I noticed something.

It was impossible not to notice.

My eyes sealed shut for a moment, as I was unsure what to say or do. He was a man working in close proximity with a naked woman. Sporting wood wasn't way off base given the situation—I'd seen men get hard from far less.

It wasn't like he was acting on it. He wasn't saying anything inappropriate or touching me or giving me creepy looks. He was my agent. My photographer at the present moment. He had a boner. No big deal.

I replayed that in my head ten times, but it wouldn't take root.

It felt like a big deal. That he'd called me in on a Sunday at the last minute, that we were the only two people here, that he was photographing me nude, hovering above me, while his hard-on bulged through his tight slacks felt dangerous.

"I'm done," I announced suddenly, sliding out from beneath him. "I can't do this."

Ellis made no move to stop me. He just rose back up, lowered his camera, and gave me a confused look as my hands scattered to cover myself. "Are you uncomfortable posing nude? Your file didn't list any hesitations over it . . ."

"No, I'm not uncomfortable with it." The more I tried to cover myself, the sillier I felt. Giving up, I got up and powered toward the dressing area. "It's just, today . . ." I didn't know what I was trying to say. Was this because of Ellis? Was it because of Soren?

Was it because of me?

I wasn't sure why I was acting so unsure—I just knew I couldn't lie below that camera for another shot.

"Today's just been one of those days," I settled on as I got redressed as fast as I could.

"Can I interest you in dinner then? I made reservations at one of the best places in the city, but the person who was supposed to go with me can't make it. People usually have to make reservations months in advance—it's exactly the type of place I go to when I'm having one of 'those days.'" Ellis sounded like he was moving around the room, switching off the lights.

"Thanks for the invite, but I've already got plans." So it was kind of a lie, but not totally. I did have plans. To be alone so I could figure out what I was going to tell my roommate when I saw him again.

"These plans rate higher than dining at a five-star restaurant with me?"

My finger stopped tying my sneakers. Was Ellis implying he was so great? Or the restaurant was? The combination was? However he meant what he'd said, it made the offer that much less appealing.

"Sorry. I can't cancel them," I said, tugging on my jacket before emerging from the dressing area.

"Too bad more women aren't like you." The room was dark now, just a wash of light diffusing in from the outside windows lining the office.

"Aren't like me?" I said, moving toward the door.

Ellis shoved off the wall, following me. "The type who don't cancel once they've committed. Hardworking." Ellis's hand made it to the door handle before mine. He held it there for a minute, but the door stayed closed.

He was staring down at me—I could feel it, but I didn't look back. Something about this whole afternoon was off. Wrong.

"Intoxicating," he added, leaning in and taking a slow breath.

"I really have to go or else I'll be late." My voice gave away nothing, but everything inside me felt like it was trembling.

"You have plans with him tonight, don't you?" There was a bite to his words, something unsettling. I didn't have time to answer before he opened the door, adding, "Don't waste everything you're about to become on a nothing like him."

I didn't say anything else as I moved through the agency toward the elevators. Ellis didn't follow, but the adrenaline charging inside made me feel like I was being chased.

What in the hell was that about? That shoot had to qualify as the single, most creepy experience of my life. I wasn't sure if Ellis's dinner invitation had been intended as a date or as a business meeting. I wasn't sure what his whole cryptic act and words had been about either. He seemed almost jealous of whatever relationship he assumed Soren and I had. But he was Ellis Lawson. What did he have to be jealous about when it came to two young kids?

The men of the world seemed determined to screw with my head.

First Soren. Now Ellis. Although, in fairness, I was responsible for the whole mess with Soren. If I'd just kept my mouth closed the way I'd been doing for weeks, we'd still be on a roommate basis instead of a roommate-plus-question-mark one.

By the time I'd left the agency and was moving down sidewalks, my head started to clear, and by the time I'd found a hotel to stay in for the night, I'd convinced myself I was making a way bigger deal out of the Ellis encounter than I needed to. He was quirky, mysterious, different . . . just like the majority of other people in this industry.

Once I'd slid into the comfy hotel bed and thrown the covers over my head to block out the world for a few hours, I felt much better about the Ellis cluster.

The Soren one I felt exponentially worse about though. Especially when I'd fired on my phone for a few minutes—to make sure I hadn't missed any emergency calls from my family or the agency—only to find I'd missed dozens of calls and texts. All from him. I powered off the phone before I read or listened to a single one.

Tomorrow, I'd confront Soren.

Tonight, I was happy to play ignorant to the whole mess I was responsible for creating.

CHAPTER

Thirteen

My mess was waiting for me just inside the doors of the K&M building the next morning.

I didn't see him until I'd already whisked through the revolving door. The moment I did, I froze, one foot wanting to carry me backward, the other wanting to propel me forward.

My decision was made for me when Soren's gaze fell on me. His shoulders fell as a heavy breath spilled from his mouth. He looked . . . relieved.

Why was he relieved?

Why did it look like he was about to throw his arms around me as he dashed toward me?

"You're okay. Thank god." He dropped his backpack and baseball bag on the floor when he stopped in front of me, his arms going around my back as he pulled me into his chest.

My arms were frozen at my sides as he held me a few moments before letting go. His eyes roamed me when he stepped back. He looked exhausted, like he hadn't slept. Bloodshot whites of the eyes, dark hollows, a couple days of scruff dotting his face. Even his shirt was on inside out.

"What happened? Where have you been? Are you okay?" His eyes did another careful sweep, checking me over again.

"Soren, I'm fine," I said after swallowing the ball in my throat.

He'd been worried about me last night. I should have called or shot him a quick text to let him know I was okay and spending the night with Jane and Ariel or something.

"Where were you? You never came home last night. I tried calling you a million times." He rolled his neck, making it pop a few times.

"Can we talk about this later? I've got a meeting in a few minutes."

He slid in front of me when I tried to move around him. "What the hell is going on?" His hand drilled into my stomach when I tried moving by again. "I was up all night, losing my shit that something had happened to you, and here you are this morning, just fine, and aren't going to give me any kind of an explanation?" He moved his head so it was in front of mine. "You owe the guy who called every hospital and minor emergency clinic in this city an explanation."

The ball was lodged right back in my throat. I guessed it wouldn't go away for a while. "You called hospitals? Soren, I was fine."

"But how in the hell was I supposed to know that? I get home last night, knowing we were supposed to have a serious discussion, and you're not there. I try calling you, probably more times than one guy has ever tried calling a girl in a twelve-hour period. You don't answer. I freak the hell out. What else am I supposed to do besides start calling every friend, family member, and hospital I can get a hold of?"

I couldn't look him in the eyes. I thought that was making him more upset than my unwillingness to explain what had happened last night.

"No one knew where you were. No one had a fucking clue. Do you know what I went through last night?"

Something he'd said caught up to me. "Did you say my family?"

Soren's head moved. "Yeah. I called them."

"You called my family to ask if they knew where I was?" My voice elevated. "How did you get their number?"

"I looked up a Hastings, Nebraska, phone book online. It wasn't hard."

My hand shoved into my purse, searching for my phone to turn it on. My mom was already under the impression New York was full of thieves and murderers. "They're probably freaking out."

"Yeah, they probably are. That's what people do when people they care about suddenly disappear." Soren's voice had risen as well, his face flushing from what I assumed was anger.

When my phone powered up, I found I'd missed a bunch of calls from my mom. I needed to call her to let her know I was okay—I wouldn't put it past her to be on her way now, ready to search every dumpster and back alley if need be.

"Why did you do that?" I asked, feeling my own pulse of anger.

He blinked at me, his expression suggesting I couldn't be seriously asking that. "Because you didn't come home last night. Because I couldn't get a hold of you. Because I fucking care."

When I glanced at the time on my phone, I knew he was missing his first class of the day. He'd probably miss the second too. He'd gotten no sleep. He'd called hospitals, friends, and family trying to find me. He looked like he'd journeyed through the depths of hell and just made it out, barely alive.

Guilt poured over me. An endless stream of scalding, petrifying goop.

I hadn't just made a mess. I'd crafted a catastrophe.

"We can talk later," I said, pushing his hand away and trying for the elevators again.

I didn't make it far. Soren's hand formed around my wrist, stilling me. "Like we were supposed to talk last night?"

My chest ached, imagining what last night could have been. Then I forced myself to harden, encasing myself in impenetrable armor. "You were planning on something else last night." My voice was poison in vocal form.

His jaw worked, his hold around my wrist staying strong. "I was planning on whatever you needed last night."

I knew that. But I couldn't admit that when I was trying to push him away. "Obviously, I needed to be alone," I stated slowly. "That should answer your question."

"And what about everything you said? Everything you admitted? What was that? Make-believe? Something I just conjured up in my imagination?"

People were staring at us as they moved by, but I didn't care that we had an audience. Maybe a public setting was better than being alone with him because being alone with Soren was a bad idea. For so many reasons.

I stopped pulling against him, twisting around so I was directly facing him. Then I gathered up whatever wits I had left to get out the next part. "I was drunk." My shoulders lifted as I crossed my arms. "That's why I said all of that. And . . . did all of that."

The corners of Soren's eyes creased, his feet carrying him a few steps back. "You were drunk?"

Biting the inside of my cheek, I nodded.

"You had two glasses of champagne over the course of a few hours. That's not drunk." His hand went behind his head, adjusting the ball cap lower on his head. "Your inhibitions were lowered. You said and did exactly what you wanted to do. Exactly what you'd been too scared to say or do for weeks."

My feet shifted. "I'm sorry, but you've got it totally wrong. I don't see you like that at all."

His head fell back into the cradle of his hands as he shook his head at the ceiling. Then he collected his backpack and baseball bag, his gaze sticking to me before moving toward the doors. "Fine." The word echoed in the spacious lobby. "You want to play this game? You want to play *the* game? I'll play along."

My chest ached again as I watched him move away from me, realizing I'd successfully pushed him away. "I'm not playing a game."

"Sure, you are. First point goes to you, but don't get cocky." He paused at the revolving doors, his mouth twisting into a dark smile. "I'll win."

In short, today had sucked. In detail, today had topped the charts of worst day ever, going back to ancient history, spanning into distant future.

Getting through a long work day with Soren's confrontation at the front of my mind was next to impossible. I'd only made it thanks to copious amounts of caffeine and denial.

The first thing I'd done after Soren shoved out of the revolving door, was call my mom and assure her a thousand times that I was okay and apologize for "worrying her sick." After fifteen minutes of repeating I was okay, she finally seemed to accept that no disaster had found me.

The next matter of business had been texting my friends who'd also been worried about me, letting them know I was accounted for and unscathed. I didn't realize Soren knew who all of my friends were until I had to get back to just about every contact in my phone.

When Ellis handed off my updated portfolio later that morning, he wasn't acting any different than usual. He was back in his suit and barely had five minutes to spare for me. I'd totally let whatever happened last night get blown out of proportion in my head. Nothing creepy or unusual had gone down. Other than my own behavior.

After flipping through the new photos he was passing on to the "colossal" client, I realized he'd only added the nude poses from the start of the shoot. The ones where I'd gone out of my way to ensure my lady bits and pieces weren't displayed. He said my expression looked awkward in the more revealing shots.

No wonder. It had been awkward being naked and hovered over by my agent who was sporting wood an arm's length away.

It was after ten at night by the time I emerged from the subway tunnel close to the apartment. It had been a busy day, and I might have gone out of my way to make it extra busy since I was dreading whatever was waiting for me inside the apartment.

Soren had gotten some stuff off his chest this morning —but I knew there'd be more. He wasn't the type who boxed stuff up or swept it under the rug.

My eyes wandered down the hall toward Mrs. Lopez's apartment, and I wondered when I'd finally catch a glimpse of her. Next, I found myself wondering why I felt so heartbroken over pushing away the guy who was possibly banging the neighbor next door?

The bathroom door was closed, the sound of the shower cranking. With it being Monday, I knew Soren had worked a shift at the pub after school and practice. I'd been hoping to come home and find him passed out at the table, asleep on his books like I found him some mornings. He hadn't gotten any sleep last night and had had a packed schedule today. He had to be tired.

Maybe after the shower, he'd be too tired to talk. Maybe he'd just want to crawl into bed. Maybe if I kept getting home late enough for the next couple of weeks, he'd just forget about the whole thing. It would become a distant memory. Never surfacing again.

Maybe not, I realized as I moved past the bathroom into the apartment. For doing a decent job of keeping his mess under wraps, he'd really let loose tonight. Baseball gear and his dirty uniform were scattered around the floor, his jockstraps hanging from the ceiling fan again. Dishes were scattered around the table and the kitchen, wads of crumpled up homework paper placed everywhere besides the inside of the garbage can. If this wasn't his way of sending a message, I didn't know what was.

I wasn't sure if it was more a fuck you or a fuck me, but it unmistakingly gave the fuck it vibe.

Sighing, I did my best to ignore the disaster and headed for my clean, organized area. After changing into my pajamas, I waited a few minutes for him to finish his shower. Wasn't happening. No way there was any hot water left. He'd been in there forever and who knew who long he'd been in before I got home.

Meandering back out into the apartment, I passed a few more minutes by pacing. I was tired and wanted to go to bed, but I couldn't stand going to bed without brushing my teeth, and my toothbrush was in the bathroom.

As I paced, my eyes kept flickering to the jocks hanging from the fan. *Mr. Giant.* Jane's latest nickname for Soren kept playing in my head until I found myself stepping onto one of the chairs and reaching for the nearest swinging jockstrap. Goodness gracious, what was I doing? I chided myself even as my fingers clasped the small tag inside the cup region so I could read . . .

XL

Mister Giant.

My legs teetered on the chair, practically spilling me over before I caught myself. Letting go of the tag, I lowered myself back to the floor, my face on fire as I glanced toward the bathroom to make sure he hadn't caught me spying on the size of his jockstrap.

Why was I behaving like this? Like a shallow, petty girl who messed with a boy's heart—and jockstraps—and played games like a seasoned pro? I didn't play games. I'd heard of them, but I didn't know the first rule or requirement of them.

Was I though? Playing some game? Playing a bunch of them?

Yeah, I liked Soren. No, I couldn't be honest with him about that. It wasn't a game I was playing; it was a matter of survival. The only man I'd been close to and loved had left. My dad. I never wanted to open myself up to that kind of pain again. I didn't want to be left. Abandoned. I didn't want to hurt someone because of those fears.

I couldn't fall in love with Soren Decker. There was no deceit in that—it was one of the few truths I knew.

"Soren?" I made my way to the bathroom door and rapped on it.

No answer.

"Soren?" I tried, louder this time.

"Yeah?" he called from inside, the shower still blasting.

I pushed past the pain in my chest from hearing his voice. "I need to brush my teeth and go to bed. How much longer are you going to be?"

"A while."

My forehead fell against the door as I calculated how long it would take me to get to the twenty-four-hour convenience store a half a mile away.

"You can just come in and brush your teeth if you want. I don't care."

Something about the way he said the last part made me shift in place. "You're going to still be a while?"

"Yep."

"And you're not doing your . . ." I cleared my throat. "Self-love right now?"

"Took care of that earlier," was his immediate response, making me glare at the door like Mrs. Lopez was about to show up with a plate of cookies and wearing lingerie.

"You sure you don't mind?"

"Hayden, I don't care what you do, okay?"

All right. So much for playing whatever game he'd thought I was interested in. He was not looking to score any points or win whatever game this had been as of this morning.

"Coming in," I announced, opening the door and stepping inside. A plume of steam rolled over me, instantly coating my skin in a hot, dewy shield. "Hot shower?"

"Hell of a lot better than the cold one I took a couple of nights ago."

His voice echoed off the walls as I focused on squeezing a glob of toothpaste onto my brush. It was difficult. I found myself quite distracted by the knowledge he was naked behind that thin shower curtain, a whole three feet away.

Just as I was about to stick my toothbrush into my mouth, the shower cranked off, the curtain whipping open right after.

Soren. Wet. Exposed.

Giant.

My eyes clamped shut, but it wasn't fast enough. From the low chuckle he gave, he hadn't missed my two-second gape.

"Soren!"

"Sorry. Water got cold."

I gave him a few seconds to cover up before I opened my eyes and got back to brushing my teeth. He hadn't covered up though.

"What are you doing? Grab a towel." My arm flailed in the direction of where we kept our fresh towels hanging from the rack. My eyes felt like they were about to go crossed from staying focused on my reflection instead of his naked one in the same mirror.

"Out of fresh towels. Haven't gotten around to the laundry." He moved up beside me at the sink, reaching for his own toothbrush. He was standing so close, his wet arm was brushing against mine.

Don't look down. Don't look down. Don't look at the giant—

Crap. I looked.

He was grinning at me as he brushed his teeth, my face crimson thanks to what I'd glanced at.

"See anything you like?"

My body was still buzzing from what I'd seen that I liked. I kind of hated him for calling me out on it though. I kind of even hated him for having so much to like.

"I know what you're doing." My eyebrow rounded as I got to work brushing my teeth too.

He spit in the sink, somehow winding up closer to me when he leaned back up. "Air drying?"

My eyes narrowed in the mirror at him. "Trying to change my mind."

He stared back, brushing his teeth in all of his naked glory, a cocky tenor to his expression. Once he finished brushing, he rinsed his toothbrush and turned toward the door.

"I don't need to change your mind," he said, pausing when he was directly behind me.

When he turned, I swore I could feel his arms coming around me, pulling me into the shelter of his strong body. An involuntary shudder spilled down my back. He didn't miss that either.

"I just need you to speak it instead of lying about it." His eyes dropped to the back of my neck, where I knew he could see the raised flesh. I knew, because one side of his mouth lifted.

Bracing my hands on the sink, I didn't blink as I locked eyes with him in the mirror. "It takes a lot more than washboard abs and a giant . . ." Crap. Something else. "*Ego* to get my attention."

Soren leaned forward, his hands framing around the outsides of mine, his arms running the length of mine. His chest didn't touch my back, but I could feel its expanse hovering above it. "I've already gotten your attention." His eyes dropped from mine to my chest. Where it was rising and falling noticeably hard, my nipples pushing through my camisole. "I'm looking for something else."

Another shudder, this one spilling down my legs. "What?"

His crooked smile changed into a cryptic one before he leaned back and opened the door. "You'll see."

"Soren—"

"Don't worry. I'll tell you when you give it to me."

My fist curled around my toothbrush as I turned toward him. "I'm not giving you anything."

"You're giving me something right now." He didn't glance back before leaving the bathroom. Did he really need to have that nice of an ass when he already had a glorious package? I was screwed. "This point goes to Decker."

CHAPTER
 Fourteen

Push-ups in his underwear the next morning. Practically right outside of my divider, so I had to lunge over him to head to the bathroom. Later that night, I came home to find him shirtless in those low-slung sweats, going between studying and knocking out pull-ups on the bar he'd screwed into the wall.

Later that week, there were a couple more instances of him emerging from the shower naked and walking around the apartment like we were in some nudist colony, and there was no end to the countless episodes of him brushing by me closer than necessary or reaching over me to grab the ketchup or reaching around me to get a spoon. He wasn't easing up, no matter how many days went by. In fact, he only seemed to be getting more persistent.

"Hayden?" A knock came outside the bathroom door. "I need to shower before work real quick."

I accidently squeezed too much shampoo from the bottle when I heard him. It was early evening, and Soren always went straight from practice to the pub when he had a shift. I hadn't been expecting him back until later tonight, when I'd conveniently be asleep. "Why didn't you shower after practice like you always do?"

I'd just climbed into the shower and was sudsing shampoo into my hair. I wasn't just going to hop out because he was in a hurry and had totally changed his schedule on me.

"I didn't have enough time," he answered.

"You didn't have enough time? Soren, that makes no sense at all. You had time to come back here to take a shower instead?"

"I had to grab a change of clothes."

"What happened to the ones you were wearing before practice?"

"They got dirty." His voice wasn't coming through the filter of the door anymore.

"Soren, what are you doing? Get out." I stuck my head out from behind the curtain to find him sliding past the door. "Why are you wearing swim trunks?"

He held out something familiar. "Here. Put this on."

"Why do I want to put my swimsuit on when I'm in the shower?" Shampoo suds were starting to run down my forehead. I needed to rinse it out before it got in my eyes.

"Because I didn't think you'd want to be naked with me in the shower. That's why I put on my swimwear too." He pinched at his swim trunks, moving closer.

My eyes rounded when I realized what he was proposing. "You are not hopping in the shower with me."

"Yeah, actually, I am. If I'm not out of here in ten minutes, I'm going to be late, and being late at the pub is like asking to be fired. I need the money, so put on the suit or don't." He waved the bikini my direction. "Thirty seconds before I'm climbing in."

"Soren, I was here first. This is insane. This isn't a community shower."

"Actually, it is. The bathroom is a community space, a shared one." He started counting seconds off on his fingers. "If you ever need to shower when I'm in there, go for it. I won't mind."

Ripping my suit from his hands, I ducked back into the curtain. "I'm sure you wouldn't," I grumbled, sliding into the bottoms first.

"And five . . . four . . ."

"So help me, god, Soren . . ." My arms twisted behind my back, madly working to tie the top together.

"Three, two, one," he said in one breath, shoving into the shower right after.

I was still working on getting my top tied and adjusted.

"Need a hand?"

"A compacted one aimed at your face would be a good start," I said, glowering at him.

His eyes lifted as he reached for the ties I'd been working to secure. "May I? I'm going to have to actually touch you to complete the task though."

"Fine. Like I care if you touch me."

"You've been going out of your way this week to avoid it, haven't you?" As his fingers tied the back of my top, they only brushed my skin a few times, but each instance made my lungs malfunction.

I'd been hoping that I'd become immune to his touch if I went long enough without feeling it. Of course, the total opposite was true.

Once he'd finished tying, I made sure everything up front was covered before turning around so I could rinse the shampoo from my hair. I didn't close my eyes as I did though, knowing this shared shower wasn't thanks to happenstance.

He swallowed as he watched me rinse my hair, but his gaze stayed north of my neck. He had better willpower than I did, I realized with chagrin. As much as I hated it, every time he'd swagger by shirtless or something-less, I couldn't *not* gawk at what was on display.

"Shampoo." He pointed at the bottle before reaching around me to grab it.

His forearm grazed my shoulder, and from my reaction, I'd have thought he'd just slid his hand inside my swimsuit bottoms. Jolting, I moved aside so he could stand under the showerhead. However, since the shower was maybe double the size of my high school locker, I had to smash against him as we switched positions. My hands found themselves dropping to his chest for support so I didn't tumble out. His found theirs pinned around my hips.

As soon as we were switched, his hands let me go. Mine lingered a moment longer before falling away. He got straight to wetting his hair, shampooing it right after.

His eyes didn't travel my way the whole time. It was like he was taking a shower by himself for all the attention he gave me.

When he reached for the soap, my eyes might have drifted to his swim trunks. Did the man own anything that didn't like to hang low off of his hips? My god, my pulse felt like it was visible in my neck from the way my heart was firing. And what evil plot had God been aspiring to when he created a man with those sloped muscles and that trail of hair all leading to one very "manly" part?

It was like having a flashing neon sign to advertise the goods.

When my eyes slid a little lower, I didn't find any of the "goods" straining through his shorts. No bulge. No wood. No signs of arousal.

Crap. Maybe this really was just about a shower.

"Would you mind getting my back?" He shook the water out of his hair, opening his eyes as he held out the bar of soap.

"What do you do when you take a shower by yourself?"

He lifted my hand, dropping the bar of soap in it. "I call the shower fairy."

Exhaling, I rubbed the soap around in my hands to form a lather before setting it down and lowering my hands to Soren's back. *Just skin, muscle, and bone. Human anatomy. Perfectly natural.* My mind chanted those reminders over and over as I washed his shoulders and back. Unfortunately, my body felt differently.

That familiar ache between my legs spurred to life. The desire to have him shove me up against another wall was overwhelming. My body was charging with energy, my mind dizzy with need.

I wasn't sure how my hands wound up around in front of him, slowly traveling down the planes of his stomach until my thumbs where just slipping inside of his shorts. I wasn't sure what would have happened if he didn't quake, a ragged groan vibrating in his chest.

Instantly, my hands left him, my body backing into the wall behind me. He stayed angled toward the shower for a moment, another shudder spilling down his back, before he turned around.

The look on his face wasn't the one I was expecting. He was gloating. Like he'd just won some game I hadn't known we were playing.

My blood rolled to a boil. "I know what you're doing." My eyes narrowed more when his tipped smile became even more crooked.

"Trying to get clean?" His gaze ran down me, like he could see every nerve still firing in my body.

"You're trying to catch me in a weak moment." I pushed off of the wall, trying to prove to him his proximity to me had nothing to do with anything. Of course, that was a total lie. "You're trying to seduce me with your body, but I already told you. It's going to take a lot more than that to break me."

Giving himself one last rinse, he pulled the curtain open to exit. "Counting on it."

I'd booked the client. The colossal one. The foreign one everyone in the Free World had heard of. The same client whose brand everyone wanted to have hanging off their shoulder or slung around their feet, and the very one whose success had come from a select few being able to afford it.

Ellis had sent me an entire case of champagne to celebrate, which seemed odd since I was still two years below the legal drinking limit, but it had been a thoughtful gesture. I was sure Soren would have plenty of the opposing opinion to say.

The thrill of it was still fresh and hadn't quite settled in. I wanted to celebrate—in a way that didn't involve marinating my liver in bottles of champagne. Jane and Ariel had offered to take me out dancing, but that wasn't really celebrating to me. It was just a workout that took place outside of the gym. Complete with meatheads trying to get all up in a girl's business when they weren't selling anything to begin with.

I wanted a celebration. The kind that involved going out and eating a good meal, capped with the best kind of dessert, followed by wandering around the city and taking in the sights late at night. Something more serene than the newest, chicest club in Manhattan.

That was what I was daydreaming about when I heard the click of the lock turning over before the door swung open. Soren's heavy, familiar footsteps echoed inside. He'd just gotten off work and would probably be up late studying, like he had all week. He had midterms coming up and was stressing with all of the time practice and work were taking up.

"Hungry?" I asked as he walked by the kitchen, where I was standing with the fridge door open, looking for something "celebratory."

His head shook as he dropped his bags in the hall. He was back to leaving his stuff scattered around wherever it landed.

"Long day?" I closed the fridge and turned into the hallway.

He was already opening up his books and pulling out a pencil. His answer came in the form of another head movement.

"I was just heading to bed, so . . ." I started for my partition, hating how awkward things were between us now.

After a few more attempts at seducing me—compliments of his hard, very seduction-invoking body—Soren had backed off. It had only been the past few days, but I couldn't figure out why he'd come on so hard and strong only to bow out so suddenly.

Had he finally realized I was a lost cause?

Had he gotten bored?

Had he accepted I really wasn't worth all of the effort?

Had I imagined the whole thing?

Stupid questions. They'd riddled me into a state of paranoia lately.

"Hey, my mom asked about you coming to dinner again this Thursday." Soren sounded as tired as he looked as he pulled a bunch of crap from his pockets, crumbling up most of it and aiming it at the wastebasket. Most of it landed outside of it though.

"Soren, I don't know. I don't think it's a good idea." I headed toward the garbage can.

"Come on. She's been asking every week since you moved in." He lobbed one last crumpled wad toward the garbage. Missed that one too. Good thing he played baseball. "Besides, she doesn't know anything about the stuff that's gone down between us. She just thinks we're roommates and you're a long ways from home."

"The stuff?" I echoed.

Soren's shoulder lifted, gesturing for me to correct him on it. The thing was, I didn't have a better term for what had or was still going on between us. There hadn't been a term created for a relationship like ours. If you could even call it a relationship.

"Come on. Mom throws down an insane meal, and I can promise you my brothers will be on the best behavior they're capable of if you come around." He tucked the pencil behind his ear. "She won't feed them dessert if they aren't."

"I've got a late shoot this Thursday." I shot him an apologetic smile as I crouched to toss the garbage in the actual garbage.

"If I give her one more excuse for why you can't come, she's going to think you either hate me or you hate them." He sighed, sliding out of his sneakers. "You've got to give me something I can give her so when I tell her you can't make it again this week, she doesn't break down in tears."

"Your mom's not going to cry because I can't make it to dinner."

"She might. She really wants to meet you."

Inhaling, I did a mental scan of my schedule next week. I didn't actually have anything on Thursday night, and Soren's mom *had* been extending the invite to have dinner at their place ever since I moved in. She did Thursday night dinners for the whole family, and even though Soren and his brothers couldn't make it back every week, they made it as often as they could. When he didn't have late practice or have to work a shift or have a test the next morning.

As I was tossing away the crumpled wads, I noticed a trend. "These are all phone numbers. *Lots* of phone numbers." I'd already tossed half a dozen cocktail napkins and still had as many more to go.

"I get a bunch of them every shift." His face read *no big deal* as he wandered into the kitchen.

"And you just toss them out?"

"What else am I supposed to do with them?"

"Call one of them." I wadded the one with an XOXO below the number into a small ball before throwing it in the wastebasket.

"I'm not looking for some relationship with a girl I met working in a pub," he said as he riffled through the cupboards, no doubts about what he was searching for. I swore he ate half a package of his beloved cookies every single night, yet he still looked like he could be a cover model for any fitness magazine out there.

"The kind of girls who stuff their phone number in some strange guy's hand probably aren't looking for a long-term commitment. At least not all of them." I glared at the extra mile "Candy" had gone by scribbling a couple of hearts around her number.

"I'm not looking for that either."

"No?"

"I'm into someone else," he said through a mouthful of Nutter Butter.

My arm froze. Was he talking about me? The look he shot me from the kitchen left no question to it.

I made myself look away. "You're not going to get that from her either."

"I'm not looking for that from her. I'm looking for something else."

"Not looking for that?" I arched an eyebrow at him as he roamed back into the room, a stack of cookies piled in his hand.

His eyes sparkled. "Okay, well, maybe I'd be down with that after she gave me something else first."

When he held out his cache of cookies, I took one. It was weird, but Nutter Butters were growing on me.

"What something else?"

He crouched beside me, collecting the last few napkins and dropping them in the garbage. He stayed there for a moment after, waiting for me to look at him. "She knows it. She's just not ready to say it out loud."

I could only hold his eyes for a heartbeat. They were too intense. Suggesting too much. And he was too damn close for me to trust myself to not do something I was going to regret all over again.

"You've never called one of these girls?" I stood up, casually backing away a few steps. "Not once?"

His head shook as he rose. "Why settle?"

"Because you're a guy."

His half smile suggested he knew something I didn't as he moved toward the table. "I'm a man. I know what I want. And I'm going to get it."

My heel tapped the floor as I watched him settle in for another long night of studying. He went sans shirt again, as he'd been most every night since . . . that fateful one. I knew why he was doing it. To wear me down. As much as I wanted to believe no amount of bare skin could get to me, I knew better.

"Thursday night. If I agree, will you stop with the half-naked to fully-naked antics?"

Soren was in the middle of ripping out a piece of paper when he paused, looking as surprised by what I'd said as I was.

"I'll stop," he said quickly, waving at where I was glued to the wall away from sans-shirt Soren. "It didn't seem to be working that great anyway."

It was working. "And these phone numbers aren't some attempt to push me into some jealous rage?" My toe tapped the side of the wastebasket.

"Give them a call. Find out for yourself." He got back to what he was doing before dropping into his favorite chair. "You might claim you didn't mean anything you said to me that night, but I meant every word. I'm not going anywhere." He extended his arms like that was that. He wasn't going anywhere and I could just believe him because he'd said it. If only trust was that simple.

"What if *I* do? What if I go somewhere?"

"No problem." He shrugged. "I like the chase too. Stay, and I'll wait. Or run, and I'll follow. Either way, you're not getting rid of me. Accept that, so you can rework this plan you've been using to try to push me away." In his eyes was a fire—a challenge. "I'm not easily moved."

My stomach was misbehaving from the things he was saying and the looks he was giving. "Soren—"

"Gotta hit the books now. Test in the morning."

"Soren—"

"What?" His grin stretched wide as his eyes roamed me in the way a predator might assess its prey. "You didn't like me trying to seduce you with my body. Let's see how you fare against my mind."

CHAPTER

Fifteen

Of all the days to be running late, this wasn't the one. It was Thursday night, and I'd told Soren I'd meet him at the apartment at five. It was five fifteen by the time I started busting up the stairs to the sixth floor.

"Soren! I'm ready to go, sorry I'm late!" I announced after unlocking the door and flying inside.

The apartment was still dark. Shuffling the bouquet of flowers into my other arm, I wrestled my phone from my purse to find I'd missed a text from him a few minutes ago. *Running late. Meet me downstairs at 5:30?*

After punching in a quick reply, I took advantage of those few minutes to gather up the garbage to take downstairs. Soren had said his mom was serving dinner at six, so I knew we'd be pushing it to make it in time. His practice must have run late, as seemed to be their habit. He was on the road this weekend and had heard rumors that some scouts might be in the stands, so he'd been putting in extra time at practice lately.

The garbage wrangled into one bag, I grabbed the flowers again and left the apartment. As I was locking it back up, I noticed a door down the hall open. The very door I'd been waiting to open for what felt like forever.

Number sixty-five. Mrs. Lopez's unit.

Stalling with the lock, I waited until a figure floated into the doorway before turning. Let's see what the woman my roommate had been "helping out" looked like.

The garbage bag fell out of my hand when I saw her, my jaw falling too.

Mrs. Lopez. She wasn't anything like I'd pictured her. Not one bit.

For starters, she was old enough to have been my grandma, if not my great-grandma. She was barely topping five feet and had her silver-white hair combed back from her face. She wasn't wearing a crimson, form-fitting gown and kitten heels like I'd conjured up in my mind—she was wearing a house dress in a pastel floral print, and navy corduroy slippers that looked like they'd seen better days.

Wait. Maybe this wasn't *the* Mrs. Lopez. Maybe this was her mother or great auntie or . . . since she was shuffling a bag of garbage outside too, a housekeeper.

"Mrs. Lopez?" My thoughts manifested verbally.

Her attention turned my way, an easy smile forming when she saw me. "You're Soren's roommate, right?"

I nodded as she teetered down the hall toward me. "That's right. I'm—"

"Hayden," she said, a glint of recognition sparking in her eye. "Hayden Hayes. He talks about you all of the time."

Moving away from the door, I headed toward her to take her bag of garbage. It was half the size she was. "He does?"

"Won't shut up about you most of the time he's over helping me out."

She thanked me with a smile as I took the garbage, while I wrestled with feeling like the biggest jerk in the whole entire world. I'd been assuming he'd been hooking up with the sexpot neighbor next door, when really, he'd been helping an old woman out around her apartment.

I needed my head examined. By a team of specialists.

"Soren's a good guy," I stated, still reeling from the revelation.

Mrs. Lopez's head shook. "Soren's the best type of human being there is, honey. I've been around a long time, seen a lot more—people like him are hard to come by."

I found myself leaning into the hall wall with her, feeling a surge of clarity come over me. The haze of hesitation, the fog of uncertainty, evaporated. Everything felt so clear now. So glaringly obvious.

"It's nice to meet you." I smiled at *the* Mrs. Lopez before moving toward the stairs with both garbage bags in hand. "Finally."

"Nice to *finally* meet you too," she replied with a wave, shuffling back to her apartment.

The whole journey down those six flights, my head wouldn't stop shaking. Not just because of Mrs. Lopez, but because of everything else. What was I so afraid of? Why had I been so afraid?

Yes, Soren was a man, but that was the only quality that matched my dad. Soren went home for family dinners, even when his schedule was so busy sleep came low on the priority list. He helped out old ladies. God, he helped me out. All. The. Time.

That wasn't a person who ran away. That wasn't a man who bailed when the mood struck.

I was so buried under the barrage of revelations, I hardly noticed the cab pull up to the curb beside me as I was heading back into the building after dropping the garbage in the dumpster.

"Please tell me you aren't just coming back from the dumpster, tucked in the back of the building, alone, and it's practically dark." Soren's head popped out of the back of the cab, giving me a look I was familiar with.

My body instantly responded—my stomach swirling, my heart racing, my mouth turning up. "It's *barely* dark." I headed for the cab. "And someone had to take the garbage out before it started radiating toxic gases."

He scooted over to let me slide in. "I was planning on doing that tonight after we got back."

"Now you don't have to worry about it." As I slid in beside him, I realized what we were in. "I thought we were taking the subway?"

Soren and I took the subway everywhere. Even though my cash flow had improved dramatically since moving to the city, we still kept to the underground for our preferred means of transportation. I was especially surprised he'd chosen a cab for tonight's journey since his family lived outside of the city.

He motioned at his ankle. "I broke myself at practice earlier. Figured it would be a good idea to keep as much weight off of it as possible until the swelling goes down."

My eyes bulged when I saw his ankle. It wasn't just swollen; it looked like someone had blown up a small balloon inside it. He was still in his practice uniform, but had slid the pant leg up to his knee and had his red sock bunched down below his ankle. When I lightly brushed my fingers across his ankle, Soren shifted in his seat. It was already starting to bruise.

"What did you do?"

"End of practice. We were all leaving the field and I stepped on a damn stray ball lying on the ground."

My face pulled up as I leaned down to give it a closer look. "Damn stray balls."

The corner of his mouth pulled. "They can really ruin a person's day."

"What did your coaches say? Are you sure you can still go to dinner tonight? Shouldn't you rest it or elevate it or something like that?"

His eyes lifted. "Please. If I called to say I couldn't make it to dinner because I rolled my ankle, my brothers would never let that go. Ever. They'd still be going on to my grandsons about the time their grandpa hurt his ankle and instead of shaking it off and getting on with things, he cried and cancelled dinner." He motioned at his ankle like he'd barely hurt it. "And I didn't tell my coaches. I don't need them getting overzealous and benching me this weekend."

"You didn't tell your coaches?" I blinked at him as I dug some hand sanitizer from my purse to put on.

"It's fine. It'll be good by tomorrow. There was no reason to get everyone worked up over nothing."

"Soren, your ankle looks like it swallowed a cantaloupe. This isn't nothing." Leaning back into the seat, I settled the flowers beside me and patted my lap.

When he took a moment to think about it, I gently lifted his leg and rested his ankle in my lap. At least it was elevated now. We'd just have to wait for the ice until we got to his parents' place.

"Sprained?" I guessed as I took another look.

"Twisted," he stated, shifting so his back was pressed into the door.

"It looks like it hurts."

Soren's foot nestled a little deeper into my lap. "It's feeling better now." A goofy grin stretched across his face as his eyes went from his foot in my lap to my eyes.

Every nerve inside me stood on end as he appraised me in a way that hinted at the very same things I felt when I looked at him. Possession. Desire. Reverence.

His face, like his uniform, was streaked with dirt and sweat. The ends of his light hair curling around his ball cap were extra pronounced tonight. The scent of him was all man and so strong that being stuffed into the back seat of the cab with him made me feel drunk from it.

"What?" he said, still staring right back.

My head shook in an attempt to break the spell. "Nothing."

He leaned forward, his hand covering mine. "What?"

Letting my fingers tangle through his, I let go of the breath I'd been holding. "I'll tell you later tonight."

His fingers squeezed mine. "I'll be listening."

After that, the ride went quickly. I did my best to keep his ankle from bouncing around, and he made it a point not to wince at the slightest movement. I knew he was in pain—just looking at his ankle made mine hurt— but there was something oddly appealing about the way he was capable of shrugging off anguish like it barely registered. Survival of the fittest or something primal like that.

And men were the supposed brutes . . .

"You brought my mom flowers," Soren noted when the cab pulled up in front of the house he'd grown up in. "She's going to love you even more now."

"You say that like she already has some reason to love me." Pushing open the door, I crawled out and turned to help Soren if he needed me.

"You put up with me. That's plenty of reason to love you in Mom's book." Soren slid across the backseat after snagging his bag and set his good foot down on the street outside.

I held out my free hand for him to grab and pulled him up. "Watch your head."

Too late.

Rubbing the spot on his forehead where he'd hit the doorway of the cab, he hopped a couple steps forward. "Maybe everyone will be too busy staring at the knot on my head to notice the cantaloupe lodged in my ankle."

I grimaced when I lightly touched the fresh red mark on his forehead. We were going to need two bags of ice.

After Soren paid the driver, I made him sling his arm over my shoulder so I could help him.

"So this is where you grew up?" I took a moment to inspect the house we were approaching, unable to keep from smiling. It was a modest house with a small yard, like most of the houses near a big city would likely have, but it had been taken care of. Around back, I could just make out an old, rusted swing set. Around the yard, a few flowers were just starting to push through the soil.

"Dad and Mom brought all four of us home from the hospital to this place. Dad taught me how to throw a ball right out here"—he indicated the front yard we were passing through—"and my brothers taught me how to how to run fast and estimate the number of stitches I'd be getting while en route to the emergency room." Soren's arm slung more around my neck than my shoulder, drawing me closer to him. "Mom pretty much taught me everything else."

When we made it to the bottom of the few stairs leading to the door, we paused.

"Want me to get one of your brothers to help?"

He snorted as he started hopping up the stairs like he'd done it a thousand times. He moved up them as quickly one-legged as I did on two. "Help, in my brothers' book, would be greasing the stairs to see how many I could make before wiping out." When we made it to the front door, Soren paused with his fist in the air before knocking. "Ready for this?"

I sucked in a breath. "Ready."

After Soren knocked, footsteps could be heard moving inside. A few moments later, the door opened and a woman was standing on the other side of it. I knew where Soren got his smile from.

"Sorry we're late, Mom. It was my fault." Soren pulled the screen door open, waving me through first. "This is Hayden. Hayden, this is my mom."

Soren's mom waved us inside then wrapped her arms around me as soon as I made it through the door. "I also have another name—Caroline, not Mrs. Decker like I could tell you were about to call me." She nudged me as Soren moved through the door. "I'm a former Midwest girl too."

When I realized I'd been about to call her Mrs. Decker, I cleared my throat. "Thank you for having me. These are for you."

Her hand covered her chest when I held out the flowers. "Gorgeous *and* thoughtful. Who would have thought a girl could be both? Isn't that right, Soren?" Mrs. Decker—*Caroline*—lifted an eyebrow at Soren as he leaned in to kiss her cheek.

"Subtle, Mom. Real subtle."

"Soren always used to complain that it was impossible to find a decent girl in this day and age. I told him he just had to be patient." She patted his cheek a few times. "And look, his patience paid off."

Soren and I exchanged a look, his leaning toward apologetic. "Hayden's my roommate. We share the same living space. We're friends. Let's not make her uncomfortable before she even makes it past the front door."

I waved it off, but yeah, kind of awkward. Especially with the realizations that had poured down on me an hour ago.

"Your dad and I were friends," his mom said, turning toward the kitchen. "One marriage and four grown children later . . ."

"Mom," Soren groaned, following her with me.

The smile fell from her face when she noticed the way Soren was moving. "What did you do now?"

"Nothing."

Her hand went to her hip as she pulled a vase from one of the kitchen cupboards. "You're limping."

"It's nothing. Just a little twist." Soren stopped moving and leaned into the kitchen doorway. "Where are they?"

"In the living room. I told them they had to stay in there to give Hayden a chance to settle in before they all came at her at once." Caroline filled the vase with water and unwrapped the bouquet. "Your dad's in there with them, making sure they behave."

Soren huffed. "Good call. Do you mind if I take a quick shower before dinner? I didn't have time after practice, and well, I stink." His nose dropped to his armpits and he took a whiff. His face scrunched up.

"Sure. I figured you'd be running late, so I stalled." Caroline gave him a look that was all mother. "You've got a half hour."

"Do you have a couple of baggies I could steal to fill with ice?" I asked as she arranged the flowers.

She opened the cupboard where the baggies were. "Did he hurt more than his ankle?"

I glanced at the red mark forming below his hairline. "His head too."

"Of course he did," Caroline chided good-naturedly. "Ice is in the freezer. We don't have one of those fancy ice makers yet."

"Thank you." I freed a couple of baggies from the box before moving to the freezer.

Soren stayed in the doorway, waiting for me.

"Do you need any help with anything?" I asked as I cracked a couple of ice trays to fill the baggies.

"I'm just waiting for everything to finish cooking. Why don't you go with Soren and let him give you the grand tour?" She pushed her sleeves up higher as she finished arranging the flowers. "Make sure he keeps those bags of ice on longer than thirty seconds, would you? I have a feeling you'll be a more convincing nurse than I could be."

Soren tipped his chin out of the kitchen at me, looking like he was even more uncomfortable with the conversation than I was.

As we moved toward the stairs, I whispered, "Your mom's really nice."

"She's also really pushy when it comes to her family," he whispered back. "Sorry if any of that made you uncomfortable."

"I'm good."

"Yeah, she just knows you're great, and she thinks I'm great, so she's going to try really hard to get all of that greatness to come together." He sighed, rolling to a stop at the bottom of the stairs. "If it gets to be too much, just let me know. I can talk to her."

"Soren, it's fine. You *are* great. She's totally right in her estimation."

His hand caught mine as I started up the stairs. "I'm great?" His eyebrow disappeared into his ball cap. "Me? Is this your opinion or you repeating my Mom's?"

"Please. You know you're great."

"But you just said 'you are great.' So does that mean you think I'm great too?"

My instinct was to turn and disappear up the stairs before I had to answer. I forced myself to stay and look him in the eye. "I don't think you're great. I *know* you are." I wiped at a smudge of dirt streaked across his cheek. "Happy now?"

He blinked a couple of times. "Bewildered now."

I laughed, pulling him up the stairs. "Come on. Let's get you iced up."

"Hey, Butt Munch? Is that you?" a voice boomed from the room behind the stairs.

"Of course it's him. He laughs like a girl," another voice replied.

"You heard what your mom said. Be nice," an older male voice rumbled next.

Soren looked like he was bracing himself as a thunder of footsteps moved toward us.

"Did your imaginary model roommate bail on you, little brother?"

"Yeah, did she have some photo shoot she was at and couldn't make it?"

Soren turned, putting his back toward me as three guys appeared at the base of the stairs. Their smirks disappeared the moment they noticed me lingering behind Soren.

"Hey." I waved at the three of them, about as different-looking as brothers could be. "I'm Soren's imaginary model roommate."

One of them elbowed the brother on his right. "I'm seeing things, right? Please tell me I'm imagining this, because if baby brother tagged and bagged a mega hottie before any of us, I'm going to kill myself."

The other brother blinked at me a few times then shook his head. "You're not seeing things. Mega hottie at your twelve o'clock."

"You live with Soren?" the first one asked.

"We're roommates," I answered slowly.

"You do anything else with Soren?" he continued.

That was when Soren went into action, shoving the three brothers back like he was trying to create a perimeter.

I decided to play along though. "I do plenty of other things with Soren."

The scuffle came to an instant halt.

"Do explain," one of them asked. "In great detail."

I had to look down to keep from smiling at the scene in front of me. Limbs and fists tangled all together, four heads turned my way, waiting. "Why should I explain when your imaginations can do a much better job?"

Soren's mouth was the first to fall open. Three more followed.

"I use my imagination all the time—"

"Every night . . ." one of them muttered, which was answered with a fist to the arm.

"My imagination would love a break, so please, do tell. Talk slowly. Use particulars."

Soren grunted as he shoved the brother who was currently speaking. "Are you kidding me right now? You guys promised you wouldn't behave like a bunch of miscreants if I brought Hayden home. What do you call this?" Soren gave the other two a shove for good measure.

"Chill, baby bro. We're not cursing, we're wearing nice shirts, and we haven't starting spilling all of those juicy stories no dude wants his girl to know about."

"She's not my girl. She's my roommate."

Three sets of eyes lifted toward me. I answered them all with a shrug.

"Since paranoid and possessive here isn't going to get around to introducing us, let me do the honors." The tall, dark-haired one shoved around Soren with one of those smiles that had probably charmed the pants or skirts off a good handful of girls. "I'm Ben, firstborn and the favorite. Let me add that I'm also single. Very single."

His dark eyes were drifting down my body when Soren slid in front of me, stepping onto the stair below me.

"That's Michael, number two, and Tobin, number three." Soren's finger counted off the other two before finding my hand and moving up the stairs. "You've met everyone now except for Dad. That can wait until dinner."

"We hate to see you go, Soren—"

"Not," another grunted.

"But we love to watch Hayden leave."

Soren's hand went behind his back, his middle finger waving down at his three brothers. I didn't realize he'd been walking up the stairs instead of hopping until we made it to the top.

I glanced at his ankle, shaking my head. "Macho much?"

"You just met the heathens I was raised with. Macho was a side effect of growing up with them."

The jeering and whistling had come to a quiet downstairs, but I was still shaking my head over the whole thing. I had that much more respect for Caroline that she'd survived twenty years of that.

"Sorry about them. I tried to warn you, but there's just no way to warn a person about that." Soren's hand stayed in mine as we moved down the hall. "They're animals, and they clearly don't know how to act around a girl, so yeah. If you want to leave right now or hide out in my room with a stomachache or something, I get it."

My arm bumped his as we stopped in front of a closed door. "I don't scare easily."

His eyes dropped to where my hand was still secured in his. "Obviously."

"Plus, they make you look good. Really good."

He fought a smile as he opened the door. "Then maybe we should hang around them more often."

"I think I'll like your brothers best in small doses."

"That's something we have in common." He moved inside the room, his limp more pronounced thanks to his jaunt up the stairs. "The room of my boyhood. In all its sports paraphernalia and denim glory." Soren grunted as he waved at his room.

"Wow. You really must have loved balls growing up."

I stepped into the middle of the room and did a slow spin. The walls were lined in a border decorated with footballs, baseballs, and basketballs. There was an entire bin filled with the real thing beneath one of the windows trimmed in, you guessed it, ball curtains. Even the twin-sized bed had a baseball diamond comforter, complete with a couple of throw pillows in the shapes of a mitt and a bat.

"Yeah, my mom has a tough time accepting we're all grown men now. With me being the baby, it's especially bad." He motioned at a stuffed bear propped on top of the dark blue dresser.

"Aww. It's so cute." I nudged him in passing before snagging the stuffed bear from its perch.

"She still comes in here every week to vacuum, dust, and change the sheets." Soren closed the door and slid off his ball cap. His light hair was plastered to his head.

"She loves her baby boy."

"But at the same time, she's trying to fix her 'baby boy' up with the first girl he brings home." Soren moved toward the adjoining bathroom, kicking out of his sneakers as he went.

The baggies of ice started to slip from my fingers. I decided to set them on his nightstand before they fell. "Am I the first girl you've brought home?"

Soren answered with a shrug.

"Me?"

"Would you be eager to bring someone home if you had three siblings like mine to contend with?" He disappeared in the bathroom, the sound of a shower cranking on following. "I had to make sure the first girl I did bring home was tough enough to handle it."

"I think that's a compliment, so thanks?" I settled onto the edge of his bed, clutching the old bear to my stomach.

"That's definitely a compliment." His head appeared past the bathroom door. "I'm going to take a quick shower and then I'll be out to ice. Scouts honor."

"You shouldn't even be moving around on that ankle."

"Please. I was riding my bike with a broken leg a week after they'd put me in a cast."

I heard the slide of a shower curtain and tried to focus on something other than the fact that Soren was, yet again, naked in the shower. This time, it was while I was resting on his childhood bed.

"I'm just going to wait here. Enjoying your balls." I bit my lip when I heard his chuckle echo against the shower walls.

"My balls are always willing to volunteer for your enjoyment."

CHAPTER

Sixteen

After that, I had to lie back. All of our banter and tension and emotion had come to a head. I knew it was only a matter of time before it all came to fruition and the anticipation of that had me squirming in his bed, unable to get comfortable.

A couple of minutes later, the shower cranked off. A few seconds after that, Soren emerged from the bathroom, covered in nothing but a white towel around his waist. At least this one was bigger and fluffier than the ones at our apartment. I swore those ones were so thin, I could see every muscle and movement of his anatomy beneath it.

"For the record, this isn't some half-naked ploy to seduce you, I swear." Soren tugged at the towel as he walked by me toward the dresser. "I just didn't want to change back into that nasty uniform." He pulled open a couple of the drawers and riffled through them before pulling out a few pieces of clothing.

"I believe you," I said, feeling seduced no matter his intentions. If I had to be tormented by another low-slung towel or pair of sweats, I was going to lose my mind.

When he glanced at me, he froze.

"What?" I asked, sitting up on my elbows.

"If I tell you the truth, you're going to think I'm a perv."

Now I definitely wanted to know. "I already think that."

He rolled his head, cracking his neck a couple of times. "It's just that when I was younger, I used to fantasize about finding a girl in my bed like that. Baseball diamond comforter and all." His forehead creased as he looked like he was second-guessing what the hell he was confessing to me right then. "I guess it just took me by surprise seeing you like that."

I lie back down, all the way, turning my head so it was facing him. "What did you fantasize about?"

"No lady should ever be given a sneak peek into the depraved mind of a teenage boy." He grunted, his head shaking. "No way I'm opening that door for you."

Why in the hell was I so turned on right now? I felt like what resided between my legs had taken over for my brain and was controlling my whole body. All facets led to him.

My eyes closed so I could try to focus on something other than my hormones. "Ice. We need to ice your ankle." *And I need to ice my libido.*

Soren limped over to the bed, his jaw moving when he stopped at the edge of it. The way he stared at me alone felt capable of making me come undone.

"Here." I cleared my throat and slid off the bed. The more vertical I got, the more blood flow seemed to return to my brain, which was so totally counterintuitive.

Soren took my place on his bed as I shuffled a few pillows behind his back. When he lifted his swollen ankle, I stuffed another pillow beneath it, as gently as I could.

I caught him smiling at me as I placed one bag of ice over his ankle. "What?"

One eye squeezed shut as his head shook. "Perv mind."

My eyes lifted as I reached for the other bag of ice. "You're totally picturing me in one of those cosplay nurse outfits, aren't you?"

"I totally am."

Grumbling, I set the other ice bag on his head, giving his chest a shove. His hand formed around my wrist before I could pull it away.

"What's going on?" His voice, like his expression, was different now. All lightness was gone.

"What do you mean?"

"This. Tonight. Right now." His other hand formed around my same wrist, his light eyes connecting with mine. "Something's different."

When I shrugged, he waited.

How could I explain it? How could I even go about trying to explain it? Putting the way a person felt about another into words was quite possibly the most daunting task known to mankind.

Instead of trying to explain it with words, I came at it from a different angle. Settling onto the edge of the bed beside him, my hand floated to his chest. I took a moment to memorize the warmth of his skin, the push of his ribcage against my palm as he inhaled. Then I leaned forward, my eyes holding his up until the last moment, when my lips touched his.

A quick rush of air sucked in through his mouth, right before one of his hands released my wrist to wind around my waist. His mouth moved against mine in slow, deliberate pulses that spurred me into a frenzy of wanting all of him all at once. My hands roamed his body, fingers curling into flesh, palms kneading muscle as they explored him. His hands remained where they were—tied around my wrist and behind my waist—squeezing every time our tongues joined together.

"Wait." His head fell back suddenly, his chest moving as hard as mine was. "Just wait." He gave himself a moment to catch his breath, his hands staying tied around me. "The last time this happened, there wasn't a verbal explanation of these feelings, and after that whole mess, I really need to hear you say it." His eyes found mine. There was excitement flashing in them, but also something else. Uncertainty?

"Say what?" I asked.

"Whatever you need to. Whatever you've been hiding." He slid a sheet of my hair behind my shoulder, letting his fingers comb through the ends. "I need to hear it this time."

I had to look away to form a rational thought. I probably should have moved my hands away from him too, but they felt super-glued into place. "I like you, Soren." My forehead creased as I tried to make sense of the feelings storming inside me. "As more than a roommate. More than a friend."

When I stayed quiet after that, he made a continue motion with his hand.

This next part required a deep breath to get out. I felt like I was about to unzip my chest and hand my heart over to him. "I have feelings for you."

That note of doubt left his eyes. "What kind?"

"What kind?" I groaned in frustration.

I slid a foot down the bed to keep temptation from overcoming my better judgment. He was fresh from the shower, wearing nothing more than a towel, and laying in the boyhood bed he'd apparently had filthy fantasies about. Temptation at its most potent.

"Do you really want me to give you an exhaustive account of them all right now? Because I'd much rather spend the few minutes we have left before dinner kissing you." I glanced at the time on the alarm clock beside his bed. We couldn't have much longer before we were expected downstairs. "Would you settle for strong? *Strong* feelings?"

Soren's eyes flicked to the same alarm clock. His grip tightened around me as he pulled me back to him, hoisting me so I was straddling his lap.

"Strong works for me," he said in a rush before his mouth crushed against mine.

My thighs squeezed him as he kissed me in such a way, I felt like we were making love right then. This wasn't the kiss of a boy making out with a girl. This was the kiss of a man making love to a woman, on the cusp of spending himself inside her.

When Soren adjusted below me, I felt his erection through the towel. With the way I'd landed on his lap, the hem of my dress had scattered around him, nothing but my underwear and his towel keeping our bodies from joining. When I slid my hips up his length, a ragged sound spilled from his mouth into mine. When I ground back down him, his mouth fell away, his head hitting the pillows behind him.

"If you do that again, I'm going to lose it." Soren's neck went stiff as I rubbed up his shaft again. "I'm going to be that guy who gets off when a girl barely touches him."

Realizing how turned on he was had me rocking into him again. "You've got a towel close by, at least."

Another sound echoed low in his chest, his hips rising to meet mine this time. "I don't want to get off in a towel. I've gotten off in a towel a million times." He managed to lean up onto his elbows, his hand fitting around my neck so he could pull me toward him. His mouth settled beside my ear. "I want to get off inside you."

Chills spilled down my whole body, my thighs squeezing together when his words hit my subconscious. I wanted to have sex with Soren Decker so badly at that moment, it felt like a sickness. The kind that would kill a person if they didn't find the cure to end it.

I knew what the cure was in this instance. His body. In mine. Rising and falling together until we came apart in each other's hold.

Turning my head so my mouth was near his ear, I pushed against him once more. "I want to feel you get off inside me."

When I swiveled my hips over his, a curse hissed through his teeth, followed by another moan. This one wasn't so muffled.

"Hey, Butt Munch. Dinner." The sound of footsteps pounding down the hall. "Is that moaning? Are you jacking off in there?" The door flew open as Michael stepped inside the room. His face ironed out when he took in our position on the bed, right before a warped smile formed. "You devil. I'll leave you to it." Michael started backing out the door then stopped. "Hayden, as the first girl to take pity on my brother, let me offer my condolences. Suggestion? You might want to kick the tires and check the motor before you take him for a test drive. Number four. Just saying. All our parents' good DNA went to us first. He got the leftover scraps."

Before he could disappear out the door, Soren had freed a pillow from behind him and sent it flying toward Michael. It nailed him in the back before he got the door slammed.

"I'm telling Mom you're playing footsie with a girl in your bedroom."

Soren's head rolled back. "There's a quick way to kill the mood."

270

Leaning forward, I kissed the red bump the ice pack had fallen off of, then I slid off his lap. As tempting as it was, this wasn't the time—not when five members of his family were waiting for us around the dinner table. I could tell I was already in his mom's good graces, and that was a position I'd like to keep.

"Clothes." I picked up his scattered items and handed them to him while he adjusted his towel.

"Where are you going?" he asked as I headed for the door, making sure my dress was in place and my hair was laying where it was supposed to.

"Downstairs."

"Don't you want to wait for me? I'll just take a minute."

My hand dropped to the doorknob. "If I stay in this room with you while you attempt to get dressed, it's going to be just that. An attempt." My eyes dropped to where he was about to tug his towel loose. His arousal was still tenting the white terry cloth.

"You're totally turned on by me right now, aren't you?" A smirk smoothed into place as his pinkie skimmed beneath the place where his towel was knotted. "I bet if I did this, you wouldn't be able to control what you did next."

I was out the door, sealing it behind me when I heard the wet towel smack the floor.

Once I was in the hall, I took a few deep, clearing breaths before heading down the stairs. I felt bad that he'd have to make it down the stairs on his own, but it wasn't like he would have made it down them anytime soon if I'd stayed either.

Maybe one of his brothers could be coerced into coming up to give him a hand.

Or not, I thought as I rounded into the kitchen to find them all around the dinner table, nodding at me with stupid smiles and leading me to the conclusion Michael had told them all what he'd walked in on upstairs.

"Where's Soren? Still recovering?" Ben asked, trying to keep a straight face.

I shot him a tight smile. Mr. and Mrs. Decker were nowhere to be found, not that I could blame them with this bunch.

"Could one of you go help him down the stairs? He hurt his ankle."

"Physical harm too?" Michael tipped his chin. "Bad kitty."

"You're how old again, Michael?" I crossed my arms as I marched up to where they were stationed around the table. They were an intimidating bunch, not that I'd let them know it. I might have been biased where Soren was concerned, but the other three hadn't struck out in the looks department either.

Michael held out his arms. "Twenty-two."

"Hmm," I mused, looking him over. "It doesn't show.'"

The two brothers stationed around him slapped his back.

"I just ordered my subscription to *Vogue*," Michael announced, all formal-like.

"Sounds like you'll be in every edition for a while."

When I didn't answer, he lifted something from his lap. It was this month's edition. Then he flipped it open to a marked page. It was a photo of me, the client being an Asian swimwear company. It looked like the type of swimsuit a person would wear in outer space and the pose wasn't the least bit provocative, but three sets of eyes devoured it like I was a centerfold.

"Like *Vogue* goes well with your *Playboy*s." Tobin gave Michael a hard enough shove, he almost fell out of the chair.

When Michael went to push him back, Tobin moved. "Fresh spank bank material is always welcome in my household." He twisted the magazine around for me to see, his brows moving.

"You mean your rat-infested flat in Tribeca."

"Better than that cardboard box you sold hand jobs for."

I was just about to ease out of the kitchen to wait for Soren when the back door opened and Mr. and Mrs. Decker came in. Soren's dad was holding a tray with a few barbecued chickens, and his mom was holding a package of foil with hot mitts. It smelled like corn on the cob.

Caroline's mouth dropped when she noticed the magazine. "Michael, what are you doing with that out? Put that away right now. Hayden's going to think we're some kind of stalkers or something and never come back."

Michael handed over the magazine when his mom held out her hand. Or hot mitt. She put the magazine up on the fridge, where there were a few other magazines.

"Soren lets me know what magazines you're in so I can pick them up when I go to the grocery store," she explained when she caught me looking. "It's silly, I know, but it's just so neat to look at this elegant woman in a fashion magazine and think that's my son's roommate."

My chest gave a little pang. I hadn't realized Soren listened when I gushed to him which magazines had campaigns I was in. And here was his mom, making sure to pick up a copy of those magazines just because I was the girl who shared an apartment with her son.

Although now, I guessed I was more than that.

"Have I made you totally uncomfortable now? If my sons didn't already manage to do so?" Caroline set the foil container of corn on the counter, half of her face pulling up.

My head shook. "You, not at all. Your sons, at least these three? Maybe."

The three brothers nudged one another like they were proud of themselves.

"Hayden." Mr. Decker approached with an easy smile after setting down the tray of chickens. "I feel like I already know you, but it's nice to officially meet you." Like his wife, he gave me a hug instead of a handshake. "Sorry, we're huggers in this family."

I was just shaking my head to show I didn't mind when a trio of chairs shoved away from the table, three bodies rising right after.

"You know what? We *are* a family of huggers." Ben grinned, moving around the table toward me.

"Thanks for the timely reminder, Dad," Tobin added, following his brother.

That was when someone stepped into the kitchen from the hallway, walking like his ankle wasn't the size of a small planet. "Take a seat. All three of you," Soren said, crossing his arms.

"How's that ankle doing, sweetheart?" Michael winked at Soren as everyone started to settle around the table.

Soren made sure I was on the opposite end of the table from his brothers before he slid into the chair beside me. "Better than you're going to be doing in five seconds if you don't shut up."

"You should come around more often, Hayden." When Ben reached for the stack of corn Caroline set on the table, she blocked his hand. "You really bring out the testosterone in Soren. Nice to see he's not really a little girl."

"This little girl never had a problem kicking your ass." Soren scooted his chair a few inches closer to me, his hand finding mine under the table.

Energy surged from my hand up my arm as I took a moment to wrap my head around the fact that Soren and I had made out, intensely, one floor above, five minutes ago. He was just holding my hand, but I could feel more in that touch. The anticipation of what was to come? The reminder of what already had? The comfort of knowing he was there?

There was a lot in that palm-to-palm embrace.

"Soren, I don't know why you're acting all King Kong about with your roommate. She's way too tall for you." Michael got up and grabbed some beers from the fridge.

"Yeah, and she's way too smart for you, shithead." Soren winced, tipping his head back at where his mom was while I grinned into my drink. He was sensitive on the height/intelligence topic. "Sorry, Mom."

She waved it off like trying to get four boys to behave had been a failed endeavor years ago.

"If she's so smart—no offense to you, Hayden, all offense directed at the moron to your right—what's she doing . . . *hanging* out with you?" The way Michael's eyes gleamed as he said it left no guessing as to what kind of hanging out he was getting at.

Soren leaned toward me. "You ever noticed how the bigger the dick, the smaller the penis?"

"Soren," his mom chided as she and Mr. Decker carried the giant tray of chicken to the table.

"Sorry, Mom," he popped off again, the response trained into him from the sounds of it.

"It would be nice if we could have a dinner guest over who is able to make it through an entire dinner without arriving at the conclusion that I am an unfit mother based on the way you four talk and behave." Mrs. Decker gave my back a gentle squeeze before she slid into the chair beside me.

"I don't know about those ones"—my gaze moved down the line of brothers across the table before I nudged the youngest beside me—"but this one turned out pretty great. You're an awesome mom."

Her face softened as she folded her napkin into her lap. "Okay, you're coming to dinner every Thursday night."

"All for this motion," Tobin boomed in an authoritative tone.

His brothers stabbed their arms into the air.

Across the table, Soren waved his middle finger at them.

Mrs. Decker just sighed. "Behave. All four of you."

A chorus of "Sorry, Moms" circled the table.

"Freezing rain." Mr. Decker came back in, one last foil packet in his hands. "The grill already had a good crust of ice on it before I got it under the canopy."

"Freezing rain? It's almost April, for Christ's sake." Ben groaned, checking the weather app on his phone. "This is supposed to keep up through the night. Great. I've got an early morning meeting in the city."

"It's supposed to warm up through the night. You'll be able to make it back in the morning, but tonight—" Mr. Decker peeked out the kitchen window after setting the foil packet on the empty platter on the table. "Doesn't look like anyone's going anywhere unless you've got ice skates."

I twisted in my seat to look at the same window. "I've got a morning meeting too." It was with one of the campaign managers for the new client I'd booked. I did not want to show up late or not at all to my first meeting with them.

"Don't worry. I'll get you back in time." Soren's hand tightened around mine.

"Why don't we all eat, and then figure out what to do about this fine, April weather?" Mrs. Decker suggested, opening the other foil packet. It had a heap of marinated red potatoes inside.

My eyebrows pulled together as I stared at the meal on the table. Soren must have noticed.

"Mom asked if there was something special you might like for dinner," he whispered. "I remembered you saying your mom used to make this for your birthday every year—how much you liked it."

My eyes burned. "You remembered barbecued chicken, corn on the cob, and roasted red potatoes?" I'd probably mentioned that random fact to him weeks ago, not thinking he'd recall any of it, let alone all of it.

"And biscuits. Homemade biscuits." Soren held out a basket, opening a checked cloth to reveal a pile of biscuits.

That homesick pang I could never quite seem to shake dispersed. At least for a while. It was such a simple meal, but it had felt like such a big deal every year when Mom made it for me. Meat, even the cheap cuts, was expensive for our budget back then. Casseroles, soups, noodles, that had been our standard fare, so dining on food like this made us all feel like we were royalty or something.

Here I was, in one of the biggest cities in the world, having just signed a modeling contract that would keep me comfortable for years to come, and there wasn't any other meal I'd rather have.

"If it's any consolation, Hayden"—Ben settled the beers in front of his seat, Tobin's, and Michael's. He

278

mouthed *underage* at Soren—"we're only giving you two such a hard time because we're a bunch of jealous pricks who wished we were the ones bringing home a girl like you."

Mrs. Decker let out another sigh as she dished some chicken onto my plate.

"Thanks?" I replied.

Michael nodded like we were square as he lifted his beer. "To baby brother. The first of us sorry suckers to get himself good and pussy-whipped."

Four sighs circled the table as two more beers stabbed into the air. "To baby brother."

CHAPTER
Seventeen

"**A**re you sure you don't want the guest bedroom? I can kick Michael out of there. We've got plenty of couches," Mrs. Decker asked as she turned down the blankets in Soren's bedroom.

The freezing rain had only gotten worse over the course of dinner and the couple hours that followed. Cabs weren't operating, and the subway station was too far away to make it on foot with the ice skating rink that had developed outside. Especially with Soren's ankle. Mrs. Decker had insisted all of us spend the night, and we could head out early in the morning when the temperatures were supposed to warm up dramatically.

"No, I'm fine. I wouldn't know what to do if I slept in anything bigger than a twin-sized bed." After sliding out of my sweater, I helped her fold the sheet down. Since I hadn't planned on spending the night, I didn't have any pajamas. At least the dress I had on was comfortable.

"I bet when you agreed to come to dinner, you didn't think you'd be spending the night." She smiled at me as she fluffed the pillows.

"It's nice of you to let me stay." Sitting on the bed, I took off my ballet flats, my teeth sinking into my lip.

Because that was when someone else lumbered into the room, carrying a big red sleeping bag and a pillow. The way he appraised me when he saw me on his bed made my stomach drop and my legs squeeze together. *Not okay, Hayden.* I should not be having those kind of thoughts about the woman's son when she was five feet away, still fussing over the bed I was about to spend the night in.

I wouldn't be alone.

Not that the sleeping bag being rolled out onto the floor suggested that.

"Are you sure about this, Hayden? I know you're both adults and everything, but Soren can take the floor downstairs." The way she looked between us, it was almost like she knew we'd crossed that line of roommates who were just friends. Moms always had good intuition.

"No, it's okay. I'm used to Soren sleeping ten feet away." I glanced at him where he was kneeling above his sleeping bag, adjusting his pillow. When he caught me looking, he tugged his T-shirt over his head.

He wasn't going out of his way to make this any easier.

"I suppose you are." She came around the bed and wound her arms around me. I rose so I could hug her back. "Okay then, sweet dreams."

My mind wasn't thinking sweet things—it was veering in the opposite direction.

"Sweet dreams, baby," she said as she moved on to Soren, kissing his forehead after letting him go.

"Night, Mom. Thanks for everything," he replied before sliding into the sleeping bag, but not before giving me one more look that had my insides jellifying.

"Lights out?" She paused in the doorway, her finger on the light switch.

I scooted onto the bed, tucking my legs under the covers.

"Lights out," Soren answered for us.

The room went black, the door sealing closed a moment after. Some light came in through the windows from the streetlights outside, but it took my eyes a while to adjust before I could really see anything.

It was almost eleven, but I hadn't been tired when we'd all finally decided to crawl into our assigned beds for the night. The instant the lights went out, I became even less tired.

The air had the feel of an electric storm coming, making the hair on my arms rise. All of my senses became sharper too. I could hear his even breath, slightly faster than I was used to hearing it at night in the apartment. I could almost make out his heartbeat, pumping only a beat or two slower than mine.

When the sleeping bag rustled as he shifted, I practically jolted in bed.

As my eyes adjusted, I was able to make him out stretched across the middle of the bedroom floor. His arms were crossed behind his head, his bare upper half sticking out of the bag, his eyes wide open, aimed at the ceiling.

It didn't look like he had sleep on his mind either.

"Soren?"

A sound of acknowledgment rumbled in his throat.

"Where's your parents' bedroom?"

"Downstairs."

"Good." I didn't bother to throw off the covers. I just slid out from beneath them and tiptoed toward him.

"What are you doing?" he asked as he threw open the sleeping bag to let me in.

Lowering over him, I wedged myself into the sleeping bag with him. My lips ran up his jaw. "You."

His body trembled beneath mine, his hands finding their way to my waist. "By that, do you mean . . .?"

My hand slipping beneath the waistband of his sweats seemed to answer his question. A breath hissed past his teeth when my fingers circled him. He grew even harder as I let myself touch him, taking the time to revel in the size and strength every part of his body possessed. One of his hands slid up my waist before settling around my breast. When he palmed the sensitive area, a gasp escaped from me, making his dick kick in my hand.

"Are you sure?" He lowered his head back onto the pillow so he could look up at me, his hands freezing where they were. "I don't have any expectations. We don't have to rush if you're not ready."

His throat moved when my hand circled down him again. "I'm not rushing," I said, leaning back so I could gather my dress in my hands. "I've been waiting months to be with you like this."

After I finished pulling my dress over my head, I tossed it behind Soren's head. He was staring at me, his eyes wide, his mouth parting from how hard he was breathing. Taking one of my hands, he guided it to his chest and flattened it over his breastplate.

"Feel that?" he whispered, his eyes returning to mine after they finished their long journey over my body. "That's what you do to me."

My mouth moved. His heartbeat was so fast I couldn't count the beats. "This is what I do to you when I strip out of my clothes while I've got you pinned to the floor?"

His head shook slowly, keeping my hand where it was. "This was what you did to me the first time I saw you. This is what you do to me anytime you're around." His fingers circled tighter around my wrist. "This is what you do to me anytime I think of you."

I leaned down to leave a trail of kisses along his jawline. "Are you saying that because you're about to get laid?"

He finally let go of my hand, letting it roam other parts of his body. "I'm saying that because I need you to know before I get laid."

"You need me to know what?"

His head turned toward mine as I lowered my chest over his. "That I love you."

The world stopped.

His words rolled over me, entering me until I was swimming in them.

My lips responded—not in word but in action. Finding his, they kissed him frantically, until I felt so oxygen-deprived, my head felt fuzzy and my legs numb.

His body moved below mine, twisting until I found myself on my back below him. His chest and hips rolled over mine, pinning me to the floor as he ground into me, his kiss never breaking. His arms came around my legs, tying them behind his back. When he ground into me again, he drew a whimper from me that made my mouth sever from his.

He grunted against my neck, his hips pitching into mine again. "Make that for me again."

When I did, not from his request but from reflex, his body calmed as he took a deep breath. Soren went back to kissing me, his hips sliding off of mine as his hands brushed up and down the sides of my arms.

This man could kiss. Good god almighty, the combination of his lips and tongue could drive a girl up a wall, but I'd had his mouth several times already. I wanted something else.

"Soren?" I pulled back just enough to look him in the eyes. "What are you doing?" When he gave me a funny look, his hand gliding down my side, I added, "Why are you slowing down?"

His lips touched mine. "Foreplay," he breathed as his hand made the return journey up my back. "It's a thing, right?"

My hand moved beneath the sleeping bag to find his. Guiding his hand down my body, I slid our joined hands beneath my underwear, skimming down, down, down . . .

When he felt me, his body went rigid.

"I don't need foreplay." My fingers tangled with his as they explored my body together. "We've had three months of foreplay."

One of his fingers moved just barely inside me as his other hand gripped around the side of my underwear, working it down my body. As soon as they were off, he settled back over me, his hips working mine open.

"Good point," he rasped. "Me either."

His wet fingers trailed along the ridge of my hip bone, curling around it as he slowly pushed himself inside me. Soren's head moved above mine so he could watch me as he claimed my body. I struggled to stay still as he moved deeper, his eyes bore as deep inside of me as his manhood was. The look on his face as he made love to me mirrored the look on my face, I imagined.

A ragged exhale poured from his lips when he could go no deeper, and the same came from mine right after. My body trembled, triggering his arms to form around me.

"I've got you," he whispered against my skin. "I won't let go."

My arms circled his back, my fingers curling into his skin as he started to move inside me. When my leg wound around his, my foot twisting against his, Soren flinched.

"Ankle. Sorry." My foot untwisted instantly. "Do you want a pain reliever or something?" I knew better than to offer him more ice bags when he was under the same roof as his brothers.

He pushed inside me, his head falling. "Or something."

My chest moved against him. "Men. It's like a girl could cure cancer with what resides between her legs."

"What? Sex is the best kind of pain reliever there is." Like he was making his point, he pushed back inside me. "All of those positive endorphins. Best drug around."

Trying to laugh silently, I made another sound I tried to keep silent when his hips circled against mine, somehow managing to find something inside me I hadn't even known existed until that moment.

When he heard my gasp, combined with whatever he saw on my face, he tied my legs around his back again and threw the sleeping bag open. "Yeah, me too."

Lifting me, his arms cradled my body as he carried me over to his bed. His uneven steps reminded me again

. . .

"Soren. Your ankle. Take it easy."

"I don't want to take it easy." He lowered me onto his bed, his body still connected with mine.

"You're not in peak shape. Just take it down a few notches."

He gave me an obstinate look, staring at my body spread out below him. "It's my ankle that's busted." His hips pitched into mine, driving deeper. My head lolled back from the erotic pleasure of having a man so deep inside me. "My dick's working just fine."

Adjusting our bodies so my head was on the pillows, he layered the blankets over our bodies as he slid over me. My mouth pulled as I noticed the baseball print sheets fall around his shoulders.

"What are you doing?"

His brows moved. "Boyhood fantasy." His hips found a gentle rhythm, mine rising to meet him with each pulse. It wasn't long before his body stilled, his hands holding my hips in place as he looked like he was trying to catch his breath.

"You're stopping." My head lifted, my body still charging forward. "Why are you stopping?"

"Not stopping." His head shook once as he wiped the beads of sweat dotting his forehead. "Slowing. Pacing."

My head tilted as I ran my fingers through his hair. It was damp with sweat. "Reason?"

His hand cupped one of my breasts, his thumb caressing my nipple until it formed into a bud. My body tightened around him, pulling him deeper into my body. His eyes squeezed shut at the same time he blew out a loud breath.

"Because I'm really, *really* enjoying myself. I'd like to prolong that sensation. And I'd like to make sure you really, really enjoy yourself because I'd really, really, really like to do this again with you. In, I don't know"—his eyes moved to the alarm clock shaped like a baseball hat on the nightstand—"say five minutes?"

My fingers kept combing through his hair, wondering what I'd done to deserve the man above me, making love to my body and mind at the same time. "That's a lot of reallys."

He kissed my breast, his tongue taking the place of his finger circling my nipple. I felt myself clamp down on him again. His hand braced at my hip tightened.

"Doesn't even begin to describe how this feels," he rasped.

My hips rocked against his, then away, setting the pace since watching him take his pleasure from me, feeling it as it happened, was more stimulating than experiencing my own right then. Soren's fist balled into the pillow beside my ear as his head fell beside mine. His breaths were labored, every exhale a grunt as I moved my body against his.

"Okay, so about how much longer are you hoping I can hold out?" he asked, his voice strained. "Ten seconds? Maybe twenty?"

My head turned toward his, waiting for his eyes to find mine. I was trying to hold myself back, to wait until I felt his body give up the fight, but I couldn't. The moment his eyes connected with mine, I lost control of whatever measure I'd been clinging to. I lost myself.

"Soren," I cried, my back lifting off the bed as a surge of pleasure drove through my body.

"Holy fuck," he exclaimed when he felt my body pulse around him.

My mouth lifted to meet his in an effort to quiet the sounds our shared release was drawing from us. His tongue shoved into my mouth as he sheathed himself so deeply in me, the headboard banged against the wall. He held himself there, unmoving, as his body quivered around mine, our mouths moving as we swallowed each other's cries of pleasure.

We stayed like that for a while after, our mouths slowing, our bodies still joined. I could feel the result of our lovemaking rolling down my body, and the feel of it turned me on all over again.

When Soren's mouth separated from mine, his eyes opened to meet mine. His thumb brushed down the slope of my neck. "That was so much better than I ever thought it would be." His voice was a bit hoarse, his back quivering when I touched it. "Even hearing all the locker room talk, knowing how good it felt when I gave it to myself . . . so much better than I imagined." Soren rolled off to the side, gathering me in his arms as he did.

I lifted my head, looking down at him. "Than you imagined?"

One of his shoulders moved. "You were my first." A grin stretched into place as everything seemed to catch up to him all at once. "In case that wasn't obvious."

My whole face went flat. Did that mean . . . ? Was he . . . ? Had he been . . . a few minutes ago? "Actually, it wasn't."

"Really?" The skin between his brows creased.

I went with the Soren approach to confessing one's sexual history. A shrug. "I don't have anything to compare it to."

That grin flattened.

"You were my first," I said, in case he needed it spelled out.

His face stayed frozen for a minute, then he sat up, his eyes widening. "Shit. Did I hurt you?" His gaze swept down my body, a wince pulling at his expression. "I never thought to ask. I never would have thought . . ."

My hand settled against his cheek, waiting for him to look at me. "That there was a nineteen-year-old virgin left out there?"

His hand slid behind my neck. "Aren't we just a couple of late bloomers?"

When I gave a soft laugh, his smile rose back to the surface. He pulled me to him, and I found a comfy spot on his chest and closed my eyes. My body ached where he'd just been, but it was a kind of pain I'd never felt before. A kind that made me hungry for more.

"Soren?"

"Hmm?" He sounded as tired as I felt.

"Thank you for being my first."

His hand dropped over mine resting on his stomach. His fingers tied through mine. "Hayden?"

My body curled closer. "Yeah?"

"Thank you for being my only."

CHAPTER
Eighteen

The storm from last night had passed by five the next morning. The sky was blue and it was pushing fifty by the time I crawled into the cab waiting outside of the Deckers' house after breakfast. Soren slid in behind me, refusing to limp as all of his brothers were perched on the porch, jeering at us as we left. Michael was waving an old pair of crutches, and Ben had what looked like a yellowed box of Power Ranger Band-Aids.

Soren was about to give the one-finger salute back when his mom stepped onto the porch. He went with a wave instead as the taxi pulled away from the curb. I thought about how we'd arrived only a little less than twelve hours ago, and it felt like the whole world had changed.

"Do you have time to head back to the apartment to change, or do you need to get to the agency?" Soren asked as he settled his bags at our feet. I smiled when I saw he'd left the wrap I'd taped around his ankle in place. The swelling had gone down, but half of his foot was blue and purple from the bruising he'd woken up to.

"The agency. I don't want to chance it and be late."

Soren leaned forward to give the address to the driver, then he settled back into his seat. When he glanced at me, my stomach twisted into a million knots. We'd barely woken up in time to shower, get dressed, and throw down a few bites of breakfast before the cab Soren's dad had called for us arrived. There had been no time to recap or replay any of what had happened last night, but with the way he was looking at me right now, I could practically feel him moving inside me all over again.

"Glad you could finally make it to dinner with the family." One side of his mouth twitched.

"Now I understand why you were so eager to get me there."

"Nothing says romance like two parents one floor below and three obnoxious brothers, right?"

I combed through my purse to grab a few items to get myself ready for the day. "Well, that, and baseball twin-sized sheets."

Soren chuckled. "Works every time."

"Or at least one time, Mr. Saving Yourself for Marriage."

"You're one to talk," he jousted back, glancing toward the driver. He was on his cell phone, speaking a different language. "And I wasn't saving myself for marriage. I was saving myself for the right one."

"The right one?" I raked a brush through my hair, lifting my eyebrow at him.

Soren lifted his eyes. "Why am I the only hopeless romantic in this relationship?"

"Because it's 'hopeless,'" I fired back with a smile.

Soren was about to nudge me when he stopped. I was in the middle of brushing on a couple coats of mascara.

"My parents kind of brought us up believing that there was one right person out there for us, you know? That there was one person for everyone," he continued, shifting. "It wasn't like they said that around the dinner table or anything. We just saw that with the way they are together. I think we all realized we weren't going to waste our time pretending. We'd hold out for that just right one."

I twisted the cap on the mascara and tucked it away. "You believe that? There's only one perfect person for each of us?" It was a beautiful idea. One I wished I believed in—but I'd never once witnessed it. Relationships, at least the romantic kind, always seemed to be more of the opposite. My dad's leaving, my mom's failed string of relationships that followed—it made a cynic out of the softest of souls.

"Partly, yeah"—he nodded, rolling his hand—"but I think it has more to do with what we *choose* to believe more than how it actually is. And for me, yeah, I choose to believe that there is one right person for me. One woman I was meant to love."

That hardened cynic inside me started to melt. "Why?"

From the way he was looking at me, it was like he expected me to know. Or was waiting for me to figure it out. "Because that's the way I want to love someone. Like she's irreplaceable. Like I'd wait forever, search forever, until I got to be with her."

My throat moved, but the ball lodged in it stayed. "Okay, I get that," I said, my voice giving away my emotion. "And you are so getting lucky tonight."

Soren fist pumped in celebration before reaching for me. His hand folded over my shoulder, and he tucked me into the shelter of his chest. "There. That feels right." When he exhaled, it was like he'd been holding his breath for a while.

"Putting your arm around me?" I asked, winding my arm over his stomach and sliding closer.

His head nodded above mine. "Before, I'd get the urge to pull you close or hold you or touch you, and I had to catch myself before I did it. Now, I get the urge, and I just do it."

His lips touched my head. Everything else touched something deeper inside me.

Closing my eyes, I imagined everything would work out between us. "It does feel right."

With all of the days I worked late, this was one time I really could have benefitted from getting off at a normal end-of-day hour. Even for work-weary New Yorkers, I was getting off late.

I'd texted Soren earlier to let him know I wouldn't be home until after nine, maybe ten, and apparently he'd been running late too. His coach had tacked on an extra practice, and he had to finish up a lab after that.

The meeting with the client had gone well. Better than expected. I might have lost a liter of fluid via my armpits, I was so nervous, but we walked away from the day with them still wanting me to be the face of their new campaign.

My feet were screaming as I climbed the stairs, even in my flats, so I kicked them off somewhere between the third and fourth floor and journeyed the rest of the way barefoot. Soren had told me to text him when I hit the subway so he could meet me at the stop by our apartment, but I hadn't. He was busy enough without having to escort me to and from a subway station. Besides, the days were getting longer, and by his definition, it was still dark, since there'd been plenty of people out on the sidewalks.

Unlocking the door, I braced myself for him to be upset about me not texting him, but instead I found a quiet apartment. A couple of lights were burning, but I didn't see or hear him until I rounded into the kitchen.

He was at the table, sitting in his favorite chair, books and notebooks spread around him. He was almost snoring he was sleeping so hard.

I'd been looking forward to seeing him tonight. I'd been really looking forward to doing more of what we'd done last night. No family within earshot, no pictures of an eight-year-old Soren holding a baseball bat over his shoulder staring at me from the walls.

But he had to be exhausted if he'd fallen asleep the way he had. With school, practice, and work, he'd barely been averaging five hours of sleep a night. He needed his rest, however he could get it.

As I headed to my area to get changed into pajamas, I noticed he was still in his practice uniform. He'd gone through two practices, kept it on to finish a lab at school, and was still in at when he'd come home?

I realized why when I checked behind his partition to find an ungodly pile of dirty laundry. He'd been too busy for laundry too.

Since I could sleep in a bit in the morning, I decided to tackle Mt. Soiled Soren. I'd been planning on spending a couple hours tonight with him anyway—maybe not doing his laundry, but it was something he needed taken care of, regardless.

Thankfully, both washers were open when I carried the first heap into the laundry room at the end of the hall. After getting those first couple of loads started, I headed back to the apartment to tackle a few other projects.

Six loads of laundry, twenty ready-to-go meals, and one spotless apartment later, I felt like I was about to fall asleep in the chair across from Soren as I rolled the last pair of his socks together.

I was trying to tuck one of his undershirts between his head and his textbook "pillow" when he jerked awake. He blinked a few times before he shot up in his chair, grabbing his phone to check the time.

"Fuck," he grunted as he bolted out of his chair.

He didn't realize I was beside him until his chest rammed into mine.

"You're here." His hands formed around my arms as he blinked the last bit of sleep out of his eyes. "Christ, I fell asleep. I'm sorry." His neck rolled as he rubbed at the indents on his face from the textbook. "Why didn't you text me? You didn't walk back by yourself, did you?"

I exhaled. "The subway station is maybe a third of a mile away from here. I managed just fine."

"Hayden—" He cut himself off, rolling his neck again. "Why didn't you text me so I could walk with you?" His voice was more composed, his face less harsh.

"Can we please not talk about this right now?"

When I turned to walk away, his hand grabbed mine. Before I knew what I was doing, I was pressed up against him, my hands and mouth covering him. Hoisting me up, Soren's other hand slipped between my legs, and a tremor spilled down him when he felt my body already ready, waiting for him.

He lowered my back onto the table—it shook when he did, pencils and paper scattering to the floor. My hands worked at his buckle as he slid my shirt up my body, exposing my breasts. Once I'd yanked the button of his white practice pants free, I ran my hands along the sides of his jockstrap before working it down his hips.

"I need to feel you." He grunted as my hand circled his shaft when it sprang free.

I had barely nodded before his fingers hooked my sleep shorts and underwear with one finger, sliding them just enough aside so he could . . .

A primal cry spilled out of me, my back lifting off the table when he thrust into me. The legs of the table squeaked across the floor when he moved into me again. His chest covered mine, his face settling above mine as he fucked me. The screech of the table legs moving with each thrust, the sound of our gasps as we drove closer, the noise or our bodies pistoning together . . . my orgasm surged to the surface instantly.

"Look at me when you come," Soren commanded. "Let me see the look in your eyes when my cock makes you come. I need to see it."

My fingers raked down his back, my body writhing below him as I let loose. I kept my eyes open as my release fired through me, letting him watch.

"Watch me now, Hayden. Watch my eyes."

The muscles running through his neck went rigid as he thrust into me one more time, holding himself deep as his orgasm released into me. Watching him come, feeling it as I stared into his eyes, spurred my second orgasm. I was so surprised by it, I thought I was having a heart attack, right before the familiar explosion of pleasure charged through me, making its way into every dip and hollow.

By the end, I was trembling in his arms. I felt broken apart and whole all at once. Soren's eyes didn't leave mine for another minute, his body still claiming mine long after our desire had been spent.

Our bodies were clammy with sweat, our chests moving as erratically as our breaths. His lips covered mine in what might have been the sweetest, most gentle kiss to have ever been given, before he lifted me and carried me across the room.

I trembled against him again. "Your bed or mine?"
His arms held me tighter. "Our bed."

CHAPTER
Nineteen

ow was it possible to miss someone I'd only been "official" with for a week as much as I had over the past seven days?

That dull ache of separation didn't take a single break my whole trip to Paris. Even when I slept, I'd wake up to the same heaviness. It was only one week, but it didn't feel like it. I'd be leaving again for Paris in a couple of days, and that would be the trend for the next long while. The colossal client was in Paris, which meant most of my work life was now in Paris. Halfway across the planet practically—and here I thought I'd moved to the fashion capital of the world.

Of course I'd get booked by a client based internationally.

Soren had to hit the road later tonight with his team for an away game in the morning. Which meant we had a couple hours of overlap. Two hours in a week. I wasn't experienced in relationships, but I knew that wasn't a good way to start a new one.

My flight had come in late, so instead of swinging by the apartment to drop off my suitcase and link up with Soren before we headed to whatever he had planned for us, I told him I'd meet him there. I didn't want to waste time since, in our case, each minute was precious.

When the cab pulled in front of the restaurant Soren had picked, I realized I was slightly underdressed. Leggings, a tunic, and flats weren't cocktail dresses and designer heels.

Grabbing the small suitcase I'd carried on, I moved out of the cab after paying the driver. I felt jet-lagged from the time changes, tired from working twelve-hour days, and exhausted from missing him.

The instant I saw Soren moving through the restaurant's door toward me, all signs of fatigue disappeared.

He didn't say anything; he just wound his arms around me and pulled me close. The suitcase fell from my hands so I could wind mine around him. We stood like that for a minute, holding each other in the diffused light of a streetlamp on a dark street, until our breathing had synced.

"God, I missed you," he said.

My body felt like it was melting into his from how close he was holding me. "Missed you more."

His lips touched my temple before he stepped back. "Impossible." His arm draped behind my back as he lifted my carry-on in his other hand to head back inside.

"I don't think I'm dressed for the occasion." I glanced at Soren, who was wearing dark slacks and a button-down shirt. "Maybe I should change," I suggested as we moved by the restrooms stationed up front. I had a dress and heels in my carry-on that would suit this place better than my international flight attire.

"Don't be crazy. You look perfect." Soren wove us through the crowd of customers staggered through the waiting area, moving toward the hostess.

"Says the man who's probably so desperate to get laid, he'd say that if I came in wearing a paper sack and galoshes."

"You know me so well." He winked at me before turning to the hostess. "Decker. Reservation for seven o'clock."

The hostess ran a pencil down the clipboard she was holding, her forehead creasing when she reached the bottom. She started at the top again. "I'm sorry, sir, but I don't have a reservation for Decker at seven."

Soren's head shook. "I called last week and made the reservation. I know I made one."

She read through the reservation list again, her gaze drifting into the busy waiting area right after. "Is there any chance you could have given a different name?"

His neck rolled. "No."

"Soren, it's okay. We can go somewhere else."

He scooted closer so he could see the reservation list. "No. I made reservations here, because I read they were one of the best restaurants in the city to have a romantic dinner."

"We can go to that burger joint by the apartment and bring a candle and a rose to set on the table."

My suggestion didn't draw the response I was going for. His hand raked through his hair as he waved into the restaurant. "I made a reservation. If you want to see the call on my phone, I can show you. There's just two of us. Can't you squeeze us in?"

I hadn't noticed out on the street how tired he looked as well. He'd shaved and his hair, usually hidden by a cap, had been combed, but there were dark shadows under his eyes. From the calls and texts we'd exchanged this week, he'd probably put in sixteen-hour days to my twelves.

"I'm sorry, sir. We're fully booked tonight. If you like, I can suggest a few other options close by, or I'd be happy to make a reservation for you for a later date—"

"A later date won't work," Soren didn't quite but almost snapped. "I leave tonight. She leaves again on Monday."

The hostess was getting flustered, Soren already was, so I slid in front of him in an attempt to convince him we could go somewhere else. Anywhere else. I didn't care, because we were together. I would have been in bliss if we grabbed a couple of hot dogs and sodas from a street vendor and parked it on a curb, because after the longest week on record, we were together again.

The annoying roommate I used to make a point of keeping my distance from was now the one I wanted to be as close to as possible.

"Hayden?" a familiar voice called right before Ellis appeared over Soren's shoulder. "What are you doing here?"

Soren's jaw worked before he turned.

"What did you think of Paris? I already know how much the client loved you." Ellis didn't seem to care how close Soren was hovering beside me. He leaned in and gave me a quick hug. It wasn't anything outside the realm of casual friends, but from the look on Soren's face, Ellis might as well have shoved me up against a wall and stuck his tongue in my mouth.

"Paris was good. I'm glad to be home though." I leaned out of the embrace before he was ready to let me go.

A blonde woman in a couture gown waited behind him, but Ellis made no effort to introduce her.

"From the sounds of the shows and campaigns they want to use you for, Paris is going to become your home away from home soon."

Soren's head twisted toward me. He knew I'd be back and forth to Paris for a while. I just might have left out how frequently, and how long of a duration, that would be. I'd really only just found out this past week that the client wanted to keep things open until they had a chance to work with me. From the sounds of it, I'd impressed them. Some awkward girl from Nebraska was going to be the face of an iconic international fashion brand. The news was still sinking in.

"Did you just finish dinner or are you just about to sit down?" Ellis asked after his prior statement remained un-addressed.

"Actually—"

Soren's hand dropped onto my back, moving me away. "We're just leaving."

"Did you have a nice dinner? This is one of my favorite places."

I sealed my lips, letting Soren answer however he wanted to. Even if that meant walking us out the door.

"They don't have the reservation I made. So we're heading somewhere else."

Ellis chuckled, moving up to the hostess table. "Yeah, sometimes they do that when certain people arrive."

I hoped Soren had missed the way Ellis said *certain people* like it was an affliction. He hadn't.

After having a short conversation with the hostess, Ellis leaned in to press a quick kiss to her cheek. "You're all set. Melanie here has a table ready for you."

Again, I waited for Soren's lead. He wasn't exactly fond of Ellis, so if he wanted to leave instead of accept some favor, I was good with that. Instead, he took my hand and moved up to where the hostess was waiting for us with menus in hand.

"Are you sure?" I whispered to him.

His head moved. "I wanted to take you somewhere nice. I'm sure."

Ellis clapped Soren's shoulder as we passed. "Be sure to add their bill to mine. Let the server know, would you?"

Soren stopped. "I've got it. Thanks."

Ellis waved that off. "Please. Don't spend a month's paycheck on one dinner. Let me take care of it. Hayden is my top girl right now. I have to make sure she gets treated right."

Soren's shoulders stiffened beneath his dress shirt. "I'll take care of our bill," he said, his eyes having no problem holding Ellis's unyielding stare. "I'll take care of her, too."

Ellis shrugged, stepping aside so we could follow the hostess. Soren's hand felt rigid and hot in mine. This wasn't how I'd been hoping to spend our two hours together.

"This is a really nice place, Soren."

By the time I was sliding into my chair, the hard lines on his face had started to disappear. He made sure I was settled in my chair before moving toward his. "I'm glad you like it."

My eyes about fell out of their sockets when I saw the menu. To be exact, the prices listed beside the menu items. I was rolling in some good money now, a six-figure income I'd only dreamed of one day making. Still, that didn't change who I was or how I felt about a prawn cocktail costing fifty dollars. My mom used to feed four of us for two weeks on fifty bucks.

"I'm paying for dinner tonight, okay?" I kept my eyes on the menu, knowing this wasn't going to go over well.

"No. Not okay."

"Soren—"

He leaned across the table. "Hayden, I'm paying."

Half of my face pulled up when I saw the three-digit prices besides the entrees. "Dutch?"

A groan echoed across the table. "You can't take one more manly thing away from me. No way. You insist on wearing stilts whenever we go out in public together— most of the time," he added, when I flashed my flats outside of the table. "You're not picking up the dinner tab too."

My teeth worked over my lip, doing a rough tally of how steep the bill would run tonight, even if we only ordered dinners. I knew roughly how much he brought home every month, and this one dinner would tear through almost a quarter of it.

"Please. I wanted to do something special for you. To celebrate this big deal you just landed. To celebrate you being on the fast-track to supermodel status." He lifted his water cup at me, toasting.

I lifted mine and clinked it against his. "We should be celebrating you being on the fast-track to the pros too, right?"

"It's way early to assume any of that—to even hope" —his eyes sparkled across the table at me—"but I played one hell of a game when those scouts were in the stands watching."

"You always play one hell of a game." My hand stretched across the table when he held out his. "How was the ankle injury?"

"What ankle injury?" he asked, straight-faced. Then he chuckled. "The ankle was great. Didn't feel a thing. Your healing touch worked wonders."

My legs squeezed together from the look he gave me. It was the same one I'd stared at the night he'd taken me on the table in the apartment. Penetrating. Domineering.

"Speaking of healing touches . . ." I leaned across the table and lowered my voice. There was a dull roar in the restaurant and the tables were spaced generously, but still.

"I figured you'd have other plans for us to spend our two hours together. Plans that didn't include dinner." I wetted my lips then whispered, "Or clothes."

His neck stiffened, looking like he was in physical pain from what I was suggesting. "Yeah, I just wanted to prove to you—to show you—that that's not all I want from you. That I value more than just that kind of intimacy with you."

The menu lowered from my hands. "That's pretty much the sweetest thing I've ever heard."

"Thank god." A loud breath blew from his mouth. "Because you have no idea how hard it was to say. Or do. Or, you know."

I took a sip of my water, trying to cool the heat swelling inside me. I wanted Soren's body so badly I felt nauseous from it. I wanted him, all of him, even more. Maybe he was right—maybe it was a good idea for us not to spend those few coveted hours we got together only one way. Our bodies worked like a damn dream together—we'd already figured that out. We needed to get the rest of the relationship components to fuse just as cohesively.

"So . . ." I leaned farther across the table. "No sex?"

He winced. "You make that sound so bad." The lines of his face creased deeper. "But yeah, no sex. Not tonight. Let's just . . . be together. Like this." His hand turned mine over so he could caress the underside of my wrist.

I'd never known how erotic a thumb touching my wrist could be until right then. Especially when it was matched with the glint in his eyes appraising me.

"I'm sorry about Ellis back there. I know he's not your favorite person, and he can come off as an arrogant ass. What he said to you, that was rude."

Soren shrugged it off, though his eyes didn't come across so dismissively. "People are always going to try to put you in your place. I know exactly where I stand."

My feet slid against his, every part of my body feeling drawn to him. The only thing keeping the rest of my body separated from his was the table between us. "And where do you stand?

"In the very spot every guy on the planet wants to be." He lifted my hand and kissed my knuckles. "Right beside the most stunning creature in creation."

Paris again. Another microscopic hotel room with thin walls and unique smells. For as glamorous of a life most people seemed to think models had, the opposite was true. The early morning shoots, the hours spent being pulled on, prodded, brushed, and styled in a chair, the long days where a bathroom break was considered generous. It wasn't a glamorous lifestyle, not even as a model who was supposedly "rising to the top." That was okay. I'd known that going in. I wasn't a diva and was familiar with hard work.

The hard part was being away from him. Another couple of weeks had passed, and the time we had spent together had been through the filter of a phone. His season was at its peak, so he was traveling a ton too. Combine that with the time difference, and it made squeezing in a few minutes to catch up a scheduling nightmare.

He always told me just to call him whenever and not to worry about what time it was where he was. He'd happily wake up to hear my voice. But I knew how little sleep he was getting, and I didn't want a selfish whim to be the reason he approached the next morning like a zombie.

The silver lining to all of this was that he and his team were having a great season and everything was going great with my new client. In fact, my career was going so great, Ellis was having to turn down offers from other fashion designers and companies thanks to my schedule being too full.

Both of our dreams seemed to be on the cusp of fruition, but sometimes it felt like the cost of being apart was too great. Especially at night. When I was alone, stuffed inside some small, foreign hotel room, trying to tune out the voices and shouts spoken in a language I didn't know.

I'd be flying back to New York in a couple of days, and Soren and I'd have one whole day together before he was back on the road for a game. Two days. I could make it.

I could . . .

My hand grabbed my phone and punched in his number before I'd made a voluntary decision. It was almost one at night here, which meant it was dinnertime'ish there. I thought.

"I was just thinking about you," Soren answered.

"You always say that." My mouth turned up as I rolled onto my side in bed.

"That's because I'm always thinking about you. So it's always true."

Hearing his voice made everything better. Everything. Two days suddenly didn't feel so far away. Two weeks didn't feel like it had been forever.

"Are you at the apartment?" I asked.

"I'm at school still, actually. Had to come in early to make up a lab I missed last week from being on the road."

"What time is it there?"

"A little after seven. Which means it's . . . one o'clock there? Hayden, you should be asleep. You need to take care of yourself." In the background, I heard voices, noises.

"I can't sleep." I twisted onto my other side, unable to find a comfortable position on the bed. I was used to sleeping on some unpleasant surfaces, but this bed was bad. I probably would have been better off on the floor.

"Want me to sing you a lullaby or something?" Soren whispered something to someone before it sounded like he was moving away from the noise.

"I'm beyond the reach of a lullaby. Or a glass of warm milk. Or even one of those sleep pills all of the girls keep telling me to get a prescription for." I groaned, turning back over again. The less sleep I got, the less willing to fall asleep my body seemed. It was a vicious cycle.

"I can think of something else that always seems to put you right to sleep." Soren's tone had changed, his voice quieter.

"What's that?" When he stayed quiet, I realized what he was talking about. "How's that supposed to help me when you're thousands of miles away?"

"Physically, yeah, but I'm talking to you right this very moment. You've got a good imagination, right?"

His voice and what he was suggesting had me sitting up in bed. "Are you implying . . .?"

"Don't play coy with me. I know what you're capable of, and reserved isn't part of it."

Crap. I could already feel my body responding to him. Half a world away. "You're in a lab filled with other people. Not the ideal time to pop our phone sex cherry."

"Was," he replied, the sound of a door whining open following. "I *was* in a lab full of students."

"Where are you going now?" My heart was hammering—so much for sleep. Although he did have a point—there was nothing like an orgasm to knock me out.

"The teacher's lounge."

"The teacher's lounge?"

"Nobody's in here this late anyway."

My head shook. "You're going to have phone sex in the teacher's lounge?"

"Hey, another boyhood fantasy about to get checked off the list."

I made sure to sigh loud enough he heard it. "The depths of your perversion know no end."

"Oh, yeah?" The sound of another door creaking open came through the phone. "Then why don't you slide that pretty hand of yours inside those panties and tell me whose perversion knows no end too."

"Soren," I hissed.

"Time to close your mouth now, girlie. Time to open your legs."

My throat went dry.

"Touch yourself. I want to know how wet you are." There was some noise in the background, rustling, and then I heard the telltale sound of a zipper being lowered. "I want to know how bad you want me right now."

"Did you seriously just unzip your pants in the teacher's lounge, Soren Decker?"

"I seriously just did. But don't worry, I locked the door." His voice hitched, followed by a low rumble I was familiar with.

"Are you . . . ?" I swallowed.

"Mm-hmm," he answered on speaker now. "Are you?"

Holy everything unholy. He was touching himself right this very second. He was stroking himself, thinking of me, imagining moving inside me . . .

My hand dropped to my stomach and slid beneath my underwear as I turned on the speakerphone. I'd barely touched myself and could feel that familiar spiral of release. He didn't miss the whimper that crested from my lips.

"How bad do you want me right now, Hayden? Tell me how bad you want it."

My nipples pressed through the cotton of my nightgown as my hand moved lower. I was so wet, my finger slipped right inside, sending my back off the mattress when I imagined him moving inside me instead.

"I want you so badly, Soren." I whispered his name the way he liked to hear me say it when we came together. As my reward, I heard his rough growl. "I'm fucking myself with my finger right now, pretending it's your cock."

"Shit," he grunted. "I love that filthy mouth. We should have given this phone sex thing a try weeks ago."

"Enjoying yourself?" My other hand slid around my breast, squeezing it as my finger continued to shuttle inside my body.

"You have no idea. I am so close to coming; I'm going to ease off until you're close."

My legs fell open wider as I pictured him above me, holding them open as he pushed inside. "Even when it's over the phone, you insist on us coming together?"

"Twice the fun, Hayden."

If I really focused, I could hear him moving. I could hear his hand thrusting down his cock, the sound of his uneven breaths. The picture of him became so vivid, I could see him inside the teacher's lounge, stretched out on a couch, his zipper undone, his body ready for mine.

I imagined going to him, stripping as I went, sheathing his body inside of mine the moment I covered his lap. It would only take a few strokes before I'd feel him kick inside me, his release filling me as he held himself deep inside, his eyes demanding my own.

A cry rose from my chest, his name right after.

"Come for me, Hayden. Let me hear it," he ordered.

I didn't hold my cries back. I didn't hold anything back as my orgasm surged through me. I wasn't thinking about thin walls or anyone listening in. All I thought about was him. Giving me what I needed, exactly when I needed it.

Soren's release tangled with mine, his groans of pleasure more subdued. For a few minutes after, there was only the sounds of our breaths. Hard and heavy at first, tapering into a more level balance.

"Suddenly, this long distance thing doesn't seem so impossible." Soren's voice was low and hoarse, his chuckle the same.

My body was still buzzing from my orgasm as a wave of sleepiness came over me. Curling into my pillow, I pulled the blankets around me.

"Nothing's impossible. Especially you and me." As I closed my eyes, I realized I'd said that more to convince myself than to agree with him.

CHAPTER Twenty

missed him. Not just in yearning this time, but in actuality.

I'd physically missed him.

My damn flight home had arrived late, which had become the trend. What were these airlines doing in business if they couldn't get an arrival time right, or even close to right, three times in a row?

My mood was beyond sour by the time I'd claimed my bag and flagged a cab outside of the airport that afternoon. If my flight had arrived on time, like, I don't know, people planned on, that would have given Soren and me one hour and forty-five minutes together before he had to leap on the team bus to head to Pittsburgh for their games this weekend. Or was it Providence? I couldn't remember.

One hour and forty-five minutes. It had been ten days since we'd seen each other, and it would be another eleven before we could see each other again. Yes, I was counting, and yes, that one hour and forty-five minutes was every-thing when we had nothing else.

The journey up those six flights of stairs seemed im-possible. The only reason I'd flown back home for two days was so I could see Soren for barely two hours. Now I wasn't going to see him. I should have just stayed in Paris and caught up on sleep. Or seen some of the sights every-one had been telling me to give a try. I'd spent weeks in Paris and had yet to see more than the inside of a hotel room, a cab, or the interior of some building I was either shooting in or walking inside of.

Eventually, I made it to the sixth floor. Eventually, I made myself unlock the door and move inside.

The apartment was quiet and empty, as I'd known it would be. The scent of his soap and shampoo lingered in-side the bathroom, which made me want to lock myself in there and breathe it in until there was nothing left to breathe.

As I passed the kitchen, I noticed how tidy it was. The faucet was even shining, it was so spotless. When I rounded into the main part of the apartment, I didn't notice how clean it was. All I saw were the flowers he'd left on the table for me. White daisies. He'd propped a little note beside it that read, *You're worth the wait.*

My eyes burned as I reread it. We'd been together almost a month now and had shared only a couple days together. The rest had been filled with short phone calls and scattered texts.

The daisies were perfect. He'd recalled the time we'd walked by a flower vendor, and I talked about how undervalued daisies were. Simple, overlooked, considered cheap and passé by most, but they were hardy and steadfast, far outliving their floral rivals. A little water, and they could last forever.

I was just about to head to the kitchen for a vase when a knock thudded at the door. When I reached it, I checked the peephole as I could hear Soren instructing me to do if he'd been here.

I wasn't expecting anyone, and I definitely wasn't expecting this guest.

"Mrs. Decker," I greeted as I pulled open the door. "You just missed him. He left a few hours ago."

Mrs. Decker stood in the hallway with that warm, open look I'd seen so often on her son. I didn't know I'd been about to cry until I felt the tears on my face.

"Oh, sweetheart. Come here." She didn't wait for me to come to her; she came to me, her arms winding around me securely. She patted my back and stayed quiet, letting me get out the tears and emotions I'd been holding inside for weeks. Finally, she gave me another squeeze before leaning back so she could look at my face. "Long distance relationships aren't popular for a reason. They hurt like hell."

Soren had told his family about us a few weeks ago. The not-just-roommates us. I hadn't seen any of them since the time I visited for dinner, but Mrs. Decker had the kind of spirit a person could go years without seeing and feel right at home with when they reunited.

"I miss him," I said, wiping my eyes as I took a few breaths to calm myself down.

"And he misses you." She brushed the back of her hand across my cheek. "You miss each other so much because you care about each other so much. That's a good thing. I know it doesn't feel good all the time—times like these—but believe me, that's a rare feeling to have for another human being. A rare one for them to feel in return."

I took the tissue she pulled from her purse to wipe my nose. I was a sobbing, snotty mess. "Yeah?"

"Trust my fifty-plus years of life experience." She nodded. "Absolutely."

"It feels like we're having a long-distance relationship living in the same, small apartment." I glanced over my shoulder, teeth sinking into my lip when I noticed he'd washed and folded a pile of my laundry while I'd been gone. "Right when life brought us together, fate's trying to keep us apart. Like it's trying to tell us something." My hand rubbed my arm as I shifted in place. There were probably better people to have this conversation with than the mother of the man I cared about, but she was right here, and I felt as though I needed to get all of this off my chest right now.

Her hand went beneath my chin, tipping it up. She had a soft smile on her face. "The only thing it's telling you is that you're going to have to fight for what you want. That you've got something special to fight for." Her light eyes—the same shade as Soren's—shone and made me miss him more. "Soren, he's a good guy, the best kind. He'll love you forever, no matter what happens. He fell in love with you—he'll stay in love with you. He won't let the distance come between you two. It's up to you if you'll let it."

A small weight rolled off of me. The distance was daunting, but it wasn't the only obstacle we faced. It wasn't the one I feared most. My abandonment and trust issues ran deep. They felt woven into my character. I wished I didn't have them, I wished I could wish them away, but that didn't change the reality of their effect on me.

Soren hadn't left me. But why was he always gone?

He hadn't abandoned me either. But why did I feel so alone?

"I recognize that brooding look. I've seen the same one on my son's face a lot lately." Mrs. Decker's arm linked through mine before she steered me out of the apartment. "You know where I take him when he's missing you so badly it looks like he's about to lose his mind?"

My head shook as I locked the door.

"His favorite bakery. It's amazing what a little conversation and a lot of peanut butter pie can do to brighten even the darkest of moods."

CHAPTER
Twenty-One

F inally. I was about to see him. Not through the filter of a FaceTime app either. I was about to hear his voice—not through the speaker of a phone. I was about to touch him—have him touch back—instead of imagining what it felt like.

The fall handbag campaign we'd shot in the French countryside had wrapped up a few days earlier than expected, which never happened. My flight had arrived on time too, which also never happened.

It was almost like fate had decided to stop fighting dirty and give us a hand.

I hadn't bothered to pack a bag this time. Instead, I'd rushed to the airport, found the first flight to New York I could get on, and smiled the whole flight home. That smile deepened when I arrived at the baseball stadium.

Soren had home games this weekend, and I was going to them all. I wasn't going to let him out of my sight until I had to board the plane back to Paris on Monday. I'd been racking up some serious frequent flyer points over the past couple of months. The client flew me back and forth as needed, but they didn't view "as needed" as every or every other weekend to see my boyfriend back in the States.

So most flights I shelled out my own cash for, but other than sending money back home and stowing some away for a rainy day, it was the best money I spent.

It was a warm day, and the stands were pretty full for a community college baseball game. I guessed it had a lot to do with Soren's team setting some new records and there being talk about the team's starting catcher getting serious attention from pro scouts.

Soren didn't like to talk about it too much—he said he didn't want to jinx it and claimed baseball players were superstitious for a reason—but I bragged about him to anyone who would listen. He was going to do it. His dream. He was going to achieve it.

At the same time I was thrilled for him, I couldn't ignore the nervousness I felt when I thought about what that meant. Soren would be done with school this spring. From there, he'd either be moving on to a four-year degree or getting signed by a major league team. He might not have talked about it in detail, but that didn't mean I didn't know what was coming.

Where would he go? Would he go? What would it mean for us?

Those were questions we were both happy to ignore, preferring instead to live in the moment. The future was too damn uncertain.

It took me a while of scanning the home side benches to find a space I could squeeze into. He didn't know I was coming, and I couldn't wait to surprise him. After excusing and squeezing myself into the free square of bench a few rows behind the dugout, I surveyed the scoreboard. The Devils were up a few runs, and it was the seventh inning stretch. Which explained why no one was out on the field, though a handful of players tossed a ball back and forth in front of the dugout.

I didn't see him at first—he was warming up with one of the team's pitchers down the right field line. My chest ached once I did see him. My lungs hurt from realizing all of those miles that had kept us apart all came down to these last few yards.

He had on his catcher's mitt, crouching low as he focused on each pitch coming in. The smack of the ball as it hit his mitt. The whoosh it made as he sent it flying back. The intent look on his face under his mask, the curl of his hair around the brim of his cap, the muscles working beneath the snug uniform. I had to catch myself from leaping over the fence and running to him right then.

Security probably would have frowned on a crazed woman charging the field toward the team's star player.

Folding my hands in my lap, I adjusted the red Devils hat Soren had picked up for me, determined to stay in my seat. My plan faltered when I noticed someone emerge from the dugout and walk toward him. It wasn't another player—it was a girl. She was wearing a team jersey and a pair of khaki slacks—clearly she was a part of the team—but I felt my hackles rise.

Especially when I noticed what was bouncing rather impressively as she ran toward him. The girl had it in the front and in the back, curves where I had planes. I wasn't the only one in the stands staring at her either. Half the male spectators were too.

Even her shiny, blonde ponytail bounced as she jogged toward him.

When she paused beside him, Soren lifted his hand at the pitcher to stop him. She was holding out a water bottle. When he nodded and tipped his head back, she sprayed a stream into his mouth. Once he'd swallowed, she said something else, to which he nodded, followed with another squirt of water directly into his mouth.

It looked like he said thanks after that drink, and she smiled and gave his shoulder a squeeze.

My blood felt scorching hot when her fingers curled into his shoulder. I felt very possessive of that shoulder at the moment. That was *my* shoulder.

With a wave, she flounced back to the dugout, bouncing her hard-to-ignore assets as she went. Weren't water girls supposed to be, I don't know, not so perky and pretty?

Soren was already back to throwing the ball with the pitcher before she'd moved away—his eyes never strayed from the ball—but none of that could calm the jealous lunatic who had busted out of her straitjacket.

After a few more throws, he rose and moved toward the dugout. He only made it a few steps before he froze in place. He'd seen me. Even through his mask, I could see his eyes blink a few times, like he was clearing his vision, before they rounded.

When he slid his mask up over his ball cap, his grin took up half of his face. Moving like he was running the bases, his direction changed from the dugout to where I was stationed at the fence. People in the stands were starting to notice, and the ones closest to me on the bench stepped a little aside, like they were expecting his next move.

They were right. Soren didn't slow or say a word when he made it to the fence—he just leapt over it in one smooth motion, his body smashing into mine as soon as he'd cleared it.

A note of surprise managed to escape me before his mouth covered mine at the same time his arms circled me, one at a time. I didn't care who was watching or how many were. I didn't care about anything besides the man holding me, his lips trying to make up for days of separation. His mitt pressed into my back, drawing me closer, and somewhere in the midst of my hands running over him, I managed to knock his catcher's mask from his head.

A cheer rolled through the crowd as we kissed. When they started chanting "Charge!" Soren's smile curved against my mouth.

"That's one hell of a hello." My arms were tied around his neck, and I wasn't sure I could let go so he could finish a few more innings.

His lips touched mine once more. "Just getting warmed up." His hips barely tipped into mine to reveal just how warmed up he was getting. Even through his cup, I could feel him.

"Hey, Lover Boy!" An older man wearing a uniform emerged from the dugout, waving at the two of us sandwiched together against the fence. "You've got a game to finish."

Soren lifted his arm at his coach, dropping his forehead to mine and taking one long breath. "Thank you. Best surprise ever."

After leaping back over the fence, he snagged the mask that had toppled over it and started toward the dugout, running backward so he didn't have to look away.

"Hit a home run for me." I fought a laugh when he bumped into the edge of the dugout.

He rubbed his shoulder mindlessly, a permanent smile on his face. "How many?"

My eyes rolled. "Show-off."

After he disappeared into the dugout as the other team took the field, I needed a minute to put my feet back on the ground. That might have been the best welcome in the history of welcomes. My toes were tingling from that kiss, and everything else tingled from the relief of having him close again.

It was hard to go back to sitting on a bench, but I loved watching Soren play baseball. I didn't know much about the game, other than the basics, but I didn't come to watch the game. I came to watch him. His passion for the sport was evident in everything he did on the field—he moved with the kind of ease that suggested he'd been born to play the sport.

When he emerged from the dugout a couple minutes later, he took a few practice swings before making his way back over to my area of the fence. "You want that homer going over right, left, or center field?"

I leaned forward in my seat. "Your ego's showing. Might want to cover it up a bit before you offend someone."

Soren tapped his cleats with the end of the bat, his mouth working. "Where do you want it?"

"What's going to be the hardest?"

His shoulder lifted, like left was just as easy as right, as was center.

"Ego level, obscene."

"I'd do anything for you, including lie, cheat, steal, and kill. Hitting a home run is nothing."

Holding my stare until the last second, he turned to move into the on-deck position. I thought that was what it was called anyway. Deck something.

As Soren took his place at home plate, he looked perfectly calm. Focused. The first pitch the pitcher threw, he swung at. There was the crack as the bat connected, the whiz of the ball driving deep, then the roar of a crowd jumping to its feet as Soren Decker added another home run to his stats.

Before he rounded first, he glanced over at where I was glued to the fence. He winked, a smirk already in place.

The last couple of innings went the same way. Soren managed to knock one more out of the park before the end of the game, along with catching a couple of fouls at the top of the ninth.

It was hard to watch anyone else on his team. I wasn't the only one drawn to number twenty-three's every move though. He stood out. A lot. His team was good—god knew I'd had to listen to him brag about them all season—but they looked like a bunch of little leaguers compared to Soren. He played at a different level. It wasn't just the filter I saw Soren through that led me to that conclusion—it was the way it was.

Soren was going to make it. He was going to live his dream of playing for some professional team. At the same time my eyes welled with pride, they stung from the tears of bittersweetness.

My dream had come to life. His dream was about to.

What neither of us seemed to want to acknowledge was that those dreams would rip us apart.

After the game wrapped up—another impressive win by the Devils—I went to wait for Soren outside of the locker room. He must have taken the world's fastest shower in the history of locker rooms, because I'd only been waiting for a minute before the locker room door threw open and out he came. Or out he *ran*.

His gear bag over his shoulder, he wrangled me under his other arm and turned to leave the park. His lips met mine as we moved.

"Kissing and walking can be dangerous."

His arm rung around my neck deeper. "I'll take my chances."

"Good game, Soren!" someone shouted from behind us.

When I glanced over my shoulder, I found *her*—waving and smiling and focusing on him.

My man. Mine.

Because I clearly didn't have a possessiveness issue or anything.

"Thanks! Catch you later," he called back before weaving us through the park fences. "Now, where were we . . ." When his head turned to kiss me again, he didn't miss the look on my face. "We weren't there. Definitely weren't there."

"Who is she?" I asked.

"Who's who?"

My eyes lifted. "That girl who just called for you in a crowd full of people when you were kissing your girl-friend."

He had to clear his throat and look away because he was about to smile. Glad my jealous streak amused him. "That's Alex. She's a PT student, so she gives the team a hand if anyone's injured or anything like that."

"So, what? She gives you deep-tissue massages?"

"Is the follow-up to that question going to involve something about candles, oil, and nudity? Because you seem a little . . ."—when he noticed my eyebrows raising, he cleared his throat—"*sensitive* on the subject."

"I'm just asking a question."

Soren wound my braid up in his hand as we moved onto the sidewalk. "No deep-tissue massages. Bags of ice, heat packs, stretching us out, that kind of thing."

"Stretching you out?" I repeated, although not in the same innocent tone.

"I am not going to be able to say anything right when it comes to this topic, so can we stop talking about Alex now, please? She helps out the team and is a total science nerd."

"How do you know that?"

The corners of his eyes creased. He took a few moments before answering. "Because she's my lab partner."

I stopped moving down the sidewalk. "She's your lab partner? So she's not just on your team, icing and heating and stretching you guys out, she's also buddied up with you every week in lab?" His arm fell away when I moved in front of him. "The lab partner you've been spending hours with over the past couple of months?"

I moved a step back and crossed my arms. It wasn't really him I was upset with; it was our situation. Soren and I had had a small handful of hours together over the past month, while some other girl had gotten loads more. I hated that. I hated that I hated that to begin with.

"Why didn't you tell me?" I asked.

His head was tipped as he watched me, his hair still dripping from the shower he'd rushed through to get to me sooner. I felt like an idiot for having this conversation on a busy sidewalk, but I also knew I couldn't let it go without getting it out. Communication was what all of those relationship books said was the key to making a relationship work. Sometimes I wondered if they needed to add a preface to that, like *constructive* communication.

"I didn't tell you because I didn't think it mattered."

"You didn't think it mattered that some woman who looks like a playmate is a part of your team and also your lab partner?"

Soren's hand reached for me. Like a magnet, mine reached back. "No," he stated.

"Why?"

"Because I don't see her like that."

"You don't see her as being Miss December if this whole science nerd thing doesn't work out?"

A corner of his mouth jerked up. "No, I don't see her. I don't see anyone else." Soren stepped toward me, his eyes on fire. "I see *you*. Only you." Each word was slow, its own statement. "Everyone else blurs into a kind of homogenous stew."

I let him pull me tight against him, my anger already melting away. "We're not a melting pot anymore apparently. We're a tossed salad—that's the PC way to describe Americans now."

He slid my ball cap so the bill was backward, just like his. "I'm not talking about Americans. I'm talking about what you brought up—other girls." He pulled me to the side of the sidewalk to give us some privacy. "And I didn't say melting pot. I said stew. Homogenous stew."

"How's that different?"

"Every bite looks the same." His thumb brushed the inside of my wrist. "Inedible."

"Inedible?" I smiled. "I don't think that's the word you're looking for. You don't eat girls."

His eyes flashed, a challenge in them. "I'm planning on eating the one standing in front of me as soon as I get her behind a locked door."

My gaze moved around us, making sure no one overheard. "Behind a locked door and on top of our bed?"

Soren's mouth dropped to my neck. He gave a slight yank on my braid, arching my neck back to give him better access. When his lips touched me, a jolt shot down my spine. When he started to suck at my skin, his tongue breaking through every few pulses, it felt like he was between my legs right then from the way my body started to spiral out of control.

"Up against the wall," he whispered against the throbbing patch of skin. "I want to be on my knees in front of you right now." His hand tugged my braid hard, his mouth sucking at my skin once more. "That's the way a real man worships his woman."

CHAPTER
Twenty-Two

"I'm pretty sure I'm going to get drafted in June. Coach has been hearing things." Soren's hand hadn't stopped moving up and down my back as we lay in bed after . . .

After lots of things—sweaty, noisy, great things.

"With the way you play?" I replied, glancing up from where my head was resting on his chest. "Any team in the country would be stupid not to want you to play for them."

He smiled, staring at the ceiling. "It's really happening."

It really was. I wanted this so badly for him—I just wished time would slow down or our circumstances were different. I wished it wouldn't mean the end. "You'll probably get signed to some team in California or somewhere far away."

His hand stopped moving. "I'm not your dad. You know that, right?" He tipped my chin up just enough I was able to look at him. "If I get drafted—"

"When," I said.

"When I do, it's a conversation we'll have. We'll make that decision together."

My eyes left his, my leg tangled tighter around us. I needed to be preparing myself to let go, instead of holding on tighter. I needed to focus on falling out of love with him instead of falling more in love. My life was here and in Paris. His life was going to be somewhere out there, and if luck had anything to do with where he was drafted, it would be in the city farthest from New York. That was my personal history with luck and the men in my life.

"This is your dream, Soren. It's not something you discuss with a girl you've been dating a couple of months."

His body tensed below me. "Yeah, this is my dream." His words were just as tense. "That's exactly why I *will* discuss it with the woman I love when it comes to that."

My teeth worked my lip, trying to keep the tears away. "We'll see," I whispered.

"Yeah," he said, not a whisper at all, "we will."

After that, we were quiet. Neither of us might have wanted to talk to each other right then, but we stayed close. His arm didn't loosen around me, his chin tucked back over my head, and I worked my body a bit tighter around him.

Our time together was too rare and too valuable to spend it apart when we were both in the same zip code. Our time felt that much more valuable when I counted the weeks until June. There weren't many.

I didn't know how soon Soren would have to move to the city of the team that picked him—I didn't know much about any of it—but instead of asking, I stayed ignorant. It felt better not to know than to be overwhelmed with looming dates and details.

Twilight was straining through the windows, which meant hours had passed since we'd burst through the apartment door, tugging at each other and tearing off clothes. We'd blown way past dinnertime, but I couldn't think of anything important enough to leave this bed, to leave him.

Food. Water. The call of nature?

None of it appealed to me the way he and that bed did.

A couple of months ago, Soren had taken down the partitions and dragged our twin beds together to create whatever size that was. It was a little strange having a big seam going down the center of our bed, but Soren always took that spot, letting me have one side or the other. In the corner he'd shoved them, the partitions had started to collect dust. The walls had been taken down, but they weren't gone. They were still there. Waiting for us to put them back up.

Or, I supposed, waiting for me to put them back up.

"You never talk about him—your dad." Soren's voice pushed into the silence, his words hesitant. "But I feel like he's somehow always in the room with us."

"Because that's not creepy." I pinched his side, attempting to keep this topic light. I couldn't do heavy—not when it came to the man who'd brought me into a world he wanted no part of.

"You know what I mean."

So much for the attempt at light and easy. Time to address it from another angle—the dismissive one. "I let go of him the same way he let go of us. That's behind me."

Soren's throat moved against my head. "How does anyone ever put that behind them though?"

I wasn't expecting tears. That's what gave them their chance. "He left us."

I was able to swipe the first tear away before he noticed, but the rest came too quickly to intercept. They fell down my face onto his chest, down the hollows his ribs formed. He held me as I cried, his clutch feeling impossibly strong, yet it wasn't the least bit confining. He shared his strength instead of exerting it over me.

"No warning. No note," I continued. "He just left for work one day and never came back. One wife, three daughters, he left it all behind to go live a different life."

Soren didn't say anything right away. I'd counted five times his chest had fallen, five times it had risen before he replied. "How do you know something didn't happen to him?"

It would have made all our lives easier if something had happened to him like that. I'd often wondered if it would have even made his own easier.

"Every year on our birthdays, he'd send us an envelope with a five-dollar bill in it. No card. No note. Just a crumpled bill that smelled like cigarettes."

My stomach turned when I remembered that smell. So strong, it seemed toxic. Each one of those five-dollar bills I received had been ripped into dozens of uneven pieces and burned in whatever fire I could find. Five dollars was a lot of money for us back then, especially for a girl who never had the luxury of extra spending money, but I'd never been tempted to keep one of those bills. Not once.

"My mom doesn't have a degree or anything—they got married right out of high school when she got pregnant with me, and after that, she was too busy having us and raising us and working." A few more tears spilled when I admitted to Soren that I was the reason my parents had married.

If she hadn't gotten pregnant with me, if they hadn't felt obligated to "do the right thing," both of their lives could have been different. My mom had dreams. She must have. What eighteen-year-old didn't? He'd probably had some too. Both had given them up because of me.

I didn't want to have that kind of guilt on me again. Especially not from someone I loved the way I loved Soren. I wasn't holding anyone else back from living the life they had planned pre-me entering the picture.

"Is that why you've never had any serious relationships?" Soren asked, his hand busy twisting through my mess of hair. "Because of your dad?"

"Would you be eager to get tied up in one after experiencing that?"

My head moved when lifted his shoulders. "I guess not."

"I wasn't the only one who waited forever to get involved with someone. What was your reason?" I asked, beyond eager to shine the conversation light on him after that surprise interrogation.

"I was too busy with school, sports, and a part-time job to squeeze in time for girls." His fingers broke through the last couple of plaits left of my braid. "And I was waiting."

"For what?"

"We've been over this." He sighed in a way that made me picture his eyes rolling. "For you."

As a smile formed, I wiped the last remnants of tears from my face. "You say the most romantic things to me when we're tangled up naked in bed together."

His arm hooked around me harder, dragging more of my body over his. "Best time to say them."

"More like the most opportune time to say them," I replied, wiggling against him to hint at what I meant.

"So very opportune." He grinned at me, rubbing himself against me a few times.

"Last time you imbued yourself upon me, you claimed it was because the third time was a charm." My hips straddled him as I sat up, taking control as I rubbed myself against him. "What's your excuse this time?"

"Fourth time's just for fun." His hands curled into my hips as he stared down at me sliding against him. His smile folded into a smirk when he saw his steel wet and shiny from my body's arousal. "Just for fucking fun."

"Are you using that as the verb or the adjective?" When his brows came together, I explained, "Are we supposed to have fun fucking, or have a fucking fun time? There's a difference, so how do you mean it?"

He tipped my hips, positioning himself. "I'll show you how I mean it. If you have any questions after, feel free to voice them then." When he pushed into me, my cry filled the apartment. "If you have any voice left when I'm done with you."

Just as I was almost seated over his lap, a hard knock sounded at the door.

Our faces went blank as we must have both arrived at the same conclusion as to who it might have been.

Soren relaxed a second after. "My mom's out of town for the weekend with some girlfriends. It's not her."

"Thank god," I breathed, sliding off him. The look he gave me as I did reminded me again how much power I had over him. Especially when it was my body doing the talking. "Two-minute intermission."

He sat up and reached for his sweats. As he tugged them on, he looked like a child who'd just been told they wouldn't get dessert for a month.

"Why am I answering the door again?" he asked when he glanced at me trying to untangle the covers to throw over myself.

I answered with a shrug.

His groan echoed into the room as whatever he must have seen through the peephole warranted a door opening. I reached for his shirt to throw on in an emergency. He greeted someone at the door, and the person who responded didn't sound familiar. There was some shuffling, something about needing a signature, and two good-byes.

"Delivery." Soren's voice was guarded which, naturally, put me on guard. "For you." When he rounded into the room, he was holding a giant bouquet of flowers and a rectangular silver box.

My forehead pinched together. The bouquet was so large, it blocked his face and most of his upper half. "Are they from you?"

After he'd set them on the table, his gaze automatically drifted to the bouquet of daisies he'd picked up for me on the last visit. They were still going strong, the water looking freshly changed in the clear vase. Soren's gaze moved between the two bouquets, reading too far into it if I was interpreting the look in his eyes correctly.

"No. They're not," he finally answered.

Rising from the bed, I padded toward the table and took the silver box from him when he held it out. "Who would send me flowers?"

"Pick a male name out of any phone book and you have an answer." Soren's arms crossed as he watched me open the box.

Inside was a stack of this upcoming month's edition of French *Vogue*. There was a sticky note on the cover of the top one that had "Page 42" scribbled down.

Soren pulled the notecard from the bouquet, his expression darkening as he read it. Flipping it around, he recited it. "'On to bigger and better things.' Since it's signed with a giant E, I can take a guess who these are from. I don't know a lot of tools who think they're such a hotshot, they can send a girl flowers and sign their name with one letter and call it good."

Even I felt a little annoyed he'd done this, but I couldn't let Soren know that. It would only make him more pissed. "He sent them as a congratulations. For my first official spread in an international magazine." I lifted the copy on top for him to see.

Soren gave the bouquet one more suspicious look before taking the magazine and flipping through it. "Your first international spread?"

The dark notes had left his face, his eyes shining when they met mine. He was excited for me—proud of me. I was so wrapped up in that, I forgot which spread I'd shot. I really could have used those few seconds to prepare him for what he was about to see.

I knew the moment he found the right page. The look that broke across his face was the exact one I guessed any boyfriend would have when he saw his girlfriend pictured as I was in an international magazine.

"You're . . ." He blinked at the photo, moving it around like it might change in a different light.

"I was shot nude," I said in the best even, straight-forward tone I could. "The client wanted the focus on their accessories. They felt clothing would distract from that objective."

"They wanted the focus on their accessories?" Soren rolled his neck, cracking it a couple of times. "And they thought putting them on a naked woman was the way to achieve that?"

I had to chew the inside of my cheek to keep from grinning because he kind of had a point. "Three things," I said, giving a preemptive wince as he flipped to the next page. His eyes went dinner-plate round. "One, it's tasteful nude. Nothing that you're worried about showing is showing in any of those shots. Believe me, I checked."

"Believe me, I'm checking too."

Again, I had to chew the inside of my cheek to keep from laughing over the irony that he was getting upset over some tastefully posed nude shots of me in a magazine when I was standing two feet in front of him, just as naked with everything showing.

"Two, the accessories actually do stand out if you are able to step out of those subjective, concrete boots and try on a pair of objective loafers."

He made a face that suggested he doubted that.

"And three, Europeans are different about nudity than we are. It's natural and respected over there, instead of taboo and dirty the way we make it over here."

"This is supposed to make me feel better about my girlfriend being naked on . . ."—he counted off the pages of the spread, one by one, a new crease forming in his forehead with each one—"ten pages?"

"Would it make you feel better if you knew that French *Vogue*'s target audience is ninety-five percent women, and that other five percent are men who—this one's for you, baseball player—bat for the other team?"

He was still gaping at the pages like he'd just found out I was the centerfold in one of the trashiest porn magazines on the market. "Does it look like any of that makes me feel better?"

My feet padded toward him. "No." Slipping my hands behind his back, I tried to press myself against him and distract him from the magazine. It wasn't working. "Does this kind of stuff make you uncomfortable? Is this something I should have talked with you about or warned you about?"

I swallowed because part of me already knew I should have talked the shoot over with Soren. Not because I felt like I needed his approval or because he was the type who felt like he needed to give it, but out of respect for him.

He stared at the last two pages of the spread for another minute before setting the magazine on the table. He didn't put it face down though; he left it open. His eyes moved between the flowers and the magazine, emotions warring on his face.

"Congratulations." He found a smile as he hooked an arm around me and pulled me to him. "A ten-page, and believe me, I counted three times, spread in French *Vogue*."

"You say that like you know all about French *Vogue*."

"I might not be a member of that five percent male demographic, but I've learned enough from you to know a major model moment when I see one." His lips pressed into my forehead, but they felt a little stiff. Forced. "I'm proud of you."

I breathed in the scent of him. The heady aroma of sweat, man, and sex. "You looked like you were about to rush to every magazine stand in the world and pull all the French *Vogue* from the shelves." I inhaled him again, my hands gripping him tighter. "You don't have to pretend to like everything I do. You don't have to ever pretend with me."

He shifted against me. "I'm not going to tell you not to pose naked again—that's not the guy I am, and you're not the woman who'd let herself be told by a guy what to do either—but I don't have to like that anyone on the planet can turn to page forty-three and see my girl without her clothes on."

We both seemed to relax after he voiced what he had. His arms hung more naturally around me. Mine felt more secure around him.

"It's not like I'm full-frontal and spread eagle." I prodded him.

The last lines bled from his face before he stepped back so he could motion at me standing in front of him. "This should be, like, proprietary or something."

If he hadn't been fighting a smile, that would have earned him a glare or a box of magazines sailing his direction.

"Proprietary?" I repeated, trying to keep a stern face.

His eyes wandered over my naked body as he nodded the entire time. "Seemed better than saying mine." His eyes flashed when they met mine. "Less uncivilized."

"Uncivilized? You?" I didn't temper the sarcasm in my voice. "Never."

"I'll show you uncivilized," he said, palming his erection straining through his sweats. Just as I took the first step toward him, eager to pick up where we'd left off at "fourth time's just for fun," he cleared his throat. "Right after you try to explain to me why your agent sent you flowers, *red roses*, the very same day you made it home to your boyfriend at the very address you live at with him."

This conversation was not going to end well. No matter how I answered, it wouldn't change the conclusion he'd arrived at.

"Because he's my agent? Because he wanted to say congrats for my first big spread in the most iconic fashion magazine in the world?"

The veins in his forearms were showing through his skin. They did that whenever we got into an argument or Ellis was the topic of conversation. "Why the question mark in your answer?"

"For the same reason there was an exclamation mark in your accusation," I fired right back. "Because this is an argument neither of us is going to win."

Soren's hands secured at his hips, his neck rolling. "He needs to back off. He needs to back the fuck off before I make him."

My arms lifted at my sides. "He's my agent. The one who's done really big things for my career. How am I supposed to get him to 'back off'?"

"There's a difference between having a professional relationship and some man twice your age sending flowers to your apartment with some note that doesn't leave a lot to the imagination of what 'bigger and better things' are." My face must have looked blank because Soren blinked. "*Him.* He's waiting for you to move on to bigger and better him. Waiting for you to leave small, insignificant me."

"You're being insane. These are congratulations flowers."

"They're foreplay flowers. So when you run to him like he's planning, you're going to run straight into his bed. Also what he has planned."

"Disgusting. Stop it."

"Why else does an old skuzzy dude with his reputation send a young, naïve girl flowers?"

My back tensed. "I'm not naïve."

"You're proving you are right this minute by pretending these flowers and everything he's done to try to come between us isn't because his endgame is winding up between your thighs."

His words sent me staggering back like they'd shoved me. "You're jealous." My lip quivered. "Stop taking your insecurity out on me."

Soren's jaw moved beneath his skin. "This isn't jealousy. This is concern. This is me wanting to protect you."

My lip wobbled again as my eyes cast down. I knew that. God, I knew that, because he was good and selfless and didn't deserve this.

"I'm not jealous of him," he said, his finger stabbing toward the ground with each word. "If you were with him, then I'd be jealous of him. I don't trust him. I wouldn't trust him with a houseplant, let alone the woman I love. *That's* how I feel about him."

If I bit into my lip any harder, I was going to draw blood. My palms already felt like I'd broken the skin from the way my nails were digging into them. "You haven't heard me tell you that one girl you're always hanging around needs to back off, have you?"

Soren's brows came together. "What girl are you talking about? The only girl I'm always hanging around is you."

"We hardly see each other anymore." My voice was louder than I'd intended.

"Exactly." He motioned at me backing into the wall away from him. "You're still the only girl I'm hanging around."

My nails dug deeper into my palms as her name rose in my throat. "Alex. Your lab partner. The team's water girl, doctor, physical therapist, star-player blow-job bestower."

Soren backed up a step. "What did you just say?" The way he was looking at me was new. Like he didn't recognize me.

The storm inside me wouldn't quiet though. "Just because it hasn't happened doesn't mean she isn't ready to do it at the drop of your pants."

Now his veins were showing through his neck too. He made himself take a couple more steps back. "And I'm supposed to be the jealous one?"

I bit back what poured onto my tongue. That would have been useful a handful of sentences ago. "I'm sorry. You're right. I'm being petty and immature. I don't know what I'm saying right now." Moving around the apartment, I started to gather up my clothes. "I need some fresh air. Alone. To clear my head."

As I started for the bathroom, Soren broke in front of me, blocking my path.

"Soren, let me go."

"No."

"Soren—"

"Not without a fight."

"Isn't that what we just got into?" My arm flailed behind me, trying to dodge around him only to be blocked again. "I need a break before getting into another."

Soren's head fell back, a frustrated roar rumbling in his chest. "For Christ's sake, you're nineteen. I'm twenty. This is both of our first serious relationship." I rammed into his chest when he dodged in front of my next attempt to get around him. "Jealousy and immaturity are easy traps to fall into, so we're going to have to fight it, Hayden. We're going to have to fucking rise above all of that petty shit our peers get wrapped up in, because this, us"—he gestured between us—"deserves more than that. I'm not going to lose you over some stupid argument. I'm not going to let you lose me because I'm jealous of some guy who sends you flowers. We're not going to do that shit."

The fight to leave drained out of me. Instead of trying to push him away, my hands started pulling him closer.

"We just did all of that shit." I sighed, letting my head drop to his shoulder, the anger melting off of me.

"But we're not going to do it again." His hand sealed behind my neck, holding me to him. When I nodded against him, he said, "Promise?"

My eyes closed. "Promise."

"I promise too," he vowed in my ear. "I love you too much to lose you over something so little."

CHAPTER
Twenty-Three

That promise stayed with me, a piece of him I could take across the Atlantic and hold close at night when his arms couldn't hold me. He loved me too much to lose me. I loved him too much to lose him.

That was the truth.

Love wasn't enough was also a truth.

We needed more than that to keep us together. So much more. Our relationship was strained, delicate enough the way it was with him still living in New York. What would happen if—*when*—he was drafted? Even if we could survive him relocating to another state, there was so much more that came with being a professional athlete. The practice schedule was intense, the travel schedule was insane, the girls vying to land a pro baller were incalculable. We were both young; this was our first relationship. We'd started out as roommates and haphazardly fallen for each other.

This wasn't a recipe for a long-term relationship.

I knew that. I thought there were moments even he knew that.

I just wondered when—if—we'd go from knowing that to living it.

My flight home was on time—I considered anything within an hour of expected arrival on time—but the smile vanished from my face the moment I turned on my phone as the plane taxied the tarmac. Soren's team had been held over in Massachusetts, where they'd been playing this weekend. The game tonight had been cancelled due to lightning, so they'd rescheduled for the morning. He wouldn't get back into the city until late tomorrow night. My flight back to Paris left tomorrow night.

Tears burned in my eyes, exhaustion giving them their chance to surface. I'd only taken this flight because it had been two weeks since my last visit and I knew it would be another two before our schedules would overlap again. As it was, I'd spent a total of thirty hours on airplanes and in airports to spend twenty-four hours with him.

It was worth it. Half that amount of time would have been worth it.

But it wasn't worth coming back to an empty apartment and leaving it just as empty.

The apartment. I couldn't stand the thought of going back to another empty space.

As I moved through the airport at the pace I usually used when I was preparing to leave, I pulled out my phone. My thumb hovered over the list of numbers in my contacts. Most were business acquaintances and clients. I knew better than to call my mom and sisters. They were already worried about me with all of the traveling I'd been doing and that "dead" tone to my voice, as my mom called it.

I came close to calling Ariel and Jane, but our friendship had been waning over the past few months. I didn't blame them at all. It was hard enough for me to keep Soren's and my relationship going and I spent all my time with him when I did come back. I knew they'd answer if I called and I knew they'd invite me out if I asked, but I didn't want to feel like someone's tag-along tonight. I wanted to feel like someone's first choice, the way he made me feel.

Just as I was about to put my phone away, it rang. Soren had told me to call him the second I landed, but I hadn't been able to. Not yet. I needed a couple of hours for the disappointment to numb me before I called him.

"Hi, Ellis," I said after I'd debated answering it for so long, it almost went to voicemail.

"Hello, beautiful. Land safe and sound?"

I paused inside the baggage claim area, not sure where to tell the cab driver to go when I climbed in. "Safe and sound."

"I'm throwing a party tonight and wanted to invite you since your being Stateside is a rarity these days." Ellis's voice sounded out-of-character cheerful, which meant he'd probably already downed a couple of drinks at this party. "You can bring him along, of course. I'm sure he wouldn't like it if I tried pulling you away the moment you landed."

My chest ached. This was usually where Soren met me. Right here, inside the sliding glass doors of the baggage claim. Where he'd start running as soon as he saw me, throw himself against me so hard it made the air rush from both of our lungs, then he'd tangle my legs around him and wouldn't stop kissing me until we risked falling over from lack of oxygen.

I wiped the tear I could feel on my cheek, but my hand came away dry. It was a phantom tear. Kind of the way Soren felt right then.

"Actually, Soren got held over for the night with his baseball team."

"Too bad," Ellis clucked. "But the invitation still stands."

"I'm not really dressed for a party," I said, even though a party didn't sound like a bad idea. I'd done my best to keep as much distance from Ellis as I could out of respect for Soren—for *us*. He was my agent, which made total distance impossible, but I'd made strides in keeping our interactions limited to occasional phone calls, keeping to emails mostly.

"It doesn't matter what you're wearing. Trust me." The way he said it made it sound like there was a punch line. "Come on. You'll enjoy yourself, I guarantee it."

"You guarantee it?" My feet were moving through the door, like they'd made the decision for me.

"I won't allow you to leave until you have. I'll make it my personal mission."

I almost smiled, which was better than a certain frown. "I'm coming."

"So soon?" There was a note of amusement in his voice before he said good-bye.

When the cab finally rolled up to Ellis's place, the driver had to tell me we were there. I'd been trapped in a haze of contemplation ever since I settled into the back seat and gave him the address. I wasn't thinking about what I would tell Soren when he asked what I'd done to-night. I was thinking about the future, however much longer we had. My mind even hiccupped over my dad for a moment, before I could shuffle him back to the end of the deck where he belonged.

After thanking and paying the driver, I moved toward the front doors. The night Soren and I had been here, lines of cars and cabs had been staggered around the grounds. Tonight, there wasn't a single car in sight. Although, based on the size of the garage, Ellis could have parked twenty cars inside if he wanted to. It must have been a smaller dinner party or something.

Which suited me just fine. I was all for the distraction a get-together would provide, but I wasn't sure I could handle hundreds of people and the noise and endless intro-ductions that came with them.

After I rang the doorbell, the sound of footsteps ech-oed from inside. I was expecting one of the housekeeping staff Ellis seemed to have no shortage of, so I was sur-prised to find him capable of answering his own front door.

"That *was* quick." He greeted me with a tipped smile, dressed the way he had the day of our Sunday photo shoot. It must have been a casual party, which was even better.

He stepped aside to wave me in, holding out the drink he held as he closed the door. When I glanced at the golden liquid sloshing in the crystal glass, he said, "It's fresh."

"I'm okay right now. Thanks."

For some reason, Soren's voice from that first night I'd visited him at the pub echoed in my mind. When he'd given me the lecture on dark versus night, not leaving my purse open when I walked down the sidewalk, and never accepting an open drink from a guy.

Ellis wasn't just a guy though. He was my agent. The person who had my best interests in mind.

"So where's the party?" I asked as we moved through the house, ending inside an empty room that I supposed was a living room but was the size of an airplane hangar.

Ellis waved into the empty room before setting the drink on a table.

"I thought you said you were having a party." I swallowed as I scanned the empty room again.

"I am." He paused beside a table set with crystal bottles and poured a different drink. Lifting the glass at me, his expression flashed with something that made my gut uneasy. "A party of two."

I stayed in the doorway as he leaned into the table and emptied an inch of the glass in one swallow.

"Have you made your decision yet?" he asked.

My head shook as I forced myself to relax. We were having a business conversation; he was asking me the same question he'd asked over every phone call and email the last month. "No."

"You're becoming the face of European high fashion." He circled his glass at me before he took another drink.

"I know."

Ellis's shoulders lifted beneath the light linen shirt he'd left the top couple of buttons undone on. "Don't throw this all away. Especially on some boy who doesn't count."

My breath caught. "I know you're not talking about Soren."

Ellis's mouth moved. "You know I am."

"He's about to be drafted. He's about to make it big."

"Yes, yes, so I keep hearing. He's going to be the All-American athlete, and you already are the European supermodel." A chuckle rocked his chest. "How's that supposed to work, I wonder?"

It was one thing to have my own fears—it was another to have someone laugh at them in front of my face.

"Ellis, I'm leaving."

As I moved toward the front door, his chuckle followed me, somehow getting louder with every step I took away. I didn't realize why that was until I felt someone grab me from behind, before not-so-gently pushing me up against the closest wall.

"But I guaranteed you'd have a good time. I promised I wouldn't let you go until I gave it to you." His body pushed into mine, leaving nothing to speculation about how he had intended to do so. His breath reeked of alcohol; his face was flushed from it. He wasn't exactly holding me against my will, but he wasn't making it easy for me to get by him either.

Inhaling, I focused on his eyes, hoping I looked braver than felt. "You've crossed a line."

"No." He clucked his tongue, his eyes dropping to my mouth. "But I'm about to."

Inside my purse, my phone was vibrating against my hip. It was him. I knew it was. Whether he knew or had a feeling or a subconscious awareness of what was going on, Soren was calling to check on me. Because he cared. Because he wanted to protect me.

Because he'd been right all along about the man breathing against my neck right now, trying to charm me with his money or sway, his booze or his body.

"Let me go. I'm leaving."

"I can take your mind off of him. I can do more." His hips thrashed into mine, making me jolt. "I guarantee I can fuck better than some boy who was just discovering he had a dick while I'd was using mine to find supermodels' G-spots."

"Ellis, stop." I shoved his chest, which managed to give me a window of space to finish rushing to the door.

"I'm twice the man he is. You don't know what you're walking out on." From the sound of his voice, he'd stayed where I'd shoved him. He wasn't chasing me any longer.

"I know what I'm walking toward." I didn't look back as I threw the door open. "And you are *nothing* like the man he is."

After slamming the door, I rushed as far away from it as I could get before the adrenaline waned and my body felt limp. Pausing just outside the front gates, I leaned into one of the big brick pillars and let myself catch my breath as my tears expelled their own form of release. I had to lean forward from the emotions pouring out of me, my body trembling like I was hot with fever.

In my purse, my phone vibrated again. I couldn't answer. Not until I'd made it back to the apartment, taken a shower, and had a cup of tea. Not until I'd composed myself enough that I wouldn't break down in shaking sobs the moment I heard his voice. I knew when he found out what had happened, it would take a ton of convincing to keep him with his team so he could play the game tomorrow instead of jumping on the first bus, train, or plane out of there.

If he heard me crying as I described it, he'd run back to New York if he had to.

After I forced myself away from the front gate, I wanted to walk for a while before flagging a cab. The exertion felt good; each step seemed to drain another drop of emotion out of me in a way that didn't involve my tear ducts.

By the time I found a cab, there was a subway station nearby, so I decided to take that route instead. I'd missed the New York subway. I'd missed the smells and the people, the sights and the memory of the first time I'd ever taken one, when he'd stayed right beside me the entire time. Even then, protecting me from . . .

Myself.

My worst enemy. He hadn't been just trying to protect me from Ellis, but from my misguided impressions of the type of man Ellis was. He hadn't just been attempting to protect me from the creatures he swore lurked in the night, but from my small-town illusion that nothing bad could ever happen to me.

He'd protected me by using himself as a buffer.

By the time I'd crawled up to the sixth floor, I knew I couldn't wait for a shower and a cup of tea. I had to call him now. I had to hear his voice and feel that film of protection close around me, snug and airtight.

As soon as I shoved through the apartment door, I dialed his number. It rang a few times, which was unusual. He always picked up on the first or second ring. Roaming through the dark, empty apartment, I switched on every light I passed as his phone went to voicemail.

Punching his number again, I stopped when I noticed the glass vase filled with the bouquet of daisies. They were dead. A scatter of petals surrounded the base of the vase. Taking a closer look, I could see there was no water inside. From the look of how dried out they were, the water had been gone for days.

Why was I about to cry all over again over a bunch of wilted daisies?

I didn't have time to analyze my answer before the other end clicked.

"Hello?" It wasn't a voice I was expecting to hear.

Checking my phone, I made sure I'd punched in the right number. Soren's name was at the top of the screen.

"Hell-oo?" The same voice, just the most impatient version of the word.

Before I could reply, I heard some shuffling in the background. "Hayden?"

My lungs released. Okay, this was the voice I'd been expecting to hear.

Those lungs contracted back up when I realized a girl had answered Soren's phone.

"Who was that?" I asked.

He sounded like he was trying to move somewhere quieter. "I've been trying to call you all night. Did you make it into New York?"

My head shook. "Who just answered the phone, Soren?"

From his silence, I knew before he said it. "Alex. That was Alex."

My hand dropped to the table, needing it to support me. "Why is Alex answering your phone?"

He exhaled. "She wasn't supposed to answer my phone, but she took that upon herself since I left it on the table when I ran to the bathroom."

Nothing he was saying was making me feel any better. "Where are you?"

"Some pizza parlor next to the hotel we're staying at for the night. The whole team came over to have dinner."

Pizza. Dinner. The team. I repeated that to myself a few times to calm myself down after hearing some other woman answer my boyfriend's phone. The very woman I already had a thing or two against, based on the fact that she looked at Soren like she wanted to make him hers.

I was trying to figure out what to say next when I noticed something scattered around the table. A big envelope was ripped open, the contents spread out around it. All of it, from the one-way plane ticket to the condo listings to the ball cap, had one thing in common—Miami.

"Are you still at the airport? Your flight must have come in late again, right?"

Soren's voice drifted into the background as I shuffled through the rest of the papers. One of the condo listings pages had one of them circled with the words "all yours" scribbled by the pending sale box. A list of city highlights, the team's stats—there was even a demographic sheet of the city's occupants. Another circle over the ratio of single males to females, the number of woman staggeringly outnumbering the guys.

I crashed into the chair behind me, curling into my stomach for the second time that night.

"Because I need to talk to you about something before you head to the apartment. I need to—"

"Tell me you're leaving?" My eyes lifted to the one-way airline ticket on top of the pile. "In eleven days?"

On the other end? Silence.

"Why didn't you tell me? You promised you'd fucking tell me." My back shook as familiar pain coursed through me. "When were you going to tell me? When I flew home the next time you weren't here to meet me and I walked into an empty apartment?"

"Hayden—"

"You swore you wouldn't do this. You promised me you wouldn't bail on me the way he did. You swore to me!" My back shook as sobs erupted, despite the lack of tears left to shed.

"Hayden, what's wrong?" His voice was concerned, anxious, not at all the one I'd expected to hear from him right now—the one that accepted he'd just been caught. "What happened?"

My head fell into my hands, my eyes clamping closed. I needed to tell someone. I needed to tell *him*. But I couldn't. He didn't deserve my secrets anymore. He didn't deserve my dark, and he didn't deserve my light. I'd given them both and he'd let them wilt where he'd left them.

"What happened is that I just realized what a fool I've been for letting myself fall in love with you."

"Why does that make you a fool?" From his voice, I could tell he had to force his jaw to unlock with each word.

"Because you're not the person I thought you were. You're not the man you promised me you were."

"And you've realized all of that from some paper-work scattered around a table? Papers you have no idea what they have to do or not do with me?" Anger was coming through in his voice, which only spurred my own into being.

"Given the name S. Decker is listed on the front of the envelope all of this junk came out of, yeah, I think I know exactly what all of this has to do with you."

"You *think* you know," Soren said slowly, a puff of air coming from him right after. "Ellis told me about Paris. Did you know that? He told me about the flat you've put a down payment on."

"What?" The turn in the conversation shocked me out of my anger. "When did he tell you that?" My fingers rubbed my forehead as I felt my whole life falling down in pieces around me.

"A while ago. Another play to take me out of the game, no doubt." He paused, sounding like he'd just shoved through some door. "I figured you had your reasons. I gave you the benefit of the doubt that you'd explain your side of it to me when the time was right instead of calling you up and flaming you over the phone."

I'd been waiting for—*dreading*—this moment from the beginning. But I never would have guessed that this would be how we'd end. With an emotion-fraught phone call on the same night we'd planned to spend together.

"I haven't decided on Paris. I haven't made my decision." When I found myself staring at the wilted daisies, I made myself look away. "But clearly you *have* decided."

He'd been about to say something but stopped himself. All I heard was his uneven breathing for the next few moments. "I keep telling you I'm not your dad. Stop treating me like I am."

My dad. He was behind me. Why did Soren want to keep pulling him to the front?

"Then stop acting like him." An explosion erupted from me then, resulting in me shoving the table as hard as I could. Its legs whined across the floor, and half the contents on it toppled to the floor when it came to a stop.

"Yeah." From his voice, I knew. I'd lost him. "And I finally just accepted that you're never going to believe me."

Neither of us said a word, but it was deafening.

My jaw worked. "Say it."

"You're the one who made the call. You say it."

Saying the words wouldn't change anything—but it would give us both closure. And they were the words I always knew I'd have to say to him—they were the ones I'd practiced in my head. I knew it. He was learning it too.

Love like this didn't last. It couldn't. It was only a matter of time, similar to planting a flower in the dark and expecting it to flourish. Life couldn't bloom from darkness. I'd never realized how much of it I carried inside me until I was forced to confront the end of our relationship.

"It's over, Soren." I spoke each word slowly, like a vow.

"There wasn't anything to be over, Hayden. I just realized that finally too." Where mine was empty of emotion, his voice swam with too much. "You've been trying to tell me that the whole time, right? Message finally fucking received."

I pushed myself from the chair, forcing myself to turn my back to the life we'd created inside this small, crummy apartment. "Enjoy Miami."

"Enjoy Paris." He'd barely finished before the line went dead.

CHAPTER
Twenty-Four

What we fear losing most, we almost always wind up losing because of that fear.

That was something I'd learned over the past month from talking to someone about my issues stemming from my dad's departure. Those same issues I'd spent years convincing myself I'd tucked away so they didn't affect me, were the same ones that had been steering my life's ship for years. I'd tried so hard to put him behind me, and in so doing, I'd only given him that much more power in my present.

Of course I'd realized that a month too late to do any good for my relationship with Soren, but as my counselor reminded me, if I hadn't lost something so big, I might never have realized I had a problem that needed to be addressed.

That was what was on my mind as I climbed out of the subway tunnel near the apartment. It was a hot, muggy day, a stark contrast to the first day I'd arrived.

My fear of being abandoned had driven him away before he could leave of his own choice. The better-to-leave-than-be-left mentality of people who struggled with the issues I did. It had cost me dearly, and I never wanted to pay the same price again. I wanted to fix myself as much as I could. That was why I talked with someone twice a week and currently had an impressive, virtual stack of self-improvement books on my e-reader. I'd made it through most of them already too.

I wasn't foolish enough to think that spilling my guts to a therapist or devouring self-help books would cure me of my demons, but they'd opened a window to healing myself. It was up to me to keep clearing the dead spaces to make room for new life.

As I climbed the steps to the sixth floor, I found myself taking each one slowly, almost savoring them. This would be the last time I'd ever climb these endless, decrepit things. Funny how the things we thought we despised could become nostalgic through the scope of new eyes.

I hadn't been back to the apartment since the night I'd left it in such a hurry a month ago. I'd been in France the whole time. He hadn't tried to call or make any kind of contact. Why would he? I'd pushed him away, and he'd stayed where I'd driven him. Away.

He must have been in Miami by now. I didn't know for sure, and another wave of nostalgia overcame me when I reached the top floor and accepted that the person I'd cared so deeply for had a life I had no claim in anymore. I didn't have the right to know where he was or what he was up to or how he was doing.

That was exactly why relationships were so damn hard. One minute, a person could be your everything, and the next, they were gone.

As I turned the key in the lock, I found myself glancing down the hall toward Mrs. Lopez's apartment. I wondered, now that we were both gone, if anyone gave her a hand. I hoped so. From the way her door looked freshly painted, I guessed someone had stepped into the empty space Soren had left.

Steeling myself before entering, I reminded myself I could do this, then I moved inside the apartment. I was surprised to find myself feeling relief instead of the opposite as I breathed in the familiar scents and took in the familiar sights. It was the sensation of coming home.

To say good-bye.

I'd brought a few boxes to pack up my belongings—the old duffel I'd arrived with could hold the rest. I'd put this off until the last possible day. Tomorrow was the last one of our lease.

When I glanced into the kitchen, I was surprised to find some dishes and cups still scattered around the counter. I saw the same thing when I came into the main space. All of Soren's things were still there—at least most of them.

The ache in my chest that manifested from seeing an old pair of his sneakers against the wall sent me back a few steps. My eyes traveled to his favorite pillow he used to share with me—or swing at me, depending on the mood we were in—still resting on the mattress.

He'd left it all behind. He didn't want any of it.

Accepting what he'd left made me wonder what I was doing there. What was I there for? I'd left nothing of value to be packed. Clothes, secondhand dishes, a mismatched assortment of décor.

Memories.

Those were here too. In everything I looked at. Each and every item had some memory attached to it, and there was its value. That was what I was packing to take with me.

The memories. They were all I had left of Soren Decker. They were more than I was entitled to.

The first box had just been folded and taped when the sound of the lock turning over in the door made me still. It was probably the furtive landlord come a day early to check on the place, but when I heard the first few steps move inside, I knew who it was. I'd memorized the way he moved before I'd accepted that I'd fallen for him.

He moved into the room, distracted by the mail he was sorting through. He didn't notice me until he was passing by the table. He stopped abruptly, his whole body stiffening. When his head turned, his hands curled around the mail.

"What are you doing here?"

Those were the first words he'd said to me in thirty days. Not hello. Not good-bye. Not how are you doing.

What are you doing here?

It made me ask myself the same question. *What am I doing here?*

Trying to act like the pain of seeing him wasn't about to murder me, I got back to pretending to arrange items in the next box I had sitting on the table. "Packing. I'm sorry. If I'd known you'd be coming back today to pack too, we could have worked out different times so we didn't have to . . ." I swallowed. "You know. Do this."

"I'm not here to pack." Soren's voice was guarded as he stayed where he was, a distance away from me.

"Then why are you here?"

"Because I needed a shower."

When he motioned at himself, I noticed the state he was in. Dirty, sweaty, disheveled—like he used to come home from practice. Instead of the red-and-white one I was used to seeing him in, he was wearing a black-and-white uniform today. The gear bag had changed too. A different number was embroidered below his name.

He must have caught me staring because he patted the new number before dropping the bag on the floor. "I got drafted."

"To which team?"

"You already know which team, right? That's what you shouted at me over the phone last month, at least." His eyes refused to come my way, his body seeming of the same mind. I noticed him backing into the wall behind him.

"I owe you an apology for that call."

"You owe me an apology for a hell of a lot more than just that call." As soon as it was out, he grimaced, grinding his jaw.

"So the team in Miami?" I stayed focused on packing so I didn't fixate on the pain surging inside me.

"Good luck to them. They're going to need it when playing against me."

My head lifted.

His shoulders moved. "The Miami team was hoping to sign me. *Hoping*. If I made it to number three in the draft." That was when his eyes finally met mine. They didn't stay there long. "I went number two."

"Number two?" I repeated, struggling to make sense of what he was saying.

"Some leftie pitcher got the number one pick." Soren huffed. "Too bad for him, because Texas sucks in the summer."

My hands were still wrapped around the vase I'd been setting in the box. "You aren't leaving?"

He scooted his hat farther down when I caught his forehead creasing as he watched me pack. "I'm not leaving."

He wasn't lying or messing with me. I could tell by his face. I'd been able to tell from the very beginning, actually. Soren was the open book—I was the sealed shut kind.

"But . . ." That was all I could come up with. I had nothing else.

"You have no idea how the draft works, do you?"

"You get drafted?" I said, still reeling. I might have known a bit more from what I'd learned from Soren, but not much.

"I explained it all to you." He shoved off the wall and wandered into the kitchen. "That one night after . . ."

Thankfully he was in the kitchen, so he didn't see the heat rush into my face from what he was getting at. Having the mattress right in front of me made it that much easier to picture.

"I might have fallen asleep," I said. "Like I tended to do after . . . that."

He snorted. "Probably not the best time to go into a drawn-out explanation of the complicated draft process."

My feet shifted. "So you have no say at all?"

"In team? Not really." His voice echoed from the kitchen. "But I do when it comes to saying yes or no, and I meant what I said when I told you it was a conversation we'd have together if I got drafted by a team way the hell away from here."

When he emerged from the kitchen, he had a couple bottles of water and a fresh package of his favorite food. I'd never been able to pass a display of Nutter Butters in a grocery store and not think about him.

"Of course we break up and I get drafted by a local franchise." He ripped open the end of the bag after setting the waters on the table. "God, I hate irony."

Letting go of the vase, my hands curled around the edge of the box. He wasn't moving to Miami? A local team had picked him up?

Everything I'd feared happening hadn't happened at all.

I'd lost him, but for all the wrong reasons.

I shook my head as I got back to packing, pretending my life wasn't falling apart all over again.

"You got picked second?" I asked in an attempt to carry on a casual conversation as I finished what I needed to get done.

"Pretty great, right?" His chin lifted as he pulled a handful of cookies from the package.

I gently placed my favorite coffee cup into the box. "Actually, I can't believe you didn't get picked first."

He was quiet for a moment, watching me. "See? That's what I love—*loved*—about you." He cleared his throat and took a drink of water. "Always thinking I was better than anyone else did. Even myself."

"That's because you are. You *are* better than anyone else." My hand gestured at him, but I was having a difficult time looking at him. It was hard to look at what I'd lost—especially when it was three feet away. "I'm sorry for what I said—the way things went down. I should have given you a chance to explain instead of ruining this—us." A sigh sneaked out as I focused on packing one item at a time. "The best thing I had going for me in my life."

"Also had that international supermodel standing, too." Instead of stuffing his mouth with that handful of cookies, he set them on the table. It was the first time I'd seen him too distracted to devour a fistful of his beloved cookies.

"What we had? So much better."

"Dream lost its shine now that you've achieved it?"

My head shook. "No, I still love what I do. I just loved us, you, that much more."

He was staring at me, standing so close. My body felt like one aching bruise from having him so close yet accepting he was totally out of reach. I needed to finish packing and get out of here before I said or did something truly pathetic that would end whatever dignity I still had, and put him in the uncomfortable position of letting me down gently. Or not so gently, as I supposed he'd earned a right to.

"Are you not packing up your stuff?" I asked, indicating the two other boxes I'd brought along but wouldn't need. "Isn't this the last day we have on the lease?"

Soren slid into one of the mismatched chairs circling the table. Not his old favorite, I noticed. Instead, he'd picked the one that used to be mine. "It was. Until I renewed it for the next year."

"You renewed the lease? On this place?" I thought he was joking until I saw his face. He wasn't. "Why?"

He rolled his neck, staying quiet for a moment. Then his eyes wandered the apartment. "Because of the memories. Because it's where I met you. Where I fell in love with you." His brows squeezed together like he was reliving something painful. The emotion ran its course quickly. "Where we did something I didn't think physically possible against that very wall." Now he was smiling at the wall opposite us, his brow rising at me. "How could I just let someone else move in here with the history I have with that patch of wall?"

That wall. This table. This whole apartment. It was all connected to some moment, some memory. Some piece of us. "Soren—"

"Plus, I'm going to be making crap for the next two to three years minimum," he continued. "So at least I know I can afford this place."

"You just said you were the second pick."

He blinked twice at me. "You really didn't hear a word I said that night, did you?"

I gave him a sheepish look as I scanned the memory bank. Other than knowing there was a draft and that draft applied to him, that was the extent of my knowledge. "Would it make you feel better if I said, the better the sex, the harder I go out?"

"A little," he grumbled, twisting the cap off the second bottle of water and sliding it across the table toward me. "So yeah, I'll be making dick working my ass off for a minor league team for a couple of seasons minimum, but thankfully, my signing bonus will keep me well stocked in Nutter Butters and Pop-Tarts." He patted his adored cookie package.

"So you got a signing bonus at least?"

"Seemed the least they could do for paying me fifteen hundred bucks a month for the next couple of years in this city." He was smiling as he said it because I knew Soren wouldn't care if they paid him in peanuts—he loved the game. He would have played for free.

"How much?" I asked before catching myself. "I don't know—is that not a question a person should ask someone?"

"You're not a person asking. You're *you* asking." Soren adjusted his black hat back on his forehead, still fussing with it like he couldn't find just the right spot for it. I guessed it would take a while before this one was as broken in as his old red one. "Three and a half million dollars."

My eyes went wide. "Three and a half million dollars? And you chose to live in this dump for a whole other year?" My nose creased as I scanned the small, outdated apartment.

"Where else would I go?" He paused just long enough, it was almost like he was giving me a chance to reply. "What about you? Have you moved into that flat in Paris yet?"

"Actually, no. I sold it. I decided after my contract ends with this client, I'm going to stay Stateside for a while."

He was quiet, watching me pack. When I glanced up, I wasn't expecting to find the expression on his face I did. He looked upset—tormented.

"Fuck irony," he said, smacking his hands on the table hard enough it made it shake. "You and I both wind up back in goddamned New York in the end, and we're no longer together to make it count."

My eyes stung, but I forced a smile. "Yeah"—I nodded once—"fuck irony."

Soren forced his own smile, lifting the package of cookies toward me. "Want a Nutter Butter? I've attempted a lot of self-soothing with these over the past month."

"This calls for two." I wrestled a couple from the package and took a bite out of one right after the other. Somehow, they'd become my favorites too. "I'm with a different agent now. I'm not working with Ellis anymore."

I finished my bite and packed the last couple of things away. "You were right about him. So right." I took the roll of tape he was holding out for me.

"Good," he said, watching me tape the box shut as his forehead creased again. "At least that's one less thing I'll have to worry about when I think about you."

Unsure what to say next, I moved around the box to lift it. I'd come here planning on packing up so much more, but I couldn't stay another minute longer. They rest would have to stay here, with him, because I couldn't.

As I started toward the door, choking on the good-bye trying to rise, I heard him shove out of his chair. The sound of his footsteps followed me.

"Hey, Hayden?" His voice. This was the one I remembered. This was the one I heard in my dreams. "Before you go"—he paused for a fraction of a second—"I still love you."

My heart. It couldn't take any more. It wouldn't survive this. Glancing over my shoulder, I knew how to say good-bye now.

"I still love you too." Taking one final look at him, I finished the last few steps to the door.

"Then what are we doing?" His voice chased me, the sound of his feet doing the same. "Why are you moving out? Why are you walking away?"

The doorknob. It was within reach. Just open the door and leave.

My hand fastened to the doorknob, but I couldn't twist it open. "I don't know."

Suddenly, he was there, right behind me, his hand dropping over mine on the door. "I don't want you to go."

His touch was my undoing. It had been before, and it proved it still was just now. Squeezing my eyes shut, I whispered, "I don't want to hurt you again."

His fingers forced their way between mine, removing my hand from the doorknob. "I'll take my chances." His fingers knotted through mine, our palms pressing together. "I'm not going to leave you. I'm not him." He lifted our combined hands in front of me. "If this isn't proof, I don't know what is."

"I know you aren't him. I always knew that." Warmth spread up my arm, nestling deep into the rest of my body. "My fear was bigger than my faith."

Holding my stare, he took the box out of my arms and set it down against the wall. His hands found mine, one at a time, and pulled me to him at the same time he brought himself to me. When our lips connected, I felt all of the fear I carried melt away. In its place, courage swept in.

My head barely had a chance to haze from the kiss before he broke it, moving toward the door with me. "We need a redo. Let's take this from the top. From the start." He threw the door open, a grin on his face as he guided me just outside of the door.

"Take what from the start?" I asked, letting him place me where he wanted me.

"Just knock on the door like you're showing up on that first day again." He waved at the door, still hanging on to one of my hands.

"I didn't knock on the door. You found me standing around its general area after you emerged from Mrs. Lopez's apartment with your fly down." I motioned down the hall. I guessed I had my answer as to who had applied that fresh coat of paint.

His eyes lifted as he stepped back inside. "Just play along. You're ruining my whole vision of this."

When he closed the door, though not entirely, I decided to go along with his crazy scheme. Rapping on the door, I waited a whole half second before it flew open.

"I heard you were looking for a roommate with benefits." Flashing a grin, I stuck my thumb into my chest. "I've come to apply for the position."

He fought a smile as he reached for my hand. His eyes were lighter than they'd been when he'd first entered the apartment. "Hayden Agatha Hayes," he said all solemn-like, his gaze intense, "will you be my roommate?"

My mouth twitched as I gave him a funny look. "Um, yeah?"

He leaned in to whisper, "You're supposed to say 'I do.' Or, 'I will'—whatever feels truest to who you are. Let's try it again."

Leaning back, he cleared his throat, flashing a wink when I shook my head. Crazy. I loved him for it too. Every last crazy, insane, irrational fiber of his being.

"Hayden Agatha Hayes"—his hand squeezed mine—"will you be my roommate?"

Standing up straight, I gave my answer just as formally as he'd voiced his question. "I will." We stood like that for a moment longer before I glanced over his shoulder.

"Can I come in already and get unpacked while you explain what this was all about?"

He slid aside to let me pass, flagging me inside. "Just practicing."

"For what?"

He had the door closed the instant I cleared it. "When it comes time to ask you another question."

My feet froze to the hallway floor. "Soren. I'm nineteen. I'm not becoming a teenage bride." When I glanced back so he knew how serious I was, the grin on his face wiped the serious right off of me.

"Always ruining the romantic mood I'm trying to set."

My finger lifted in a stern way, since I couldn't hold my serious face. "I will not say yes until I'm in my twenties. You can ask all you want, but you're not hearing a yes until I've officially reached that milestone."

As he locked the door, his brows moved. "So I'm getting a yes?"

When I realized what I'd just given away, I groaned. "Soren . . ."

Both of us smiled. How many times had I sighed his name in that exasperated tone? Those were memories too. Good ones. Some of the best. As he took my hand and led me by the boxes, I realized we didn't have to pack any of them and carry them away. They could all stay here—with us.

"Just come here for a minute. I want to reenact something over here, too." Turning into me, his body pressed into mine, backing me up into . . . "Right here against this wall."

My hands tied behind his back as he lifted me into his arms. "What is it with you and this wall?"

"It's not the wall. It's what I'm holding between me and it." His arms secured around me tighter, feeling capable of carrying me through whatever challenges would come.

"Me?" Other than air, there was nothing between him and this wall he was so fond of. "The person who did everything you warned me not to and made a huge mess? The person who destroyed the great thing we had because I stumbled on a few pieces of paper and assumed I knew what they meant? The girl who let her fear of losing you be the very reason she did?" I had to take a breath. "Is that who you're referring to?"

"You." His lips touched mine. "Also known as my whole entire world."

I gave him the most convincing look of apology I could, tying my legs around him tighter. I wasn't letting go. Not for anything. "I'm sorry your whole entire world is such a hot mess."

He chuckle rumbled in his chest. "If the person you love doesn't want to make you breathe fire and pull your hair out every once in a while, she's not the right one."

My eyebrows knitted together. "And what's your logic behind that?"

"Because I want her to love me so damn much, she wants to roast my corpse over a spit for lying to her—for even *thinking* I'm lying to her," he added, catching the protest rising from my lips. "I want her to care about me—care about us—so much it drives her up a fucking wall."

"Roast corpse. Up a fucking wall," I counted off, debating a moment before giving a nod. "Accurate assessment."

Soren pressed closer, like he was trying to leave his imprint on me. But he already had. Months ago. On the first day I moved in and knew all of my dreams were about to come true.

"Good," he whispered against me, "because I feel the same damn way about her."

The End

Thank you for reading
ROOMMATES WITH BENEFITS
by NEW YORK TIMES and USATODAY
bestselling author, Nicole Williams.

Nicole loves to hear from her readers.
You can connect with her on:

Facebook: Nicole Williams (Official Author Page)
Twitter: nwilliamsbooks
Blog: nicoleawilliams.blogspot.com

Other Works by Nicole:

MISTER WRONG

HATE STORY

TORTURED

CRASH, CLASH, and CRUSH (HarperCollins)

UP IN FLAMES (Simon & Schuster UK)

LOST & FOUND, NEAR & FAR, HEART & SOUL

FINDERS KEEPERS, LOSERS WEEPERS

STEALING HOME, TOUCHING DOWN

COLLARED

THE FABLE OF US

THREE BROTHERS

HARD KNOX, DAMAGED GOODS

CROSSING STARS

GREAT EXPLOITATIONS SAGA

THE EDEN TRILOGY

THE PATRICK CHRONICLES